A Jaime Azcárate adventure

TURNED TO STONE

JORGE MAGANO

TRANSLATED FROM SPANISH BY SIMON BRUNI

This is a work of fiction. Names, characters, organizations, places, events, and incidents are either products of the author's imagination or are used fictitiously.

Text copyright © 2014 Jorge Magano
Translation copyright © 2015 Simon Bruni

All rights reserved.

No part of this book may be reproduced, or stored in a retrieval system, or transmitted in any form or by any means, electronic, mechanical, photocopying, recording, or otherwise, without express written permission of the publisher.

Previously published as *La Mirada de Piedra* in 2014 in Spain. Translated from Spanish by Simon Bruni. First published in English by AmazonCrossing in 2015.

Published by AmazonCrossing, Seattle

www.apub.com

Amazon, the Amazon logo, and AmazonCrossing are trademarks of Amazon.com, Inc., or its affiliates.

ISBN-13: 9781503946347
ISBN-10: 1503946347

Cover design by Scott Barrie

Printed in the United States of America

In the fields and along the paths, here and there, he saw the shapes of men and animals changed from their natures to hard stone by Medusa's gaze. Nevertheless he had himself looked at the dread form of Medusa reflected in a circular shield of polished bronze that he carried on his left arm. And while a deep sleep held the snakes and herself, he struck her head from her neck. . . . He told of his long journeys, of dangers that were not imaginary ones, what seas and lands he had seen below from his high flight, and what stars he had brushed against with beating wings.

Ovid, *The Metamorphoses*

THE BIRTH OF A MONSTER

1656—Naples

The block of marble seemed to glow as Andrea Bolgi stood it upright on the bench and gazed at it, lost in thought. A burning passion took hold of him as he looked deep into the stone. He thought he could see the monstrous smile of the creature encased within. Emulating old Michelangelo, his task was to free it from its prison and release it into the world.

Bolgi often forgot that he was no Michelangelo.

Though the great master worked with agility, seemingly without effort, guided by his instinct—or divine power, as he believed—Bolgi's methods were often criticized by his colleagues as being too coarse. They considered his work cold and static, at odds with the expressive, dynamic, theatrical trends of the time. But Bolgi did not care what others might say. He was euphoric as he worked on his new piece, a commission for the wealthy merchant Domenico Corsini, who had built a garden to house his sculptures of mythological subjects. The ancient gods' world of love and conflict had seduced Corsini, just as it had inspired Cardinal Scipione Borghese to commission some of Gian Lorenzo Bernini's finest works years before.

After this, nobody will doubt my ability, Bolgi thought with stubborn naiveté as he set to work on the block. On several occasions the flying chips of stone struck his bare arm, but he ignored the pain and kept chiseling. The task would take weeks, but he would not rest until it was finished. For the first time in his life, Andrea Bolgi was determined to push his gift to its limits.

On the third day of this work, a tall man with a bushy black mustache walked into the shed and stood beside the artist, watching him sculpt. "I see you're making progress."

Bolgi stopped and looked up. Recognizing his patron, he gave a hint of a smile and wiped the sweat from his brow.

"It's coming along. I want to finish as soon as possible. I'm sure you'll be satisfied, once it's done."

"With this final piece in my collection of monstrous creatures, my garden will compare with that of Emperor Hadrian himself."

"I have absolutely no doubt you are right," Bolgi assented, though deep down he was not so sure. He bent and picked up a portfolio from the floor. "This is what it will look like."

Domenico Corsini examined the sculptor's charcoal sketches, half closing his eyes as he studied the images. Never before had he seen such expression: the wild hair; the creature's violent, bulging gaze and twisted features; the contrast of light and shade. Never had he seen such a brilliant portrayal of monstrosity. He admired the drawings in silence for several minutes, and then slapped Bolgi on the shoulder.

"I truly cannot wait to see it finished, so I will leave you to your work. Next Tuesday I'll return to see what progress you've made. Arrivederci, Andrea."

"Arrivederci, Domenico."

For the next several days, Bolgi worked to form and contour the figure. After polishing away the marble's impurities, he recalled what his master, Bernini, had taught him.

The marble must not resemble marble. You must make every surface and material true to life, imitating its texture and light.

Bolgi, who had taken ten years to complete his Saint Helena for the Vatican, did not want to waste time now, so he dismissed his master's advice and left the marble as smooth as it had been when it was cut from the quarry at Carrara. When the figure was finished, he compared the sketch to the sculpture one last time. Satisfied with the result, he covered the marble with a cloth and went to rest before Domenico's next visit.

"What do you think?" the impatient artist asked when Domenico arrived a week later.

Domenico Corsini removed the cloth and walked around the bust several times, inspecting every detail closely. He ran his hand over his face and hair a couple of times, then pulled it away, looking disenchanted. Finally he shook his head at Bolgi.

"You see, Andrea, when you showed me the sketch I was astounded by its expressiveness. It captured that spark of life found only in the great art of the ancient world. But I'm afraid the final result is disappointing. The ancient sculptures in my garden have lives of their own. You must have seen this for yourself. Aphrodite emerges from the water and the transparent liquid runs down her body; Hercules's mace looks as if it was made of wood; the nymphs' garments look like delicate cloth, not marble—I do not wish to denigrate your work, Andrea, but this sculpture is nothing more than cold stone. It no more deserves a place in my collection than a half-starved mule belongs in my sumptuous stables."

His self-respect mortally wounded, Bolgi begged the merchant to give him another chance with the gorgon, assuring him he could do much better and faithfully capture what he had sketched, but he needed more time. Domenico was lenient and granted this to him, but Bolgi imposed one condition.

"I would beg you not to enter the shed for one week. I will have finished the piece by then, and you may reject it or give me your approval."

The demand surprised Domenico, and he nearly refused there and then, but the sculptor's determination moved him. Agreeing, Domenico took his leave, promising not to return until the appointed day.

When Domenico returned a week later, he found a smiling Andrea Bolgi leaning on an object draped in cloth. The artist's proud expression suggested he had fulfilled his promise. Domenico hoped that was the case. He had no desire to reject the piece again.

"Here it is, as we agreed," said Andrea with a tone of complete confidence. Before Domenico could say anything, Bolgi pulled away the drape and bared the statue.

The bust wore the same terrifying expression Domenico had seen in the drawing and on the first version of the sculpture, yet this time there was a vital difference. Now, the wrinkles on the face and neck were like those of a real person. The tangled hair was no longer simply hair but glistening serpents that writhed in an orgy of movement. The gaze—hard, wicked, demonic—made Domenico shudder.

He could not believe his eyes. He placed his hand on the woman's neck, but after holding it there a brief moment, he snatched it back in fright. The marble felt almost warm, and he imagined he could feel the flesh somehow throbbing. He glanced back at the artist, who was still smiling.

"I must admit I'm impressed," he said in a low, almost reverent, voice. "Bravo, Andrea! You have done an extraordinary job. It truly is the most terrifying thing I have seen in my life. And what movement—it is as if it could turn its head at any moment to gaze at me!"

The sculptor ran his hand through his hair, combing out little drips of sweat.

"Do you accept it for the garden?"

Domenico lifted his eyes to the artist's face, and after scrutinizing him, turned back to the gorgon, feeling another reflexive spasm when his gaze met hers.

"I never thought a lump of marble could embody evil so savagely! I can almost believe that anyone who looks upon it will be turned to stone."

Corsini's words about the sensual savagery of the statue could have applied just as well to the young woman who, a week later, moaned and writhed beneath him in his bed. Since they'd met a couple of years earlier at a party at the Royal Palace, their private bacchanals had become a most pleasant habit for the hedonistic, womanizing merchant. He enjoyed beautiful companions as much as he admired a beautiful poem or sculpture, and Constanza was one of his greatest pleasures.

"Domenico," she told him, "if you keep wearing me out like this, soon there will be nothing of me left!"

His eyes idled down her body. "There's still so much of you to explore, Constanza."

"Much? Don't tell me there's something you'd like to do that you haven't done already."

"And if there is? Will you refuse me?"

"There's only one way to find out," she countered, cocking her eyebrow suggestively.

Corsini fell against his lover, exhausted, and burst into laughter. "Grant they or deny, yet they are pleased to have been asked."

Constanza rested her head on her hand, her elbow sinking into the straw mattress. The firmness of her naked body captivated him. She was a stunning young woman, with eyes like hot coals that echoed the heat of her unruly, flame-colored hair. "Ovid," she declared, drawing out each syllable.

The points of Domenico Corsini's mustache lifted as he smiled. "You never disappoint me, Constanza. You can recognize any quote from antiquity, however obscure."

"That's why you want me. My head excites you more than my chest," she said, juggling her breasts in her hands. "You couldn't care less if my beauty fades, as long my mind remains intact. Maybe you should find another woman to satisfy your base desires."

"There is nothing worse than a woman, except another woman," Corsini recited. Seeing his lover's look of feigned anger, he added: "according to Aristophanes. Anyway, I already have another woman, though I doubt she will satisfy me the way you do. Get dressed; I want you to meet her."

They went out into the garden and strolled among its impressive collection of mythological sculptures. Corsini had begun assembling his collection as soon as the palazzo's architect, Cosimo Fanzago, had finished building the stately mansion. It was one of the many buildings constructed under the auspices of the Spanish Habsburgs, who had ruled the viceroyalty of Naples since 1516. The city had become an important cultural and artistic center, where nobles and wealthy merchants led opulent lives in the new palazzi that presided over the newly built streets and squares.

"Here you have it, my most recent acquisition," said Corsini, stopping in front of the marble pedestal that supported the head of the gorgon Medusa.

It was not a cold day, but Constanza wrapped her arms around herself as if suddenly chilled. She paled and looked at her lover with disgust. "What monstrosity is this?"

"Impressive, isn't it? It's a piece by Andrea Bolgi, a sculptor from Carrara. He's not very famous, but he was a disciple of Bernini and worked at the Vatican."

"It's horrifying. Get rid of it, Domenico."

"What do you mean? It's sublime. Look at the work on the snakes, the expression in the gaze, the ferocity of her countenance . . ."

"Take it from me—it can only bring you misfortune."

Corsini was surprised by the alarm in her voice. Constanza was an erudite woman, not at all superstitious. When he pressed her on the issue, she explained that as a child, while she was playing in a sown field, she had found a medallion that bore the image of the same being. A friend of the family, a priest, told her that it was the work of the devil and that she must throw it away, for it was imbued with evil powers. But Constanza wanted to keep it, and she hid it in a cabinet at her grandmother's house. The next day the house burned down.

"My beautiful Constanza," Corsini said. "That was undoubtedly a fatal coincidence, nothing more."

"It was not. The priest was right and I was foolish. The medallion was cursed. The monster brings bad luck, and this statue will bring it again."

Corsini tried to reassure her, but she could not be talked out of her distress, nor of her demand that he destroy the sculpture that very day. He refused, and she left his house, never to return.

. . .

Four months later, the moon's rays fell on the façade of the house as the front door opened and a frantic figure bolted into the hedges. If any of the many eyes that watched the garden had belonged to a being of flesh and bone, a witness could later have described the moment when Domenico Corsini, naked and out of his senses, scampered among his brood of nymphs, satyrs, gods and monsters, reciting verses by Petrarch and Ovid. But all the eyes were of marble, and none could appreciate that Corsini's mad gallop followed a predetermined course to the front of the pedestal supporting the bust of Medusa.

There, the Neapolitan merchant fell to his knees. "Infernal monster!" he declaimed, trembling with fever. The buboes on his neck had burst and were oozing a blackish fluid. "Bastard daughter of Poseidon! I curse the day you were created. That sculptor tricked me. Oh, poor Constanza! She said you were cursed, and now she is dead, with hundreds of others! But your victory will be short-lived. Before I die, I will defeat you. Your reign of terror is over."

The gorgon's bust stood motionless on the pedestal, immune to the reproaches and threats. Corsini arose clumsily and rained blows on the marble with his fists until his hands bled. "Oh gods!" he whimpered. "My strength fails me. But if Perseus could destroy you, so can I. I just need . . ."

His words were lost in the night. Corsini was rendered mute: horror-struck by Medusa's face, bewitched by her chilling expression. He screamed, and his cry was heard in surrounding Naples as its inhabitants fought against the plague that would kill half of them.

Corsini's servants didn't find his body until the next day. It was floating in the pond, its black skin covered in cuts and scratches, its fingernails broken, and several locks of hair pulled from its head. A short distance away, the gorgon Medusa stood upright on her pedestal, defiance flashing through her stony expression, as if warning that her kingdom of shadows would reign for many centuries to come.

PART I
ACCURSED MEDUSA

1

October 2013—El Burgo de Osma—Soria (Spain)

When Jaime Azcárate walked into the rustic restaurant on Calle Mayor at three in the afternoon, the last thing on his mind was the possibility that he was about to get himself into one of his frequent scrapes. Some people run away from problems and lead peaceful, mundane lives from the day they're born until they die; others seek out excitement and danger, even when simply popping out to buy bread. Jaime Azcárate belonged to a third category of people: those who, without ever intending to, act as magnets for conflict, mysteries, and trouble.

That afternoon, Jaime was looking for none of these things. All he wanted to do was try some of the region's culinary specialties, perhaps *castellano* stew or some pickled partridge. He was famished after touring the Hospital de San Agustín, the university façade, and the Episcopal Palace, and had wandered the streets extensively, taking in the touristy atmosphere of the town. It had been difficult to find accommodations because the cathedral's *Ars Homini* exhibit had attracted crowds from all over Spain. But after much searching he'd found an available room in a modest guesthouse where there'd been a last-minute cancellation.

In the end, Jaime opted for a salad and a peppered tenderloin steak. As he waited for his lunch he scanned the small dining room. Of the seven tables, five were occupied, including his: two were taken up by families with noisy children; a couple sat in silence at a third; and at the table at the back, a man sat alone and ate as he typed on a tablet. Jaime thought he looked too professional to be a tourist and could not help feeling for the man.

For once, life's injustices belong to someone else, he thought. *Other people have to work, and I'm here on vacation.*

That is . . . more or less on vacation, he corrected himself. Though the trip to see the exhibition had been planned for pleasure, he knew that Laura Rodríguez, editor of *Arcadia*, would ask him to write a few lines for the magazine's next issue.

For several weeks now he had felt an inexplicable inner turmoil. He didn't know whether to attribute it to all the changes happening around him or to how little he himself had changed. At some point he had decided that the journey of life was more important than the destination, and ever since, he had felt fulfilled, free, and happy. His work at *Arcadia* made it possible for him to enjoy his independence while simultaneously making use of his training as an art historian and realizing his vocation as a journalist. Still, for reasons he didn't understand, he'd been feeling a void for almost a month, which was why he had decided to take things easy and get away from his usual surroundings for a few days.

The waiter brought out the salad, and Jaime dressed it in oil and a splash of vinegar. He'd just pierced an asparagus spear and was lifting the fork to his mouth when he heard a timid cough off to his side.

Jaime turned and saw the man who a few moments earlier had been eating and working at the back table. Now, he was standing as stiff as the asparagus still quivering on Jaime's fork. The man smiled with perfect teeth, and his bronzed skin was covered in tiny scars, like furrows on a sown field. The graying roots of his blond hair suggested he was in his fifties, and the body under the brown suit appeared strong and fit. His computer tablet was now tucked under his arm, and he wore an expensive-looking pair of leather gloves despite the warm temperature in the restaurant.

"I'm sorry to bother you," the man said, "but are you Jaime Azcárate?"

Jaime did not know what to say. If he said no, he'd be lying, but if he said yes, he would be forced to talk to the man. The last thing he wanted right now was someone pestering him.

Curiosity won out. "Yes. And you are?"

"My name's Amatriaín. Vicente Amatriaín. I'm with the EHU. Do you mind if I sit down? You can eat while we talk."

Jaime did not need to be told he could eat while another person sat at his table, but out of politeness he merely gestured at the empty chair in front of him.

"Thank you," said Amatriaín.

"Who did you say you're with?"

"The EHU—the Europol Heritage Unit. Europol is the European Police Office. I'm sure you've seen us in the news."

"I filled the TV with water and turned it into a fish tank long ago. I don't know what you're talking about."

"Excuse me?"

"Okay, not really. But I wouldn't mind, given the crap they put on TV nowadays . . ."

"Allow me to explain. The Europol Heritage Unit was set up six months ago. It's like the Narcotics or Homicide Department—but more sophisticated, shall we say, and operates throughout Europe." Amatriaín showed his perfect teeth again. "It's comprised of investigators and officers from all the security forces in the European Union. As you well know, a fanatical artifact thief can be as dangerous as any drug trafficker. Could you bring me a *café solo*, please?"

This request was directed at the waiter, who had used so much gel and hairspray, his head appeared shellacked. He had positioned himself near the table, making it impossible for them to speak privately. At this request, however, he nodded and withdrew, leaving Jaime and Amatriaín alone.

"I hope you'll forgive me for disturbing you," Amatriaín said, with a concern that seemed genuine to Jaime. "But I need to speak to you about a case we're investigating."

"How did you find me?"

"Your boss told me you were here on a trip."

"Really? How discreet of her. I must remember to post my naked photos of her on Facebook."

"I had to lean on her a little," Amatriaín confessed. "She's a tough woman."

"Tell me about it."

"Are you here alone?"

"People say a joy shared is a joy doubled, and a problem shared is a problem halved—but if you ask me, having the freedom to travel without considering anyone else is a problem joyfully solved."

Amatriaín looked down at Jaime's salad as if meditating on what he'd just heard.

"You said Graciela told you I was here," Jaime prompted him.

"Yes. When I contacted the Center for Historical Research a few days ago, Dr. Isidro Requena confirmed that he and some of his researchers are prepared to cooperate with us. When I explained the case yesterday to your employer . . . sorry, what was her name?"

"Graciela."

"Forgive me, but I thought *Arcadia*'s editor was named Laura."

"And forgive *me*, but I had no reason to believe you'd actually met her. Now I do."

Jaime popped a slice of boiled egg into his mouth while Amatriaín processed what had just happened. Glancing at him sideways, Jaime thought the white-toothed blond appeared annoyed.

"You're quite clever," said Amatriaín.

"And you're beating around the bush. Why don't you tell me what your problem is and why Laura let you come and find me on my weekend off?"

"A well-deserved break, if you don't mind me saying so. I've been reading your articles, and the one you wrote a few years ago on the Brotherhood of Saint Fructus and Solomon's Table was an excellent piece. It's a shame you had to leave out everything related to the Mossad agents' involvement in the operation."

Jaime's knife and fork fell onto his plate with a sharp metallic ring. At the table with the silent couple, the girl turned around and looked at him. Jaime gave an awkward smile by way of an apology.

"How do you know about that?" he asked.

"That's not your concern. Anyone who works at the EHU knows these things. And remember that yesterday—"

"Yes, yes. I imagine Dr. Rodríguez embellished the story."

In fact, Jaime knew that Laura Rodríguez never exaggerated; on the contrary, she tended to play down the adventures of her most zealous contributor. That was the only way she could stay out of trouble with her superiors—and with the law. Jaime felt certain that she would not have told this man half of what had happened to them at that accursed finca—an episode he would just as soon forget.

He made an effort to calm himself as he picked up his cutlery again. Amatriaín reached into the inside pocket of his jacket and pulled out a piece of paper that he placed in front of Jaime. "Do you know this work of art?"

Jaime identified the subject of the pencil drawing the moment he picked it up. It was a bust of Medusa, the creature from Greek mythology best known for being cursed with snakes in place of hair, and for turning to stone anyone who looked her in the eyes. The drawing itself had quick, precise strokes; it showed that the artist had a good command of volume, shade, and perspective.

"Very nice," Jaime said after a while.

"It doesn't tell you anything?"

"What's it going to tell me? It's a drawing. Did you do it?"

"Yes."

"Congratulations. It's very good."

"Thank you. But you don't know the piece?"

"At first glance, no. It looks like a bust of Medusa. The sculpture is baroque—Italian, I'd guess."

"I don't know if I believe you. Are you telling me this particular piece doesn't ring any bells?"

"Señor, it's obvious from the way you're insisting that you know I'm familiar with it. Why don't you just hurry up and tell me what you want?"

"Let's see," a voice broke in. "One peppered tenderloin here. And one café solo there."

The waiter with the impressive hair had arrived just in time to ease the tension. Amatriaín seemed to realize that he was going about things the wrong way, because when the waiter left he cut straight to the chase. "Two years ago you wrote an article about this statue, attributing to it a curse that has caused many of its owners to die under strange circumstances."

"What's wrong with that? Readers go crazy over wild stories."

"There's nothing wrong with it. But the article's bibliography included an essay you wrote with someone named Paloma Blasco, published in the *Revista Complutense* in 1999. In it, you attributed the work to the Italian sculptor Andrea Bolgi."

"An essay, you say?"

"An essay on classical iconography in Italian baroque sculpture. And don't tell me you don't know what I'm talking about. Laura Rodríguez—"

"Laura Rodríguez may look like an alien, with that red dye she puts in her hair, but she's actually a human and she does make mistakes. Sorry, but if you don't mind I'm here for a few days' relaxation and—"

"Just one moment." Amatriaín turned on his iPad. "You claim you have never written an essay on Italian baroque architecture—"

"Because it's true."

"Then can you explain this to me?"

Jaime froze when he saw the PDF document shown on the screen: "Gods and Monsters in Italian Baroque Sculpture." By Paloma Blasco and Jaime Azcárate.

Hit and sunk by damn technology. "All right," he conceded. "Am I supposed to feel guilty about this?"

"I suppose not. But I'd like to know why you lied to me."

"Because my tenderloin's going cold."

"It's a serious question."

"And a serious answer. I've had a tough few days, and I'm trying to unplug from work."

"I understand. But what can you lose by giving me a few more minutes? I'm sure you already know the bust of Medusa disappeared last month from the museum where it was on exhibit."

Jaime admitted that he'd seen it in the news. The Pontecorvo House Museum in Verona. A robbery in the middle of the night, a security guard killed, and the statue gone. Amatriaín gave him a look. "Didn't you say you don't watch TV?"

"I get my news on Twitter." Jaime realized right away that he'd put his foot in his mouth. What if this bore decided to follow him online? He sliced off a piece of tenderloin and tried it. Immediately, he regretted not ordering the pickled partridge. What part of "medium rare" had that chump with the haircut not understood?

"Both the plundering of archeological sites and thefts of works of art are on the rise," said Amatriaín. "Since 2004, the number of cases has risen fivefold. While there have been isolated cases like the remarkable robbery at Oslo's Munch Museum, most of the thefts have been from houses. This incident at the Pontecorvo is one of the rare occasions when thieves have been bold enough to break into a museum."

"The Pontecorvo House Museum is hardly the Louvre," Jaime pointed out. "Force a door, load the sculpture onto a wheelbarrow, and breeze out of there the same way you came in. It doesn't seem like a particularly spectacular feat."

"That's the thing: there wasn't even a broken window. No forced door. Nothing. The morning after the robbery, everything except the statue and the poor security guard were in their places."

"What happened to the security guard, exactly? The press was vague on that point."

"The girl in charge of opening up the museum found him on the floor. His back was broken from a fall. He was still alive when they took him to hospital, and en route he kept muttering something about being attacked by a woman with snakes for hair. He died two hours later."

"How many security guards were there?"

"Just him. It's a small museum, so they don't need more than one."

"Clearly they do. Any other leads?"

"The autopsy revealed something strange in his blood—a toxin that couldn't be identified. Tests on the Aperol Spritz he had drunk that evening revealed traces of an extract of *Psilocybe semilanceata*."

"A hallucinogen." Jaime showed no sign of surprise.

Amatriaín nodded. "I'd heard that you were a capable mycologist."

"An enthusiast, nothing more. My grandfather was the expert on fungi. I simply learned a few of their names when I was a boy." Jaime smiled. "There are some things that, for better or for worse, one never forgets."

"In this case, for better. As you said, *Psilocybe semilanceata* has potent hallucinogenic properties. Combining it with alcohol, especially for a man nearly seventy years old, is almost certainly fatal—not because of the interaction between the two substances, per se, but because the subsequent disorientation poses a high risk of accident for the person who consumed them. That is precisely what occurred. The disorientation also explains why he thought Medusa herself attacked him."

"The curse of Medusa. Since you've read my article—"

"Let's not play games, Azcárate. This was a robbery and homicide, nothing more."

"And that seems trivial to you?"

"Not at all. The main suspect was the girl, of course; she was the last person besides the victim known to have been at the museum. The carabinieri questioned her thoroughly, but could find nothing linking her to the robbery. According to her statement, the poor man was sitting near the main entrance when she left. When she returned the next day, she found him lying on the floor, in the throes of death. It was only later that she realized the statue was no longer in its place. Her innocence is almost beyond doubt; she has alibis: the wife of the deceased security guard, who saw her outside the museum that night, and a boyfriend."

"Of the security guard?"

"Of the girl."

"Right." Jaime wolfed down another piece of tenderloin and chased it with a gulp of wine. "You make this robbery sound like the work of a genius. How far do you figure the security guard must have moved away from the main entrance for him not to have seen anyone come in?"

"Not far. As I said, it's a small museum. It doesn't even have cameras installed."

"If your description is anything to go by, this isn't a difficult case. Investigate the employees. I bet someone has a copy of the key. They found a way to drug the old man's Aperol, waited until he was out of his head, then opened the door and snuck into the museum. After they took out the guard, they grabbed the sculpture and left. No need to call Sherlock Holmes. Now, if you'll excuse me, I'm going to order dessert then head back to my hotel for a nap. I'd like to see the exhibition this evening."

"Don't bother. Have you seen the line? It goes almost all the way around the cathedral. If I were you, I'd wait until tomorrow morning."

"Perhaps." Jaime fixed him with a look. "And what do you suggest I do in the meantime to keep boredom at bay?"

For a moment Amatriaín was confused. Speaking to Jaime Azcárate was like playing tug of war with an opponent who had complete control over the rope.

"Well . . . you could help me."

"Help you what?"

"Come on, Azcárate. You studied this almost undocumented sculpture, then wrote about it in a university essay and an article for *Arcadia*. For better or for worse, that makes you the world's foremost expert on the piece. Maybe you could tell me why the thieves were so interested in it."

"I've already told you everything I know. It was created by a minor sculptor about whom very little is known. Who stole it and why? I don't have the faintest idea. Why should there be a special reason? You said yourself that thefts are on the rise. This case doesn't seem all that complicated to me. What do you need me for? And I'll remind you: I'm here to enjoy a brief and well-deserved vacation."

"But doesn't it seem odd to you that someone would go to so much trouble to steal this particular statue? There are far more valuable works of art at that museum. And if a museum employee is responsible, why would that person risk losing their job and going to prison? There must be more to this Medusa than meets the eye."

Jaime listened sleepily, his arms crossed, then gave a rather unenthusiastic laugh. "All right. You win. No doubt the Medusa is the key to finding a treasure of incalculable value. Or perhaps the secret to eternal life. With your imagination, you should write a series of mystery novels set in the art world. For a while they were quite fashionable—"

"Azcárate—"

"—although lately their popularity has dropped, and I hear publishers aren't taking on unknown writers anymore."

"Hey—"

"But why don't you give self-publishing a go? You could try your hand at mommy porn. Or perhaps that new thing with dinosaurs?"

"Azcárate, I'm being serious!"

Jaime called over the helmet-haired waiter, paid the exact amount of the bill plus a two-euro tip, then stood and, with a polite nod of the head, turned and left the restaurant.

Amatriaín sat looking at the money and empty plates, trying to understand what he had done wrong, why the conversation had not panned out as he expected. Then suddenly he pushed aside the dishes and looked under his iPad. A glint flashed in his eye.

It appeared that Jaime Azcárate's lack of interest was all an act.

He had taken the drawing.

2

The bartender's cleavage threatened to spill from her neckline, but somehow stayed in place as she served a gin and tonic to the stranger who had found himself in the bar.

Looking resigned, Jaime stared at the transparent liquid that sparkled in his glass. The alcohol could not distract him from the fact that his current crisis did not fit any of the previous patterns. It had been almost ten years since he hit the milestone age of twenty-five; he had just six to go before he reached forty. He lived on his own, he had fantastic friends and a job that he was passionate about, and he was accountable to no one but himself. So what was going on with him? What was the cause of the emptiness he'd been feeling for some time now and the source of the whisper in his ear that said he was throwing his life down the toilet?

The darkness seemed blackest when he was alone with his pillow at night. He spent his days working at the magazine and busied himself searching for mysteries and hidden treasures. But when he finished an article or returned home from an expedition, he felt as if the earth was swallowing him up. His mother, the few times she'd seen him recently, had noticed the change. She had attributed it to a single cause, asking:

"Why don't you find yourself a nice girlfriend?" Jaime had burst out laughing. He didn't think that was a good solution. At best, he'd simply infect someone else with his pessimism. Instead, he'd sold his old Renault 21 and was learning to shoot a gun. A positive way to deal with what he was feeling? Who could say?

And now there was this business with the Medusa . . .

God knew Jaime had tried to forget about the damn statue and enjoy his weekend, but good intentions weren't enough. From the moment he'd arrived back at his guesthouse, he had been lying on the bed, looking at the drawing of the sculpture and thinking about the university study. He hadn't exactly lied to Amatriaín when he said he'd never written an essay on Italian baroque sculpture, but that didn't mean that no such study existed. A person who Jaime once had been very close to kept popping into his mind and then disappearing again after delivering a look of disdain and a single message:

Moron.

That one word, mysteriously conjured from the past, tormented him now just as it had after arriving by text message more than a decade earlier.

He grabbed his gin and tonic, leaned back against the bar, and looked around the room. On the dance floor in the back, just visible through dense smoke tinted with green light, a group of girls dressed in skimpy Friday-night attire danced to Shakira, Britney Spears, and El Canto del Loco. Jaime wondered whether they were just there to dance or they had something else in mind. It made no difference to him either way. He'd never been the type to approach a woman in a bar.

Or almost never: the one time he'd tried, his friend Roberto had been forced to step in to keep him from making a fool of himself. Since then, Jaime had always waited for women to take the initiative—something that, men know, almost never happens.

As he was mulling this over he felt a presence next to him at the bar. He turned to find himself next to one of the most beautiful women he'd ever seen.

She was tall, almost as tall as Jaime, with wavy black hair, bronzed skin, and bright, almond-shaped eyes accentuated by violet eye shadow that gave her an exotic look. Her sleeveless black dress was cut low enough to drive the bartender's cleavage from his memory, and her legs were long and strong-looking. If she had looked any more appetizing, thought Jaime, she'd have to be served up on a toothpick.

"Hello!" she said with a disarming smile. "Don't I know you from somewhere?"

Jaime racked his brain, but it was pointless. If he'd crossed paths with this woman before, her image would have been etched into his memory. He could have said that, but he replied, "Nah. You're mistaking me for my womanizing brother. I'm the intellectual one."

The girl laughed, and Jaime, seeing the effect humor had on her, relaxed and readied his weapons of seduction: a series of silly phrases and amusing stories that usually worked on girls who were easily entertained. "That was a lie," he corrected. "Actually, I have a sister, but she doesn't look anything like me."

"Too bad for her."

"That's what I always say."

Jaime tensed when the stunning brunette began to flirt with her eyes. What was this? It wasn't unusual for women to notice him. He was tall and slim—handsome even, his mother would say—but this was too easy. He wondered if the girl was Vicente Amatriaín in disguise, and he was tempted to stick his hand under her dress to find out. "What's your name?" he asked.

"Sandra."

"Nice. I think you're the first Sandra I've met."

"Shame. They say good things come in threes."

"Maybe they don't in my life."

Sandra laughed again. "And you are . . . No, wait. Let me guess. Jorge."

"Almost: Jaime."

"Hey, I was only . . ." She counted with her fingers and laughed again, "three letters off. But I could still swear I've seen you before."

"You're sure?"

"When you say it that way, I guess not."

There are few things more stupid than a conversation between two strangers in a bar, Jaime thought. Which was precisely why he decided to relax and play the game. He put on his most carefree expression and bought the woman a drink. After all, that was what she was looking for.

After two martinis and a couple more gin and tonics, Jaime gleaned that Sandra was of Milanese origin, which explained her musical accent, and that for several years she had been living in Soria. She worked as an administrative assistant for an insurance company and had travelled to El Burgo de Osma for the weekend to get away from work pressures. She also mentioned a lawyer she'd been living with for two years, who had left Sandra for a colleague who was five years younger than her. Since then, Sandra said, she had stopped taking men seriously and now only used them for sex. This last part, said in such a self-assured, natural way, came as a pleasant surprise to Jaime, who in a short span of time had come to know all about the private life of this stunning brunette. She hadn't even bothered to ask where he was from.

She drained the contents of her glass through lips painted violet to match her eyelids, then slowly leaned toward Jaime's ear and whispered something.

"What did you say?" he asked over the crowd noise and music. "Speak louder!"

Sandra's sudden laugh was a bit too enthusiastic. Clearly the martinis had gone to her head.

"I said, shall we leave? It's so hot in here!"

"If you like. I'm easy prey today."

She laughed again, and as she stepped back, bumped into a girl who was arguing with her boyfriend. Jaime recognized them as the angry couple from the restaurant, but he had no chance to acknowledge them, because Sandra had grabbed him by his belt and was dragging him, stumbling, toward the door.

The night was cool, and Sandra covered herself in the red overcoat she had reclaimed from a peg on the bar. As they walked together, Jaime listened to the rhythmic clacking of her heels and tried to guess her age. She might have been four or five years older than him, but her beauty and spirit made her age irrelevant. When they'd reached Casa Genaro, he opened the guesthouse door slowly to avoid any creaking sounds. "Don't make any noise. The landlady might not like me bringing a drunk woman back to my room at this time of night."

Sandra could not contain herself and let out a burst of laughter just as Jaime put one hand over her mouth. He scooped her up, one hand behind her knees, and carried her up the stairs. She smelled good, like berries. At the door to his room, he stopped and put her down. "It appears that you like me," she said, giggling at the bulge below his belt.

"Don't get too excited," he replied, reaching into his pocket and taking out a big key that was chained to a domino. "But my pants *are* starting to feel tight."

Sandra ran her tongue over her lips. "Maybe you should take them off."

"Shh, be good for a minute. Once we're on the other side of this door, you can be as bad as you like."

Under the alcohol's influence, Jaime wasn't even surprised by his good luck. He hadn't expected to go to bed with anything but his pillow and his own drunken self, so the unforeseen encounter was boosting both his self-esteem and his virility. However, the thrill was short-lived.

He hadn't yet managed to get the key in the lock when an alarm bell rang in his mind. Something was not right.

He looked at Sandra. Her expression had turned cold, and the "sweet girl" mask was gone, leaving a face as hard as granite. Jaime still didn't understand what was happening until he felt a metal object pressing into his side over his leather jacket. Slowly, he dropped the key into his pocket then held up his hands.

"Very good, Einstein," she said in a deep voice Jaime hadn't heard before. "Now walk in front of me and down the stairs. Slowly and quietly."

3

Sandra's Italian accent had moved to the foreground, as if she'd suddenly reclaimed her ethnic roots. Jaime walked down the stairs, encouraged by the gun barrel pressing into him from behind. Adrenaline began to overcome the dulling effect of the alcohol on his brain and he became more aware of what was happening. His arms and legs trembled and his heart was beating at twice its normal speed, but his fear didn't paralyze him. His biggest regret was having taken such obvious bait. Sandra was a textbook femme fatale.

Who do you think you are, fool? Brad Pitt?

He made an effort to breathe deeply, trying not to let panic set in. Near the bottom of the stairs he turned around with his arms still raised.

Sandra didn't even blink. "Keep walking."

"What is this, anyway? A holdup?"

"Just turn around and walk."

Seeing that she wasn't in a talking mood, Jaime obeyed. When they reached a closed door at the opposite end of the guesthouse lobby, Sandra shoved him inside. After waiting a few seconds to make sure all was quiet, she followed him in and closed the door behind her. "Very good. Now tell me who you're working for."

Jaime blinked as he tried to take in the absurd question. "Working? I'm here on vacation."

Though he was past the initial shock, he was still dazed and confused. He feared that the alcohol's effects would make him appear braver than he really was and he'd end up with a bullet in him for talking too much.

Looking around, he saw that they were in the guesthouse kitchen. Strings of garlic hung from the ceiling, and the remains of a rabbit rested on the countertop. The only light came from a streetlamp, filtered in through the translucent glass of the door to the outside.

"If you're on vacation you must work somewhere."

"All right, I'll tell you." Jaime took a breath and, without thinking first about what he was going to say, he let the alcohol do the talking. If she got mad, so much the better; the more noise she made, the more likely she was to wake the guesthouse owners or some other guest. "I'm police. The chief asked me to investigate all the horny brunettes in Castilla-León and find out whether they'd be prepared to screw our informers to make them talk. Or the captain, to help him let off some steam. Or all of us, so we stop demanding a Christmas bonus . . ."

The whole thing didn't come out as witty as Jaime would have liked. Fearing imminent payback, he threw up his hands to protect himself. But the woman was no fool and she didn't make a move toward him. Instead, she started laughing. He felt ridiculous.

"You're wasting your breath. No one's coming down here until tomorrow morning, so I have all night to find out what I want to know."

"Oh yeah? Well I warn you, I charge by the word."

"For me you'll do it for free."

"You wish."

"Oh, you're going to tell me what I want to know and you're going to be quick about it. There are plenty of things in this kitchen I can use to help with your interrogation."

"You're going to gouge my eyes out with a spoon? If you do that I'll scream."

"If you scream, I'll blow your head off."

"And if you blow my head off . . ." Unable to think of a way to finish the sentence, Jaime abruptly thrust his hand under her dress. Sandra turned red and slapped him.

"What the hell are you doing?"

"Nothing, just checking something." Jaime stroked his chin.

Sandra pushed her pistol against his forehead.

"Enough games. I'll repeat the question: Who are you and who are you working for?"

It occurred to Jaime that he could save himself a lot of misery if he just followed this psychopath's instructions.

"If I tell you, will you explain what all this is about?"

Sandra stood motionless, still holding the weapon as Jaime looked back in a stupor. She cut a striking image: a beautiful and dangerous woman in a black dress and red overcoat, pointing a gun at him. All that was missing was the wailing of a saxophone. And a Dashiell Hammett signature.

"All right," she said, lowering the pistol.

"My name's Jaime Azcárate. I work for the magazine *Arcadia* and I'm here to see the *Ars Homini* exhibition. I'm a Libra, I live in Madrid, I don't have a girlfriend, and my mother insists I should find one. Though if she met you, I'm certain she'd change her mind."

"A sensible woman. What's your relationship with Vicente Amatriaín?"

There it was. The little light that had been flickering in his mind began to blaze. Two events as unusual as these happening in one day? Of course they were related.

"Amatriaín? If you'd asked me that earlier you could've saved me the trouble of reaching under your dress."

Ignoring the comment, Sandra deftly dug through her purse with her free hand and took out a crumpled piece of paper.

"And he gave you this?"

Jaime winced upon finding himself face-to-face again with Medusa. He had done his best to forget all about the business of the statue, but everything was working against him.

"If I'd known you were already acquainted with my hotel room, I'd have suggested going to your place."

"Did Amatriaín give you this drawing? Yes or no?"

Jaime quickly explained that Vicente Amatriaín had approached him in the restaurant and asked him for help in the case of the stolen sculpture. He emphasized what he'd told Amatriaín: that all he wanted to do was relax and forget about things. That, Jaime told her, was why he had gone into that bar at such an unlucky moment.

Sandra regarded him silently for a few seconds, looking not at all convinced. "You're saying you didn't already know him."

"I'd never seen him before. I'd remember those white teeth and nasty scars."

"Yet you both happened to be in El Burgo de Osma at the same time, and then in the same restaurant, where he took a liking to you and gave you a drawing of the statue he's searching for. Either I'm stupid or I'm missing something here."

"Or both. What does the sculpture have to do with you?"

"It's a long story—one I'm not about to tell you."

Jaime considered the possibility that this was a case of mistaken identity and that, despite how things looked, Amatriaín, not Sandra, was the villain in the story. He recalled that Amatriaín had not shown him any identification. What if all that stuff about the EHU was a lie and he wanted Jaime to help him find the sculpture for some other, unknown purpose? He decided to resolve the matter directly. "Are you a cop?"

Sandra smiled at his naiveté.

"Do you really believe that's a possibility?" She looked at the clock and then aimed at Jaime again. "Sorry, *caro*. Time's up."

Jaime tensed. The woman's stony glare could mean only one thing. "You wouldn't shoot me here," he said.

"Shoot you? What we have in store for you is far more subtle."

"We? Who's we?"

Her weapon still pointed at him, Sandra made her way to the walk-in freezer located at one end of the kitchen. When she opened the door, a cloud of frosty air floated out, then quickly dissolved. She signaled for Jaime to step inside. "You're going to freeze me?" he asked in disbelief.

"You know the castle on the hill, at the entrance to the town? In three hours your lifeless body will be outside it. You'll be taken for a foolish, drunken homeless person who fell asleep out in the open and froze to death. The autopsy will reveal nothing abnormal and there'll be no investigation. How's that for subtle?"

"No, no, wait. You're making a mistake. Amatriaín gave me the drawing but I don't know anything about it and I never wanted to. I left it in my room, wadded up in a ball, just the way you found it. I don't want anything to do with that Medusa's head! What else do I have to say to convince you?"

"To tell you the truth, this plan was for Amatriaín, but he's managed to get away. Don't worry, though. He'll join you soon enough."

Jaime began to breathe heavily. He lifted his arms and walked around the kitchen, trying to hide the fact that his legs were trembling again. "They'll never believe I was a drunken tramp."

"I don't give a damn what anyone believes. I'll be long gone by the time they discover the truth, if they ever do."

"Why are you doing this? I'm telling you—I have nothing to do with Amatriaín. What is it about this Medusa that's so important?"

Just as she was about to reply, the translucent glass in the door lit up, and a dreamlike shadow was projected onto it.

Someone was coming. Jaime took his chance.

Quickly, he launched himself against Sandra, who could not keep her balance in those heels and immediately fell backward and hit the wall. The pistol flew out of her hand and Jaime managed to grab it. Suddenly the rules of the game had changed: now he was the one aiming the weapon at the startled woman in the red overcoat. "You should be more careful," he said, smiling.

"You don't say," she said, smiling back.

Her lack of concern alarmed Jaime, but his apprehension came too late. By now the door had opened and the figure he had seen through the glass was standing beside him, holding a long object. The man was dressed in black and wore a demented smile beneath his mustache. *"Buona sera,"* he said. "Can I help you?"

Jaime felt a sharp blow to the head and an intense pain, and then he was overcome with the sensation of falling into a deep, dark spiral.

4

Madrid

The ringing of the telephone broke the silence in the room like a train sounding its horn in a desert. On the third ring, a hand reached out from between the sheets and grabbed the wireless handset from its base.

Still half-asleep, *Arcadia* editor Laura Rodríguez spoke without rising or even opening her eyes. "Mmm . . . Hello?"

Given her languid tone, the man on the other end of the line might have reasonably assumed he'd reached some kind of sex line. But instead of cursing and hanging up, he asked, "Dr. Rodríguez?"

"Who is this?"

"It's Vicente Amatriaín."

"Who?"

"Amatriaín, from the EHU. Remember?"

Laura opened her eyes, sat up, and planted her feet on the floor. As she turned on the lamp and looked at the clock, she brushed away the curly cascade of red hair that fell across the right side of her face. "It's one thirty in the morning," she said in an icy voice.

"I've been calling your cell phone all evening."

"The battery's dead. Who gave you my home number?"

"I took the liberty of finding it myself, since no one at your office would put me through to you."

"I was in a meeting with the CHR bosses. I told you I would contact you. I have your number."

"Yes, of course, I know. But . . . Look, I'm sorry to bother you so late, but I have to talk to you about your contributor."

"Jaime? What is it?"

"I was with him a few hours ago. And to be honest, his attitude disappointed me."

"I don't follow."

"To put it nicely, he didn't show much willingness to help us."

"Perhaps you didn't ask him the right way."

Amatriaín waited for Laura to advise him about his next step.

"Listen, Señor Amatriaín," she said. "As we discussed the other day, the Center for Historical Research will back your plan and do everything possible to help you recover the lost works of art. To be honest with you, to me, the idea of *Arcadia* publishing a report on your methods seems opportunistic, exhibitionistic, and inappropriate. But from a purely selfish point of view, I realize this could pull in readers and benefit us, too. I'll call Jaime in the morning to bring him up to date."

"I already did that, but the outcome wasn't as positive as I'd hoped."

"You're a total stranger and I'm his boss. And by the way, Jaime is within his rights to refuse."

"But you told me—"

"I know what I told you: Jaime is curious by nature and easily enticed by a good mystery. But he doesn't accept commissions from strangers just for the hell of it. I'll call him, okay?"

Laura was about to hang up when Amatriaín's voice stopped her. "Wait."

Laura wavered, holding the phone halfway between its base and her ear. After a moment, she chose the latter. "I'm listening."

"Azcárate insisted that he knew nothing about the study you mentioned."

"That doesn't surprise me."

"But you—"

"I said what I said, but that study was credited to two people, one of them being someone Jaime did not end on good terms with. Leave this to me. I promise I'll talk to him and we'll get things sorted out."

"But when?"

Laura moistened her lips with her tongue and, despite how tired she felt, smiled. "Don't worry. He'll contact you."

After hanging up, Laura jumped out of bed, turned on her cell phone—which was at full charge—and dialed Jaime's number. It didn't surprise her when a businesslike voice told her that the person she was calling could not take her call right now. She left him a message, even though she knew she wouldn't get a response, and then looked up the number for Hotel Virrey Palafox in El Burgo de Osma. Before being reunited with her pillow, there was one thing she wanted to check out. The receptionist who answered her call sounded friendly, but when Laura asked to be put through to Jaime Azcárate's room, the woman told her nobody by that name was staying at the hotel.

Laura sat on the bed for a few moments, a blank stare on her face. Then she dialed another number. The phone rang seven times before someone grunted in her ear. "Grmph."

"I don't believe it. Were you asleep?"

"Are you kidding?" a gruff, powerful voice replied. "I was just fighting off a zombie attack in the east wing. It's no end of excitement here tonight."

If Laura had been in better humor she would have laughed at Roberto Barrero's banter, but her worry had affected her mood. She pictured the bald, potbellied security guard slumped against the desk in the CHR lobby, his eyes glassy, white drool collected at the corner of his goatee-encircled mouth, the cobwebs of his slumber slowly falling away. "Well, get rid of those zombies quick because I have a question for you: What do you know about Jaime?"

"That he's a jackass. That he can't comb his hair. I don't know, a lot of things. You'll need to be more specific."

"I mean, has he called you, or have you spoken to him?"

"Not since he went gallivanting off to El Burgo de Osma, no. Why? Has something happened?"

"Just that he's taken his gallivanting a bit too seriously and seems to have disappeared off the face of the earth."

"Gallivanting should never be taken seriously," said Roberto. "All right, Jaime's a jackass. But lately his head's been a mess, and this vacation was well deserved. I could use a break myself, by the way."

"Talk to your bosses about it."

"If you were my boss, I'd be doing that already."

Laura ignored the dig. For years, Roberto had been trying to talk her into hiring him at the journal as a photographer, but *Arcadia*'s finances kept her from taking on any more staff.

"But I'm not your boss. You'll have to take this to someone who can help you."

"I already have. By this time next week, you'll see neither hide nor hair of me—not that there's much hair left to see."

"I'm thrilled for you. Now listen, I need Jaime back here as soon as possible for a briefing. You know how he is—when he's on vacation his house could be burning down and he wouldn't know because he won't answer the phone."

"What do you expect me to do? He didn't tell me where he was staying, what he was doing—nothing. All he said was that he wouldn't miss me. You know how that son of a bitch is. I don't know why I'm bothering to teach him to shoot."

"To shoot?" Laura was horrified.

"Yeah, but don't worry. He's a dead loss. If he was hunting King Kong he wouldn't even hit the Empire State Building."

"Please don't tell me these things." Just the thought of Jaime with a weapon in his hand would give her nightmares for months. "But see what you can find out, okay? Do you know whether he drove his car?"

"What car? He sold that old beater he had. He's so cheap, he probably took the bus." Roberto exhaled loudly. "Look, I'm not his mother. Isn't there anyone else you can call?"

"Not at this hour."

"Great. You know the name of his hotel, at least?"

Laura felt a knot in her stomach. She swallowed and told Roberto the name of the place Jaime had said he'd be staying.

"I'm not promising anything," Roberto said.

"I didn't ask you to promise. But if he sees it's you calling, he might actually respond."

"I'm sure he will. But he shouldn't get his hopes up—my heart belongs to someone else."

Laura said good night and hung up. Despite their very different natures, Roberto and Jaime had been friends since their paths first crossed five years earlier, when Jaime was working on a story in the Sepúlveda area. She was certain the two men shared more secrets than they admitted, but Roberto had sounded sincere about trying to reach Jaime. She just hoped he would have more luck than she'd had. As she switched off the bedside light, she felt a twinge of apprehension.

"Jaime, please tell me you haven't got yourself into trouble again," she prayed into the gloom.

5

El Burgo de Osma

The cold air woke him.

Jaime was lying faceup in the dark, and something under him was digging into his back. When he tried to sit up, he realized that what he'd felt were his own hands, tied at the wrists. The darkness was eased only by a vaporous glow from somewhere above, and the only sound came from the whirring fans that dispersed freezing air throughout the chamber. His head hurt, and he felt as if millions of needles were stabbing him all over his body. Gathering his strength, he straightened his back and sat up on the cold floor. The fact that he was alive told him he hadn't been there long. Fortunately, his captors had left him in all his clothes, including his leather jacket. It occurred to him to scream for help, but the freezer's insulation immediately absorbed the sound of his choked voice.

Shivering almost unbearably, he dragged himself backward, trying to find an edge sharp enough to cut through the rope wrapped around his wrists. Though his limbs were nearly numb, he could feel that his assailants hadn't tied the cord too tight—in order to avoid leaving marks, no doubt. Yet it was tight enough to prevent him from untying himself.

As he scooted backward his back hit something hard. Feeling around with his hands, he determined that the object was a wooden crate. He tried to slice the rope by rubbing it against one of the box's corners, but the edge proved too blunt. As he slid himself along the floor again, something poked his right side, causing a sharp pain. Carefully, he turned and ran his stiff hands over the object, discovering an irregular surface full of razor-sharp projecting parts. The feel was familiar. He'd experienced something similar in his hands and between his teeth on more than one occasion. He gave silent thanks for that bony discovery; the hard vertebrae of a dead animal would be the perfect tool for cutting through rope.

"I don't know what you were in life," he said to the unhappy row of bones, "but if I get through this, I promise I'll go vegetarian."

Making conversation with a cow's skeleton wasn't exactly a sign of sanity, but Jaime knew from experience that talking to whatever was in front of him could help him fight against panic. In the past he had chatted to lamps, spoons, shoes, and even rain—and on all those occasions he'd managed to keep his situation under control.

Once free of his bonds, he started flexing his hands to restore their circulation and soon began to feel a pain that, despite his discomfort, he gladly received. "Welcome back," he said to them, eager to talk to anything now.

Still using the cow's ribcage as a saw, he freed his legs from the rope and then tried to stand, but weakness and poor circulation caused his first attempt to fail. Lying on his back, he pumped his legs in the air as if riding a bicycle before trying again, and on his next attempt managed to stand and dodder toward the freezer door. He felt the surface of the door from top to bottom, looking for a way to open it, but he was out of luck. His kidnappers had tampered with the handle and it now hung uselessly from the door.

He felt around in his jacket pocket and scowled when he found that they'd taken his cell phone. "Hey!" he cried out. "Can anyone hear me?"

But he knew no one would hear him calling out. The walls of the freezer were lined with thick sheets of aluminum, rendering useless any attempt he might make to get help from inside.

That was when it hit him that he was completely alone.

No friends or family knew what hotel he was staying at. Even if they did, they'd still have no idea he was in danger. He'd been left to his fate in an icy, hermetically sealed death trap.

Sandra had told him his body would appear three hours later near the castle on the hill. He held his watch closer to the weak light overhead and saw that it was now ten past two. He guessed that they would come to collect his frozen body around four o'clock. As an art history major, Jaime didn't consider himself a natural scientist, but even he knew he couldn't survive the cold for two more hours.

As he shivered, he tried to locate a switch to turn off the fans, but either the switch did not exist or it was beyond his reach. He had to find a way to turn off the refrigeration, and he had to do it quickly, before the cold began to paralyze him.

Tracing the current of cold air back to its source, he found an opening that concealed one of the fans. The cavity was located in a corner of the ceiling, three meters up. Drawing upon the little bit of warmth left in his body, he made his way back to the corner where he'd found the wooden crate and discovered an entire tower of them. He stretched to reach the top one, hobbled back to the other side of the freezer with it, and set it down on the floor. By standing on the crate he was able to reach the metal grille that protected the fan. Jaime stuck all his fingers into the holes and pulled with all his strength, but the grille was screwed into the ceiling and wouldn't budge. He cursed the freezer's manufacturers and their security measures. What had they feared would happen? That a group of frozen cows would attempt to reenact *The Great Escape*?

He then noticed the dark cables running across the ceiling. These came out of the fan nearest to him and crossed to the other fan, located in the opposite corner of the freezer. If he could destroy the cables, perhaps he could shut down the fans' motors. Using the cow's backbone as a lever, he managed to pop out a refrigeration tube and tear out one of the cables at the point where it attached. Then he grabbed the box and put it under the other fan, repeating the process. Once the cables were hanging from the ceiling and the tubes had been split in half, Jaime was relieved to see that the fans had stopped. Exhausted, he threw himself to the floor. Unbelievably, he was sweating. However, the satisfaction of destroying the refrigeration system was fleeting, because it felt to Jaime as though he'd done nothing more than raise the temperature from absolute zero to freezing. The huge quantity of frozen food and the freezer's effective insulation would soon turn his sweat to frost.

Thinking it might help to have a shelter, he improvised one using the wooden crates. But within five minutes he'd crawled back out from his refuge, knowing that he had to do something to warm up or there'd soon be two stiff carcasses in the freezer. He had to find some way to keep warm until his would-be murderers came to collect his body. When they opened the door he would attempt his escape, but he had to survive another hour and a half of cold first.

Desperate, he looked around again for something he could use to force the door open, but found nothing. The sweat on his chest had become a breastplate of ice. He unbuttoned his shirt and beat himself until the frozen perspiration fell from his body.

Then he remembered a warning that his mother used to give him as a boy: If you sweat and then get cold, you'll get sick.

Of course! He had found the solution. He looked at the wooden crates, knowing what he was about to do would be tough but that it was his only chance. But he figured he'd been meaning to join a gym, anyway.

At four o'clock in the morning, a white van bearing an egg company's logo stopped in front of the entrance to Casa Genaro. A man dressed in black climbed out and crossed the pavement as nimbly as a grasshopper. The light from a nearby streetlamp fell on his face, revealing blue eyes over a long nose and a large mustache. As he reached the guesthouse door, he heard one of the van's windows being lowered and turned back toward it. "Be quick about it," said the dark-haired woman inside the vehicle. "The sun's about to come up."

The man spread his arms and smiled. "Don't worry! When has your cousin Clark ever failed you?"

The woman snorted. The man strode into the guesthouse humming a tarantella and then headed down the stairs to the kitchen, where just a few hours before he'd whacked that poor unfortunate on the head. His hands turned the wheel on the freezer door and then pulled it toward him. The cloud of freezing air that came from the gap was much smaller than it had been earlier, but he didn't notice this detail and quickly slipped inside, taking care to prop the door open with a stool.

A strange feeling came over him when he saw that the body was not where they'd left it. In its place there was a strange structure built of broken wooden crates. As he approached he could hear a sobbing sound, accompanied by the chattering of teeth.

It seemed that the wretch was alive, albeit at death's door.

He peered behind the pile of crates, expecting to find a dying lump of frozen meat, but all he saw was more boxes. The body had to be buried under them. "May I ask what you're doing? I hope you haven't injured yourself or broken any bones; the boss will be furious."

As he began to remove one of the crates, he realized that only the ones forming the outer structure were made of wood. The crates covering the moaning, shivering body were made of polyurethane and were much lighter. "Hey you," the man with the mustache called out. "Stop playing games and come out of there or I'll—"

Just then a long object shot out from between the boxes and whistled past his face. Cartons and plastic flew everywhere as his intended victim clambered to his feet, retrieved the object, and tried for a second time to strike him with what looked, unbelievably, like a cow's backbone.

To Jaime's dismay, the man with the mustache moved with agility and evaded his second lunge as easily as he had the first. Before he could attack once more, he felt the vertebrae cut into his hand as the improvised weapon was violently snatched from him.

"You're clever, kid," said the man. "Very clever. But you have no idea who you're messing with."

Jaime knew that in his weakened state he was no match for this dockyard goon, and he had no desire to hang around and get beaten to a pulp. He ran toward the freezer door, but the man struck him on the leg with the backbone, throwing him to the floor.

"Hey! What did I tell you? Come on, get up from there."

Jaime rolled over and saw the man advancing toward him with the bony club held high above his head.

"I wasn't supposed to hit you," the man said, "but now you're really pissing me off."

As the cow spine traced an arc through the air, Jaime rolled his body away to evade the blow. As he stood up, he found himself at the end of the freezer opposite the door, near some shelves with boxes on them. Knowing that the thug was between him and the door, he decided to escape upward. He jumped to his feet and started to climb, moving himself beyond the reach of the man, who was now laughing heartily.

"Go on, keep climbing. The higher you go the harder you'll fall."

Jaime crouched at the top of the shelves as the man moved toward him.

"Ready to come down?" Grinning, the thug grabbed the shelving with both hands and pulled until he'd torn it from the wall. As he looked up, he expected to see the terrified face of his victim.

But what he saw was a box full of ice bags flying toward him like a meteorite and then smashing into his face.

The man crashed to the floor, his septum shattered, blood gushing from his nostrils.

Jaime jumped down from the shaky shelving and grimaced at the sight of the man lying faceup on the ground. He assumed this must be the person who'd delivered the blow to his head earlier, when he'd been aiming the gun at Sandra. He was about to run out of the freezer when he glimpsed a metal object protruding from his assailant's belt. Jaime bent down and grabbed the automatic pistol. When he stood and turned, he found himself face-to-face with Sandra, who was staring at him in disbelief.

"You!"

"Yup, me."

She looked thoroughly confused. She'd undoubtedly expected to find a dead body. Instead, Jaime was very much alive. He was not frozen, although he was weary, his breathing was agitated, and his brow dripped with sweat as if he'd just run a five-thousand meter race.

"How . . . ?" she stammered. She had exchanged her black dress for camouflage pants and a fleece jacket, but despite her change of attire and shocked expression, Jaime thought she still looked dazzling. "It's impossible!"

"Nothing's impossible," he said, pointing the gun to direct her out of the kitchen.

The sun had yet to rise when Jaime, standing outside on the sidewalk, noticed the white van parked in front of the hotel entrance, its engine still running. He pushed Sandra inside and climbed into the driver's seat.

"Where are we going?" Sandra asked as he put the vehicle in gear and drove toward the center of town.

Jaime waited a few seconds before responding. He hadn't bothered to tie her up, assuming she wouldn't dare do anything stupid while the van was in motion. He glanced over and saw her gripping the seat, her knuckles white and eyes wide open.

"Where are we going, you ask?" Jaime didn't know the answer to the question himself. Then it came to him. It was a crazy idea, but there could be no better way to accomplish what he intended. "How about we stick to the plan?"

"The plan? What plan?"

"Your plan. Hold on tight. Next stop, Osma Castle." A triumphant smile spread across his face. "I'll just need to make one small change. It turns out that the person who will be found dead won't be a homeless man. It'll be a homeless woman."

6

They sped past the cathedral and crossed the River Ucero, leaving behind the town and its sleeping inhabitants. Jaime eased his foot off the gas only when he saw the lights of two vehicles approaching from the opposite direction. As the cars passed, he saw they were filled with young people returning from a night out, and they saluted him with a honk of the horn. He returned the gesture, adrenaline flowing through his veins and warming his body, a feeling more welcome to him than anything else in the world.

"How did you do it?" Sandra asked.

Jaime kept his eyes on the road, which was still illuminated by streetlights. Ahead, the castle ruins were silhouetted against the dark sky. "It's a trick of the human body: if you exercise, you keep warm."

"What did you do?" Her tone was mocking. "Sit-ups?"

"Oh, much better than that: I built my own weightlifting bench and used boxes as weights."

Jaime stopped along the riverbank and then, still clutching the pistol, he hauled Sandra out of the van. He gestured to her to start walking in front of him. It didn't seem like a good idea to have the discussion inside the vehicle, in case a passing driver glanced inside and noticed a haggard-looking man pointing a weapon at a woman. The hilltop, however, was the perfect spot for what he had in mind.

They began to climb the promontory upon which the eighth-century castle had been built. Floodlights illuminated the crumbling remains of the structure that had played a crucial role in a battle between Christians and Moors waged eleven centuries earlier. Jaime thought about all the people who had fought and died in that place, and it amused him to think that more than a thousand years later he'd narrowly escaped joining them. But why? It looked like he was about to find out.

He and Sandra entered through a great collapsed stone archway and into the small open space that formed the main body of the castle's structure. The smell of urine on the ground made the site an unpleasant place to linger, but Jaime already knew this would be no friendly chat. "Okay," he said to Sandra. "So what are you going to tell me about this Medusa?"

"I don't know anything. My job was to find out what you knew. Now I see we were mistaken about you."

"You don't say. But *who* was mistaken?"

"I can't tell you that. It's a secret investigation into art thefts. We saw you speaking to Vicente Amatriaín and—"

"Who is Vicente Amatriaín?"

A shadow of disbelief fell over Sandra's eyes.

"You don't know?"

"I know who he told me he was. Now I want you to tell me."

Sandra swallowed. Her features softened a little and Jaime detected a hint of relief in her expression. "He's a thief. An art trafficker who's stolen much of my family's property. When we saw you together, we figured you were mixed up with him."

"And where does the Medusa come into it?"

"The Medusa's ours. He stole it."

"Right. So if he stole the Medusa, why did he ask me to help him find it? Is he so stupid that he lost it?"

"He didn't want you to find it, idiot! He wanted to know what *you* knew about it, in case you were a threat to his plans."

Jaime thought for a moment. It was true that Amatriaín had shown more interest in the university study than he had in recruiting Jaime to search for the piece itself. But what about the statue would make a thief compromise himself? Sandra might be right about Amatriaín, but something still did not add up.

"Let's assume you're telling the truth," he said, "and you belong to a family organization searching for missing works of art. Then why kill me? How would that have made the sculpture reappear? Please, Sandra—or whatever your name is—tell me something I can actually believe, or the finger on my right hand is going to start to shake."

The woman's black eyes flashed in the first rays of sunlight that crept over the horizon. "We didn't want to kill you. We wanted to catch Amatriaín. It was a mistake, okay? We got it wrong."

"No shit. And now you apologize, and we shake hands and act like nothing's happened?"

"Please. I just follow orders. Don't . . ."

Sandra fell to her knees and held her face in her hands. Jaime thought she looked like she might throw up at any moment. She appeared genuinely distressed by her circumstances, but he already knew her to be a convincing actor.

Suddenly, she looked up and threw a stone that she'd picked up from the ground. Jaime dodged it, but by the time he'd turned back toward her, Sandra was already sprinting out of the ruins and back downhill. Jaime followed, hot on her heels.

Her luck ran out when her foot found a hole, and she lost her balance, her flawless body getting bruised, cut, and scraped as she rolled down the hillside. From his vantage point above her on the hill, Jaime didn't think she would get up, but Sandra quickly leapt to her feet and continued to run toward the van. Jaime felt in his pocket for the keys and then slowed his pace, reassured that she couldn't go far.

Unfortunately, he stepped in the same hole and also fell to the ground. He was unhurt, but by the time he got to his feet Sandra was in the middle of the road, flagging down an approaching motorcyclist.

Jaime cursed and broke into a run. Was this yet another accomplice of hers? He couldn't let her get away, or he'd never know what this whole thing was about. By the time he'd reached the bottom of the hill, the motorcyclist had stopped and Sandra was screaming. "Please, help me! This man kidnapped me!"

The motorcyclist pulled off his helmet, revealing a large, melon-shaped head and bulging eyes. He was tall and broad shouldered; his gloved hands looked powerful enough to crush walnuts.

Jaime swallowed hard. This was no associate of Sandra's, but that didn't make him feel any better. "Don't listen to her," he said. "She's the one who attacked me!"

"He has a gun!" Sandra cried.

"The gun was hers!"

"Shut up!" bellowed the motorcyclist with some difficulty. It was clear he'd been drinking, and not mineral water. "Get away from her right now."

"But I didn't—"

Before Jaime could finish, the motorcyclist leapt on him with fists flying, and the pistol flew from his hands. The biker smelled of sweat and alcohol and clearly wasn't someone who could be reasoned with.

"Stop! Ow!" Jaime curled up in a ball and tried to make himself heard between blows. "She's lying! Will you listen to me, you idiot? Ow!"

"I can't stand jerks who take advantage of women!" The man alternated words and punches. One blow hit Jaime on the shoulder, causing him to wince in pain; another to his cheek almost knocked him senseless.

"You damn fool! Don't you see she's . . ." Jaime paused as something caught his eye. "She's stealing your bike!"

The big man kept throwing punches until a familiar roar made him stop. Turning toward the road he saw the woman he was trying to protect speeding away on his motorcycle. "Hey!" he cried. "That's my bike!"

Sandra's only response was to wave as her silhouette, backlit by the rising sun, disappeared over a bump in the road. The biker turned back around with his mouth open, trying to find answers in Jaime's bruised face.

Jaime smiled through split lips dripping with strings of blood. "You just can't trust some people."

7

The café at Hotel Virrey Palafox bore no resemblance to Casa Genaro's rustic dining room.

A polished wooden bar, paneled ceiling, and chairs that had been expertly carved to fit the human backside gave it a sophisticated, stately appearance. At least, that was how it seemed to Roberto Barrero as he sat his large body at a low table in the back. As he tried for what felt like the millionth time to reach Jaime by cell phone, Roberto dipped a bit of croissant in his *café con leche* and stared without interest at the muted television mounted above the café's entrance.

He yawned. He'd left Madrid at six that morning, after he'd finished his shift at the CHR. The receptionist at the Hotel Virrey Palafox told him there was no Jaime Azcárate staying there, so he'd made the rounds at the nearby hotels and guesthouses. At one, the desk clerk remembered a rangy-looking journalist who'd tried to rent a room and said she'd recommended he try Casa Genaro.

There, he learned that a Jaime Azcárate had indeed checked in, but no one had seen him since the previous evening, and nobody answered when Roberto called Jaime's room. Finally he'd decided to return to the

Virrey Palafox and get a decent breakfast after his night shift and long drive in the van.

What're you doing here, fatso? You should be at home sleeping, he thought in a bad temper. *Or playing Lego Batman.*

Laura's call had unsettled him. He knew she was prone to exaggeration and worried too much about Jaime, but Roberto had been more than willing to do as she asked. He'd been a security guard for too long—first at a jewelry store in a shopping mall, and now at the Center for Historical Research—and despite the considerable size of his backside, he remained as restless as he'd been during his years as a photojournalist or when he stole relics to make ends meet.

It was during the last of his clandestine missions that he'd met his crazy friend Jaime Azcárate. Roberto's first impression of Jaime was that he'd been born without a common sense gene. Although the art historian–cum–journalist could be easygoing and reasonable, he didn't seem to consider the consequences of his often reckless actions. After Roberto had lost his job at the shopping mall, Jaime had persuaded Laura Rodríguez to give him a job as a photographer for the magazine. The job hadn't lasted long, but he still felt indebted to Jaime, and at least he'd managed to find work as a security guard at the CHR. And Laura, from time to time, still managed to sneak one of Roberto's photos into the publication.

He looked at his watch. For ten full minutes he'd been dipping his croissant in his coffee, which was now no warmer than the River Ucero. He gulped down what was left and, wiping his goatee with the back of his hand, pulled out his wallet to pay. He had a five-euro note halfway out when someone walked into the café.

Were it not for the bags under the man's irritated eyes, the red nose, and the slight limp, Roberto would have sworn he was looking at the highly regarded coordinator of *Arcadia*'s Mysteries of Art section.

"You've proven it again: you're actually crazier than I am," said the new arrival. The words sounded strange through his swollen lips.

"Holy shit, man! What the hell happened to you?" asked Roberto.

"Nothing good."

"I can see that. Come sit down. I'll buy you a coffee."

Barrero ordered two coffees from the waiter.

"How did you find me?" Jaime asked. "They said at the guesthouse that some foulmouthed fat guy was looking everywhere for me."

"Foulmouthed, my ass. I've been all over this fucking town after staying up all night. But before you tell me anything else, you should know that Laura's about to call the police."

"Well, she could have left a message for me. I've just come from the station."

"Here we go. What've you done now?"

"Nothing. I went to report a stolen motorbike."

Roberto knew Jaime would happily provide a long, embellished version of his adventures, so he decided to introduce a shortcut. "All right. I heard you didn't spend the night at the guesthouse. Where did you sleep?"

"Sleep? What makes you think you're the only one who was up all night?"

The waiter left the two coffees on the table.

"Let me guess," Roberto asked. "Were you alone?"

"Nope."

"With a girl?"

"Not in the way you think. But, yeah."

"I knew it! I suppose she looked like Monica Bellucci and you spent the entire night discussing epistemology? I wouldn't put it past you."

Jaime pulled a tissue from his pocket and blew his nose. "Not a bad guess. She was a stunner, all right: dark eyes, tight black dress. And yes, in fact: Italian, like Bellucci. As it happens, we did spend the whole night talking, though not exactly about epistemology."

Roberto leaned in impatiently, ready to press his friend for details. Jaime raised one hand as if to stop him.

"Before your imagination runs away with you, let me explain what really happened."

Jaime diligently recounted his strange night. When he had finished, Roberto's face was contorted with astonishment, like a Balinese mask.

"All that really happened? Are you sure you didn't fall asleep with the TV on?"

"Do you think I'd look like this if I'd been in bed all night?"

"I don't know." Roberto stroked his goatee. "It depends on what you did in it."

"There was nothing like that. The woman asked a bunch of questions, though I still don't know what she wanted. The key to all of this is Vicente Amatriaín. It seems they were after him, but he got away and they figured I'd do."

"You'd do? Do for what? You don't look good for shit right now."

"I'd 'do' to be murdered in cold blood. Quite literally, in fact." Jaime laughed at his own unintentional wordplay. "They thought Amatriaín and I were accomplices or something."

As he turned and sneezed, Roberto tried to absorb everything Jaime had told him. "And her partner? The thug with the mustache who you locked in the freezer? If you want, I could go defrost him with my fists."

"Too late. I've just been at the guesthouse. The owner told me that when her husband opened the freezer this morning, someone ran out. That guy's staying power is impressive, though of course the freezer wasn't the same after I wrecked the fans. Poor Señor Genaro still hasn't recovered from the shock. I pretended not to know anything, and they called the police. After a while they told me you'd been there looking for me and said you'd be waiting here."

"At least the bastard got what he deserved. Poor Señor Genaro—all that food gone to waste. What did the police have to say?"

"Not much," said Jaime. "The van's stolen, the license plate's phony. Luckily they left my cell phone in the glove box so I won't have to buy another; I've already lost three this year."

"Did they say anything about that Sandra woman?"

"They said they'll look for her. But she could be in Guadalajara by now."

"Wait till Laura hears about this. I bet anything you just took your last vacation."

"I accept your bet. Actually, I'm hoping Laura can shed some light on all of this for me, at least about Amatriaín. She's the one who told him I was here and that I'd written an essay on the Medusa."

Roberto looked away.

"You know something," said Jaime.

"Me? Don't be silly."

"Really?"

"Well, security guards do hear things . . ."

"And what did you hear?"

"Fuck me, what is this? Some kind of interrogation? It's just that Laura and Amatriaín had a meeting a few days ago. It looks like they're up to something, and the CHR and the journal are involved."

"Up to something?"

"That's all I know, I swear on my grandmother's life. Last night Laura called during my shift. I thought she was unreasonably worried about you."

"Sure. That's why you jumped in the van and drove straight here?"

Roberto took a sip of coffee. "I couldn't sleep. Anyway, I thought you'd need some help with all the booze and women."

"Well, you weren't wrong about that."

Roberto glanced at his watch. "We should go. Laura wants to see your face as soon as possible. Though the way you look, she might regret it."

"It's not even ten o'clock yet. Laura can wait a little longer. I have to do something first." Jaime stood.

"Where are you going?"

"We're off. You're going home to sleep, and I'm going to the Prado Museum."

Roberto frowned. "What a hipster. You're going to see paintings *now*?"

"No. Not paintings, exactly."

8

Madrid

It was just past two in the afternoon when Paloma Blasco walked out of the Prado Museum's new building. The statue of Goya stood solemnly, impervious to the passing of time. A group of tourists pointed their cameras at it as the sun projected the statue's immortal silhouette onto the grass. Paloma was wearing dark sunglasses and didn't even notice.

But Amanda Escámez wasn't fooled by her coworker's outward calm. She knew Paloma had just come from a meeting that may have sucked the life out of her, and she had a gut feeling things hadn't gone well.

"Paloma!" Her voice was like a thunderclap to the people passing by, but the person she was addressing just kept walking. Amanda's ample body broke into a run. When she caught up to her friend, she tried again.

"Paloma, honey. Are you okay?"

Paloma didn't answer immediately. The two kept walking, one beside the other, until they reached the crosswalk on Calle Felipe IV, where a crowd of pedestrians waited for the light. Paloma looked at Amanda through her tinted lenses and nodded.

"I'm fine." Her voice was thin.

"Yeah, right. You want to talk about it over lunch?"

"I told you, I'm fine!"

Amanda sized up the situation and shrugged her shoulders. "Suit yourself. See you tomorrow."

She was walking toward the statue of Neptune when she heard a shaky voice behind her. "Amanda, I'm sorry."

At just that moment the light turned green, and the crowd started marching across the street. If any of them had been facing Amanda and Paloma, they would undoubtedly have sighed with emotion at the sight of the two friends hugging each other as if making up after a decade-long quarrel.

Both women were of average height, but that's where their similarities ended. Amanda, were she standing nude with a cupid beside her, could have been the model for Rubens's *Venus at a Mirror*, while Paloma, petite and graceful, would have blended in perfectly among the handsome festivities of a Watteau painting. Their fashion choices further identified them as people of contrasts. Amanda wore a tight purple top that showed off her generous figure. Her body was abundant, but not obese, and passersby couldn't help but look at her. Her calves showed beneath a floral skirt that contrasted with her tall leather boots. A lock of dark blonde hair fell provocatively over her right eye, forcing her to blow it out of her face every few steps. Paloma, on the other hand, cut a darker figure. Her hair was bobbed, and she wore a gray suit and black raincoat.

"Were you going to see your mom?" Amanda asked, releasing Paloma from her embrace.

"No, she's eating with a friend today. And you're going to do the same."

"What?"

"Eat with a friend."

They crossed the Paseo del Prado arm in arm and strolled past the touristy souvenir shops toward a restaurant they liked near Plaza del Emperador Carlos V. It was the definitive place for *platos combinados* and *menús del día*, where Japanese tourists could be found eating paella at all hours of the day. A waiter in a white shirt and black apron greeted them and showed them to a table surrounded by a semicircular couch. When Paloma took off her sunglasses Amanda's suspicions were confirmed. "So you were fine, huh?" she said, noting the mascara marks around Paloma's honey-colored, unusually reddened eyes.

Paloma gave her a sad smile and shrugged her shoulders.

"Do me a favor and let's have a stiff drink before lunch, like in *Sex and the City*." Amanda waved the waiter over. "Excuse me, do you make cosmos?"

He smiled. "Vodka, Cointreau, and lemon juice."

"And cranberry."

"Of course. Two?"

Paloma nodded and the waiter disappeared into the forest of tables, occupied primarily by pink-skinned tourists who had burned in the Spanish sun. Only when he'd completely disappeared from sight did Amanda turn her attention back to Paloma.

"So tell me. Is this about Oscar Preston?"

Paloma nearly choked at the sound of that name. "Who? That bastard? No, this has nothing to do with that creep."

"Well, start from the beginning then. How did the meeting go?"

"Honestly, it could've gone better. Ricardo Bosch told me a bunch of stuff he's said to me before: he's delighted with me, he's bearing in mind my doctorate, my thesis, and my master's in museum studies—"

"And your command of English and Italian," Amanda added.

"He didn't say anything about that, but I'm sure he's taking that into consideration, too. No doubt he's taking it all into account, including my decision making, my teamwork, my art courses in Rome . . ."

"Honey, that's great. So what's the problem?"

"Well, now, after a month of making us jump through hoops to compete for the new deputy director position, he suddenly says this isn't an easy decision and he's going to need to assess our research credentials."

"You've lost me. What does that mean?"

"He's going to take into consideration the articles and studies we've published in journals and catalogues. And that's a real bitch for me. Preston has published at least a dozen."

"You've published some, too, I've read them."

"Nothing compared to what Preston has done. But wait for it: Ricardo also wants us to submit an original piece of research at the end of November. One that, in his words, 'will serve as a dissertation.' I mean, what does he think? That we're still at school or something?"

"But honey, that sounds exciting. Do you know what you're going to write about?"

"Yeah, I have an idea . . ." For a moment Paloma stared ahead blankly, as if someone had pushed "Pause" on her thoughts. Then her expression hardened. "But I'm worried that there isn't any point. Preston kisses Ricardo's ass every chance he gets, and Ricardo likes that. I'd be too ashamed to do that. It'd make me feel sick."

"Just be patient. Ricardo's not stupid. I bet he realizes what's going on."

"Realizes? What's he going to realize, Amanda? Preston's been working with him for years and he's the apple of Ricardo's eye. Ricardo probably decided long ago and this project is just for show. When we were alone, he actually started telling me that Preston—a graduate of Princeton and Chicago, no less—had been the top student in his class and has curated exhibitions at the Met, MoMA, and I don't remember where else." Paloma paused when the waiter delivered their drinks. "So there you go," she said when he stepped away. "The shithead has everything on his side."

Amanda wasn't so sure. She knew Ricardo Bosch well and could see that he valued Paloma, not just professionally but also as a person. But right now she was distracted by a man who was talking to the waiter. He was tall and slim, with a wild-looking mop of black hair and two-day-old beard, and he wore a leather bag over his shoulder. Amanda was rarely wrong about men, and she quickly concluded that he was gay. "When did you say you have to submit the project?" she asked Paloma.

"At the end of next month. But I'm sure Ricardo's decision is more than made. He just wants to make me suffer."

"Maybe."

Amanda was still studying the new arrival. He had a bruised face and swollen lips, but what stood out to her most was the concerned expression in his brown eyes. *Too much sensitivity for a straight guy,* she thought ruefully.

"Are you listening to me?" Paloma's voice thundered as if from a distance.

"Huh? Yeah, of course." To Amanda's surprise, the stranger was now heading toward them. He stopped at their table.

"Hullo." His voice was hoarse, as if he had a cold. "May I sit down?"

Stupefied, Amanda scooted over to make room for him. Paloma almost dropped her glass when she saw that emaciated, unshaven face with its timid smile. She looked as if she'd seen a ghost, which in a way, she had. She couldn't have been more startled if the new arrival had appeared draped in a sheet with his head tucked under his arm. When her lips finally moved, they did so just enough for her to murmur, "Jaime."

"Hello, Paloma."

Paloma was in shock. Her mind wanted to travel back in time, but somehow she kept it in the present. She drew a breath. "Amanda, this is Jaime Azcárate. An . . . old classmate from university."

Despite them being the best of friends, Paloma had never told Amanda about her relationship with Jaime. Just as all their coworkers knew that Amanda was divorced and had a son, the staff at the Prado Museum was aware of Paloma's long-standing status as a single woman. But no one knew anything of her romantic past. The sudden appearance of this handsome stranger combined with Paloma's look of surprise made Amanda think there'd once been something special between them. Special and tempestuous.

So he wasn't gay after all.

"How's it going?" she asked, giving him the customary two kisses.

"Pleased to meet you." Jaime looked meekly at Amanda, who was beaming. "But I need to speak to Paloma. I hope you don't mind."

"Of course! I was just—" Amanda moved as if to rise.

"Amanda's a colleague," Paloma interrupted. "We were about to have lunch."

"Nobody's going to stop you from having lunch. I just need to speak to you for a moment. I won't trouble you for long, I promise."

As the atmosphere grew increasingly uncomfortable, Amanda excused herself to the restroom.

Jaime took Amanda's seat and studied Paloma for a few moments. She'd hardly changed since he'd last seen her, just after they graduated from university: same average height, honey-colored eyes, and black bob. Everything was still in its place. The only noticeable differences were the tiny wrinkles she'd gained under her eyes and little bit of weight she seemed to have lost. "You haven't changed," he said.

"Neither have you. Still appearing and disappearing when least expected. How did you find me?"

"I went to the museum. They told me you often eat here."

"Only during the week. On Saturdays I usually eat at my mother's house."

"Your mom! How is she?"

"She's well. But it's best if she doesn't know that we've seen each other. What do you want, Jaime?"

"To tell you something. I don't want to scare you, but it's something that affects you directly."

When Paloma lifted her gaze Jaime saw that his ex-girlfriend's eyes were almost as red as he knew his to be.

"You know what else affects me directly? You running off to Egypt without saying anything. I had to find out from Guillermo González."

"Guillermo González! Whatever happened to him? What a brain."

"He gave up studying for his doctorate and now he's helping his dad in the butcher's shop, if you must know. But I doubt you've come to see me after all this time just so you could ask about my mother and our old classmates."

Paloma's defensiveness brought back memories of a tender but draining past, and this dampened Jaime's spirits. He was too tired to argue. Roberto had driven him straight to the museum, and he hadn't slept since his arrival in Madrid. The last thing he wanted to do now was relive the kind of endless arguments he'd run away from in the first place. "Look, I'm sorry about what happened—"

"You're sorry? For what? Using me for four years and then walking out?"

"I didn't use you."

"Oh, no? Face it, Jaime: I wanted a relationship, and you wanted someone to study with—and fuck. If I called on the weekend, either you didn't answer or you said you were busy." Her eyes filled with tears of anger. "You'd been gone for a month when I learned you'd disappeared to Cairo for a dig."

"To Herakleopolis Magna. Many of the findings we made there are now in the National Museum of Archeology."

"How lovely. But you couldn't even call to tell me you were going. Were you scared of something? You were always afraid, weren't you? And when you got back? I guess you forgot to call then, too."

"Look, calm down," said Jaime.

"Calm down? But I'm perfectly calm, can't you see that? You're the one who always got nervous when you didn't know how to put me off. Or those times when you told me you couldn't meet me because you were sick, and then later I'd find out you were really off on one of your adventures. You're a coward, Jaime. You've always been scared of commitment."

Jaime raised his hands. "Now that is true," he admitted. His eyelids were heavy; he wasn't going to argue.

Paloma burst into tears.

Jaime sat staring at her, not knowing what to do. Though the moment he walked into the restaurant he'd known reproaches would be inevitable, he hadn't expected such a dramatic reaction. He had hurt her, sure, but it had happened so many years ago. He hadn't expected the wound to still be so raw for her; he felt bad for not feeling the same way. He scooted around the circular couch and clumsily put an arm around her. "Don't cry."

"Why is everything going wrong today?"

Jaime didn't know how to answer the question, but he was saved from having to try when Amanda showed up at the table and grabbed her purse. "Sorry, guys." Despite the dramatic scene unfolding in front of her, she tried to act as though everything was normal. "I have to go. My boss wants to see me right away."

To Jaime, whose arm was still around Paloma, this sounded like the lamest excuse he'd heard in his life. Paloma, who also knew her friend was lying, lifted her head and managed a smile. "I'll call you."

"You'd better."

Amanda winked—at whom, it wasn't very clear—and left, swinging her hips. Without warning, Jaime let go of Paloma, scooted back across from her, and got straight to his original point. "I have to talk to you about our second-year piece on baroque sculpture."

Paloma's face went through a series of expressions: alarm, then panic, then momentary composure, followed by anxiety. As her hands clutched the edge of the table, they turned ivory, and her cheeks went a shade of pomegranate. "The . . . essay?" She tried unsuccessfully to sound calm.

"Gods and Monsters in Italian Baroque Sculpture."

"So that's why you've come: to thank me for letting you take credit for a piece I wrote almost entirely by myself?"

"I thanked you at the time."

"How considerate. By the way, I read that trash you wrote in *Arcadia*. 'The Curse of Medusa.' You could have consulted me before quoting *my* study as a bibliographical source for that drivel."

"It must have slipped my mind. But right now I need you to listen. Someone tried to kill me because they linked me to that study and to the bust of Medusa. I don't know why, exactly, but I think you could be in danger, too."

Paloma's eyes grew bright and her grip tightened on the table until the ivory color almost reached her wrists. This lasted only a few seconds before she restored her state of feigned calm. "The statue was stolen from the museum in Verona last month."

"Exactly." Jaime raised an eyebrow. "Do you know something I don't?"

Paloma turned her gaze away. "Only what the newspapers said. But what's this business about someone trying to kill you? Is that true or just more of the same old bullshit?"

Jaime pointed at his swollen lips and the bruise on his forehead. "Do you really think this is about some old bullshit?"

"I wouldn't put it past you."

"What do you know about the Medusa, Paloma?"

"No more than you. Andrea Bolgi was a minor sculptor, virtually unknown. It makes no sense that someone murdered a security guard to get it."

"The sculpture's good. It looks ancient."

"That's not reason enough for someone to kill for it."

The waiter appeared to take their order, but Jaime asked him to come back later. Next he rummaged in his leather bag and took out a dirty, crumpled issue of an academic journal that he placed on the table. "Ring any bells?"

"Where did you get that?"

"It was in my kidnappers' van. All the pages of our essay have been marked with a cross."

Suddenly, Paloma looked a little sick. She lowered her head into her hands and started to massage her temples. After a minute she glanced back at the copy of the *Revista Complutense* but she seemed unable to focus on it. "I'm sorry." Her eyes looked glassy and tense. "I'm not well. I want to go home."

"I'll take you," said Jaime, rising to his feet.

9

Glancing over at Paloma on the bus that was taking them down Calle Atocha, Jaime felt the pangs of conscience that visited him from time to time and then disappeared again, as if they'd found no place to take root. All these years later he still didn't know whether leaving Paloma before graduation had been the right thing to do.

At first he'd justified his behavior with the idea that he and Paloma simply had different views of what it meant to be in a relationship. Jaime believed himself to be—or *wanted* to be—a free spirit, and he rebelled against the idea of someone being able to control him. He still agreed with this assessment, but how could it have been the right thing to leave without saying anything, throwing away a four-year relationship that he knew had not been a bad one? Despite Paloma's earlier characterization of their relationship, the truth was he and Paloma had travelled, laughed, cried, and made love together countless times, often in charming places like country hotels, forest cabins, gorgeous ravines, old ruins, or at lakes. Back then they'd been drawn together, pushed apart, and reunited. Just as they were now, so many years later.

They made the journey in silence. When the bus arrived at her stop, Paloma jumped off and Jaime followed, trying not to get left behind.

Her apartment was on Calle de la Cabeza, quite near the museum, though that was its only advantage. The building's entrance was dirty and covered in graffiti. Jaime contemplated its regrettable state while Paloma tried to get the key in the lock. "So you finally managed to get your own place."

"I lived with Amanda for a while, but then she got married, and..."

Jaime realized she was trembling. He took the keys from her and opened the door. A nauseating smell immediately invaded his nostrils. "It's the drains," Paloma explained as the elevator door opened for them. "They've been promising for months to get them fixed."

The climb to the fourth floor seemed endless. Over the hum of the old elevator, Jaime could clearly hear Paloma's agitated breathing. He imagined he could even hear her heart beating. Looking at their reflection in the mirror he noted that he still towered above her. How many elevator mirrors had witnessed their many expressions of affection during those years? But this wasn't the best time to revisit old memories. The sliding doors had opened.

Paloma began to unlock the door to her apartment, but then she hesitated. That one moment of doubt told Jaime that something was not right. "What's wrong?"

"Nothing." She wiggled her key too easily in the dead bolt.

"Come on, Paloma. Since when have you not locked your door when you left?"

"I must've forgotten. My mind's been all over the place lately. Thanks for taking me home, but I'd like to be alone now."

She pushed the door open and was about to go in, but Jaime stopped her. "Are you crazy?" he whispered. "They could still be in there."

"Don't be silly. There's no one there."

"They're going after you, Paloma."

"Leave, or I'll scream."

"Very well, we'll both go. But first we'll call the police."

"Since when do you call the police?"

"Good point." Jaime reached into his bag and took out the shiny object he'd kept as a souvenir from his adventure in El Burgo de Osma.

Paloma gave a start when she saw it. "Where did you get that?"

"From the Italian mafia. Now let me go first, and stick close."

"Sorry, but no. You're not going into my home with a weapon."

"Wanna bet?" Jaime pushed the door open with his foot. Together they stood at the threshold, listening.

The only sound was the noise from the street, four floors down.

And then, suddenly, a sneeze.

"Excuse me," Jaime said, wiping his nose with the back of his hand.

"I hope there really isn't anyone in there," Paloma whispered, sounding irritated. "Because if there is, they sure as hell know we're here now."

"I'd like to see *you* not sneeze after spending three hours in a freezer."

"What?"

"Never mind."

Jaime advanced, holding the pistol in both hands like he'd seen people do in the movies, and stretching out his arms every time he walked through a door or turned a corner in the hallway. Followed closely by Paloma, he checked the kitchen, bedroom, and bathroom, then returned to the entrance hall. "There's nobody here."

"What did I tell you?" Paloma said. "Now can you leave me in peace?"

"Why the hurry?"

"You've seen there's no one here. You're as paranoid as ever. I'm grateful for your concern, but I'm not in any danger. So do me a favor and get that gun out of my house."

"You always bolt your door, Paloma."

"I told you, I must have forgotten."

"Forgotten? Remember that time I picked you up at your parents' and we went to see *Gladiator*? You made me go back and make sure you'd locked the door, even though the movie was about to start. I missed the entire opening battle."

"Look, Jaime, I'll ask you one last time: go. I'm not in a good place at the moment. I'm barely holding it together. This isn't a good time for you to show up and try to drag me into some James Bond adventure."

"Why don't we sit down and you can tell me all about it?"

"I don't have anything to tell you!"

Jaime noticed that his vision was starting to blur. He hadn't had a great day, either, and he needed to get some sleep before he did irreparable damage to himself.

"Suit yourself. But if you want to talk, call me."

As the door closed behind Jaime, Paloma ran to her bedroom and opened her desk drawer. Her data CDs were gone.

Preston. That son of a bitch Preston.

Her heart accelerating, she ran to the shelves where she kept her music CDs and took down Handel's *Water Music*. Back at her desk she pressed a button on the old computer that had belonged to her father and still worked as if it were brand-new.

It didn't turn on.

The apprehension Paloma had been feeling since she got home multiplied a hundredfold. She pressed the button several times, but the damn computer didn't respond. Crouching down, she realized that the cable was unplugged. With a trembling hand, she reconnected it, and the speaker beeped. Feeling calmer, she sat down and fiddled with the keyboard and mouse as a succession of messages informed her that the system was cranking up. When the computer was ready, Paloma inserted the Handel CD and clicked on the icon for drive D. Within a few seconds another menu appeared. Paloma clicked on an unnamed document and opened it.

She was relieved to find everything in its place, and at last breathed more freely. But this lasted only for a moment, and then she burst into tears, overwhelmed with anxiety.

A young brunette holding a bag and a man with his nose in a plaster cast watched from farther down the street as Jaime Azcárate exited the building. "That was a close call," she said.

"This guy is everywhere," the man grumbled. "We should've waited for him in the apartment and cut his balls off."

His companion gave him a look of disgust. "You'll get your revenge, Clark."

"What's the problem, cousin? You hot for this guy?"

"Don't talk crap. You're on your own for now. Leonardo wants me to get the disks back to the *Phoenix*. You stay here and wait for instructions."

The man was about to complain, but the woman silenced him with a wad of hundred-euro notes.

"For the inconvenience. I don't want to know what you do with it."

And then she disappeared into the crowds walking toward Calle Atocha, while her cousin stared shamelessly at her backside.

10

After sleeping through the remainder of Saturday and much of Sunday, Jaime left his attic apartment on Calle Jesús del Valle, deep in the Malasaña neighborhood. After taking the metro to the CHR building, in the heart of Madrid's university district, he took the elevator up to see Laura. Based on what Roberto had told him, he guessed that his imminent meeting was meant to serve some convoluted purpose—a feeling that was confirmed when he looked into the great lagoons of concern that were Laura's green eyes. "Good God, Jaime. You look like you've been dragged backward through a bush."

"Yeah, and a particularly thorny one."

Laura didn't smile. For as long as Jaime had known her, she'd possessed a restless, productive personality, one that had fueled her promotion from president of the society to editor of its magazine. Many of her contributors had known her since her previous job, so her old job title had stuck as a nickname; it wasn't unusual for her close friends, including Jaime Azcárate, to address her as "La Presidenta."

"Are you going to tell me what all this is about or do I have to guess?" Jaime asked.

"Let's head to the lecture hall. Isidro Requena's waiting for us."

Jaime looked at Laura in surprise. Although *Arcadia* operated under the auspices of the Center for Historical Research, CHR director Requena rarely meddled in the magazine's affairs. "This sounds important."

"It is. Jaime, you should know before we go in there that they're going to propose something unusual, and of course you're well within your rights to refuse."

"Can I refuse to go to the lecture hall? I need a coffee more than I need air."

"There'll be time for that later."

"There won't be a 'later' for me if I don't get some coffee."

Ignoring his complaints, Laura led the way to the elevator, and they descended to the second floor. The lecture hall was an elongated room filled with blue armchairs and a dais where talks were delivered and the CHR's projects were discussed. The walls were wood paneled, and portable partitions kept too much light from coming in through the windows.

As Jaime was walking into the room, a blonde woman with fair skin and blue eyes was just coming out. She looked to Jaime to be just shy of forty, and she gave him a polite smile before disappearing down the hallway.

Laura figured that if Jaime kept devouring the woman with his eyes, pretty soon there'd be nothing left of her, so she took him by the arm and led him into the hall. "Who was that angel?" he asked, continuing to follow her with his eyes until Laura shut the door behind them.

"That's Sonia Durán," replied Isidro Requena in his booming voice. The director of the CHR stood in the center of the room, dressed as always in a gray suit that matched his hair, mustache, and character. "The Center's new hire. She's an expert in heritage management, and I don't want to see you or that fat security guard you hang out with anywhere near her."

Jaime shrugged his shoulders. "I'll do my best. I can't speak for Roberto."

Laura gestured toward a second man in the room, whom Jaime had not yet noticed. The man standing beside Requena was tall and blond. He was neatly dressed in a dark suit and tie and his scarred faced smiled at Jaime with perfect white teeth. Jaime almost retched at the sight of him. "Jaime. I think you already know Señor Vicente Amatriaín, from Europol's Heritage Unit."

Amatriaín shook Jaime's hand. He was wearing leather gloves, just as he had been in El Burgo de Osma. "How are you, Jaime?" Unlike at their first meeting, this time he spoke informally. "I've heard you had a terrible experience. I'm very sorry to hear it."

"It was your fault," Jaime replied.

"How do you mean?"

"The people who grabbed me were after you. I hope you feel terrible about it. And that you've taken precautions."

"Someone in my position can never be too careful. I'm truly sorry for the incident, and I can assure you we're doing everything possible to establish the facts and catch the perpetrators. That's part of the reason I asked your boss to arrange this meeting."

"If Laura sends for me, I drop everything."

"I'm glad to hear it," Requena said in his gruff voice. "There's a lot at stake for all of us in this operation. I personally don't think *Arcadia*'s involvement is necessary, but Señor Amatriaín considers it essential."

"If not exactly essential," the Europol officer replied, "it is at least convenient, and an interesting offer for all parties involved. Anyway, the idea wasn't mine; it came from my superiors."

Laura suggested they sit. She and Jaime lowered themselves into armchairs in the front row of the hall, while Amatriaín and Dr. Requena stepped onto the dais and took office chairs. Jaime found it ridiculous that four people were meeting in a lecture hall when they could've met in a café surrounded by coffee and buns, but he said nothing.

Dr. Requena's deep voice filled the room, creating a menacing effect. "You may not be aware of this, but a few days ago a meeting was held in this very room to prepare an action plan—one that will help us combat the plundering of heritage. The EHU is a recently formed unit, and it has many excellent investigators, but very few art experts. That's why they've turned to us and to other centers and universities around Europe. Mr. Amatriaín will now explain about an initiative to recover stolen artwork, approved by the European Commission just last Thursday, for which they've asked our help."

Amatriaín cleared his throat. He stood stiffly and his eyes darted from Jaime to Laura, as if quickly trying to gauge their reactions. His gaze came to rest on Jaime, whose attention was noticeably elsewhere.

Jaime was aware of his distracted state, but did nothing to hide it. In his condition he had no desire to listen to this man ramble on about an operation that they clearly wanted to involve him in. They probably needed him to write a report on the methods the European police used to track down stolen art, something he had no wish to do. He still had a cold and was exhausted, even after spending a weekend recovering, and his attention span was short. His thoughts were still drifting between Sandra and Paloma. He'd have liked nothing more than to go home and sleep for ten hours straight, but eventually curiosity got the better of him. He rubbed his tired eyes and tried to focus on Amatriaín, who was arranging some documents on the table.

"Right, well, I won't waste time explaining who we are or what we do—I did that at our first meeting and there's plenty more information on the Internet. Europol is the organization that coordinates the fight against crime within the European Union, its headquarters are located in The Hague. It was first formed to fight drug crimes, but since then its operations have expanded. One of its most successful missions was the dismantling of a child pornography network, but there have also been several antiterrorism operations and even an investigation into the trafficking of stolen cars in Spain. You're probably wondering what all this has to do with art. The answer is in the unit I represent, which was created a year ago."

Jaime nodded. Amatriaín's words had rekindled a memory. He had seen something in the news. It happened in Amsterdam. A guy stole a painting from the Van Gogh Museum and then destroyed it when he found himself cornered by the police. The media had laid into those responsible for the operation. Jaime had no doubt that one of those men sat in front of him right now.

"We've conducted a couple of minor missions to date," said Amatriaín, "but we plan to expand our area of operations. We've secured the cooperation of all the security forces of the member states of the European Union, with whom we constantly share information. At this very moment we are launching an operation whose main objective is to recover works of art stolen on European soil in recent months. Here's the situation."

Jaime made an effort to listen more carefully, presuming the important bit was about to come.

"You're probably wondering what all this has to do with you. As Dr. Requena said, we met a few days ago with some colleagues in the CHR, and that was when it was decided that the magazine you work for should play a central role."

Amatriaín gestured to Requena, who pressed a button set into the table. The overhead lights went out and the screen behind the dais came on, showing a photograph of a man with shaggy white hair and a wrinkled face.

"This is Nelson Krupa, known as Nelson the Pole, initiator and boss of one of the largest organizations in art contraband. In April 2012, two seventeenth-century oil-on-board paintings fortuitously appeared at El Rastro flea market. The Civil Guard's Heritage Squad opened an investigation and found that the two paintings had been taken from a church in Terrazos de Bureba, in the Burgos province. Eventually two men were detained, and they helped facilitate the arrest of the Pole and his associates. They're now serving prison sentences." Amatriaín paused for effect. "Since then the number of art thefts has fallen dramatically, until a month ago."

The photograph of the Pole disappeared and was replaced on the screen by an image of Bolgi's Medusa. Jaime shivered.

"On September 14 of this year, this sculpture disappeared from the Pontecorvo House Museum in Verona. Our experts suspect the robbery could be the work of a member of the Pole's group who is still at large. Our intention is to follow the trail of the statue to the thief and dismantle this criminal organization once and for all."

By now, Jaime was awake enough to ponder what he'd just heard and formulate one or two questions. Five across, six letters, a thief of baroque sculptures and member of the Pole's missing gang? Only one answer fit the puzzle: S-A-N-D-R-A.

"Something doesn't add up. The group's thefts were big news for a long time, but as you said yourself, all of those pieces were taken from churches or private collections. This sculpture was taken from a museum in the middle of the night, and a security guard was murdered. There are other, more valuable and more portable works of art in that museum, and yet the thieves broke in, poisoned the poor guard, and snatched the Medusa without touching anything else. It's not the Pole's modus operandi—his group would be more likely to grab the first thing they thought would find a buyer on the black market. What's so special about this statue?"

A hyena-like smile formed on Amatriaín's lips. "That's what I wanted to know in El Burgo de Osma and, in fact, what I still want to know."

Jaime rolled his eyes as he realized why Amatriaín had thought specifically of him for this mission. An image of Paloma Blasco popped into his head, spat in his face, and faded away again.

"Oh, no. You're not going to start going on about that blasted essay in the *Revista Complutense* again, are you?"

"It included a chapter about the sculpture," Requena pointed out.

"One page," Jaime corrected him. He made eye contact with Laura, hoping for some assistance. "We mentioned it in the section on Bolgi simply because the rest of his works, other than the Saint Helena at the Vatican, are barely of interest. That doesn't make me the ultimate expert on baroque sculpture."

"*You* might not be. But your coauthor, Paloma Blasco—"

"Leave Paloma out of this. She just put her name to it. I was the one who did all the work." This was a massive lie, but his intention was to protect Paloma. Although she could undoubtedly be a big help to Amatriaín, Jaime wanted her kept out of it. She seemed to have enough problems already, whatever they were.

"Which is why I must insist on your help," said Amatriaín. "Don't forget the article you wrote years later about the supposed curse of Medusa. For better or for worse, that damn statue seems to follow you everywhere. We're certain that the solution to the mystery is in your research."

"Well, there you have it. Both the essay and the article are in the public domain. Study them and draw your own conclusions, but leave me in peace. And please, someone bring me a coffee."

Ten minutes later, Jaime Azcárate emerged from the room in a foul mood, feeling more tired than ever, and sworn to silence about everything that had just been said.

11

"Man, it's a good thing you didn't have to use that pistol. You're hopeless," Roberto Barrero said after confirming that none of Jaime's six bullets had come near the target.

"I told you: I'm for making love, not war. Plus, I've still got a cold."

"In that case you should be at home, especially after the rough time you've had. Here, watch and learn."

Roberto put on his ear protection and picked up the revolver. He loaded six bullets into the cylinder, cocked the weapon, and started pressing the trigger. There wasn't much paper left at the center of the silhouette when he was done. "Impressive," Jaime admitted.

"It's just practice."

"Let me try again?"

"No, that's enough for today. If anyone catches you here they'll have my balls."

"But aren't you the instructor?"

"Yep. And aren't you the dickhead without a license?"

"I'm hoping to get one soon."

"Well, it could take a while. Guns are like cats: some people love them and others are allergic. Come on, let's grab a beer."

"They let you drink beer here?"

"Not before practice. But afterward, yes."

"I'll just have a juice."

As they seated themselves at a table in the firing range café, Jaime let out a groan.

"You're still wiped out," Roberto observed.

"I can't sleep. This whole EHU thing has gotten to me. Paloma won't answer my calls. Worst of all, I can't stop puzzling over that damn Medusa."

"Why? I thought you already were the world's foremost authority on it."

"Don't be a dick, Roberto. We both know Paloma's the expert, and she's not talking."

"But hang on—all she did was go to the museum in Verona to study the bust, gather all the technical documents, write an essay that got you both top grades, and get it published in the university journal. What's all that compared to what you did? 'The Curse of Medusa.' Now *that's* impressive!"

"Nice of you to say so." Jaime smiled as he pulled a brown folder from his backpack. Inside were several sheets of paper, stapled together. "I've reviewed the article and done more research. This is everything I could find. Plenty there for a story."

Roberto exhaled loudly. When Jaime said "plenty there for a story," it invariably meant he was about to spin a yarn that fell somewhere between *The War of the Worlds* and *The Wonderful Wizard of Oz*. "Don't tell me you actually believe the things you write."

"You know what they say: anything that can be imagined exists."

"Including the curse of Medusa?"

"It's not the only case of its kind. There have always been deaths blamed on some curse from an ancient object or work of art. Remember the Hope Diamond, or the monks of Lokrum? The diabolical amulet in *The Exorcist*? The curse of Tutankhamen?"

"Oh, that's a classic."

"Well, now it has a challenger. The death of that museum security guard is going to make our Medusa's curse a critical and box-office success."

"That explains the theft. Who wouldn't go crazy for a cursed statue?"

"Go crazy? Die, is more like it. In every place the sculpture's been exhibited, someone has met their death."

"There it is."

"What?"

"That look."

"What look? I'm just telling you what I know."

"Maybe, but when you start talking about these things, you lose touch with reality. Let's review: Most of the people involved with Tutankhamen died naturally. One had an accident, another was sick. Lord Carnarvon, who funded the dig, was an old man who got bitten by an insect. It's the same with this statue. Through all the years it's been exhibited, a lot of people will have died, but that doesn't mean we should blame poor Medusa. She's got enough problems with that hair."

Jaime sipped his orange juice. "If you stop interrupting me I'll tell you what else I've found out."

"All right, I'll be quiet. But just so you can tell me about that woman again."

"What woman?"

"The one Requena said we had to stay away from. What did you say her name was?"

"Sonia Durán. She's an expert on heritage management and her legs are longer than both of ours put together, and much shapelier."

"Speak for yourself. When are you going to introduce me?"

Jaime ignored the question and consulted his notes. "Let's see . . . The statue is credited to Andrea Bolgi, a seventeenth-century sculptor who was a disciple of Bernini. They called Bolgi 'Il Carrarino' because he was born in 1605 in Carrara, the land of marble. He apprenticed at Pietro Tacca's workshop, and in 1625 he moved to Rome, where he encountered the sculptor Francesco Baratta, who was desperate to gain access to Bernini's circle. Baratta finally did so and worked with Bernini on one of his masterpieces: the Fountain of the Four Rivers, for which Baratta sculpted the figure representing the Río de la Plata. In 1627 Bernini commissioned Bolgi to help with the Vatican's famous baldachin." Jaime raised his glass of juice, as if he were Laurence Olivier holding up the jester's skull in *Hamlet*, and recited: "What the barbarians did not do, the Barberini did."

Roberto gave him a blank stare. "What the fuck was that?"

"That's what Romans said when the Pope stripped a bunch of ancient Roman monuments for the bronze and other materials Bernini needed to build St. Peter's Baldachin. Pope Urban VIII's real name was Maffeo Barberini."

"'What the barbarians did not do . . .' It's an impressive turn of phrase."

"Bolgi tried to continue in the tradition of Bernini's aesthetics, but his classical style was too cold. His most important piece is one of the four statues set into the niches in Saint Peter's Basilica: the *Saint Helena*."

"Okay, great. But when are we going to get to the Medusa? I hate when you go all Wikipedia on me."

"We'll get there very soon. Unfortunately for Bolgi, he wasn't able to produce much work of note. No one liked his *Saint Helena*, not even Bernini himself, who criticized Bolgi's classicism and the excessive serenity of the saint's face. Bolgi had been in Rome for ten years without receiving a single important commission, so in 1653 he left for Naples, where he tried to imitate his master, and there he produced some of his best pieces."

"The fucking Medusa."

Jaime nodded. "He produced it in 1656 for Domenico Corsini, a rich Neapolitan merchant who collected sculptures of mythological creatures."

"There's no arguing that the curse worked back then. No one from that time's still alive."

"Well, get ready: this is where the fun starts. Bolgi himself died that year, but so did Corsini. And over half the population of Naples, thanks to an outbreak of the plague. At the time, some sources said Corsini went mad and committed suicide. Apparently he believed the Medusa was cursed. He was a strange man, what we'd call an eccentric these days—who was at odds with Catholic doctrine and fanatical about classical mythology and culture. He became so unhinged, he started to believe that the spirit of the gorgon Medusa, after drifting aimlessly for centuries, had installed itself in Bolgi's sculpture. That was the beginning of the end for him. One night, he went out into the garden and drowned himself in the pond, near the statue."

"It's guys like these that give eccentrics a bad name," Barrero complained. "Anyway, that was four hundred years ago. What happened to the sculpture after that?"

"It stayed in the garden until 1799, when an Italian named Pietro Parodi bought it for his private collection. In 1940, one of his descendants went to live in Rome and took the entire collection with him. He had no heirs, so when he fell ill in the late seventies he donated it along with the rest of his collection to the Leoni Antique Center. The statue remained there until there was a fire. Fortunately, almost all of the sculptural pieces were saved; but many paintings of great value were lost, including a Parmigianino and two Beccafumis."

"What happened to the things that were saved?"

"Years after the fire, the Petrarca Gallery bought some of the Leoni pieces, including, among other sculptures, our good friend Medusa. After the statue was transported and put on display there, three people died."

"No shit. Did the pestilence get them, too?"

"Very funny. No. One was a caretaker who'd worked at the gallery his entire life. Another was some rich guy who went often to see the Medusa."

"How did they die?"

"I have no idea. The papers didn't find the story important enough to report more than that."

"I don't see why. Medusa, the beautiful princess who turned into a monster after screwing Poseidon in the Temple of Athena, would have been the perfect subject for a serial-killer profile. What about the third person?"

"We know a bit more about this one. He was a security guard, but not at the gallery; he worked at the Leoni Antique Center before it burned down."

"A bit of a stretch, but it's still a link to the Medusa."

Jaime smiled. "You believe me now? As you see, anyone who takes an interest in the gorgon can wind up dead. This guy, Alvino Nascimbene, died in a car accident. The body was badly burned. Some Italian magazines actually published photos from the scene."

"How tasteful."

"Quite. There were even close-ups of some of the most spectacular burns. This whole business is enough to make your hair stand on end."

"So what are you going to do?"

"I tried to contact the Petrarca Gallery in Rome, but they won't answer the phone. Yesterday I spoke to Antonio Miguel Galán, an antique dealer who's a friend of my father's. He said that about a year ago the Petrarca wanted to buy a couple of illuminated bibles from him, but in the end the gallery backed out. He offered to ask around and see whether he can find out anything about the statue's history."

"That's my Azcárate. But . . ."

"What?"

"I know you won't listen, but I'll say it anyway: watch your step."

"Why?" Jaime rolled his eyes back in his head and stuck his tongue out in imitation of a mummy. "Because of the curse?"

"Don't be a shithead. I'll bet you anything there's no curse, but that some of those deaths still weren't a coincidence."

"I'll take that bet."

"All right, but be careful."

"I don't believe what I'm hearing. Are you actually worried about me?"

"Who wouldn't worry after seeing the way you shoot?" Roberto drained the last drops of beer from his bottle.

12

Coast of Sardinia

From high in the sky the sun was painting a wide, glowing trail across the calm sea. Though it was well into October, the weather was almost summery, and there was no shortage of the bathers who came to Capo Testa to enjoy a pleasant swim in the Mediterranean. A group of boys and girls were surfing near the harbor, while people of all ages enjoyed the autumn morning beneath the small forest of umbrellas that had sprung up on the beach.

One of the surfers was thrown off his board when a large wave made him lose his balance. When his head reemerged from the water, he saw that the swell had been caused by a motorboat speeding toward a large white catamaran anchored some distance out from the turtle-shaped rock near the beach. The young people waved at the dark-haired woman in sunglasses who was steering, but when they received no response they went back to their surfing.

Skillfully, the woman turned to starboard and guided the motorboat to the stern of the catamaran, cutting the engine as she reached the boarding ladder. The name of the boat was painted on its side in black letters: "PHOENIX."

A deckhand working at the catamaran's stern approached and greeted the woman with a smile. "Good morning, Miss Carrera."

The woman stood. She was tall and her black T-shirt and tight black pants emphasized her athletic figure. "My last name is Mazi," she said in a cold voice. "Tie up the boat."

The young man rushed to obey and threw her a rope. Slowly she climbed the ladder leading up to the yacht.

Rosa Carrera had changed her surname almost a year ago, but nobody seemed to have taken it seriously. She was starting to think that her attempt to put her past behind her had been a waste of time, especially since she was still doing the same things she'd done before. No matter what efforts she made to distance herself from her family, her destiny pursued her. She would always be a Carrera. Especially if she couldn't bring herself to cut ties completely.

She stood on deck for a while, admiring the vessel's aerodynamic design. Whenever she set foot on the family yacht she was filled with conflicting emotions. On the one hand, she enjoyed the sense of abundance, wealth, and danger that went with her family's activities. On the other, she was filled with self-loathing because her attempts to leave it all behind had been in vain. A luxury yacht of the highest caliber, the *Phoenix* served as a reminder of everything she abhorred, even as it offered her an exciting life. Her father, the businessman and antique expert Angelo Carrera, had been on the ship when it sank off the coast of Cyprus three years earlier. Its recovery and restoration had cost the family a fortune, but the yacht was seaworthy once more and had been rechristened the *Phoenix* after the mythological creature reborn from its own ashes.

A man of about forty, dressed in a blue-striped T-shirt and shorts, stepped through a glass door and beamed at Rosa.

"The enchanting Mata Hari has returned." He approached her with open arms. The red kerchief on his head and the ring in his left ear gave him the air of a pirate. He gave her a quick hug and led her toward the door. "Our venerable elder was just wondering aloud about when you might return."

"Then why didn't our venerable elder pick up the phone?" she said, sounding irritated. "I've been trying to call for hours."

"You know how particular Papà is. He only likes to talk to us on the boat's lounge. I spoke to him yesterday; he's hoping you have some good news for him."

"Well, he can keep on hoping," Rosa muttered, shoving her brother aside and walking through the door.

At the bottom of a set of stairs was a short teak-floored hallway that led to a spacious lounge with tinted windows. The place had the look of a miniature museum, with oil paintings depicting ancient landscapes and ruins and busts representing historical figures from Socrates to Napoleon Bonaparte. In the corners of the room were marble pedestals decorated in relief, and above those were carvings of the Four Evangelists and their corresponding symbols—angel, lion, ox, and eagle. A bartender dressed spotlessly in white offered them glasses of champagne.

"So, how did it go?" Rosa's brother raised his glass and gave her a look of genuine admiration.

"You'll find out soon enough. I don't like explaining things twice."

"Uh-oh. Little sister's in a bad mood."

"I've been away from the gallery for almost a week."

"I'm sure it's fine. Your boyfriend will have taken care of everything."

Rosa's face turned red.

"Leave Dino out of this. That poor man would run for his life if he had any idea what his fiancée really did when she was supposed to be away on business."

"Come on, I bet dangerous women like you are a turn-on for him."

"Me, dangerous? Not dangerous enough for this job. At least I won't have to quit. Papà won't just fire me, he'll disown me. And I'll be glad of it."

The man ran the tips of his fingers under the kerchief as he registered her implication of failure. "The policeman . . . ?"

"Amatriaín? He escaped from right under our noses. And so did the other guy, Jaime Azcárate."

"Two screwups for the price of one, little sister."

"It wasn't my fault," Rosa protested. "One of them disappeared and the other managed to put that moron Clark out of action and then kidnap *me*. I don't get why Papà still trusts that idiot."

"I think you're about to find out."

Rosa nodded with her characteristic self-assurance. But deep down, she envied her brother. Although Leonardo occasionally undertook fieldwork—the most recent example being the theft of the Medusa from the Verona museum—his primary responsibility was coordinating the organization's activities. Thus he spent most of the day in a luxurious cabin on the family yacht, flicking through documents while sipping mojitos and caipirinhas. Rosa, meanwhile, was the one out risking her neck, since her father figured a beautiful young woman looked less suspicious than a guy with an earring.

As a criminal mastermind, Leonardo possessed all the skill and cunning of Lex Luthor. Thanks to him and Rosa, both sides of the family organization were ruled with strength. The problem was that for years, Rosa had been trying to reform herself. After several masterstrokes had sealed the family's fortune, the youngest Carrera had decided to give up crime and devote herself to the legitimate art business. But she was still attached to her father, and he had persuaded her to take on one last mission, perhaps the most important of their criminal careers.

Rosa and Leonardo finished their champagne and crossed the lounge. A massive oak desk stood on a platform in the room and a portrait of an aristocratic-looking man wearing a proud expression hung above it, presiding over all that happened there. The man was bald and in the portrait he was leaning casually against a table, gazing out at the viewer with the indifference of a baroque monarch. Flanking the portrait, looking out of place, were two loudspeakers mounted at the height of the subject's shoulders.

Aside from this depiction, and not counting the dozen or so marble and wooden faces represented artistically, there was no one else in the room. Leonardo walked somberly toward the portrait, his sister following close behind. Suddenly, a sharp voice crackled over the loudspeakers. *"So here you are."*

They stopped in the center of the room.

"And in one piece, from what I hear," the voice continued. *"How's Clark? If he keeps injuring himself like this his medical treatment will cost me a fortune. Fortunately, very soon money will no longer be a problem."*

"Like it is *now*." Rosa looked around the yacht's impressive lounge.

"Tell me everything."

"We encountered some difficulties," she said loudly. It always made her feel uncomfortable to speak to a painting. "How are you today?"

"I'm tired," the voice said. *"But don't use that as an excuse not to tell me the search was a failure."*

Rosa felt herself grow pale under the fluorescent lights. "How did you know?"

"From the pitch of your voice. It's an octave higher than usual."

She clenched her fists to contain the rage she felt at having to speak to a person she couldn't see. "We looked everywhere. In drawers, notebooks—there wasn't even a damn USB drive. I spent the entire return trip searching the CDs I took from her room, but I didn't find anything. There was no sign of it on her computer. I was just starting a more thorough search when Clark saw her coming down the street with that journalist, Jaime Azcárate." She waved her hand dismissively. "Clark wanted to stay and settle the score, but I convinced him to escape down the stairs. We didn't have time to take the computer. One thing I can tell you with absolute certainty is that there was nothing in the documents I took even remotely related to Asclepius's *Chronicle*. Isn't it possible we've got the wrong person?"

"My dear Rosa, research is the key to all operations. That and luck. A few years ago, when I published my essay on the work of Filippo Baldinucci, Paloma Blasco came to my office with an absurd theory. I gave it a lot of thought, and the more thought I gave it, the less absurd it seemed. So I decided to conduct my own investigation, and that's how I came across the university piece attributed to her and Jaime Azcárate, who she was besotted with at the time. Maybe she still is."

"He's an interesting guy," Rosa admitted. Leonardo made a snorting sound. "What are you laughing about, jackass?"

"Nothing. 'An interesting guy.' So interesting you let him live?"

"Go fuck yourself, shithead."

"Quiet, both of you. Rosa's right: it was Paloma's feelings for Azcárate that made her want to help him and, ultimately, to conduct the study. By all appearances, he was a crackpot who thought about nothing but travelling the world and searching for treasures. She was the more sensible party. She knew what it truly meant to be an art historian. The piece was hers. She's the one who went to Rome and Naples, who studied and researched the Medusa, and discovered the truth about it."

"So then what's his involvement? Why was Azcárate in Soria on the very day we were planning to freeze Amatriaín?"

"There's no such thing as a coincidence. We were following Amatriaín and he was following Azcárate, and that's why you were all in the same place that night. Don't forget, my girl: investigation can take you anywhere. And we're going right to the top."

"But Paloma doesn't have a diary; there's nothing written down. I'm telling you I carried out a thorough search."

"Not thorough enough," was the calm but cutting reply. "The diary must be somewhere that only she knows about. I'm certain that if you'd had more time you'd have found it."

"And what if she doesn't have it at home? She might have it stored in an e-mail account. Or hidden somewhere else—the museum, for instance. How was I going to sneak into the Prado Museum?"

"That possibility had occurred to me, too. Don't worry: Clark will take care of everything."

"What do you think Clark can do?" she asked. Although she was often forced to work with her cousin, she'd never liked the brute. The feeling was mutual, especially since the day Clark took a boot to the groin for trying to get too friendly with her.

"Everything has been planned. I've put Clark in touch with a colleague of Paloma's who can get the truth out of her."

"Seriously? And who is this genius?"

"His name's Oscar Preston. Apparently there's some professional rivalry between him and Paloma. Clark shouldn't have any trouble persuading him to get his hands on her research."

"I still don't understand why this document is so important. We already know what it says."

"We know the conclusion, but it is of vital importance to our negotiations that we get our hands on the original source material. Dr. Galliano is aware of its existence and insists that our documentation include this proof of the bust's link to the legend. It's a quirk common among collectors—what can I say?"

Rosa nodded even though he couldn't see her, but she didn't feel convinced.

"You trust Clark?" she asked.

"I know you don't like him, but he's my nephew, and he has rarely failed us. He has orders to report to Leonardo as soon as he discovers anything."

"He couldn't discover a nail if it was hammered through his foot."

"Rosa, please don't talk about your cousin like that. He has always been loyal to us."

Rosa gave up. Clark had always been loyal to the family. But what about her? She was travelling all over the world, risking her life and neglecting her duties at the art gallery—and with each day, her chances of becoming a respectable businesswoman were growing that much smaller.

"All right," she finally said.

"*Excellent. Now, let me rest awhile.*"

There was a crackling sound and then the room was silent. Rosa and Leonardo stood there for a few moments, showing an almost servile respect for the voice that was now gone. Then they went back to the main deck and looked out at the town of Santa Teresa di Gallura on the Sardinian coast.

"Is there a problem with Clark?" Leonardo watched a gull soaring overhead.

"He's a madman."

"But he's good at his job. He's strong and isn't scared of anything."

Rosa gave him a piercing stare. "The fact that he's fearless is a good thing. But his pleasure-seeking, money-grubbing ways are going to get us into trouble one of these days. I think he spends his pay on whores and God knows what else."

"Every man has his particular methods and vices. But the vices don't have to interfere with the methods. Our father wouldn't have given him this mission if he wasn't sure he was up to the task."

"I guess you're right," she said.

"Of course I am. Papà doesn't take stupid risks. Now I have to leave you, little sister. I'm working on a new project that requires my full attention."

"An assignment from Papà? Another sculpture?"

A look of mischief flashed in Leonardo's dark eyes.

"Oh, come on!" she said. "Not another side operation?"

"Do you really want to know?"

"To be honest, no. But eventually you'll be caught, and I dread the fact that I'm going to get that news one of these days."

"It's possible," he said. Then he turned on his heel, military-style, and headed back toward the lounge.

13

Madrid

Two days earlier, Oscar Preston never would have guessed that his movements were being watched. But on Sunday, the day after his meeting with Ricardo Bosch, he received an anonymous call during which an unfamiliar voice intimated that it knew of his ambition to become the Prado Museum's deputy director of research and conservation. Hearing this, he felt his heart leap.

At first he was put out by the intrusion into his personal life; if fact, it angered him so much he threatened to call the police. But when the voice mentioned his rivalry with Paloma Blasco and suggested she might be taken out of the picture, Preston's curiosity was piqued and he listened to the proposal. The plan seemed quite simple: all he had to do was obtain some information and then someone would remove Señorita Blasco by peaceful means. The voice offered up no other details.

Preston spent the next two days on edge. He'd been off of tranquilizers for months, but that week he relapsed. He wondered: Was he falling into a trap? Who were these people, anyway? What did they want and why were they helping him? He quickly pushed the last part of the question from his mind. The important thing was not why but how. Aware he'd always been a bit paranoid, he resolved to stop worrying so much and give the situation time to unfold.

He was just opening the fridge door to make himself a sandwich when his cell phone rang. "Hello?"

"Good evening, Preston. Have you thought about it?"

Preston's head had been elsewhere and the call came as a surprise. "Wait—what was it I had to think about?"

"Our agreement. Now listen: At this very moment there is a gray car at the entrance to your building. Go down to the street and get in it. We'll go someplace where we can talk."

Preston gripped the phone so hard he was close to snapping it. He wasn't accustomed to receiving shady offers; he was usually the one making them. "I was about to have dinner," he said, taking in the pitiful sight of two bare slices of rye bread on the countertop.

"We can eat together," the voice said. "If the idea I present doesn't interest you, I'll pay. If you *are* interested, you can pay. I think that's a fair deal."

Despite his nasal tone the stranger sounded friendly enough. But Preston knew perfectly well that, over the course of his life—both in the United States and in Europe—he'd made dozens of enemies who would have no qualms about dismembering him given the slightest opportunity. The deal he was about to be offered might be a dream come true. Or it might not. Perhaps it was the beginning of a terrible and violent nightmare.

Suddenly it dawned on him. Why did he need a favor? It was clear that Ricardo Bosch preferred him for the position—it was an open secret. He was the best, the boss's favorite, Number One. "Señor," he said, "I've thought long and hard about it, and I'm not interested in your offer."

"But you haven't heard it yet."

"All the same, I'm not interested. Now if you'll excuse me—"

"I can assure you, you *will* be interested. Just give me a few minutes of your time to explain."

"I'm listening."

"Not here. Come down to the car."

"Why can't you just tell me over the phone?"

"Just come down, for fuck's sake!"

"Excuse me? You're starting to sound rather aggressive."

"Forgive me. Please come down and we'll have a proper chat. It turns out that your friend Paloma Blasco may be able to cause a lot of problems for you."

"Paloma's no threat to me. I'm a thousand times better than her!"

"I don't doubt it. But something's come up that could complicate things."

"Oh?"

"If you want to know, then come down and we'll talk."

The line went dead. Oscar stared at his cell phone, as if it could reveal the identity of the mysterious caller. He leaned out of the window, but his apartment was on the opposite side of the building from the entrance, and no gray car was visible. He ran to the bathroom, opened the medicine cabinet, took out a bottle of anxiolytics, and swallowed two at once.

Getting into the gray car might be the death of him, but there was another prospect that seemed even more unthinkable: not knowing. If he didn't go now, doubt would seep under his sheets every night and spread its poison through his body. That was the last thought Preston had before grabbing his keys and leaving the apartment. In the elevator he pressed the ground-floor button; he was filled with anxiety, his heart in his throat.

. . .

The man sitting at the wheel of the gray Fiat 500 watched his target come out of the front door. He seemed strange, with the faltering gait of an insecure man. When he got closer to the car, the driver could see him more clearly. His ears and nose looked two sizes too big for his face and he'd drowned his blond curls in hair gel. He wore black-rimmed glasses. This was definitely the guy from the photo his cousin Leonardo had sent. "Were you the one who called me?" the man asked through the open window, his voice trembling.

"No, it was my daddy, you idiot! Come on, get in."

Preston obeyed. He climbed in next to the driver and examined him closely. He was a dark-skinned man with a strong physique. The raincoat he wore over a black T-shirt and military pants looked out of place, and on his head he sported a black Kangol-style beret. His nose was in a plaster cast, and his unruly mustache was beginning to turn white. On his chin grew four ridiculous hairs, none of which pointed in the same direction. His light eyes bulged slightly in their sockets, and contained an amicable glint that matched his stupid smile. Preston glanced at the bulge in the driver's raincoat. "Look, if this is a trap—"

"It is!" The driver pulled out his pistol and aimed it between Preston's eyes. "You're dead, Preston!"

Preston screamed.

"Ha! Not really, wimp. Just kidding. Your face! You should've seen yourself."

"What is this? That's not funny! I'm getting out of here."

Ignoring him, the driver tucked his gun away and hit the gas, and within a few minutes they had joined the nighttime traffic on the M30.

"Where're you taking me?"

"To get something to eat. You should never talk business on an empty stomach."

"I'm not hungry. And what is this about Paloma Blasco being a problem?"

"All in good time, my friend. And how can you not be hungry? You said earlier that you were about to have dinner. Fasten your seatbelt. As you can see, I don't waste time. And your safety is very important to us."

Preston did as he was told and from then on kept his mouth shut and his eyes on the road. There was really no other option. The driver dodged between the other cars with terrifying skill, ignoring red lights, crosswalks, and stop signs. He even laughed like a madman when he narrowly missed a young woman on crutches at one crossing. He should have had the entire police force on his tail from the moment he started his car.

Ten minutes later, the kamikaze driver parked the car in an underground lot and led the way to a place with tinted windows and a sign that read "Bar Agustín." Inside, the air was thick with a greasy-smelling smoke that spread out from the kitchen, and nothing could be heard over the day's news booming from the television and music blaring from a slot machine. The driver pointed at a table, but Preston wanted to go to the restroom first. "Whatever. Just don't try anything, because I'll come after you. I know where you live."

Preston walked down the stairs that led to the toilets and locked himself inside. Looking at his reflection in the mirror, he asked it whether it was sure about this thing he was about to do. There was no answer. His reflection appeared no clearer about the whole thing than he was. He took several deep breaths, splashed water on his face, and practiced looking confident in the mirror before tucking his shirt into his pants and heading back out into the restaurant.

Back at their table he found a dish piled high with the most disgusting matter he had ever seen. The plate gave off a strong smoky stench that caused his nose to wrinkle involuntarily. "What *is* that?"

"*Chopitos.*" His companion grinned.

"Cho . . . pitos?"

"Chopitos. They're like baby squid. A bitch to catch, but so good."

Preston looked on in disgust as the man licked his lips under his comical mustache. The maniacal driving had been an early clue, and here was more evidence he was dealing with a dangerous lunatic. With some apprehension, he turned his gaze to the mountain of tiny creatures heaped on the plate. It looked like a mound of fried spiders. His eyes and his mouth worked in tandem, expressing his revulsion.

"Come on, Preston. For fuck's sake, it's time you learned to eat like a Spaniard."

"That's what the Spanish eat? I've been here over ten years and I've never seen anyone eat it."

"That's because you don't mix with the right people. You spend all day by yourself, dreaming about the ridiculous customs of North Dakota or South Carolina, your hotdogs and your hamburgers with burnt bacon." He took a swig of his beer and speared one of the little creatures on the plate using a toothpick. Oscar watched in astonishment as he put it in his mouth and chewed with passion.

"Mmm . . . delicious. You gonna eat? It'll go cold!"

Feeling intimidated, Preston picked up his own toothpick and skewered one of the critters, which somehow heightened its resemblance to a scaled-down version of the monster from *Alien*. After inspecting it, smelling it, and brushing it against his lips, he finally put it in his mouth and ground it between his teeth, careful not to let it touch his tongue.

"Good shit, eh?"

"Mmmff!"

"Excellent, now let's get down to business." Preston's companion paused to allow the waiter to serve a plate of grilled pig's ear. "We know you hope to become a director at the Prado Museum."

"Deputy director of research and conservation," Preston corrected him, looking curiously at the new dish. As with the previous item, these cartilaginous lumps looked unfamiliar to him, but—though equal in repugnance to the chopitos—it took some time to register that they came from an animal.

"Whatever. Director, deputy director . . . It makes no difference. It would be an incredible job, wouldn't it? We understand that Señorita Blasco is your biggest rival for the post."

"You already said that on the phone." Preston could feel his anxiety rising, partly because of the mysterious situation and partly because of the miniature octopuses staring back with blind eyes from the plate. "Incidentally, you haven't told me who you work for."

"Believe me, you're better off not knowing. I'll be your only contact. You can call me Clark."

"'Clark'? You're name's Clark and you're telling me to learn to eat like the Spanish?"

"It's a fake name. I was born in Spain, but my family's from—Hold on, why the fuck should I tell you my life story?" Clark glanced from side to side but no one was paying them any attention. The fact that his hand had moved to the bulge in his raincoat did not escape Preston's notice. "Here's the deal: we're offering to get Paloma Blasco out of the way for you, without violence and forever."

"I don't understand."

"'I don't understand, I don't understand.' Of course you don't understand. That's why I'm explaining it to you."

Clark dug around between his teeth with a toothpick for a minute and then smoothed out his mustache with one finger. "The thing is, Paloma has secretly been conducting a study that could bring her fame and glory within a matter of days."

Preston's eyes lit up. He felt half-curious, half-alarmed. "A study? What on?"

"That's where you come in. We want you to find out."

"Wait a minute. If you don't know what it is and you say it's a secret, how do you even know she's doing this research?"

"Señorita Blasco doesn't live underground, Preston. My boss has been watching her. We know everything about her: what she does in and out of the museum; what she eats, what she drinks; who she fucks . . ." Clark allowed himself a wink at Preston over this. "We also know that she's in possession of a document that could help convince an important client that our merchandise is genuine. We want you to get this document for us."

"Me? Impossible. Paloma won't let me get anywhere near her; she hates my guts. She even accused me of sneaking into her apartment the other day."

"We've already thought of that. Please don't underestimate us, Preston." Clark looked and sounded agitated, but he quickly lowered his voice. "We have a plan that can get you access to Señorita Blasco's research without you having to come into contact with Señorita Blasco herself."

"How?"

"We thought we might blackmail her. We've been keeping an eye on her for several months and haven't dug up a single shady affair. She doesn't put out, if you know what I mean." Another wink and a smile. "Earlier I told you we know everything about her. And it's true. She drinks, she eats . . . but as for the other thing—nothing. Zero. She's like a fucking cloistered nun. But she does have a friend—"

"Amanda Escámez." Preston nodded. "She works in the Technical Research Office."

"Well, it appears that Señora Escámez is divorced and has a son. Do you see where this is going? Is my Spanish good enough for you?"

"I don't know anything about Amanda."

"Well, you're in luck then, because we do. She's a lonely and bitter woman whose husband ran off with someone else and left her with only her job and her little boy. We can't take her job away, so we've decided to go after the one thing she loves most in the world."

Preston stared at him in horror. "Her son?"

"Tell Amanda to get Paloma's research from her or she'll never see her child again."

"But that's insane. I'm not a kidnapper! I refuse to take part in something like this."

"That's the best part. You won't have to kidnap anyone. You won't even have to lie. In two days Amanda will take her little boy to school like she does every day, but he won't come back home. You'll call her and explain what happened: a handsome stranger with blue eyes and a passion for fine dining forced you into getting the document. No, don't even say that. If she has any brains she'll know what's best for her. She'll speak to Paloma, get the document, and give it to you; you'll give it to us, and we'll give her back her son. And don't give me any shit, Preston. We know your background. It won't be the first time you've stooped this low."

"I've never done anything remotely like this. Why don't you blackmail her yourselves? Why do you need me?"

"This makes it easier to throw the cops off the scent."

"But the suspect for the kidnapping will be me!"

"Keep your voice down, will you? Without proof they won't be able to charge you. In the hypothetical case that the police come after you, you'll honestly claim you were blackmailed. Give a false description of the blackmailer, and that's that. The perfect plan: you'll be safe and so will we."

"But I still don't understand why—"

"Come on, man. You'll have to do something to earn your reward. Suppose Paloma has found something important, something that stirs up the entire art world. Your dream job will become hers, and that's just be the beginning. But what if, on the other hand, *you* reveal the discovery to the world? Here's the deal: you get the research; we make sure Paloma disappears and the research is credited to you. Now look me in the eyes and tell me you think it's a good idea. Do you think it's a good idea, Preston?"

Clark asked the question slowly, nodding his head at the same time: a crude yet effective attempt to coerce his victim. It was starting to work. The picture Clark had painted for Preston was so tempting... But he knew from experience that no one did favors for nothing. "Hang on. I still don't get it. If I do all this, I get the study and the job. But what do you get?"

Clark impaled another mini octopus and inspected it against the light before gulping it down like a whale swallowing a herring. He gave Preston a mocking look. "Us? Oh, don't you worry about that. We'll take the big prize. And you, my friend, won't ask a single question."

Then he raised his hand and called the waiter over, ready to order another round.

PART II
NIGHT OF THE *ARTEMIS*

14

"Aaaaaaaarrrrrrrrgh!"

Jaime Azcárate's ferocious howl echoed off the bathroom walls as the water spraying from the shower abruptly dropped to near freezing. This had been happening a lot lately, and whenever he asked the landlady about it, she put him off with an excuse. "The boiler's acting up," was all she'd say. Jaime had since grown accustomed to what he called "express showers," which saved him money by using less water and had the added advantage of wasting less time. But this morning he'd been distracted, and the torrent of cold water surprised him as he was mulling over everything he'd been obsessing about since the previous weekend.

He couldn't stop thinking about Paloma's reaction to him bringing up the Medusa. She had always been a little temperamental, but he didn't see why the subject should have affected her so much. When Jaime told her they'd come close to killing him because of the piece they'd published on Bolgi, she'd stood up and practically shot out of the restaurant, as if she already knew someone had broken into her home. Why? He had no answer to that, or to the question of why that damnable Petrarca Gallery in Rome, which had once been home to the Medusa bust, was refusing to answer his calls.

Nobody was helping him, everyone was ignoring him, and it was starting to depress him. He was grateful to at least have Roberto and his shooting lessons, though he was starting to worry that he might have a panic attack while his finger was on the trigger.

As Jaime was putting on his bathrobe, he realized that the toilet was blocked and full of brown water. He suspected a link between the shower and this new phenomenon. This was confirmed when he turned the shower on again and a mud-colored geyser spouted from the basin. The scientific theory behind communicating vessels came to mind as he tried to solve the problem using a rubber plunger, but the problem persisted. Jaime decided he needed something lively to help him face the messy challenge with some semblance of joy, so he went out into the living area of his attic studio and headed for the stereo. Within a few seconds Glenn Miller's "In the Mood" was blasting from the speakers. He wasn't going to let a little plumbing issue ruin his morning now that he'd finally started to feel a bit better.

Except for a slight ache in his temples and the occasional cough, he was almost back to full health. His cold had relented in the face of an onslaught of orange juice and herbal remedies, and he could even breathe again without feeling like he was drowning. His lip had also healed well, and he no longer looked like a third-rate boxer.

All that was left was the emptiness, and the unanswered questions.

He was still waging battle with the plunger when he heard the doorbell ring. *Could it be the plumber?* he wondered in a rush of optimism. Putting his eye to the front door peephole, he saw a warped image of a tall, blond man. Suddenly he was filled with a terrible desire to climb back in bed and stay there for the rest of the day. Instead, he mustered his strength and opened the door.

"Good morning." The visitor ran his fingers through the hair on his temples. "I hope I haven't woken you."

"Whatever you may think of me, I don't tend to sleep with wet hair. Come in and make yourself at home. Do you feel like unblocking a toilet?"

Vicente Amatriaín quite unnecessarily wiped his spotless shoes on the doormat and, looking a bit taken aback, followed Jaime to the bathroom. "I was wondering when you'd show up again," Jaime said as he took up the plunger. "Laura said you're not the type to give up."

"I told you we'd be in touch." Amatriaín looked at the toilet and then the shower, which was filled with standing water. "Do you have a problem with your pipes?"

"What would make you think that?"

"I think I owe you an apology for getting you into this mess."

"So now it's your fault my bathroom's flooding?"

"I'm talking about the other day. I'm sorry to have caused trouble for you."

"Don't worry. I rarely say no to anything. Any day now I'll wake up married with three kids."

Amatriaín gave him a polite smile. He glanced at the bathtub again and, observing Jaime's fruitless efforts with the plunger, said, "This has all the earmarks of a blocked siphon trap."

"Does the EHU give you plumbing training? What's this about a symphonic trap?"

"Siphon, not symphonic." Amatriaín took off his jacket and hung it on the doorknob. "I have to admit, I'm a fan of your work. I've read many of your magazine stories and I think we could achieve great things together. Do you have a flat-head screwdriver?"

Jaime left the bathroom and returned in an instant with an Ikea toolbox. He watched in amazement as Amatriaín laid a folded-up towel by a circular metal cover in the floor beside the toilet, then knelt on it. "Pass me the screwdriver. This is the cover for the siphon trap. I bet it's full of muck."

"Would you believe it, this is the first time I've noticed that." Jaime looked on as the EHU officer deftly unscrewed the cover to reveal a stinking hole full of dirty water. "I appreciate your comment about my work," Jaime said as Amatriaín worked. "Most people I know think what I write is sensationalist trash."

"I don't think that. And even if I did, it'd be trash that has thousands of devotees. I don't suppose you have a rubber glove? I don't want to ruin my leather ones."

"Would a plastic bag do?"

Amatriaín nodded.

Jaime brought a small plastic bag from the kitchen. Amatriaín removed one of his leather gloves and slipped the bag on like a mitten, briefly revealing a scarred, yellowing hand covered in marks like those on his face.

"Well, well. Look what we have here." Amatriaín pulled his plastic-wrapped fingers from the trap. He was holding a mass of hair and filth at least the width of his hand.

Jaime looked impressed.

"I guess I really am losing hair. It must be the stress."

"It's a mystery how so much stuff ends up in there." Amatriaín opened the toilet seat lid and threw the foul wad of matter into the bowl. "Right, it should work now." He returned the plastic bag to Jaime and put his leather glove back on before screwing the cover back in place. "It's true that you specialize in rather unorthodox areas of art history. But stories like yours have always had broad appeal. And if you write, it's because you want people to read what you have to say, isn't that true?"

"Actually, I write so I can afford to pay for this little palace. And while I'm grateful to you for fixing my bathroom, I doubt that's why you came here. So tell me: Why did you come?"

"To speak to you about some work." Amatriaín stood and removed his gloves again, taking care this time to turn his back to Jaime. He washed his hands in the sink, from which the water now drained freely, and put his jacket back on. "Your expert knowledge of unusual topics is exactly what's needed for this Medusa business."

"I've already written everything I know about the sculpture. And anyway, I don't understand how a sensationalist story about a Medusa that causes death, hallucinations, and plague epidemics could possibly help the EHU."

"It might not help the EHU, but it'd be huge for the magazine. And, therefore, for you."

"I appreciate your interest," Jaime said. "But I don't need to play along with you to do that."

"Azcárate, you need to understand that—"

"No. *You* need to understand that I don't need any of this, so don't come here with your underhanded tactics. You can talk straight with me or go and find yourself another idiot. Can I get you a coffee?"

"Yes, please."

In the kitchen, Jaime unfolded the table and started the coffee maker.

"The fact is," Amatriaín continued, "you seem uncomfortable with this business, but I'm anxious to have you on board. I've followed your career closely, and, as I've said, I'm very impressed."

"Thank you. But all I want is to find out who tried to kill me in El Burgo de Osma, and why."

"If the aim is noble, any motive is good," said Amatriaín.

"Who said that?"

"Me, actually. I just thought of it."

"Congratulations. And yes, finding out why someone wanted to freeze me like a codfish seems a pretty noble aim. Do you want sugar? Sweetener?"

Jaime put two coffees on the table and set out the sugar bowl. Amatriaín helped himself to a spoonful.

"What's the deal with you, anyway?" Jaime asked. "Has your life always been dedicated to bothering people while they're on vacation or have you had other jobs before this? As a plumber, perhaps?"

When Amatriaín smiled, the scars on his cheeks grew even deeper. "I've done a bit of everything. A few years ago I was an adviser for the Historical Heritage Group. For a long time my job was to hunt for missing works of art, but a little accident forced me to give that work up. Don't you think the music is a bit loud?"

"No. Go on, please. What was this little accident you mentioned?"

"I was discovered while searching a suspect's warehouse. There was a firefight, and a bullet burst a container of sulfuric acid." Jaime gave no sign of understanding, so Amatriaín continued. "It was a chemistry lab. Its owner was involved in trafficking drugs, diamonds, and works of art. I suffered burns to my hands, chest, and part of my face."

Jaime nodded. That explained a few things.

"Wearing gloves all day is uncomfortable, but you get used to it," Amatriaín told him. "They moved me to Archives, and I still dabbled in other routine work and the occasional investigation. When the EHU was formed, Europol asked all the security and investigative forces in the EU for their cooperation. I was chosen to coordinate operations in Spain and Italy."

"Given all the artwork that's disappeared, why are they mounting an operation of this scale to find this one wretched Medusa's head?"

"As I said, the EHU hasn't been active for long, and until now we haven't had the help of true specialists. Our goal is to recover every piece of stolen artwork, but the Medusa was taken most recently, so the trail is fresher. We should be able to locate it more easily."

Jaime finished his coffee and stared at the bottom of the cup. Finally he put it down on the table, and without lifting his gaze said, "Fine. I'm all yours."

"Seriously?"

"Sure. We can't let the mess you and your team made in Amsterdam tarnish the reputation of the EHU. It needs some polishing pretty badly, and I can help you do it."

Amatriaín screwed up his mouth.

"I can't say I agree with all of that, but thank you. Now we can get to the real reason I came to see you."

"What's that?"

"There's news about the Medusa. There's a good chance we've located it."

"*Now* you tell me?"

"I had to be sure you'd agree to work for us first."

"How could I refuse after all you've done for me and my bathroom?"

"According to our contacts on the Italian coast, yesterday a collection of artifacts was loaded onto a cargo ship named the *Artemis*. It's scheduled to sail tomorrow from Istanbul to New York, stopping at Piraeus to collect more freight. There's a distinct possibility the Medusa is among those works of art."

"How do you know that?"

"Our agent recognized a crucifix that was stolen from a church in Ravenna a few weeks ago. It's possible that the rest of the pieces are stolen, too, so it stands to reason that the Medusa could be among them. In order not to tip off the ship's owners, we've decided to inspect the goods in secret."

"Stolen artwork on a ship? Don't you need warrants and all that?"

"All the pieces are required to have export certificates that prove they've been acquired legitimately," Amatriaín explained. "We suspect these certificates are excellent forgeries. Our sources tell me that there's also a very good chance that a port official is involved."

"I wouldn't be surprised. Do we know who put the artwork on the ship?"

"A dealer named Vittorio Rosselli who intends to exhibit them at an antique fair in New York next month. He has no previous convictions, but my superiors insist we need to dig deeper. Unfortunately, there's not enough time for a thorough investigation before the ship sets sail, so we'll have to intervene at some later point."

"When did you say it leaves?"

"It sails from Istanbul first thing tomorrow. That gives us just enough time to get to Piraeus and inspect it there before it casts off again. Mind you, we can't stick around."

"Couldn't the authorities hold up the ship for a few days? That'd give you more wiggle room."

"Possibly, though currently there's little proof that the ship's transporting stolen goods." Amatriaín gave a vulpine smile. "However, we could arrange for it to be stuck in port an extra night thanks to some problem with the vessel and a spare part that could be difficult to obtain. Inspector Juliun Kraniotis of the Greek police is going to lay the groundwork for us. Tomorrow morning my team will head out there with an extensive list of the artifacts stolen in recent months and try to identify the goods that are on board. If we find anything from the list, we'll seize the items and arrest Rosselli."

"Can this Kraniotis be trusted?"

"Completely. He's carried out other operations for us and his service record is impeccable."

"What's the source of the inventory you mentioned?"

"It's from a database Interpol compiled and sent to every investigative agency in the world. Over five thousand pieces appear in the catalogue. Of course, the list includes only those pieces for which we have a photograph; these are the ones that can be identified if they happen to surface. Our job is to find out whether any of the pieces in the *Artemis*'s hold are a match."

"Let me get this straight: Have you come to recruit me? You want me to go with you?"

"That was the idea, yes."

"Just you and me, loading and unloading boxes and checking a database of more than five thousand pieces of art?"

"I never said it'd be just you and me. A team of researchers from the CHR is at my disposal. Once we're in Piraeus we'll have the support of the Greek and Italian police. The team includes Professor Mercedes San Román, Professor Lucas Andrade, and Señorita Sonia Durán."

"Sonia Durán?" Jaime raised an eyebrow. Requena had forbidden him from going near the attractive blonde he'd crossed paths with outside the CHR lecture hall. But what if they were thrown together in a professional capacity?

Amatriaín was looking at him expectantly. "What do you say? Any questions?"

"Just one," said Jaime. "What's the weather like in Athens at this time of year?"

15

"Hey, what are you doing later?" Amanda asked Paloma, who was sitting in front of her computer on the other side of the room. She was writing up a report on a damaged still life by Spanish artist Luis Meléndez. The two-hundred-year-old painting was one of the works affected when the Prado developed a leak the previous year. The Technical Documentation Office had to evaluate the damage before they could proceed with their restoration.

When she got no response, Amanda raised her voice. "Paloma!"

"Huh?"

"What is going on with you? You've been ignoring me all day."

Paloma lifted her hands off the keyboard and rubbed her temples. "Sorry. I'm . . . concentrating on this."

"Are you all right, honey? You seem tense."

"Yeah. It's nothing. I just didn't sleep well. It must be the new pillow I bought."

"I was asking you what you're doing tonight."

Paloma glanced nervously at her watch. It had been a long day, but it was almost over, and she was looking forward to going home. Ever since the break-in at her apartment, she'd felt a deep sense of unease whenever she had to be out for more than an hour. She had lashed out at Preston over what happened, but he denied all knowledge of it and his innocence had seemed sincere. "I'll probably just grab a shower and try to sleep," she said, keeping her eyes on the computer screen.

"How about we grab a drink? Whatever's bothering you, you can tell me all about it over a few beers."

"I can't, Amanda, but thanks. Maybe some other day."

"Why? Are you sick?"

"No, just tired. Anyway, don't you have to get home to make Hugo's dinner?"

"The neighbor who picks him up can do it this once. I think he can get by without me for one night. Even moms need a break now and then."

Paloma couldn't help giving her friend a look of reproach. At thirty-three, she still wasn't a mother, and, although it wasn't something she had wanted, her body had recently begun sending her signals. *You don't have long left,* she would suddenly find herself thinking. But she always found reasons to ignore the message and focus on work. Plus, if Amanda's life was anything to go by, parenthood appeared to be something one should enter into very carefully.

"Honestly, I can't. Another time."

"Is this about that idiot?" Amanda whispered. She nodded in the direction of Oscar Preston, who was sitting on the other side of the room reviewing some reports while listening to music on a pair of giant headphones.

"Only partly. Sorry, I have to finish this before I go home."

Amanda shrugged and went back to her workstation. She was working on a small eighteenth-century landscape painted by an English artist that had also been damaged by the leak. The piece depicted a biblical scene of the Virgin Mary, Saint Joseph, and the baby Jesus resting during their flight into Egypt. The water had affected the outer layers of paint, which had bubbled up at certain points and changed color in others, but the preparation and medium remained intact. The stereomicroscopic analysis had been completed, and now Amanda faced the task of cleaning it and repainting the affected areas.

At seven in the evening she stopped, stretched her muscles, and put her utensils away in a small black case. "I'm off," she told Paloma. "If you come to your senses, call me."

Paloma was gathering up her things, too, but hurriedly and in no particular order. When she'd finished, she stood and grabbed her jacket from the hook. Before she walked out the door, she came up behind her friend and whispered in her ear, "See you tomorrow—and sorry."

Amanda shook her head, wondering what on earth was going on with Paloma. She gave one last glance to Oscar Preston, who was still engrossed in his work and his music, and left without saying good-bye.

The night was misty and the streetlamps and car headlights glowed through a thick layer of gray paint. At least that's how it seemed to Amanda, who was used to spending her days surrounded by artwork and was developing the habit of viewing real life as if it, too, were a painting. The air was cool and pleasant, and the idea of walking home was appealing.

As she strolled, she tried to call Señora Julia, the neighbor who picked up Hugo from school whenever Amanda had to work late, which was almost every day. It seemed strange that the Señora wasn't picking up the phone—it was the third time Amanda had called that evening. The poor woman must be going deaf.

As she strolled past the Parque del Retiro, Amanda thought about how quickly Paloma appeared to be unraveling. Over the last week she'd been particularly sensitive and overanxious, looking at everyone with suspicion, and was generally keeping to herself, speaking as little as possible even to Amanda. She speculated whether the change had something to do with the man who had surprised them at the restaurant a few days earlier.

Jaime Azcárate.

Amanda wondered who he was and where he'd come from. It worried her that Paloma had never mentioned him, and it pained her that her friend didn't confide in her as much as she'd thought she did.

So lost was Amanda in her thoughts, she barely noticed that she'd arrived at her home on Calle Jorge Juan. As she took the elevator up to the second floor, she toyed with the idea of sinking into a bubble bath after cooking Hugo his dinner; her body and mind both needed the tension relief. Before taking her key from her handbag, she rang the bell to Señora Julia's apartment. No one answered.

That was odd. The Señora rarely went out, especially on days when she had to look after Hugo. She began to worry. Had someone fallen ill? Why hadn't anyone called her?

Amanda opened her own door and went in, but the place was empty. She took a set of her neighbor's keys from the sideboard and let herself into the adjoining apartment. The lights were off and no sound could be heard. She took out her cell phone and called Señora Julia. Somewhere in the apartment a ringtone went off.

Amanda felt her heart pound. "Señora Julia?"

She walked down the corridor to the bedroom, and then she heard it: a hollow banging sound, coming from the wardrobe. Amanda turned the little ornamental brass key and the wardrobe door opened. A bundled-up form fell to the floor and Amanda screamed. "Señora Julia!"

Her sixty-nine-year-old neighbor was bound and gagged. Amanda removed the tape covering her lips and the woman gasped for breath.

"Wait here. I'll . . ." Amanda ran to the kitchen and returned with a serrated knife, which she used to free her neighbor. "What happened? Where's Hugo?"

"Oh my dear. Oh good God . . ."

"Señora Julia, where's my son?"

"A man. He said he was here to read the water meter. They'd left a note this morning saying they'd come. I—I believed him. God, what an idiot I am!"

"What did the man look like? Did you know him?"

"I don't know. I couldn't see him clearly through the peephole, and when I opened the door he was wearing a mask. How could I have been so stupid? You know I never open the door to anyone. We have to call the police!"

Amanda took out her cell phone and when she looked at the screen saw that she had a text message waiting. Ignoring it, she began to dial the emergency number with trembling fingers, but then the handset started to ring. The screen showed an unknown number.

Not knowing what else to do, she answered the call.

"Hello, I can't—"

"Amanda?" The male voice was nasal, with a strange accent.

"Who is it?" The voice seemed familiar but she couldn't put a name to it. Then it clicked. "Oscar Preston?"

"Are you okay?"

"Oscar, I can't talk right now. Someone has—"

"I know. Someone broke into your neighbor's house and took your son."

Amanda felt dizzy. She sat on the bed.

"How do you—?"

"I sent you a text. Have you called the police?"

"I was just about to. But how—"

"Listen to me, Amanda. It's very important that you don't tell the police. If you do that, you'll never see your son again."

"You son of a *bitch*—What are you talking about? What've you done with Hugo?"

"I don't have him, I swear. But the man who did this is desperate. You can't mess with him."

Amanda looked at Señora Julia, who was digging her fingernails into the younger woman's arm. "What's going on?" she whispered. Amanda shook her head.

"I don't understand, Oscar. Where's Hugo? And what's your part in all this?"

"They're using me. I'm supposed to tell you to get something from Paloma. Something she's working on."

"What are you *talking* about?"

"That secret document of hers. She must have told you something."

"I've never heard anything about Paloma having a secret document."

"You're lying. You're her best friend. You must know about it."

"I swear I don't. I know Ricardo has asked you both for a research piece. Is that what you mean?"

"Possibly, yes. Amanda, you have to get it. This man isn't screwing around and we only have a few days. If I don't get that document for him by Wednesday, God knows what'll happen to your son."

Amanda took a deep breath. Everything in her wanted to scream and insult that bastard Preston, but she forced herself to stay calm. "Look, Oscar, I don't know what despicable mess you've got yourself into, but if you so much as lay a finger on Hugo—"

"I'm not going to touch him; I don't even know where he is. I'm as much a victim in all this as you are. Remember, next Wednesday."

"But I don't—"

"I'm sorry, Amanda."

The line went dead. Amanda collapsed onto her neighbor's bed.

"What's going on?" Señora Julia asked.

"I don't know," Amanda said in the voice of someone whose soul has been torn from her. "I honestly don't know . . ."

16

Athens

Just before midday, the Alitalia Boeing 777 transporting Vicente Amatriaín's team landed at the Eleftherios Venizelos airport in Athens.

Jaime had spent the nearly four-hour flight chatting with the three CHR researchers the EHU officer had recruited for the mission. There was Mercedes San Román, an expert in religious imagery; Lucas Andrade, an all-around historian who drove the CHR's Modern History Department crazy with his audacious theories about the treasure that disappeared from France during the Franco-Prussian War; and, of course, Sonia Durán, the specialist in heritage management.

Jaime's new colleagues left a wide range of first impressions on him. Professor San Román had striking chestnut hair that she wore in a spiral knot. She wore red-rimmed glasses, and, even though she'd just met him, she nearly talked Jaime's ear off. Andrade was short and reserved, with a monotonous, husky voice that had the unfortunate effect of driving people away. Sonia Durán, a Nordic-looking beauty with white skin and turquoise eyes, proved to be both intelligent and amiable, though, to Jaime's regret, she was also rather guarded and not at all open to workplace flirtation.

To Jaime, all three seemed encouraged by the faith the EHU had in them, but they remained apprehensive about the responsibility laid at their feet. These were people who spent their days conducting research in museums, libraries, and archives, and each one's expertise in his or her field was unrivaled. But the task ahead was different from anything they had done before. They couldn't help but worry when they considered that the objects they were to find and examine might be loot a dangerous criminal gang had collected over many years of robberies.

Jaime's own unease was less about the mission than about the loose ends he'd left behind in Spain. When he left home Paloma wasn't answering his calls, and neither was the Petrarca Gallery. He had left them both messages via their answering machines, e-mail, and even social media accounts, but nobody seemed to want to hear from him.

During the last part of the trip, he managed to grab a power nap. His final thoughts before he closed his eyes were of Paloma and of the gorgon Medusa, and—for no particular reason—he found himself wondering whether both history and mythology were doomed to repeat themselves.

At a quarter past twelve, the five team members walked out of the airport toward the patrol car with tinted windows that was waiting for them. A man in a suit approached and greeted Amatriaín. "This is Inspector Juliun Kraniotis, the EHU's associate and head of the operation in Athens," Amatriaín said to the others, indicating the man with the red hair and beard.

Kraniotis didn't speak a word of Spanish, so he greeted them in English, showing each person an equal amount of attention. "I'm sorry for the inconvenience this trip may have caused you," he said, "but, as I'm sure Mr. Amatriaín has mentioned, it is only through close cooperation between our countries that this investigation can produce results. My team is already waiting at the port, but if you wish, I will take you to your hotel first. You must be tired, and the *Artemis* hasn't arrived yet."

Once they were all settled into their seats, the van set off toward the center of the ancient city. They left behind a highway flanked by olive groves and entered into a confusion of stores, kiosks, orthodox churches, and sidewalks packed with pedestrians. After the driver took a few side streets, they arrived at the grand hotel where rooms had been reserved for them.

The EHU had spared no expense. The Theoxenia was the only five-star hotel in Piraeus, and with its four nine-story buildings it resembled an architectural experiment more than an apartment block. While Kraniotis checked them in, the rest of the team admired the sleek, expansive lobby, which looked like something out of a science-fiction movie. They dropped off their luggage and refueled on coffee, and within an hour they were back in the police car following a report that the *Artemis* had just docked at port.

Jaime sat in the back with Lucas Andrade, who seemed equally miffed not to be sitting next to Sonia Durán. He breathed the salty air of one of the world's most important ports and peered out of the window. There it was: Piraeus. The legendary departure point for voyages of exploration, trade, and war.

Jaime had once studied the plans, designed by Hippodamus of Miletus, in a university class on urban planning. He dug back into his memory and recalled that it was Themistocles who, five centuries before Christ, had ordered the port city built so that Athens could become a true maritime power. Years later, in 1834, after the War of Independence, Piraeus became Greece's third largest city, with over two hundred thousand inhabitants—thereby recovering the status that for centuries had been lost.

The van turned down a road that ran parallel with the wharf; before a glass-fronted building, sailboats bobbed gently on the water. Buried in thought, Jaime barely noticed that they'd turned into the Kentrico

Limani, one of three harbors that made up the port complex of Piraeus, and had stopped at the red-and-white barrier of a checkpoint. A guard approached the window of the police car and, after exchanging a few words with their driver, went back to his guard station and raised the barrier.

They passed a series of ships bearing the names *Delphos, Delphos II,* and *Delphos III*. Beyond the Delphic trilogy were other vessels whose names, painted on their hulls or bridges, said a little more about their owners' interests: *Ulysses, Zenobia, Theseus, Veronica* . . .

Finally they stopped at a small brick building. Kraniotis got out of the car first, and he pointed toward a massive ship several meters out. "There you have it: the *Artemis*."

The ship was moored alongside a gigantic crane, parallel to the old jetty and separated from it by half a meter. Its bow rose ungracefully, revealing a layer of rust that covered most of the black hull. Containers and crates of all sizes were stacked on the deck, chained to crane masts at both bow and stern.

Kraniotis led the group into the small building, which turned out to be a port police station. Its one spacious room contained a filthy, threadbare sofa and a large table in the center. In a corner were a computer and a printer. Standing near these was the team of historians from the University of Athens assembled by Kraniotis: three specialists in ancient artifacts whose names Jaime forgot the minute he was told them.

"What do we do now?" Professor San Román asked Amatriaín. She looked around for a place to put her bag and decided not to deposit it on the disgusting couch.

"A soon as I inform the EHU's head office of our arrival, we'll go on board and get to work."

While Amatriaín made the call, Jaime slipped out of the station and set off at a fast walk out of the port. As he breathed in the pleasant smell of sea and petroleum, he passed a charming restaurant filled with couples and families sampling some tasty-looking meze under a natural canopy of vine leaves. Giving them a look of envy, he slipped his cell phone from his pocket and called Roberto. After seven rings he was about to hang up, then he heard a breathless voice. "Yes?"

"Am I interrupting something?"

"No, no. I love answering the phone while I'm soaking wet and shivering, with just a towel around my waist. I get off on it, in fact."

"Too much information. I can call back later."

"No, wait a second." Jaime heard Roberto switch on his heater. "Okay. Where are you?"

"At the Port of Piraeus. We just got here."

"Lucky you. And? Found something already?"

"Nothing but a freighter that's falling to pieces. I doubt the artifacts inside it are much older than the ship itself." Jaime said. "Listen, I'm going to need your help."

"Sorry, but you're dreaming if you think I'm going to show up with my revolver to get you out of trouble again. It's one thing expecting me to drive to El Burgo de Osma, but it's another—"

"That's not what I'm asking. Do you remember the gallery I mentioned? The Petrarca?"

"Where the Medusa used to be, yes. Unlike some people, *I* actually listen when someone talks to me."

"I can't get hold of them and things are going to be crazy here for a while. Could you do me a favor, since you like to stay up late anyway?"

"There you go again, trying to drag me into your crazy plans."

"Actually, what I need is really very simple. But if you want, I can let you get back to more important things, like scrubbing your belly."

"You're an asshole. Fine, what do you want me to do, exactly?"

"Do you have a pen and paper?"

"Are you kidding? I never shower without them."

Jaime gave Roberto a series of instructions and passed on the contact information for the Petrarca Gallery. After he'd written it all down, Roberto asked, "Anything else?"

"Not for now. I'll call tonight so you can tell me how it went."

"Not tonight. I'm playing in a match." Roberto took his online gaming very seriously.

"That's how you keep watch on the building?"

"You have no idea how mind-numbing it gets at night."

"Fine. Tomorrow then."

"Not too early," Roberto pleaded.

"Hey, we're professionals and there's work to do. You don't want the EHU to think we're as incompetent as they are, do you?"

"Honestly, I don't give a rat's ass. You're the secret super agent, not me."

"I'll talk to you tomorrow. Have a good night."

"You too."

Jaime whistled his way back to the port. After waving to the now-familiar guard, he walked back into the station, where an enraged Amatriaín asked where he'd been. Jaime shrugged.

"Nature called. Can we get started now?"

17

Madrid

Paloma had just ordered a decaf from the waiter when Amanda approached, looking stricken. "Amanda, what's the matter?"

"Can I sit down?" She could barely get the words out.

Her concern growing, Paloma gestured toward the empty chair at her corner table in the museum café. "Of course. Are you all right? You look like you're about to cry."

Amanda wiped her nose as she sat down. "They've kidnapped Hugo."

She spoke in such a low, weak voice, Paloma thought maybe she hadn't heard right. "What did you say?"

"When I got home last night, the neighbor who watches him wouldn't answer the door. I called but she didn't answer, so I got her spare keys and let myself in." Amanda's voice was strained. "I found her tied up in the closet, with tape over her mouth. She said a man had taken Hugo."

"Oh my God. What man?"

"I don't know. He told her he was from maintenance or something. Señora Julia never lets anyone in, but this time she opened the door and . . ." Amanda started to moan.

"Okay. Deep breaths." Paloma pulled a pack of tissues out of her handbag and handed one to her. "What do the police say?"

"I haven't called them."

"You haven't called the police? Amanda, why?"

"I was told not to. The people who have Hugo . . . they want something from you."

Paloma straightened, as if her spine had suddenly turned to iron. "From me?"

"Right after it happened, Oscar Preston called. He told me someone had taken my son and said they won't let him go until I give them something in exchange."

"Preston?" Paloma exclaimed. "That son of a bitch?"

"He was very clear. They want you to hand over your document."

Paloma was not the kind of person who could easily hide her thoughts or feelings. Her face reddened and her eyes grew damp. She felt her breathing and her heartbeat speed up. "My document? I don't know what you mean."

"Yes you do. For a week you've done nothing but go back and forth between your place and the museum. I'm assuming this is about that project that Ricardo Bosch assigned you."

"Yes, I've picked up some old work again as part of the application process. What's so unusual about that? If you want to get anywhere in life you have to work for it. I don't understand what—"

"Don't you see?" Amanda was crying now. "If I don't hand over whatever it is you're working on by Wednesday, I'll never see my son again."

"That's what you think." Paloma stood in a rage and grabbed Amanda's hand. "Let's go and see him now. We'll call the police, get Hugo back, and that son of a bitch will go to jail."

"It's not that simple." Amanda pulled her hand away. "He doesn't have anything to do with it. They're blackmailing him to get me to do the same to you."

"How can you believe that?" Paloma reluctantly sat back down. "Preston wants that job and there's nothing he won't do to get it. He even searched my apartment."

"Are you serious?"

"The day of my meeting with Ricardo. When I got home I noticed that someone had opened the door and rummaged through my things."

"Did they take anything?"

"Some computer CDs, but most of those were empty. I asked Preston about it the next day, but he claimed he didn't know anything about it. That bastard's a professional liar."

"Paloma, please. You're my friend. Why won't you tell me what they're looking for? Maybe we can find a solution together."

"The only solution is to call the police." This argument was beginning to remind Paloma of the one she'd had with Jaime a few days earlier. *What would Jaime do in this situation?* she wondered.

"I'm not going to call them! Preston told me not to, or—"

"Or what?"

"He says he isn't the one who has Hugo, and I believe him, Paloma. If we report him, whoever really has Hugo will find out, and I can't bear to think what they might do to him. It's been hard enough convincing Señora Julia to keep quiet about this. They went into her home, attacked her, locked her in the wardrobe . . . Do you realize what she's been through? These people are dangerous and I can't afford to piss them off."

The waiter arrived just then with the coffee Paloma had ordered. "One decaf?"

Paloma pressed her hand against her mouth and stood. As the waiter and Amanda looked on, she sprinted toward the restroom, bumping into a waitress who almost dropped her tray. In the bathroom, Paloma bent over the toilet and emptied her stomach. As she stared into the bowl, all she could picture was Oscar Preston's face.

Jaime, she found herself thinking again. *What would you do if you were here?*

18

Piraeus

As he took stock of the huge number of crates in Vittorio Rosselli's container, Jaime realized that the task ahead was not going to be easy. There must have been fifty crates, and all of them had to be opened, inspected, and reassembled with the utmost care.

Kraniotis and Amatriaín coordinated their efforts while the crates were removed from the container and placed on an enormous wooden table set up in the center of the hold. They were then unpacked by the Greek team, which also was responsible for photographing and measuring the artifacts, while Professors San Román and Andrade worked with Sonia Durán to compare them against the catalogue of stolen items. Jaime's role consisted of taking notes and photos of the procedure in order to prepare a report, though he helped out with the physical tasks when his colleague needed him to.

As Amatriaín had foretold, the EHU had managed to detain the *Artemis* in port due to some problem with the engine. One of the ship's engineers had facilitated the ruse after Inspector Kraniotis had claimed it was a "matter of national security"—and offered a substantial cash reward. The team now had time to inspect the goods away from the prying eyes of the freighter's captain and crew, for whom both the intrusion and the delay were a genuine nuisance. To make up for the inconvenient holdup, the authorities had provided them with luxurious hotel accommodations, making it unnecessary for them to wait out the repairs in the ship's uncomfortable cabins.

Jaime liked all of his coworkers, with the exception of Andrade, who wouldn't take his eyes off Sonia Durán and was constantly approaching her and whispering some nonsense into her ear. Fortunately for Jaime, she largely ignored it. The expert in heritage management made Jaime's blood pump a little faster, even though she spoke little and was focused more on her work than in building relationships of any kind with her coworkers. Mercedes San Román, for her part, possessed an energy and a readiness to help that Jaime found admirable. And he couldn't help but feel impressed by Juliun Kraniotis, a strong man committed to his work, who also displayed both extraordinary professionalism and impeccable manners. Amatriaín, meanwhile, was about as friendly to the group as a rabbit is to a boa constrictor, but Jaime had grown accustomed to his dry and anxious personality.

Their work involved a great deal of effort and little satisfaction. After several hours' toil, they hadn't found a single match. The famous crucifix that had raised the suspicions of the EHU officers turned out to be nothing more than a near-perfect replica of the original stolen in Ravenna. The rest of the shipment included sculptures, paintings, and gold and silverwork, all with the necessary export papers. There seemed to be nothing out of the ordinary stored in the hold, and as the hours went by the team grew increasingly frustrated.

"This one's clear, too," said Professor San Román, confirming that the last piece in the twenty-third crate matched none of the items in the catalogue.

At eight in the evening just five crates were left to inspect. The team members were sweating and breathing heavily; many of them were stopping frequently to rub their eyes. Amatriaín wiped his brow with his sleeve, walked over to Kraniotis, and whispered something in his ear. The Athenian inspector gave him a quiet answer and Amatriaín turned to the team. "I think we should take a break."

"That's the best idea I've heard all day." Professor San Román threw her notebook onto one of the crates and sat on the floor.

"We're stopping?" Jaime asked in surprise. "But we've almost finished."

Amatriaín shook his head. "We still have three hours of work and the ship doesn't leave till tomorrow. I've just suggested to Juliun that we have dinner in the port to help us get our energy back."

Kraniotis nodded. "You've been working yourselves to death. The least we can do is feed you."

Professor San Román smiled. "I take it back. Now, *that's* the best idea I've heard."

Jaime would have preferred to get the job done as soon as possible, but it was true that everyone was tired and hungry. He shrugged. "You're the boss."

"Good. Let's finish this crate and then get some dinner."

After examining the final object, an eleventh-century ivory crucifix that Rosselli had obtained in a Paris auction, and verifying that it, too, did not appear in the catalogue of stolen artifacts, they washed their hands and headed to the port. The police car was waiting for them at the port's exit and it delivered them to their hotel, where each of them enjoyed a well-deserved and badly needed shower. After freshening up, they strolled to a simple but nicely decorated harbor restaurant where the delicious wine, octopus, and fish drove the thankless work still ahead from their minds.

The restaurant was a big place, and it had charm: two floors decorated with nautical objects and reproductions of maritime antiquities. The quality of the food, the brisk service, and the friendly owner were among the reasons why the establishment was one of the most popular in the area.

Jaime sat at one end of the table, some distance away from the others, and enjoyed the flavors and aromas in silence. Back in El Burgo de Osma, he'd vowed to the cow spine that saved his life that he'd go vegetarian. He quickly decided that because prawns and clams had no vertebrae, they were fair game. He felt strangely at ease at this table in a restaurant by the sea, far from his attic apartment in Madrid, sitting alongside a bunch of virtual strangers. For the moment, he could forget all about the void he'd face when this was all over. He wished it didn't have to end.

Something the others were saying caught his attention and brought him back to the present.

"The curse?" Kraniotis said. "Come on, Vicente. You can't believe all that stuff."

"I don't," replied Amatriaín. "But it's something that seems eternally linked to the sculpture. Ask Azcárate."

Everyone turned to look at Jaime, who felt a surge of heat in his chest at suddenly becoming the center of attention.

"Wow, Jaime." Sonia Durán gave him a wry smile. "You're an expert in ancient curses?"

"Me? Not that I know of."

"Come on, Azcárate. Don't be so modest," Amatriaín said. "You've written tons of articles on paranormal phenomena: the temple cat, the Table of Solomon, that thing about Saint Fructus—and of course an article on the curse of Medusa. The extraordinary is your department."

"Possibly," Jaime replied. "But that doesn't mean I believe in those things. Not all of them, anyway."

Professor San Román made a small "O" with her mouth, as if she'd just remembered something. "Wait a minute: it is true. I read something about it. That sculpture carries a terrible curse."

"What do you mean?" Andrade asked.

"I read it—that's it! In that magazine, *Arcadia*! Were you the author?" Jaime gave a reluctant nod. "In the article you said that the statue has caused a number of deaths and a lot of misfortune throughout history."

"Particularly in recent times." Amatriaín peeled a prawn with this knife. At no point had he taken off his leather gloves. "From its first owner, Domenico Corsini, up to the security guard at the museum in Verona, there has been a trail of victims. It's said that the spirit of the gorgon Medusa lives in the statue and brings misery to anyone who gets close to her.

"In Greek mythology, if you recall, Medusa started out as a beautiful woman who conceived two children with the god Poseidon in a temple devoted to Athena. The goddess didn't take kindly to the situation and got revenge by turning her into a being so horrible, anyone who looked in her eyes would turn to stone. Perseus, son of Zeus and Danaë, supposedly killed her and cut off her head, and later gave Athena the head to place in the center of her shield." Amatriaín smiled. "The creature we're dealing with has been through a lot. It would seem advisable not to provoke her."

Several of the others listened to Amatriaín with open mouths.

"It's a terrifying story, Vicente," Kraniotis said in a mocking voice. "Perhaps we should call off the operation?"

"Of course not, it's just a legend. But we should be considering things from every angle."

"Even superstitious ones?"

"Even those, Juliun. One thing that's not based in superstition, however, is the very real death of the security guard at the museum in

Verona. It doesn't make sense, but he insisted he'd seen blue smoke that gradually devoured him—"

"That shouldn't really come as a surprise," Jaime interrupted. "You said yourself that the liqueur he drank was spiked with hallucinogenic mushrooms. If there's one thing I've learned from my work, it's that curses 'from the other side' have very tangible causes in the real world."

He turned away from the conversation and quickly became lost in his thoughts again, which skipped back and forth between Medusa's serpents and Paloma's sleek bob. He looked up as someone sat down beside him.

"What is it? Are we boring you?"

His heart raced as he found himself looking into aquamarine eyes and a face that smiled in a cautious but friendly manner. He smiled back. "I was arranging my thoughts in alphabetical order."

"I hope you're not planning your escape. We're all in this together, you know."

"It's no secret that we all expected this mission to end in disappointment."

"Don't worry. I'm used to working hard without any reward. It's part of my job description."

She spoke with an air of detachment that surprised Jaime. It reminded him somehow of Paloma, whose humanity seemed to fade when she was buried in her work. He was addicted to his job, too, but he also tried to enjoy himself as much as possible. Both women seemed to barricade their responsibilities away from their emotions. "What do you think of the boss?" Sonia lowered her voice so as not to be heard over the murmur of the other conversations.

"Amatriaín? The job's too big for him. And his mood changes too much."

"The others think so, too. And he doesn't seem very at ease with Kraniotis."

"Inferiority complex?"

"Rivalry. They get along on the surface, but I think it's all show."

Jaime thought she was probably right. Kraniotis called the shots in the operation, but he did it with style and efficiency. Amatriaín seemed intent on proving at all times that he was the one in charge.

"Why did you take this job?" Sonia asked. "You don't seem very happy to be here."

"A few reasons. Mostly because my boss asked me to."

"I met her a while ago. Laura seems great. What are the others?"

"The other women?"

"The other reasons."

They laughed and Jaime suddenly felt even less eager for the mission to end. "I don't know—to break the routine. Because Amatriaín helped me unblock my bathroom. And because I knew you were coming."

Sonia's cheeks reddened. "Is that true?"

"As true as these clams are delicious." Jaime figured it best not to continue too far along this path until their work was done, but the prospect of where it might lead certainly was an interesting one. "What about you? What brought you to this end of the Mediterranean?"

"Like you, the change of scenery. I was tired of spending all my time in that crypt they call an archive."

"I can relate." Jaime's smile was sincere. "Before I started working at *Arcadia* I was an intern at the CHR's library. I still have nightmares about the hours I spent underground searching for books. I went without sunlight for so long, I nearly turned into an insect."

"I believe you."

Just then Professor San Román called over to Sonia. As his companion excused herself and went back to her seat, Jaime came back to reality.

After their delicious meal, the restaurant's owner tried to entice them to sample an herb liqueur, but both Amatriaín and Kraniotis declined the offer, despite the protests of the rest of the team. There was a brief discussion, but in the end professionalism won out over the desire to get drunk, and they headed back toward the ship.

Jaime's spirits soared as he enjoyed the sea air, the sparkle from the streetlamps reflected on the water, and especially the company of the woman walking beside him. For now, he needed to focus on his work. But when they returned to Madrid, who knew what might happen? Maybe he'd have good reason to consider disobeying Isidro Requena's order relating to Sonia Durán.

The walk was a short one. Sooner than he would've liked, they were back at the port and waving at the checkpoint guard.

Nobody noticed anything out of the ordinary about the *Artemis*, but Jaime was struck by the feeling that a dark aura had enveloped the ship, something strange and malevolent that he couldn't quite put his finger on. The feeling grew as a cloud passed in front of the full moon and obscured it, as if in a Romantic landscape.

The ominous feeling gave way to cruel reality when they climbed down into the hold. There, they found Rosselli's container open and part of its cargo spread over the floor.

Most of the artifacts were gone.

19

"Oh my God!" cried Mercedes San Román. "What happened?"

Kraniotis poked his head into the container and confirmed that it was empty.

"They've taken everything!"

"Nobody leaves here," Amatriaín ordered, his face etched with worry. "Azcárate, come with me."

Jaime followed him out into the passageway and up the ladder to the upper deck. There, he stepped into Amatriaín's path, blocking him from going farther. "I suppose now you'll tell me I was right and we should've finished the job instead of going out for dinner?"

"Damn it, Azcárate. You must promise me you won't say anything about this."

"What about freedom of the press? Are you afraid the public will find out we went on a seafood bender and left the ship unguarded?"

"Azcárate, don't play games with me. This is serious."

"Calm down. I won't say anything until we know what happened."

"You'd better not. It would be a disaster if the world found out all that artwork was stolen from right under our noses."

"Did you see the port guard? He waved at us as if nothing had happened. There's no way anyone could've emptied the hold without alerting him. He's in it up to his neck."

"I agree. Bribery's rampant here."

"Not just here. What surprises me is how fast they emptied the container. Maybe we should search the ship before—"

Suddenly he realized Amatriaín was looking past him, over his shoulder. In the half-light, Jaime thought he could see the man's tanned face taking on a yellowish hue. He looked like he was about to be sick. "What is it?"

Then Jaime saw it, too. He went stiff.

A bluish smoke was rising up the ladder from the belly of the ship and moving directly toward them. "What's that?" Jaime asked.

"I don't know. Could be steam."

"Steam isn't blue." Jaime wondered why the rest of the team wasn't coming out. "Wait here, I'm going down."

"Down? We have to sound the alarm. If the thieves are still here—"

"Can't you see the others aren't coming out? The smoke is probably keeping them from finding the exit."

"I'm in charge, Azcárate. I won't let you—"

Jaime didn't wait for Amatriaín to finish giving his order. Under cover of the thickening fog that was gathering on deck, he slipped through the hatch. The smoke was even heavier below deck. Jaime retraced his steps until he found the passageway wall and, pressing himself against it, advanced until he reached the door to the hold. He was surprised to find that it was closed now, and even more surprised that there seemed no way to open it.

Beneath his feet the ground began to vibrate and his limbs felt slightly numb. The trembling grew stronger until it felt as if the whole ship was shaking. He quickly realized what was happening: the engines had been started and the *Artemis* was beginning to move off in the water. He banged several times on the hold door. "Hey! You in there! Can you hear me?"

He pushed with all his might, but the door wouldn't budge. He had felt the same sense of powerlessness when he'd been locked in the walk-in freezer in Casa Genaro, though at the time he'd been fighting to save himself, not to rescue others. He missed Roberto Barrero. If the potbellied security guard were there, he'd smash down the door with his body or take out the bolt with one clean shot. In that moment, Jaime understood that his only hope was to use Amatriaín's weapon to shoot off the lock. He dashed back up to the deck and was left breathless.

The *Artemis* was already sliding past the wharves toward the open sea. Whoever had started the engines was intent on sailing away with both cargo and passengers. Then it hit him: this was more than a curse or a robbery. It was a hijacking!

He looked around for Amatriaín, but the freighter's deck, as far as he could see, was deserted. Why hadn't the police shown up yet? How could they not have noticed a giant cargo ship leaving port in the middle of the night? "Amatriaín!" he bellowed. There was no reply.

The wharves slipped past impassively. From the front of the ship, Jaime could just make out the lighthouse that marked the entrance to the harbor. Then he heard something to the stern: part human-like cry, part synthesized sound. When he turned his heart gave a leap of joy. Like a sardine swimming after a sperm whale, a little police patrol boat was pursuing the *Artemis*.

Jaime climbed onto the railing and gripped it with one hand while waving with the other at the two men in the motorboat. They were screaming through a megaphone, demanding that the ship stop. The freighter was travelling at no more than five knots, and the motorboat overtook it easily. Feeling euphoric, Jaime smiled, shouted, and waved so that the team's rescuers could see him.

Suddenly, a yellow trail streaked out from somewhere in the ship, travelling toward the patrol boat. As it struck the boat a tremendous explosion of fire and shattered metal lit up the sky and then rained down into the sea. The motorboat and its occupants had been pulverized in an instant.

A shockwave hit the *Artemis* and Jaime fell to the deck, the smile wiped clean off his face. Despair overcame him as he realized that all hope of them being rescued had died with those men.

Who had launched that projectile? And from where?

It occurred to him then that screaming like a madman hadn't been his best idea.

He heard a gunshot, and a bullet whistled past him. Jaime hit the deck and crawled between two shipping containers. He could make out the sound of a firefight in the direction of the stern. He assumed Amatriaín was trying to keep their attackers at bay until reinforcements arrived.

When the shooting stopped, he feared the worst. Their assailants might have abandoned ship, an outcome that would warrant another seafood feast. But they could just as easily have killed, wounded, or captured Amatriaín, and Jaime knew that if they had, he would soon meet the same fate.

How had he ended up in this situation? He was just a journalist who wrote about art!

It was a question he'd been asking himself for far too many years.

He was torn between the desire to stay hidden and an impulse to jump overboard. Neither seemed like a good idea. If he stayed put, he would become one of the hostages. If he jumped, he'd be abandoning his colleagues like a yellow-bellied rat.

He decided to jump. If he was lucky he could reach the shore undetected and get help.

Before he got to the gunwale, he came across a body. To his relief, it wasn't Amatriaín's, but that of a heavily built man dressed in commando gear. Jaime found it reassuring that the EHU officer had eliminated at least one of their adversaries. A pistol lay nearby. Jaime picked it up.

Its weight in his hand made him feel more confident, though given his marksmanship, he knew he'd be better off avoiding an encounter with a living enemy.

He climbed down to the hold and aimed at the door lock, but the sound of creaking timber startled him before he could shoot. Unable to see through the darkness and smoke, he aimed blindly down the passageway. All he could hear was the beating of his heart.

But he could tell someone was there.

Driven by some survival instinct, he lifted the pistol the way Roberto had taught him—arms outstretched, knees bent—and pressed the trigger. It was virtually impossible to miss in such tight quarters—but still that's what he did. The sound of footsteps grew louder. He fired again, but this time the pistol made only a metallic click. He was cornered, and he'd run out of bullets. Behind him was the locked hold door, and in front of him, an armed man drawing closer. There was no point in resisting; the ship had left port and soon they'd be on a course to Salamina.

Jaime could smell gunpowder. A silhouette appeared through the smoke. The figure, dressed entirely in black and wearing a face mask, signaled to him to walk out in front.

Reluctantly, Jaime let the masked man direct him to the deck with an assault rifle. Along the port gunwale he saw two others holding Amatriaín prisoner. Both wore the same kind of night-vision mask and held the same rifle as his captor.

What was happening? This reminded him of the video games he played from time to time with Roberto.

"They're pirates," Amatriaín said through clenched teeth. "They want the freighter and all its cargo."

Jaime turned and looked at his captor, trying unsuccessfully to make out some feature of the man's face. Neither he nor the other two men said anything. They must have been trained to remain silent, and they were doing a pretty good job of it.

"What have you done with the crew and our colleagues? Did you kill them like you did the port police?" said Amatriaín.

The absence of a reply infuriated him. His eyes blazed. "I demand to know what you're going to do with us and where you're taking this ship!"

One pirate signaled almost imperceptibly with his head and the man nearest Amatriaín dealt him a blow to the stomach with the butt of his rifle.

Amatriaín's knees buckled and he fell to the ground, panting.

Jaime clenched his fists but did nothing. This was no game. For now, his best move was to keep quiet and still.

The smoke was now enveloping the ship, making it impossible to see anything but dreamlike forms and spectral lights. Jaime weighed their chances of escaping. If there had been a slim possibility before, now there was none. He looked at Amatriaín, who remained lying on the floor, holding his side. He bent and took the EHU officer's hands in his own, causing him to groan with pain as he pulled him up to a sitting position. Amatriaín then climbed to his feet and nodded his gratitude as he rubbed his stomach where he'd been struck.

At that moment a door squeaked and a man with a red handkerchief tied over his head appeared among them.

"Just what we needed," Jaime mumbled. "Who's this? Captain Blood?"

The new arrival whispered something to one of the pirates, and the figure immediately drew back. Then he nodded at the other two, who stood at attention and then disappeared into the smoke. The man stood in front of the two prisoners and glanced from one to the other.

"Vicente Amatriaín and Jaime Azcárate," he said in a mocking tone. The words were in Spanish, but his accent was Italian. "This really is my lucky day."

Jaime stayed silent. He could think of a thousand things to say, but none of them would improve their situation. He thought he'd let the stranger explain himself, but then he realized the man was not going to explain a thing. Instead, he took a couple of steps away and then spun back around, pointing an automatic pistol at them.

"We'll be finished in a few minutes' time, but I can't leave the ship without finishing the job my sister left half-done."

As if in slow motion, Jaime saw the man's finger leave the barrel and curve down over the trigger.

It was true what people said; in the end, a person's life really does flash before his eyes.

His birth on a cruise ship in the Mediterranean, off the coast of Alexandria.

His training as an art historian at the Complutense University of Madrid, where he met Paloma. His travels to Egypt and his return. His time as a scriptwriter for a TV mystery series.

His reunion with Laura Rodríguez. His appointment at *Arcadia* and all the adventures he'd had since.

After all that, this miserable freighter was about to become his tomb. Jaime gave a wry smile. He had come into the world on a ship and he was about leave it on another, in virtually the same waters.

He closed his eyes and prepared himself for the shot, which came two seconds later. He felt no pain, just a current of air to his right. When he opened his eyes, he saw that Amatriaín had launched himself at their captor and run his throat through with some kind of grappling hook.

The pirate, his eyes bulging in horror, was bent double and blood gushed from his mouth. His expression betrayed a hatred that was even greater than his pain. *"Porco albino . . ."* He crashed to the ground like a felled tree. Jaime let out all the air he'd been holding and looked at Amatriaín, who still held the hook, dripping with blood.

"What just happened?"

"I found this by the port gunwale and figured it wouldn't hurt to hide a weapon nearby." Amatriaín was panting. He didn't take his eyes off the body. "It's one of the grapnels these bastards used to board us."

"That looks serious."

"'Serious'? He's dead."

"Not him, you!"

Amatriaín touched his shoulder and discovered that he was indeed wounded. The pirate had shot Amatriaín as he attacked.

"Hold still." Jaime took the handkerchief off the dead man and used it as a tourniquet on Amatriaín. He pulled the knot tight and examined the result, unconvinced. "That's the best I can do for now."

"Thanks," Amatriaín said through clenched teeth.

"You stay here and keep still. I'll go down and help the others, and I'll bring back a first-aid kit. Does it hurt pretty bad?"

"Azcárate, we have to get out of here. He said that the ship—"

"Tell me later."

Amatriaín clamped his hand around Jaime's arm. It was the second time he'd try to stop him that night. Jaime turned and stared at him in fury. Amatriaín's eyes were barely visible through the smoke. "What are you doing? They're going to suffocate if we don't get them out of there!"

"They're dead already! And we will be too in a minute. The ship's going down, you heard that bastard."

"And you believed him? That's the biggest load of—"

A violent explosion cut Jaime off midsentence and he fell back as the *Artemis*'s bow was momentarily lifted above the water. After a few seconds, a huge wave crashed over the ship and swept away everything that wasn't chained in place, including the two men. Water poured into the hatches and portholes as an immense orange flame emerged from the starboard side of the freighter, like a great steel dragon spitting fire.

The *Artemis* had been mortally wounded.

. . .

The inside of the hold was an inferno. Flames licked through the thin bulkheads and set fire to Sonia Durán's jacket. She tore it off and ran to the other side of the hold with the others. Discovering that the container had been looted was a blow, and finding themselves surrounded by a blue mist had been a nightmare. But that was nothing compared to the sheer terror they felt when they realized the ship was on fire.

Seconds after Jaime and Amatriaín had left the hold, Kraniotis went out to see what was happening and was immediately struck on the head by some mysterious object.

Sonia Durán screamed, Lucas Andrade froze, and the rest looked on in bewilderment. All were thinking the same absurd thing.

The curse of Medusa.

Though none thought they believed in such superstitions, they still were momentarily immobilized by fear driven by circumstances they could not understand. Finally they ran toward the door, but it closed before they could escape. They screamed and banged against it, but their efforts were useless.

Kraniotis quickly recovered from the blow to his head and tried to smash open the door with a heavy marble bust that the thieves had left behind. He had nearly succeeded when a massive explosion shook the ship under them. In an instant they felt the ground tipping, and they fell and rolled to the back wall of the hold.

Kraniotis scratched his way up from the floor and tried again to get the door open. The place was starting to feel like an oven, but he persisted. It was only when he saw great puffs of black smoke emerging from the bulkhead that he grew truly afraid.

Sonia Durán cried out in horror as the realization that they had to escape or be burned to death set in. Kraniotis removed his shirt and tore off the sleeves. He threw one to Sonia and put the other over his mouth and nose.

"Cover your nose and mouth. Don't breathe in the smoke."

The others followed suit. Kraniotis saw that the flames were now getting through the bulkhead's boards and he advanced toward them, clutching the marble bust. Slowly but urgently, he struck the wood, and eventually created a soccer ball–sized hole. A great black cloud flooded through the opening and filled the entire hold. Ignoring it, he pulled at the loose ends of the boards, which split with a crunching sound. Finally he managed to make a hole in the bulkhead big enough for a person to pass through. "Come on, get out! Fast!" Kraniotis screamed. The two women, Lucas Andrade, and the three other researchers escaped through the hole.

Because he was the last to go through, he was the last to see the horror that awaited at the end of their improvised passageway. Through the flames he saw the engine room burning and then the fire setting the fuel tank alight. The second explosion came as a surprise, immobilizing them in the face of the fire show. Suddenly a ball of flames engulfed the engine room with a heat that could be felt across the entire ship.

The men and women instantly burned to death. They barely had time to feel pain or to understand what had happened. In an instant, their bodies were turned to charred flesh and their lives were swallowed up by the hungry vortex of fire.

20

The current of seawater and spray dragged Jaime Azcárate the length of the deck, as if he were riding the flume at a water park. He was afraid he'd be smashed against the stern, which drew ever closer. On his violent journey he'd crashed into several crates; others came free from their securing lines and he barely avoided being crushed by them. In desperation, he stretched out his hand, searching for something to grab hold of. A chain attached to a container scraped the skin off his palm, but it stopped him and kept him from being smashed to a pulp. Wave after wave crashed down, pounding him mercilessly. The pressure on his chest was great, and he felt the agony of someone drowning. He scarcely had time to suck in a little air before each new wave engulfed him.

Between waves he looked around for Amatriaín, but he had disappeared from sight. All that seemed to remain was the imposing column of smoke caused by the fire, which mixed with the blue mist, creating an effect like two pots of paint thrown on a canvas.

For a full minute Jaime clung to the chain, trying to time his breathing with the waves. When they began to subside he attempted to stand, but his knees failed him and he fell back down with a splash.

Eventually he managed to clamber onto his knees, still clasping the chain. Bruised and battered, his lungs sore, he spit out water, checked to make sure nothing was broken, and resumed his search for Amatriaín.

He eventually spied him huddled against the starboard gunwale. Other than the wound to his shoulder, he appeared unscathed.

Jaime cupped his hands around his mouth and shouted, "Can you get to me?"

Amatriaín raised his hand and let it fall. The signal meant nothing to Jaime, so he decided he'd have to be the one to make his way to the gunwale. When he finally reached it he grabbed hold of it and crawled along it to where the EHU officer was lying. "Are you all right?"

Amatriaín spat out water and gave him a blank look, nodding.

In one swift movement, Jaime snatched the pistol from his holster.

"What are you doing?" said Amatriaín, alarmed.

"Wait here. Don't let go of the gunwale."

Jaime ignored Amatriaín's protests and practically flew to the hatch, from which a foul-smelling black smoke now emanated. He felt sheer horror at the thought that his colleagues might have perished, but he could not let fear paralyze him. Breathing in air and courage, he leapt into the flaming hole and dragged himself down the passageway to the hold door.

This time he aimed straight at the lock and fired three times. His eyes were watering from the salt and smoke. Fear turned to surprise when he entered and saw that the hold was empty. At first he was confused, but he felt a surge of hope when he made out a hole in one of the walls and understood that his colleagues may have escaped. It was time for him and Amatriaín to do the same.

At the end of the passageway the flames were advancing from the engine room, reducing to ashes everything in their path. If he didn't want to end his days there, he had to get out now.

Jaime felt the smoke in his mouth and nose. He felt lost and no longer had any idea where to find the ladder to the deck. His head spun and he fell to his knees. The bony hand of death pressed tighter and tighter on his lungs.

Then he made out something beside him: a blackened form alongside several others of various sizes. He realized with horror that he was looking at the charred remains of his colleagues. Professor San Román, Andrade, Sonia . . . they were all dead.

The sight paralyzed him. He knew then that it was too late. He had tempted fate and had lost. He teetered on the verge of unconsciousness and his eyes filled with tears, his throat dry. He knew asphyxiation was preferable to burning to death, so he breathed in deeply, filling his lungs with the stinking, deadly smoke.

21

Madrid

In an unknown location, hidden in the shadows, the gorgon Medusa displayed her defiant, demonic smile. There was nothing else in the mysterious room. Just her, standing proudly in the middle of her murky kingdom.

In all her existence only once had she been defeated. Perseus, son of Zeus and Danaë, had caused her to fall into her own trap. After tricking her with a bronze shield that allowed him to see her reflection without being turned into stone, Perseus cut off her head. In the wake of her humiliating defeat, the monster had sworn never to let anyone else get the better of her.

A door opened, causing Medusa to take on a tinge of yellow in the light, and a dark shape slipped into the gorgon's dominion.

Paloma Blasco heard the beating of her heart and an inner voice telling her to escape while she still could. But something was calling her onward, a force so seductive it was impossible to refuse. She advanced slowly until she was upon the creature and able to rest her hand on the swirl of serpents that crowned her head. Paloma had always imagined the snakes in motion, as if performing a hideous dance, but she found only cold and lifeless stone. If the Medusa's face had once shown emotion, that expression had since completely disappeared.

Despite her disenchantment, Paloma felt compelled to confirm whether or not the legend was real.

She felt around the monster's head with both hands, seeking some kind of opening mechanism. After several attempts she was certain that the solid bust was nothing more than a lump of marble.

With this realization, her world came crashing down. She felt that she had failed: not just in relation to the Medusa but in all she'd done with her life. She had missed her chance to get married, to have a family. Her work, her friends, her whole life was a mess. Unable to control herself, she sat at the foot of the statue, put her head between her legs, and sobbed. She had never before felt so sad and defeated.

Suddenly, the wall in front of her lit up with a weak reddish glow that seemed to originate somewhere above her head. A blue smoke came from out of nowhere and began to envelop her. Paloma dried her tears and looked up. Through the smoke she saw a pair of stern-looking but inanimate stone eyes.

Then the eyes filled with life and looked at her, reddish flashes issuing from the marble pupils. The hideous creature bent her neck and let out a howl.

Paloma screamed and threw herself toward the door, but it slammed shut, trapping her. She looked back. Medusa was advancing through the smoke, arms outstretched, with a fierce expression on her face.

"Help!" Paloma shouted to no one. She broke her fingernails scratching at the door. This could not be happening! Her face a mask of horror, Paloma watched as the vile woman devoured her from the feet up and screamed until there were no screams left.

Terror, pain, agony . . . and then the end.

It was all over.

Sweat.

The sheets were soaking, as was her body.

Paloma sat up in her bed and rested her back against the headboard, trying to slow her breathing.

As she had countless times before, she wondered if she was going crazy. This was not the first time she'd had such a nightmare, not even the first time this week. It had been happening every other night. When she wasn't dreaming about the sculpture, she dreamed about Jaime. She couldn't understand how he and the Medusa had reappeared in her life at practically the same time. Sometimes they even came to her in the same dream. And Amanda, her son, and Oscar Preston had been the next people to get embroiled in the whole business. Paloma had tried to reason with her friend and convince her to turn the matter over to the police, but Amanda was terrified by the idea that Hugo's captors could harm him. In the end Paloma had admitted that she was working on some research that was still unfinished. That research had to be what Oscar Preston wanted. She promised Amanda that together they would find a solution, but at no point did she promise that she would hand over her work.

This was all her fault. It was all because of her ambition. She'd never had much contact with Hugo, but he was her best friend's son, and if something happened to him she would never forgive herself. She hated herself for even thinking she might withhold her work. How could she even consider such a thing?

She wondered whether she should seek medical help, or just try to forget about pursuing her dreams. No. It was too late. Just a little bit longer, and it would all be over.

She rolled over, not feeling much conviction at that assessment, and tried to go back to sleep.

22

Piraeus

When the cloud of smoke dissipated, Jaime expected to see the face of the devil himself. Instead he found himself gazing at the soot-blackened features of a man who was looking at him with concern. The face didn't seem familiar, but Jaime's brain wasn't in any condition to recognize people. "No, Paloma," he muttered, battling back toward consciousness. "I promise I won't do it again . . ."

"Who's Paloma?" The stranger spoke in English.

Jaime turned his head and saw that he was lying beside a container on the main deck of the *Artemis*. The ship was stationary and had heeled over to starboard. A strange red haze kept him from seeing clearly, and when he tried to wave it away he realized there was blood in his eyes. As he sat up, pain seared his temples and the face before him split into three.

"Take it easy, buddy. You've had a good crack to the head."

The voice was deep and calm. Jaime had heard it before, but the man in front of him didn't look much like the friendly, red-bearded inspector who owned it. The beard, like the hair, was nearly gone, leaving only a charred, straw-like mass where it had been. "Kraniotis..." Jaime said. "What happened to the others?"

"There was nothing I could do for them." He gave Jaime a devastated look.

Jaime pushed himself up with his elbows and wiped the blood from his forehead. He didn't have to be an expert on freighters to know that the boat, now tilting several degrees to starboard, was quickly sinking. "What happened?" he asked.

"The engine room blew. I saw them die..."

Memories of the charred bodies came back to Jaime. "How am I still alive?" he managed to ask.

"I was looking for a way out of the inferno below when I stumbled into you. We nearly didn't live to tell the tale."

"You saved my life. What does a person say in a situation like this?"

"Nothing we have time for," said Kraniotis. "We have to get off this ship—now."

Jaime got himself to his feet. His head was spinning, so he took several deep breaths before scanning the sea in front of him. The deaths of the rest of the team had not yet fully hit him. The deep attraction he'd felt for Sonia Durán just a few hours earlier had been pushed down to be dealt with later. His main concern now was saving the lives that were left, including his own.

"How far from land are we?" he asked.

Kraniotis thought for a few seconds. "I don't know for sure. Judging by how fast the engines were going and how long we've been at sea, I'd guess we're at least twenty miles from the coast."

Jaime didn't want to think about them swimming that distance, especially in complete darkness. "The lifeboats?" he asked.

"Gone."

"How many were there?"

"Two!" said a voice from the other side of the deck.

The startled men turned toward the voice and saw Amatriaín hobbling over to them, clutching his wounded shoulder. "They loaded the artifacts onto one," he said, "and used the other to escape."

"Thank God you're alive," said Kraniotis, exhaling. "Where've you been?"

"When the ship tilted I rolled to starboard. If it wasn't for the gunwale I'd have wound up in the water."

Jaime peered overboard and looked down. The fuel that had leaked from the ship was ablaze, forming a wall of fire around the hull. Some wooden boards were floating inside the burning circle; whenever one of them came into contact with the flames, it disappeared as if it had been suddenly devoured by a sea monster.

A light breeze was spreading the flames across the ship. Amatriaín, Azcárate, and Kraniotis were trapped in a small space on the forecastle, totally surrounded by the fire. Behind them the bridge burned; in front of them stretched the sea. Under their feet, the *Artemis*, now tilting fifty degrees, was quickly sinking. The massive freighter was about to become a giant grave, and the number of deceased stood to rise at any moment. "We have to jump now," Jaime said, his eyes fixed on the water.

Kraniotis looked at the wall of flames advancing toward them and agreed. But Amatriaín wasn't so sure. He limped over to the rail, then looked back and forth between the fire and the sea. "I don't know if it's a good idea."

"You can't have seen *Titanic*, then." Jaime walked over to a damaged container that had a large wooden crate poking out of it.

Kraniotis quickly saw what Jaime had in mind and without a word he helped him free the crate. Together they removed the lid and threw it overboard. Then they did the same with another crate. Amatriaín joined in and a moment later there were three wooden boards floating in the water. "Those are our rafts," said Jaime.

"All right." Amatriaín grimaced in pain. "Azcárate, you jump first. Then Juliun. I'm hurt, so I'll wait for the ship to heel over a bit more. It'll make for a shorter drop."

They agreed this was the best course of action and Jaime prepared to jump. He took a couple of steps back so he could build up speed and then ran toward the gunwale, glancing over his shoulder to get one last glimpse of the doomed ship. When he reached the ship's edge he launched himself headfirst into the water.

The fall was brief thanks to the heel of the ship, and the water enveloped his body completely, as if the sea had swallowed him. He plunged deep below the surface then arched his back until his body was horizontal. His heart was beating twice its normal speed and he felt as if firecrackers were going off inside his head. Fire raged above him. He kicked and began to swim upward. When his head surfaced, smoke-scented air rushed into his lungs, making him cough. He tried to relax. As he waited for his breathing to return to normal, he looked at the ship just as someone jumped. It was Amatriaín.

Jaime swam toward him. "Where's Kraniotis?"

"He's still on the ship," Amatriaín replied nervously. The flames from the freighter's hull reflected in his eyes. "He said he saw movement on the bridge and went to investigate. He must've thought it was a survivor."

"There are no survivors. Why didn't you wait for him?"

"I waited as long as I could. The ship was sinking."

Jaime felt a twinge of contempt for the man in front of him. He kicked his legs to keep himself from sinking and cupped his hands around his mouth. "Kraniotis! Can you hear me?"

"Juliun!" Amatriaín cried. "Oh God, what has he done?"

Grief stricken about the fate that might have befallen the man who'd saved his life, Jaime swam around the hull. By the time he had circled back around to Amatriaín, the flames from the deck appeared to be planing across the surface of the water. He knew it was a matter of minutes before the freighter would disappear under the waves. "No sign of him."

"What could've happened? What could he have seen?"

They called his name several times, even as they carefully swam as far as possible from the freighter to avoid being sucked down with it.

Neither man blinked during the *Artemis*'s final minute. The flames went out; the ship went down; and the sea was left in silence as if nothing of great importance had happened there.

Five minutes later, the sound of rotor blades came from above and a powerful light shone down on the ship's only two survivors. The helicopter descended until it was almost floating on the water, and Amatriaín raised his hand to greet the crew that had come to their aid.

That was when Jaime knew that whatever else Vicente Amatriaín was, he was not a man Jaime could trust.

23

Madrid

As soon as Laura Rodríguez received Isidro Requena's call, she dropped what she was doing and rushed down to meet him in the lecture hall. On the way, she ran into Roberto Barrero, who was still wearing his guard's uniform. "I saw it on the news. What's happened to Jaime?" He blocked Laura from going any farther down the hallway.

"I don't know yet. Let me past."

"How can you not know?"

"I know as much as you. Something happened in Piraeus—"

"'Something'? The press is going off about a tragic incident, a hijacked cargo ship, a patrol boat sunk, several dead and wounded, and some kind of investigation."

"That's what they're saying, yes—"

"So stop screwing with me. Is Jaime all right?"

"I'm telling you, I don't know!"

Laura had been working since she got to the office at eight that morning. The recent discovery of Neanderthal remains in the Cova Negra area of Xátiva warranted extensive coverage in the December issue and she was weighing who should get the assignment. She'd just started to peruse the online news sources when Isidro Requena called her down. "So where are you going in such a hurry?" Roberto asked.

"Isidro called me down. I think he has news."

"About Jaime? I'm coming with you."

"He won't want you coming in there."

"Tough shit."

Pursued by both Roberto and her own guilt over having allowed Jaime and the other CHR researchers to participate in a mission so far beyond their purview, Laura ran toward the room where they'd met and agreed to cooperate with the EHU.

"No, Barrero. Not you," Requena said, blocking Roberto's way at the door.

"I want to know what's happened to him."

"You'll be told what you need to be told, but not now."

Roberto snorted like an enraged bull, but Requena's order was categorical. Laura gave the security guard a tense look and followed Requena into the room. Standing by the window was a short, bald man in a suit who turned toward them as they entered. His thick-rimmed glasses magnified sad, mousy little eyes. He introduced himself as Herbert Monfort, commissioner of the EHU's Spanish branch. "I'm Amatriaín's immediate superior," he said after he'd shaken their hands. "First of all, I'd like to thank you for responding so graciously to our request."

"Get to the point," Requena said. "Are our colleagues all right?"

Monfort looked like he could be a pleasant man, but he wasn't smiling now. He cleared his throat, rubbed his hands, and looked at them with sadness. "As I imagine you've gathered, I have bad news. Last night a group of armed men boarded the freighter *Artemis* while it was anchored in port. They arrived by skiff and boarded the ship using grappling hooks attached to cables. These men stole the artifacts from the container our colleagues were inspecting and then fled. But first they locked the team in the hold, started the ship's engines, and, once they were in open water, sank it with explosives."

"But why?" Laura looked at him, horrified.

"Come on, out with it," Requena growled. "What happened to our colleagues?"

Monfort took a deep breath. "They're all dead except for Vicente Amatriaín and Jaime Azcárate."

Laura felt all the strength drain from her body. Using every bit of concentration she could muster, she managed to stay put and not run straight to the restroom to throw up.

Dr. Requena sat down and dug his fingernails into his knees. "How did this happen? Who . . . ?"

"We don't have any of those answers yet. Amatriaín was struck several times and was shot in the shoulder, but he's well enough to help the Greek police in the investigation. Two police officers and two of the pirates also died. The rest managed to escape."

"And Jaime? Is he all right?"

"He has burns to his hands and is also being treated for smoke inhalation. He's under observation at one of the best hospitals in Athens. The minute they discharge him I'll have him brought home."

Requena took his hands from his knees and gently massaged the places he'd dug at with his nails. "Do you have any idea who might have done this?"

"I wouldn't say that, exactly. I spoke with Amatriaín and he told me none of the pieces they inspected appeared in the catalogue of stolen artifacts, so it seems unlikely that the crime was committed to prevent our team from finding something. The thieves took almost all of the works of art that were in the hold, so it's more than likely this was just a robbery."

Laura had stopped smoking more than a year ago, but at that moment she would have killed for a cigarette. She began to pace between the chairs. "If it was just a robbery they wouldn't have needed to blow up the ship and kill everyone. How did they remove the artifacts before sinking the freighter?"

"It appears that the pirates loaded them onto one of the lifeboats and launched it before taking over the cargo ship by force. But we don't yet know all the details. We'll know more once Amatriaín can investigate what's left of the ship and question staff at the port. Some workers may have been bribed; that's the only thing that would explain how the thieves boarded and hijacked the freighter so easily."

"My God. How is it possible that almost everyone was killed?"

"Amatriaín said that the assailants fled in the other lifeboat, so the opportunities for anyone else to escape were limited. What's more, all the victims except Azcárate and Amatriaín were locked in the container hold when . . ."

"When what?"

"When a blue smoke suddenly filled the hold. No one knows where it came from. Amatriaín and Jaime were on deck at the time, and that's what saved them from being burned to death when the engine room exploded."

"A blue smoke?"

"Like at the museum!" cried a muffled voice.

Monfort glanced from side to side. "Who said that?"

"I did!" The door to the room flew open, revealing Roberto Barrero.

Requena jumped to his feet. "Barrero, I told you, you can't come in here!"

"I didn't come in. I was just listening from behind the door. You didn't say anything about that."

"Do me a favor, and get out of here."

"Wait a moment, Isidro," Laura said. "What did you say about the museum, Roberto?"

"The Pontecorvo House Museum, where the Medusa was stolen from. In his statement before he died, the security guard said something about smoke that had a life of its own and attacked him."

Monfort blinked behind his large glasses. "Who is this gentleman?"

"He's one of the center's security guards," Laura said. "And a friend of Jaime Azcárate."

Roberto appeared annoyed. "What do you mean, *a* friend? I'm the only friend that pansy has."

"Getting back to the blue smoke . . ." said Requena.

Herbert Monfort snapped his fingers. "Someone's using the same trick."

"The Medusa!" Roberto said. "Maybe that fucking statue was on the ship after all."

Requena frowned. "Language, Barrero."

"Sorry, but you know I could be right."

"Where are you going with this?" Monfort sounded intrigued. "That legend of the curse is—"

"I don't believe in curses any more than you do," Roberto said. "But think about it for a minute: The night the Medusa was stolen, the smoke appeared at the museum. This time, it appeared on the ship. Where there's smoke, there's—well, a Medusa. This isn't rocket science."

Laura and Montfort were listening attentively, but Requena wasn't impressed. "Barrero, you've completely lost it. Go home, your shift's over. Aren't you on vacation?"

"My vacation starts tomorrow."

"I suggest you start it now. This is affecting your judgment."

"Wait—what if the smoke kept them from finding the Medusa?" Laura said excitedly. "Suppose someone was watching the team: a member of the crew, someone at the port, one of our own researchers . . . anyone who knew that the Medusa was on the freighter. When the search got too close, this person released the smoke, kidnapped the team, and then sunk the ship."

"But why?"

"It's obvious: to keep us from finding the Medusa."

"But who would want the Medusa to disappear?" said Requena in despair. "Besides, according to your theory, there had to be a mole in the team, and it could only be one of the survivors: Vicente Amatriaín or Jaime Azcárate."

"Not Jaime." Laura shook her head.

"And I can vouch for Amatriaín." Montfort looked disconcerted by the turn the conversation had taken. "He's been fighting against art theft and contraband for years, and his loyalty is beyond question. At any rate, sinking the ship just to hide the bust from us would be a rather drastic plan, don't you think?"

"Can you think of any other reason for what happened? Maybe the people who sunk the ship already removed the bust. Or perhaps they plan to dive and retrieve it."

"Forgive me, but that theory's pretty far-fetched. The blue smoke appeared when the mysterious assailants had already emptied the container. If the Medusa had been there, they would already have taken it. It would make no sense to then sink the boat and arrange all those fireworks."

Laura's longing for a cigarette intensified. Trying to banish all thought of smoking, she studied a photograph hanging over the room's dais: Isidro Requena and the Spanish minister of culture. She shook her head. "Maybe you're right. We're all losing our minds."

"We'll know more in a few hours' time," Montfort said. "Dr. Rodríguez, Dr. Requena, I'm deeply sorry for what has happened. If there is anything I can do for you, I—"

"There is something," Laura said. "Find the people responsible for this atrocity."

"You can depend on it."

"Thank you for coming to tell us in person." While Isidro Requena walked Monfort to the hallway, Laura took the opportunity to confront Roberto Barrero. "What do you think you're doing? What if Requena loses his temper and fires you for insubordination?"

"Then you can hire me as a photographer."

"Right. Like I'm in a position to hire anyone," Laura replied gloomily.

24

Port of Cagliari—Sardinia

"Impossible! What you're saying is *impossible*!"

Rosa Mazi stood among the pieces of the expensive vase she'd just dashed against the timber floor of the *Phoenix*, her eyes brimming with tears.

"*Control yourself, Rosa.*" The voice crackled through the speakers on either side of her father's portrait. "*Leonardo always understood the risks involved in our work. He took on that risk willingly and was equal to the task. But leading such an audacious enterprise on his own, without saying anything to the family, was a foolish thing to do, and foolish choices have consequences.*"

"Consequences? How can you talk like that? Your son is dead! They murdered him!"

"*He wasn't murdered. My informer tells me he fired first. All his captive did was defend himself.*"

For Rosa, things were happening too fast. It had only been a few days since she'd returned to Cagliari and joined her fiancé in making final preparations for the exhibition that would open to the public in less than a week. A crew member had called and summoned her to the family yacht, back now in its usual berth at the port, and she'd just learned her brother had been murdered while conducting a secret and unauthorized mission. "Are you trying to justify his killing?"

"Not at all, Rosa. I regret his death as much as you do. I'm not a monster. He was a good son—strong and intelligent. But his hunger for power blinded him. He wanted to be smarter than his father, and he got the punishment he had coming. I'm sure you've heard me say it a thousand times: betrayal gets the reward it deserves."

"But . . . what are you saying? He was always loyal to you. He did everything you asked. He stole the Medusa to impress *you*!"

"No one authorized him to lead that mission, and he certainly didn't have the right to do it behind our backs. He wanted to get rich by cutting ties with the family—the same family that gave him everything he had and without which he wouldn't have become half the man he was. Now what is he? A corpse at the bottom of the sea."

The rage that besieged Rosa began to give way to a deep sorrow. She felt this grief not because her brother was dead, but because she understood that she was now further than ever from the kind of life she longed for. She remembered the last conversation she'd had with Leonardo, when they saw each other on the yacht. He'd said he was working on another operation, and when she asked him what it was, he had replied with another question: "Do you really want to know?"

Maybe if she had shown an interest then, she could have convinced him it was a bad idea, and her brother would be alive.

"How did you find out?"

"*You continue to underestimate me, Rosa! I may not be able to move, but I still have contacts all over the Mediterranean. Your brother hired mercenaries to steal the artifacts and hijack the freighter, and one of them is an old acquaintance who has since told me everything. In the end, a father is always wiser than his son. Part of the merchandise seized is on its way now to the home of our best client.*"

"Galliano."

"If Leonardo hadn't been so greedy, he would have come to me. We would have made a plan together and taken every precaution, and we'd now be enjoying the reward together."

"You're no better than him if you're going to profit from his death."

"May it serve as a lesson to him in his next life! The worst thing is not that Leonardo betrayed his family and died, Rosa. The worst thing is that he died because he was deceived."

"Deceived? What are you talking about?"

"The man who hired your brother did it from the shadows. They never looked each other in the eyes. He heard that the EHU was planning to board the cargo ship, he found a way to contact your brother, and he promised Leonardo that all the artifacts in the hold would be his if he hijacked and sunk the ship."

"But why? What did he hope to gain?"

"Supposedly, his intention was to kill the researchers on board. But I have another theory. Based on what I know of Nascimbene, this entire spectacle was arranged to trick and kill Leonardo."

"Nascimbene?" Rosa sounded horrified. "The man's been dead for years."

"Don't call him a man! He's a degenerate, an enemy of your family."

"Whatever he is, he's dead."

"So am I, supposedly, and look at me."

Rosa looked at the portrait and felt stupid. Her brother was dead, and her father wouldn't let himself be seen except in the form of this ridiculous canvas. She felt like throwing herself overboard, swallowing water, and drowning herself. Better still, she'd swim to dry land, marry Dino, and disappear, never to return again.

"Nascimbene's dead. He died in a car accident."

"And I 'died' when the yacht went under. No, Rosa. I'm certain he was the faceless person who hired Leonardo to do the job. His intention was not so much to kill the EHU team as to get rid of another member of our family. When Nascimbene swore vengeance against the Carreras, he was not just referring to me. And now you, my girl—you're next."

"But that can't be right. You told me yourself: Leonardo didn't die in the explosion."

"He would have, had Vicente Amatriaín not first driven a grapnel through his throat."

Rosa felt bile rise up and stop at the back of her mouth. "Amatriaín?"

"He and the Greek inspector were heading the operation."

"I don't understand any of this. I know—" She took a deep breath and corrected herself: "I *knew* Leonardo, and he would never have let himself be tricked like that."

"Greed is blind. And it kills. Whoever had his finger on the detonator intended to kill Leonardo along with the others. The only reason he didn't is that Amatriaín killed your brother first. And there is something else you should know, Rosa."

From the tone of voice, Rosa understood she needed to steel herself against another surprise as unpleasant as the ones she'd just heard.

"Jaime Azcárate was another survivor."

"Azcárate? For the love of God! What was he doing there?"

"Supposedly, helping the EHU. But it's curious that Amatriaín and Azcárate survived two successive attempts to eliminate them."

"I don't understand any of this. It doesn't make sense—"

"It all fits: the blue smoke, the hijacking of the ship, and worst of all, the cruel and twisted killing of a Carrera. We both know only one monster is capable of all this. That snake is still alive, Rosa, there can be no doubt. He tried to kill me on board this very yacht, and he failed. Now he wants to wipe out my family. He started with Leonardo, and God knows he won't rest until you're in the ground."

"I can't believe I'm hearing this. You're as bad as he is!" Rosa exclaimed. This was too much. She wanted nothing more than to forget everything and escape forever the life of double-dealing and family pacts that could only end in a bloodbath. She thought of Dino, of the gallery, the exhibition . . . those were the only things she could allow to matter anymore.

She turned and, without saying good-bye, marched angrily out of the yacht's lounge.

25

Madrid

Roberto Barrero hung up the telephone and kicked his bare feet up on the sofa in his little apartment in the Argüelles neighborhood. He had been calling the Petrarca Gallery for three days, and the only voice he'd reached had been the one on the answering machine, asking him to leave a message.

Sick of getting the same old message in Italian, he pushed the phone away and laid his head against the soft arm of the sofa. The job Jaime had given him was boring to the point of insult for someone who'd spent the best part of his youth digging for archeological treasures in Israel, trafficking relics, and sneaking into mansions and churches to steal ancient codices. Although he was almost fully rehabilitated and his activities were now completely legal—not counting the small liberties he took in his role as a security guard—Roberto was used to action. Calling a telephone number repeatedly and never getting a response was putting him in a bad mood.

For a moment he wished he could trade places with Jaime, but he quickly rejected the thought when he remembered the nightmare his unlucky friend had endured on board the *Artemis*. Roberto didn't know how he managed it, but Jaime always found himself in the thick of things. And this time it had very nearly cost him his life.

The sound of the doorbell startled him out of his daydreaming. He took a deep breath and rose to his feet. "Time to move your butt," Roberto told himself.

When he opened the door he found himself looking at Laura Rodríguez's pallid face. "It's you, Presidenta," he said in surprise.

"Is it a bad time?"

"Only if you're still blocking the doorway when the pizza guy arrives. Come on in."

Laura walked into the living room and was shocked by what she saw: a television on mute, a cell phone on the floor, papers all over the coffee table, several dozen cigarette butts in an ashtray, and an empty potato chip bag. In one corner, standing like a silent bodyguard, a life-sized Batman mannequin—fully equipped with cape and gadget belt—seemed to stare at her through its mask. Roberto was wearing shorts and a Spider-Man T-shirt covered in holes and stains, and his feet were bare. Crumbs in his goatee and smudges on his glasses rounded off an unkempt appearance that matched the room.

"Fighting off zombies again?" Laura ventured.

"I wish. I've spent two days and two nights trying to find a woman who owns an art gallery in Rome. The guy who invented answering machines should be strung up by his balls and forced to listen to an endless recording of 'The person you are calling is currently unavailable' on repeat."

Laura straightened a cushion on the untidy sofa and sat down. "Is this about something important?" she asked.

"I suppose not. It's a job Jaime gave me."

"I thought it might be."

"If he'd stayed here and done it himself, he would've saved himself a lot of pain. He's not cut out for shoot-outs and explosions. Believe me: I know what I'm talking about."

"You didn't know him in college," Laura said. "He was the same then, and he won't ever change."

"You liked him, huh?"

"Where'd you get that idea? Not that it's any of your business."

"He's never said much about it, but he's mentioned a trip you took together to Marrakech back then. I'm guessing he liked you, though maybe not enough to try to get you into bed."

"Are you done?"

"I guess." Roberto picked up a wrinkly cigar from the table and lit it with a lighter he pulled out of his shorts. "Jaime's got more balls than a bowling alley, but he's hopeless when it comes to matters of the heart." He coughed a couple of times. "To what do I owe the honor of your visit? If I'd known you were coming, I'd have put the garbage out. Though you can take it down when you leave."

"I came to warn you that Requena's upset with you. That's two things now, and it would be a good idea if you took things back a notch."

"Two things? As far as I know, he's only mad about me butting in today."

"There's also what you do at night at the CHR when you think nobody's looking."

"Gaming's no crime," Roberto argued. "It helps a guy keep his reflexes sharp and practice his marksmanship."

"All the same, you should give it a rest. If not for yourself, for me; I'm the one who recommended you."

"Don't blame me. I wanted to be a photographer."

"You're impossible. And would you mind putting that cigar out? I'm trying to stop smoking."

"That's your problem."

Laura sighed. "Why don't you tell me what you're investigating?"

"It has something to do with the Medusa. For a while it was exhibited at the Petrarca Gallery in Rome. They won't pick up the phone or reply to my emails."

"Is this for one of Jaime's stories?"

"I'm helping out."

"Okay," Laura said, "but I'm not paying you a penny."

"Now, why would you think I'm as money oriented as you are?"

"What you are is useless. For one thing, investigating a Roman gallery by phone and email is a sloppy approach. You have to visit."

"Yeah, sure, visit the place. You'd love to do that, wouldn't you? Send me on an all-expenses-paid trip to Rome courtesy of *Arcadia*?"

"You don't have to actually go there. There's a little thing called the Internet, and I bet that gallery has a website. I'm sure that under that pile of trash, there's a laptop. Why don't you try turning it on?"

Roberto rooted under the piles of paper for his computer and was soon inputting the web address for the Petrarca Gallery.

Laura wrinkled up her nose. "Don't you ever open up the windows in your apartment?"

In response, Roberto pulled a bottle of *Star Trek* cologne out from somewhere and sprayed half the living room.

"You're such a geek. You know that, don't you?"

"Sweetheart, geeks are just intellectuals with an expanded universe."

"Sure they are." Laura turned her attention to the computer, which was covered in fingerprints, dust, and beer and Coca-Cola stains. "Here we go. Let's see what it says."

The website looked as if its design had cost as much money as the gallery building itself. On the home page, animated graphics jumped out from the four sides of the screen and swirled around in the center before joining together like a jigsaw puzzle and forming the image of a classical-looking building with walls of gray stonework and rounded,

English-style windows. Over all this was superimposed an elegant logo that read *Petrarca: Galleria d'Arte*.

When Laura clicked on the image, it broke up again and new icons emerged out of the swirl. The screen was divided into sections: *Storia, Servizi, Agenda, Artisti, Antiquariato*.

They chose the latter and were led into a world made up of marble gods and heroes. The Petrarca Gallery focused on local contemporary artists, but it also had a sizeable section devoted to Renaissance and baroque works. Bolgi's famous Medusa would certainly not have been out of tune with the gallery's catalogue.

Laura then clicked on the word *Contatto*. A window opened that included space for entering a message.

"What are you doing?" Roberto asked. "Are you sending them an email?"

"Didn't you want to ask them something?"

"Haven't you been listening to me? I've been asking them to call me for three days. It's as if I don't exist."

"No offense, Roberto dear, but do you speak Italian?"

"Sure I speak Italian. It's the same as Spanish but the words end in *i*."

"You're such a Neanderthal." Laura's fingers took up their positions over the keyboard. "Right, then. Watch and learn, Roberto. Watch and learn."

PART III
UNDER FIRE

26

Madrid

The Lufthansa flight from Athens landed on the runway an hour late due to a storm over the departure city, and the cold and damp of the morning made the passengers pull collars and scarves tighter around their necks.

His eyes underscored by dark circles, Jaime Azcárate plodded through the cabin without acknowledging the smiling flight attendant performing the polite parting ritual, or even noticing the other passengers he was following out of the plane. He ignored everyone, advancing like a zombie to the airport exit. With the little clothing he'd taken to Athens tucked in his carry-on, he had no need to wait at baggage collection to see whether a suitcase had been lost, and he beelined toward the automatic doors, which opened to reveal a familiar figure in the crowd.

At first he thought he was hallucinating, but he soon saw she was real. Her green eyes radiated concern. Jaime lifted his arm and waved like a schoolboy arriving home from a long field trip. Laura Rodríguez returned the greeting, a serious expression on her pale face.

Jaime dodged the other passengers reuniting with loved ones and walked toward his boss, who made no attempt to hide her joy at seeing him.

"How are you?" She hugged him carefully.

"I won't lie, Presidenta. I'd have rather been sent to write a story on Iberian bronzes."

"Come on. I've got the car."

Jaime felt touched by the attention. Laura didn't normally get involved in her contributors' lives, not even his. They'd initially reunited seven years before, a twist of fate that had led to Jaime getting hired at *Arcadia*. Since then, the aloofness he'd seen glimpses of back in their university days had become the most salient characteristic of his no-nonsense boss, who dined, danced, and romanced only her work. But she wasn't a monster, and Jaime had come out of his recent adventure badly. Picking him up from the airport was the least she could do.

Laura parked her black Ford Fiesta in her space at the CHR, and they made their way up to the *Arcadia* editorial office. Shifting from the concerned attitude she'd shown at the airport, La Presidenta now reverted to her usual professionalism.

"Are you fit to write a report?"

Jaime frowned.

"'A report'? What is this, the CIA? You mean a story."

"For now, let's call it a report. Then we'll decide whether this is something we can publish. A couple of hours ago I spoke to Herbert Monfort, the EHU commissioner. He told me what Amatriaín and the Greek police have found out, but I want to hear your version."

"My version? My version's that a bunch of asshole pirates boarded the ship, stole the artifacts, and sank it with everyone still on board. End of report."

"I seriously doubt you believe it's that simple."

"And you're not wrong. Pirates board freighters in the open sea, out of reach of the security forces, not when they're moored and under supposed guard. What did this Monfort tell you?"

"A team of police divers was able to recover the bodies of our team members, two pirates, and Inspector Kraniotis. They still have to search most of the starboard side, but because of the way the ship's positioned they haven't been able to access it yet."

Jaime slumped into an office chair, rolling it across the floor until it stopped against a wall. "So many dead. Why?"

Laura looked at him with compassion, wishing now that she'd taken him straight home. "You should rest for a few days. I'll call you a taxi."

"You don't need to do that. I'll grab some coffee and go work at my desk."

"Forget it, Jaime. The report can wait. Anyway, we don't have much information to work with yet."

Though he was gaunt and his eyes were swollen, Jaime managed a brave smile. "That's where you're wrong, Presidenta. I know things other people don't."

"Is this another one of your fairy tales?"

"This Monfort: Did he tell you who the pirates were?"

"He just said that they were Caucasian, possibly from Southern Europe."

"'Caucasians from Southern Europe.' So, anyone from Anthony Quinn to Penélope Cruz?"

"Anthony Quinn was Mexican."

"And Penélope's from right here in Spain. Didn't he tell you anything else?"

"What else should he have told me?"

"One of the pirates, the leader, mentioned two important things. First, that he was going to finish the job his sister left unfinished."

"His sister?"

"It seems obvious to me: he was referring to the knockout brunette who tried to turn me into a journalist Popsicle in El Burgo de Osma."

"'Journalist'? I don't know if I'd go that far. Maybe an 'art historian Popsicle.' A knockout, huh?"

"Forget it." Jaime refused to take the bait. "I can't think of any other woman who would want to kill both Amatriaín and me. I'm sure the guy was her brother. The weird thing is, he seemed surprised to see us. That makes me think he didn't know we'd be there, or maybe we weren't his main target. He probably meant for us to die in the explosion with the others, but when he saw us on deck he decided to kill us personally. Fortunately, Amatriaín was one step ahead of him and cut his throat."

"That's horrific. I guess you don't dislike Amatriaín quite so much now."

"You guess wrong. There's something crooked about him, but I'm not sure yet what it is. I imagine the accident left a mark on him."

"What accident?"

"Something involving acid, on one of his missions. Not the kind that gets you high, the type that burns your skin."

"That explains the gloves and the scars. I've been wondering about that."

"Why? You like him?"

"They do give him a manly look."

"You *are* a strange one, Presidenta." Jaime said. "And now for the second important thing. I've been chewing it over in my mind ever since the guy said it. Just before the pirate leader died, he said something like 'porco albino.'"

"Filthy albino . . . Who was he referring to?"

"No idea. There weren't any albinos on the ship that I know of."

"Could he have been talking about Amatriaín?"

"Amatriaín is a lot of things, but albino isn't one of them. His teeth might be fake, but that tan's natural. Anyway, whoever this albino is, the guy didn't think very highly of him." Jaime stood. "Still, you're right. That's not much more to go on."

"So . . . ?"

"So we should leave the matter of the *Artemis* in the hands of the authorities and focus on the Medusa. That's the key to this whole thing, and it's what falls in our territory as art historians."

"So you're not calling yourself a journalist anymore?" Laura said.

"You worry too much about titles. Anyway, I've delegated a task to a certain crazy, fat geek we both know."

"Yeah. I think Roberto has something for you."

Jaime glared at her. "You know something I don't?"

"Could be, but I'm heading into an important meeting. Talk to fatso and keep me posted. And don't forget the report."

"I won't," Jaime promised.

Jaime's cockiness vanished as soon as he walked out of the building and climbed into the taxi Laura had called for him after all. He felt dreadful, as if a part of him had died along with his innocent companions. Common sense told him he should go home, take a few days off, and put this business behind him before resuming his routine of writing about exhibitions, old statues, crumbling ruins, and ancient myths.

Common sense also tried to convince him that this whole thing was above his pay grade. That playing at being a swashbuckling journalist was one thing, but going up against someone capable of cold-blooded murder quite another.

Common sense kept up its efforts for a while, and then, fed up with being ignored, finally turned away and left.

Jaime Azcárate's drowsy mind had room only for Sonia Durán, Professor San Román, Lucas Andrade, Inspector Kraniotis, and the three Greek historians whose names he'd never been able to remember.

As a journalist, it was his job to tell the story of what had happened. He was somehow ashamed he had survived, and he felt a responsibility to discover what had cost so many lives. He believed he owed it to the victims to uncover the truth, and he planned to do so with a fire in his belly.

First he left a message for Roberto. Then he skimmed the daily news, which barely mentioned the incident in Piraeus. He spent the rest of the afternoon sitting at the little desk in his attic apartment, listening to music while roughing out his report. He recounted everything, from the team's arrival in Athens to his and Amatriaín's treatment at the hospital. Once he'd finished, he printed it and left the copy on his printer. He had no desire to reread it. He sat back in his chair and looked up at the ceiling. He could see it was time for a deep clean. He noticed the mass of papers overflowing from his desk drawer. How long had it been since he'd tidied up, anyway? He clicked the mouse cursor on the CD icon and a jazz band began to play Chet Baker's "You Go to My Head."

Still exhausted after his ordeal, Jaime very nearly fell asleep at his keyboard. But the series of events that had been tormenting his subconscious for days forced its way into the foreground of his rational thoughts: the man with the red handkerchief shooting at him, then blowing off Amatriaín's shoulder, and finally joining the list of casualties himself. And those mysterious words: porco albino.

He did an online search for the phrase and the results surprised him: pictures and videos of white pigs, a superhero fan's blog, and several inconsequential sites, almost all of them in Portuguese.

Albino. White skinned.

Like the Medusa.

Then he thought of Paloma.

Though the memory had been parked at the back of his mind, Jaime hadn't forgotten the strange way she'd behaved when he mentioned their university piece. She had looked like a seer on the verge of making contact with Lucifer himself.

He suppressed an urge to call her. It seemed ridiculous in light of all the dangers he'd confronted in the last few days, but the one thing he could not face up to was the hurt he'd caused Paloma. He would take her help only as a last resort—assuming she even was willing to give it, which was by no means certain. He hoped that whatever information Roberto had dug up, it would provide some new pieces for the puzzle. Jaime headed for the bathtub, praying that the water would come out hot, even if it was only for a few minutes.

Roberto Barrero finished shaving his head with his electric razor just as the intercom buzzed to indicate he had a visitor. It was his habit to remove the little hair he had left whenever he felt the need for a clearer head, as if the strands somehow interfered with his brain activity, and he'd never needed clarity more than he did now.

When he went down to the building's entrance, he saw someone who looked a lot like Jaime Azcárate, if a bit more singed and haggard than Jaime usually appeared. "You look like shit," Roberto said.

"You always say the nicest things to me."

"Sorry, but it's true. What did I tell you? You're not cut out for this. You're a hack, a pen-pushing shithead, not a trained investigator. Tell me at least that you didn't have to shoot."

"I fired a couple of shots at a lock."

"Moving?"

"No, stationary."

"Good."

They set off for a modest *cervecería* on Calle Hilarión Eslava, near the Moncloa bus interchange. The table they chose was near the back, by a long mirror that mercilessly reflected back to Jaime the sorry state he was in. His eyes were swollen and part of his hair had been burned away by the fire. If he wanted to listen to his mother and find a girlfriend, he'd have a hard time doing it looking like this.

After the waiter had brought their food and beer, Jaime stretched his feet under the table and looked at Roberto. "Come on. I've waited long enough. What did you found out?"

Roberto stroked his goatee dramatically. "So the detective wants information. Well, it's going to cost you."

"It's already costing me. I'm buying you dinner!"

"You call this dinner? Where are the oysters? Look at this: a plate of sausages, an egg, a few fries, three lettuce leaves, and a slice of *salchichón* . . . the information I've got is worth a lot more than this."

"Fine. I'll pay for dinner *and* drinks once you've told me what you know."

"That's more like it." Roberto pulled a small tablet from his jacket pocket.

"Did you check out the gallery?"

"Yeah, and it wasn't easy. I called and wrote about twenty times. It turns out that they were closed for remodeling. I talked to them last night."

"Wow, your Italian must've improved a lot since that time at the restaurant when you couldn't even pronounce *gnocchi*."

"Very funny, you bastard. This time I had help."

Jaime thought back to his conversation that morning at *Arcadia*. "Laura."

"She's stiffer than salt cod, but she can be pretty cool when she wants to be. One of these days you'll have to tell me what it was that happened between you two."

"There was never an 'us two.' Laura, huh? I wondered how you'd do at something that doesn't involve shooting. What did you find out?"

"The director of the gallery is named Maria Santucci, and, lucky for you, she's a talker. She said they purchased the sculpture from the owners of the Leoni Antique Center after it burned down. Remember you told me that after it arrived at the gallery, three people died?"

"Yeah. Can't you tell me something I don't already know?"

"Not just 'something'; I have all the details. One of the stiffs-to-be was a janitor who'd been about to retire and had a heart attack while watching a soccer match." Roberto looked up from his notes. "Nothing strange about that. Most people can live with getting their pay cut, losing their job, or paying a fee every time they use their credit card, but if Sergio Ramos misses a penalty, it's all over. The man's name was Martino Laszlo. He was a Hungarian widower, and he lived in an apartment near the Petrarca Gallery."

"Did they find out anything strange?"

"The old guy had suffered four heart attacks and been hospitalized three times. He had a weak heart and apparently had never really listened to his doctors."

"I think we can rule him out as a victim of the curse. Tell me about the second person who died."

"Angelo Carrera. A businessman from Sicily who began to study the Medusa when it was still at the Leoni Center. After the fire, he continued to go see it at the Petrarca Gallery. He took lots of photos and spent evenings in the library and archives, going over old documents. One day he told the director he wanted to buy it. Another person was also interested, but Carrera's offer was so generous the gallery couldn't refuse it."

"How much did he offer?"

Roberto named a six-digit euro price.

Jaime whistled.

"Carrera had a small family fortune, and he dabbled in history and antiques," Roberto continued. "One or two of his articles were even published in magazines. The gallery was having money troubles, and they didn't think twice about selling the statue to him." He dipped a large piece of bread in his egg yolk. "It was Carrera who sent it to the Pontecorvo House Museum in Verona."

"Why?"

"His daughter was the director there at the time. Apparently it was a birthday present."

"Then what?"

"He was so happy about the deal, Carrera decided to celebrate with a cruise around the Mediterranean."

"What a guy. He pays a fortune for a lump of marble and then goes for a cruise. When I grow up I want to be just like him."

"I doubt that. Right now, he's pushing up daisies. Or coral. Or whatever the hell a body would push up if it were buried at the bottom of the sea."

"What happened to him?"

"An accident very much like the one your cargo ship had."

"That was no accident."

"Neither was his."

"He was murdered? Why?"

"Fortunately, Maria Santucci isn't just a big talker; she's also more curious than the two of us put together. When she sold the Medusa to Carrera she decided she should look into his background. She was shocked by what she found. Carrera was born in Sicily, and when he died he was the thirty-first-most-powerful man in Italy. The explosion that sank his yacht may have been meant to settle some kind of score. His body was never found, and his children run his business now."

A bell went off in Jaime's head. "His children? How many did he have?"

"Two. His daughter, the director of the museum in Verona, and a son. The director couldn't find much on him except that he ran many of his father's businesses."

"What kind of businesses?"

"A bit of everything: property, stocks, antiques. I bet his kids are set for life."

Jaime pictured the man in the red kerchief pointing a gun at him on the deck of the *Artemis*.

"I'm pretty sure I've met them both," he said, considering his words. "And for some reason, both of them tried to kill me."

Roberto stopped his glass of beer halfway to his mouth. "What the fuck are you talking about?"

"The curse of Medusa, in all its splendor. What time do you start your shift?"

"What shift? For your information, I've been on vacation for the last twenty-six hours."

"Good. How about coming with me to Verona? I have a sudden urge to visit the museum."

"If it's to question Carrera's daughter, you're out of luck. She doesn't work there anymore. The director is now one Mirto Ugolini."

"Damn."

"Disappointing, to say the least. Wait a minute. Is this the woman from El Burgo de Osma? You said she's a stunner."

"She is. But she's not someone you'd want to get close to."

"Wait, I haven't told you everything. There's still the third stiff: Alvino Nascimbene."

A shiver ran down Jaime's spine. He stared at a point somewhere between his fries and his egg. Anyone observing him would've thought he wasn't listening.

"Jaime? Hello?" Roberto sounded as concerned as a NASA technician calling a shuttle crew with whom he'd lost contact. "You still with me?"

"Alvino, you say?"

"Yeah. What? You know him too? May I ask why you've asked me to investigate a story you seem to have already written?"

"Alvino . . . What am I, an idiot?"

Roberto exhaled. "You don't really want me to answer that."

"Alvino Nascimbene. Alvino, with a *v*, not a *b*. It's a name!"

"Of course it's a name. It belongs to a guy who was a security guard at the Leoni Antique Center. When it burned down, he was left without a job. He was seen sniffing around the Petrarca, and he was interested in the Medusa, too. It seems to me she's more like a siren than a gorgon, what with all the guys who were after her. Not long after the fire, Nascimbene got in an accident while driving on a country road. The car was unrecognizable, and so was his body. His family had been waiting for him at their house in the mountains. They learned about his death from the police. I don't know about you, but this has all started to sound pretty fucking serious to me."

"What family did he leave behind?"

"His wife and daughter. You want their names?" Roberto scrolled through his notes. "The wife's named Isabel and the daughter's Tamara. If you're thinking you want to interview them, you're luckier than the devil."

"And why's that?"

"Because Alvino Nascimbene died not that far away, on a country road in Extremadura. The family's house is in Trujillo: just two hundred and fifty kilometers from here."

27

Isabel Huelves was a sticklike, sickly-looking woman with disheveled hair, and she looked out at Jaime from the computer screen with eyes that appeared as though they'd never closed in sleep. Jaime judged her to be about fifty-five years old, and he was just two shy of the mark. "Isabel?" He spoke in a gentle voice and adjusted his webcam. "Good morning. Can you see me okay?"

"I can see you very well." Her voice was raspy. "I didn't realize when you called that you were so young. And so handsome."

Jaime thanked her with a smile.

"I hope you can't see the mess," Isabel said. "I've just got up."

"Everything's perfect. Thank you for agreeing to talk to me."

"Well, it's not every day a girl gets asked to do an interview, now is it? I hope you'll paint me in a good light."

The idea of holding a videoconference had been Isabel's; she'd suggested it the previous day when Jaime called from the restaurant, while he was still at dinner with Roberto. He'd originally been tempted by the idea of a trip to Trujillo, but, in the end, he'd decided the effort was probably unnecessary, and he could learn all he needed via a video chat. "Nice painting," Jaime said, referencing an abstract watercolor landscape hanging on the wall behind Isabel. "A very original use of color."

"Thank you. It's by . . . Alvino did it."

"Your husband was an artist?"

She made a dismissive sound. "Pfff. Something like that. He liked art, anyway. He always dreamed of being a painter, though he said time and again it'd never make him rich. As you can see, he wasn't wrong."

"Had he been working at the Leoni Antique Center for long?"

Isabel hesitated. "Sorry, but I'm not sure I understand what you're getting at. Yesterday you didn't explain exactly what . . ."

"Of course. Forgive me. I'm helping with the investigation of a series of freak incidents related to a sculpture of Medusa. I'm afraid your husband's death is one of those events."

Isabel's eyes briefly widened as much as her heavy eyelids would allow. "Is this a joke?"

"I'm sorry if it sounds that way. Don't worry, I'm an art historian, and I don't believe in old wives' tales or curses. But the fact is, two people besides your husband died not long after the statue arrived at the gallery where he worked. Had you not heard about this?"

"I knew about one other death. Poor Mr. Laszlo had been having trouble with his heart for a long time. Who was the other person?"

"His name was Angelo Carrera."

For a couple of seconds, Isabel's expression was impassive. Jaime suspected she'd taken some unknown substance to help relax her, but he noticed her eyes opened a fraction wider at this news.

"Angelo Carrera," she said. "It's been years since I heard that name."

"You know him?"

"How could I not? He's the bastard who abandoned my husband!"

Jaime was shocked by the intensity of her answer, but tried not to react. "Isabel, I hope I'm not making you feel uncomfortable with this conversation. I just—"

"I'm sorry. It's just that I haven't thought about this business for a long time. You've caught me a bit off guard."

"Angelo Carrera was a regular visitor to the center where Alvino worked. Years later he bought the sculpture, and, soon afterward, he disappeared in an accident at sea."

"Alvino mentioned Carrera to me only once, not long after we left Rome and relocated to Spain."

"You're Spanish, right?"

"I am. Alvino was Italian." Isabel sighed. "Alvino's life was like a horror story."

"How come?"

"Because it ended as unfortunately as it began. You're a writer; you should write his life story."

"You'll need to tell me it first."

"Tragic," Isabel said. "Miserably tragic. How else is there to describe someone who came into this world because an American soldier raped a Sicilian woman?"

Jaime could see Isabel registering the shock on his face.

"It happened in 1943, when the US Army landed on the south coast of Sicily. Near Barcellona Pozzo di Gotto, one of the soldiers murdered a fisherman and raped the fisherman's wife. The soldier was drunk and almost beat her to death. He might have, if a young Sicilian hadn't appeared and put two bullets in him. The Sicilian carried the woman back to his home, where he cared for her until she recovered. The woman stayed with the young man who'd saved her, and they fell in love. They married in Palermo. The woman was named Giulia Nicosia, and the man was Angelo Carrera."

Jaime listened to the story without blinking. He worried that they'd lose their Internet connection just as things were starting to get interesting. Isabel told him that in May 1944, the son who'd been conceived during that rape was born. Both Giulia and her husband accepted the child as their own.

"They called him Alvino, in honor of Giulia's murdered husband, and for a year he brought joy to their home. Then one day, without warning, Angelo abandoned his wife and child."

"Where did he go?"

"No one ever knew. The war was over; maybe he decided he wanted to do other things in some other part of the world. After he left, Giulia fell into a deep depression and suffered from panic attacks that made little Alvino's life a nightmare."

"In what way?" Jaime asked.

"She started to mistreat him. Her rage over the boy's father, the man who'd killed her husband and raped her in front of her neighbors, was mixed with her resentment toward the man who first saved her life and then left her. Alvino told me that his childhood was horrific. Some nights his mother would come into his room and beat him because he reminded her of the bastard who'd ruined her life. One night she hit him on the head with a ladle again and again, nearly killing him."

The breakfast he'd eaten earlier was churning in Jaime's stomach, and he changed positions in an attempt to hide his discomfort. "No one noticed what was happening?" he asked.

"They did. The neighbors called the police. They arrested Giulia, and Alvino was removed from her custody and later adopted by a young couple who'd been unable to have children: Giuseppe and Mercedes."

"So there was a happy ending after all that tragedy," Jaime said.

"Well, more or less. With his new parents, Alvino lived a peaceful life again. He knew at least that he wouldn't wake up to a hysterical woman screaming at him and beating him. But those terrible years still took a toll."

"In what way?"

"When Alvino was eighteen, his parents explained his origins to him. There was no need to do so, but they did, and this revelation took Alvino back to his traumatic past and brought out a fury that he'd never experienced before. He understood that he could never get revenge on his biological father, so he made it his mission to find the man who'd left him and his mother. After much searching, he finally found Angelo Carrera living in a mansion, surrounded by luxury and servants. This enraged him even more, and their reunion turned into an exchange of insults and threats. Carrera sent some men after Alvino."

Isabel swallowed hard. "They beat him nearly to death. After he got out of the hospital, he returned to his parents' home, but they decided he wasn't safe in Sicily. They decided to move to Spain, where Mercedes, his adoptive mother, was from."

"And that's where he met you."

"At art school, yes. He was taking a course in art curation. We lived in Spain for a while, but Alvino eventually decided he needed to return to Italy. I went with him, and he found work as head of security at the Leoni Center."

"Until it burned down," Jaime said.

"After that, we came back to Spain. Alvino started working for a private security agency and things were going well. We had a few happy years. Until . . ." Isabel's eyes welled up.

"Did Alvino hear anything more about Angelo Carrera?" Jaime couldn't help asking.

"Not after we returned to Spain, no. He was focused on just us. He went to work every day, and that was it. Sometimes they changed his hours, but he never complained. All he wanted was to be able to support our family. Everything was fine between Alvino and me. We had our girl, he had his job. After some years, we were able to plan a vacation, and that was when it happened. I still can't believe it."

"Did you notice anything strange about Alvino before the . . . ?"

"No. Well, he seemed a bit stressed, but I figured it was just work. He had spent months fighting for permission to go on vacation."

Jaime's eyes fell on a framed photograph in the background, behind Isabel. Though the photo was too far away for him to see it clearly, he could just make out a plumper and healthier-looking version of her standing with a splendid smile on her face and her arm around a tall, good-looking man. Even from a distance, the man's bright eyes stood out. A little girl hugged his leg and smiled at the camera.

"How did it happen?"

"This house belonged to my parents, and we often came here on vacation. Alvino had been offered work as a security instructor in Paris, and he took it without thinking. When his assignment was over, he told us he was coming back and said to wait for him here."

"Who was the last person to see him alive?"

"In Paris? I have no idea. The only person he knew in France was Dr. André Fournier, a frequent visitor to the Leoni Center, but I don't think they saw each other. Alvino was just a security guard; he didn't have much contact with patrons. His adoptive mother, Mercedes, told me Alvino had visited her on the day he left for Paris."

"Did she say anything about it? Had she noticed anything strange?"

"No. But one thing she said surprised me." Isabel closed her eyes partially, as if squinting back at the memory through a mist. "It didn't seem to strike her as odd, but I . . . Well, the day he went to visit, he asked his mother for money. He didn't say what it was for."

"And what do you think?"

"I thought it could have been for his accommodations in Paris, but he told me before he left that the company was covering expenses. The strange thing is, the money was never accounted for."

"How much money was it?"

"I don't remember exactly. But a lot. Enough that his mother remarked on it."

"Could he have owed the money to someone?"

"What do you mean?"

"Maybe he was involved in something. I'm sorry to ask, Isabel, but I have to explore this from all angles."

"Alvino never did anything illegal. He didn't have any contacts in the mafia, if that's what you're suggesting. He wasn't exactly passionate about his work, but he took it seriously. He loved us and did everything he could to provide for us. He wouldn't have done anything risky without talking to us about it."

Jaime wasn't so sure, but decided not to keep pushing. It suddenly struck him that it was because the circumstances of her husband's death did not add up that Isabel had let herself fall into such decline. He promised himself he would discover the truth. "What's that?" he asked. "Behind the family photo."

Isabel turned around and put her hand on the item that had caught Jaime's attention. It was a portrait of Isabel, done in charcoal. With just a few strokes the artist had manage to capture her features and melancholic expression.

"Alvino did it," she said, sounding sad. "He started drawing as a boy at boarding school, and he never gave it up."

"It's very good," said Jaime.

"That was just a sketch. Perhaps *Arcadia* could do a feature on his work."

"I'm sure that could be arranged." Jaime rubbed his hands together as he considered what he was about to say. "Isabel, I'm going to ask something that might sound very strange, but I need you to answer me honestly. Do you think there's any chance Alvino is alive?"

The question not only surprised the woman—it infuriated her.

"What are you talking about?"

"I know it's difficult to consider such a thing. But the bad blood between Alvino Nascimbene and the Carrera family was too strong for it to have simply ended. One of Carrera's sons died recently, and there are those who believe Alvino might have had something to do with it."

"Who would believe that?"

"The son himself. When he died, he said Alvino's name."

"Well, I'm sorry for his death, but either he was badly mistaken, or he had a very sick sense of humor."

Isabel disconnected the chat as quickly as she could, leaving Jaime staring at an empty screen. He glanced longingly at his coffee machine and got up from his chair. Maybe a café solo would help him process all he'd just heard. As he always said, there was plenty there for a story. He needed to let the information sink in, and he decided to devote the rest of the morning to making sense of it.

He hadn't the slightest suspicion that he was about to receive the call that would change everything.

28

This time, Clark didn't have to waste time picking the lock. After breaking into Señora Julia's apartment, he had entered Amanda's place next door and found a set of keys from when she and Paloma were roommates. Slipping into his target's apartment was quicker and easier this time, although he wasn't so sure he'd find what he was looking for there.

In Paloma's bedroom, the music CDs were arranged in rows on a bookcase opposite the computer desk. There weren't that many of them, but in an age when physical music formats were on the verge of extinction, even this small collection was big enough to catch the eye. The titles were so varied, a psychologist using them to gauge something of their owner's personality would likely conclude she was a woman open to anything. Leonard Cohen and Brahms; Manolo García and B. B. King; Bob Dylan and Andrew Lloyd Webber; Lou Reed and Enrique Morente: all coexisted peacefully on the shelves, waiting to be played whenever they suited the CD owner's mood.

Clark moved quickly. In an instant, all the discs were in his metal briefcase.

The previous day, Rosa had called him from the *Phoenix* and told him to break into the apartment and take the discs. Clark hadn't understood why, but Rosa had insisted so strongly he couldn't refuse.

He had always known that his uncle's daughter was not just gorgeous, but also brilliantly intuitive. Clark was certain that when the family fortune was divided up one day, the biggest share would go to Rosa—especially now that Leonardo had snuffed it. But he wasn't worried. When the time came, he'd find a way to make sure he got his piece. He deserved *something* as reward for getting his hands dirty for the family over the last two decades.

The assignment in El Burgo de Osma had gone badly, it was true, but his commitment to the family would be taken into account. As would his kidnapping of the brat, his coercion of Oscar Preston, and this second raid on Paloma's apartment. Angelo knew he could count on Clark for anything, and Clark did not intend to disappoint him. He had both willpower and a genetic advantage; he barely felt tired even after a full day of physical exertion. The doctors had called it an anomaly, but he considered it a gift. And he used all of it in service to the cause.

Gripping the briefcase, he locked Paloma's apartment and went looking for a place with Wi-Fi. He settled on an empty ice cream shop, where he ordered a chocolate milkshake. He pulled out a small laptop computer and inserted the disks one after the other.

The thirteenth disc brought him luck. A broad smile spread beneath his plaster-covered nose as he connected to the Internet. Within a few seconds, Rosa's face was peering back at him from the screen.

"Yes?"

"I did it."

"You got them?"

"While she was at the museum. You were right: it's all here, on a CD by some . . . Andel."

"That would be Handel, you oaf."

"No, no. It's a silent *h*. Andel. The full document is here: text and images. You're brilliant, little cousin. How did you figure it out?"

"I went to Leonardo's cabin and went through his things."

"Is that right?"

"What isn't 'right' is what he was doing. He's ripped off Papà all he could, and then some. I looked through his music collection, and inside a Megadeth album was a piece of paper listing his accounts, payments from clients—stuff like that. Business he's been doing behind the family's back for years. It wasn't the only one. I found several other similar documents. Then I remembered there were music CDs at Paloma Blasco's apartment, and thought she might have done something similar."

"They're not there anymore." Clark grinned. "Now what? Can I go back to the warehouse? I had to leave the kid by himself."

"First send me the information on the CD, then wait for instructions. I'll contact you as soon as possible. And Clark . . ."

"Yes?"

"If you hurt that boy, I'll pull out every hair in that mustache of yours, one by one."

The screen went dark. Clark felt aggrieved by the threat. He tried to be friendly and efficient, but Rosa never cut him any slack. He finished his milkshake and began to upload the data from the disc. It was received a few minutes later on board the *Phoenix*.

Rosa finished printing Paloma's document and ran from Leonardo's study to the yacht's main lounge.

"*What is it?*" came the guttural voice from the portrait of Angelo Carrera.

"We have it. We have Paloma's research."

"*And the* Chronicle of Asclepius?"

"A few scanned pages. But those are the ones that interest us."

"Dr. Galliano would've paid a handsome sum for the original."

"What does it matter if they're not the original? I've examined the pages, and they've been taken from the genuine document. They include everything Dr. Galliano needs to know in order to be satisfied with the Medusa."

"Congratulations, Rosa; I never doubted you could do it. One day, you'll be the richest person in Sardinia, by far."

Rosa looked down.

"That's not my goal, and you know it," she said in a steady voice. "You have what you wanted. Now will you please accept my resignation?"

"That, never."

"And why not?"

"Because I've never understood this attitude of yours. You've been a natural leader ever since you were a little girl, yet you insist on living a mediocre life."

"I'm thirty-nine years old; I can live whatever kind of life I want to."

"Not until you've finished what you started. Call Clark and tell him to call off the business with Preston. Now we have the document, he's no use to us anymore. Have him let the boy go."

Although that pacified Rosa, her relief was short-lived, as another grisly order immediately followed: "Once the child is back with his mother, have Clark find a way to get rid of Preston."

"Are you serious? Kill Preston?"

"It's necessary to our mission. Any complication that might compromise us must be eliminated."

"How is he going to compromise us? He doesn't know anything."

"Not yet. But all he would have to do is apply a little pressure to Paloma Blasco, and he'd discover everything. And who's to say he won't go public in order to score points with his boss? Tell Clark he can choose the method. But first send me that document. I need to see it with my own eyes."

"You're sick, Papà. And so is Dr. Galliano. Why did he have to involve Preston? Couldn't Clark have done everything himself? You're so . . ."

Without bothering to finish, Rosa stormed out and headed to the study that had been her brother's, to send her father a copy of the document. She thought again about how Leonardo's stupid ambition led to his annihilation. She wasn't like him; she needed to convince herself of that. She would be more than content to throw herself into her gallery-café-school project with Dino, the man for whom she'd left the museum in Verona—and whom she'd been deceiving since the beginning of their relationship.

Rosa cursed her father. She thought again, as she had so many times before, that she was sorry Alvino Nascimbene hadn't killed him in the attack on the yacht. As always, she instantly regretted having the thought. After she'd successfully sent the document, she returned to the lounge and looked up at the portrait.

"What do you say?" she asked, sounding impatient. "Is it what you wanted?"

"We have it!" Carrera said with excitement in his voice. *"It's genuine."*

"Excellent. So we're done here."

"Not yet. When you speak to Clark, tell him to be ready to do one last thing."

"To do what?"

"To eliminate Paloma Blasco."

Rosa felt a wave of horror overtake her, but she tried to speak calmly.

"I refuse to give Clark that order."

"As you wish. I'll give it to him myself."

"You're a psychopath! What need is there to kill Preston and Paloma?"

"Dr. Galliano insists on it. Now that we have the document, Paloma Blasco is surplus to requirements."

"I don't agree. She can generate a lot of publicity and add value to the deal. Our asking price could triple in a matter of days if she tells the world what she knows about the sculpture. After all, she was the one who discovered it. There are plenty of other collectors in the world crazy enough to pay whatever it takes to own the—"

"You're ambitious, Rosa, and that's a good thing. But in this case, we owe our loyalty to our best customer. Galliano wants the sculpture and what it contains, without that information becoming public knowledge. This is not merely a question of collecting. As a doctor, he has a practical interest in the contents of the Medusa, and we cannot let him down. Paloma's discoveries must not be made public.

"That is why the price includes her elimination."

29

As Paloma left the museum, she decided she wouldn't go to her mother's house or her favorite restaurant, as she normally would. Neither did she want to go home. Over the last few days her paranoia had grown, and there was nowhere left where she felt comfortable. The business with Amanda had hit her where she felt most vulnerable and was making her rethink everything, even the future for which she had fought so hard.

It was still over a month before she had to submit her application to Ricardo, but she was starting to seriously doubt that she would live to make it happen. Her spirits were in shreds and she felt confused. According to Amanda, Oscar Preston was both an accomplice in Hugo's abduction and a victim of someone who wanted to get his hands on Paloma's research. Paloma wasn't buying it. She was convinced that Preston himself was the brains behind the operation, and, for that reason, she didn't think Hugo was in any real danger. Oscar was an unscrupulous creep, but he wasn't capable of following through on such a serious threat. She'd tried to speak to him at the museum that morning, but the worm had managed to wriggle away. And Amanda still believed him?

She took a long walk along the streets of downtown Madrid and wound up having lunch in a Japanese restaurant near Plaza de la Ópera. In an attempt to reassert her confidence, she'd put on a pair of high heels she'd bought six months earlier and hadn't yet worn, and she soon realized that this had been a stupid idea. Her feet felt as if they'd been impaled on nails, so she decided to take the metro back to the museum.

As she stood on the platform, she replayed in her mind the conversations she'd had with Amanda over the last few days: Hugo's kidnapping. Preston's blackmailing. It was all insane. Paloma had to choose what mattered to her most: the well-being of her best friend's son or the study she had been working on for so long, which finally was about to have a proper outlet. She was ashamed that she felt so torn and was on the verge of tears.

Thoughts of Jaime came to her again, unbidden. He always knew what to do. He seemed so controlled, so sure of himself . . . At least, that's how he'd appeared at the beginning, during their first year of college. Jaime was the only man she'd ever been with, and his sudden reappearance, along with the problems he brought, evoked in her the same state of tension she'd lived in back when they were together. After their breakup, Paloma had decided that work came first, and aside from fooling around a bit on dates, she hadn't been with anyone else since.

The metro station was full of people. Caught up in a world of her own, Paloma wandered away from the crowd and stood by herself near the tunnel at the left end of the platform. Sometimes she felt as though she was holding the most important secret in the universe, and she was afraid someone wanted to steal it from her—which, of course, someone did. For this reason, she always kept her research document with her, in a little flash drive disguised as lipstick. The drive had been a present from a colleague at another museum who had chased her and then, having gotten the message that she wasn't interested, left her in peace without making a fuss.

An electronic sign above the platform told the crowd that the next train would arrive in one minute.

Paloma noticed someone position himself beside her: a man wearing a raincoat, sunglasses, and a grizzled mustache. But the most striking thing about him was the plaster cast that covered his nose.

Paloma's first reaction was to grip her purse more tightly.

The stranger's response was to grab *her*.

The roar of the train could be heard through the tunnel, and then came the glow from the headlights as it plowed down the iron tracks. Paloma tried to scream, but the man in the raincoat was pulling her against his body, his hand over her mouth. The passengers were watching the train, and most of them were oblivious to her fate. Only a couple of girls saw what was happening and ran to look for security.

Once the train's headlights had fully illuminated the tunnel, the assailant pushed Paloma toward the track, but she drove her heel into his instep. His scream made everyone turn and look.

The train stopped.

The girls who'd run for help returned with two security guards.

But there was no trace of the train, or of Paloma or her attacker.

The Indiana Jones theme song woke Jaime from his nap. He'd spent the better part of the morning searching the Internet for information about the story Alvino Nascimbene's wife had told him, but exhaustion eventually got the better of him, and he wound up snoring on the sofa.

He woke from a confused dream about Inspector Kraniotis. In the dream, Kraniotis had jumped into the water before Jaime and Amatriaín, so it was he who was saved and they who died.

Not a very nice dream, he noted as he awoke.

He had to rummage around in the cushions to find his cell phone. "Hello?"

"Jaime . . ." The voice was a tiny, unidentifiable squeak.

"Who is it?"

"It's Paloma."

Jaime was immediately brought back to reality. The dream, the sofa, a living and breathing Kraniotis—all were gone. All that existed in the world was that telephone call. "Paloma, what is it?"

"Not on the phone. I have to see you."

"Where are you?"

"At Café del Real. Plaza de la Ópera."

"Give me fifteen minutes."

"Hurry, please."

Jaime made it in twelve and a half. The ground floor of the traditional café was full, and Jaime couldn't find Paloma in the crowd, so he climbed a narrow stairway to the lounge upstairs. She was sitting in the back, pale as wax. Jaime felt a blend of fear and compassion as he walked toward her.

"Are you okay?"

Paloma wasted no time. "They tried to kill me," she said.

"Who?"

"A man. Just now, on the metro platform. He came up to me and tried to push me onto the tracks."

Jaime swallowed. They had found her, and, just as they had him in El Burgo de Osma and on board the *Artemis*, they'd tried to kill her. He searched his mind for a motive that connected the attempts on their lives, and his thoughts turned once again to the university study she had written long ago, and to which she'd attached both their names.

"Your shoes?" he asked, looking at her bare feet.

"I had to leave them. I ran here."

"What about the police? The metro security staff?"

Paloma shook her head. "You're not the only one who prefers to solve his own problems."

"That doesn't sound good. You have to tell me what you've gotten yourself into."

Paloma opened her mouth to speak, but at just that moment someone came up the stairs from the ground floor: a man dressed in black who appeared to be looking for someone. "Let's go," she said, pinching Jaime's arm.

"Is that him?"

"No. But let's go."

They hurried down to the street. Jaime took a few steps toward the Ópera metro station before changing his mind and flagging down a taxi. They jumped into the car.

"What did the man look like?" he asked as he shut the door behind them. "Can you remember him?"

"I'll remember him for the rest of my life. He was a strong-looking man in a raincoat, and he had a mustache. He looked like your stereotypical thug from the movies. And he had something on his nose, like a plaster cast."

Jaime snorted.

"What is it?" Paloma asked.

"He owes the plaster to me."

"You know him?"

"Yeah. He must be feeling pretty unlucky to have missed killing both of us. You should come to my place. You'll be safe there."

"I don't know about that. They know you. They're after you, too."

Suddenly they realized that the taxi driver was looking at them in the rearview mirror, waiting for an address. "Oh, sorry," Jaime said. "Just drive for a minute; we'll let you know in a second."

The driver nodded and looked back ahead as he stepped on the gas.

Jaime whispered, "You'd better come with me to the CHR building, then; it'll be hard for them to hurt you there."

He gave the taxi driver the address, and soon they pulled up in front of the old philology building at the Complutense University, beside which stood the headquarters of the Center for Historical Research. During the short walk to the entrance, they glanced nervously at everyone who crossed their path.

Relax, Jaime told himself. He was starting to see mustachioed murderers on every corner, where he imagined they were plotting to tear them to pieces. Though his nerves were on edge, a part of his mind was calm. Paloma had reached out to him, and this could give him the opportunity to clear a few things up.

They hurried toward the tall brick building. Paloma had never been inside it, though she knew the surrounding area well. Back when she was a student, the large building had still been under construction. When she'd passed by the big yellow sign that read "Construction Works for the Center for Historical Research," she'd never imagined that Jaime would end up working there, much less that she would one day use it to seek refuge from a potential murderer. She paused and glanced over at the nearby history and geography building, where the two of them had studied, and indulged in a few seconds of nostalgia.

They climbed the five steps to the main entrance, which was framed by a Bramantesque pavilion, and walked through the glass doors that led to the lobby. Then they took the elevator up to the tenth floor. "You'll be safe here," Jaime told Paloma.

She walked into an office full of desks with computers. The walls were covered in postcards from exotic locations like Luxor, Varanasi, Cancun, and Istanbul.

"There's no one here?"

"Not a lot of people come in on the weekend. If they have to work, most do it from home."

By Jaime's desk, a glass case nearly overflowed with books stacked in no particular order. Paloma glanced over the spines: *Gods, Graves and Scholars* by C. W. Ceram; *Atahualpa*; *Theories of Art* by Moshe Barasch; *The Holy Scriptures*; *Alexander the Great*; *The End of Atlantis*; *Art and Architecture of the Ancient Orient*, and a complete history of art collection that she knew well. She wasn't surprised to see a few issues of the journal *Mysteries of Archeology* and a thick volume entitled *Romantic Archeology: Voyages, Dreams, and Adventures*.

Paloma recognized Jaime in those books. Though they'd been leading separate lives for some time now, she'd heard from former classmates that he was a meticulous researcher, and that he knew that his profession consisted of writing reports, conducting interviews, and spending hours in the library. From time to time, he found an opportunity to work someplace under the sun for a while, out in the open air in some far-off city or on an archeological dig. He was as much of a dreamer now as he had been when they were students together, always with his head someplace else. She remembered one time a lecturer had been explaining the influences of Genoese sculpture on Spain in the seventeenth century, but Jaime's mind had been far away: following Winckelmann through the ruins of Pompeii or discovering a magnificent Mayan treasure in some lost temple of Tikal.

Paloma remembered the first time she went to Jaime's home, back when he still lived with his parents. He had shared a bedroom with Jules Verne, Walter Scott, and Robert Louis Stevenson, as well as with Ian Fleming, Michael Crichton, and Dashiell Hammett. Not to mention the companions from his movie collection—James Bond, Humphrey Bogart, Errol Flynn, John Wayne—and the giant *Raiders of the Lost Ark* poster that hung over his headboard.

There was always an exotic soundtrack playing on his stereo, Paloma remembered. He was a dreamer and yet, at the same time, a scholar. Paloma still couldn't figure out how he'd managed to combine the two different sides of his life, but he had, and that was what made him different. Maybe that was why she'd fallen in love with him. So many men resigned themselves to taking their dreams to their deathbeds, or to walking past half-open doors to changes they never would make. Jaime had made his dream come true. Through a lot of hard work, and more than a few identity crises, he had forged a personality made of fragments he'd taken from the heroes of his youth. He had been all of them and none of them, and now he was himself: a perfect Frankenstein's monster sprung from his own hopes and dreams.

She studied him. He looked at her knowingly—that look she knew so well.

"Make yourself comfortable," he said. "Can I get you something?"

"I guess a lime flower tea wouldn't do me any harm."

"I'll go get you some. Try to relax."

Jaime closed the door to the office behind him. He hadn't yet reached the elevator when an ominous voice stopped him.

"Where are you going?" He turned to look at Laura Rodríguez.

"Good afternoon, Presidenta. How's it going here?"

"The usual. Is something up? You seem on edge."

"No, it's nothing. It's just . . . I have a visitor."

"Someone I know?"

"Well . . . Paloma Blasco."

"Paloma?" Laura exclaimed. The name was well-known to anyone who was close to Jaime. "She's here?"

"In the editorial office, resting." Jaime lowered his voice. "Laura, we have to talk."

"I'm listening."

"The day I got back from El Burgo de Osma, I went to find Paloma at the Prado Museum. I had a feeling she was in danger. I wasn't wrong. Someone tried to kill her today."

"What?"

"There's a link between her attack, the Medusa statue, and the attack on the *Artemis*."

"Well, if that's true, I'm dying to know what it is."

"I still need to fill in a few details. I think Paloma will be able to help me. I was going down to fetch her a *tila*, and then I'm sure I can get her to tell me what's going on."

"Wait a minute, smooth talker. What made you think she was in danger?"

"The scumbags who locked me in the freezer had a copy of the essay on baroque sculpture that was published in the *Revista Complutense*. Paloma did all of the work. I just put my name on it."

"You should be ashamed."

"Don't think I'm not. I'm guessing someone has followed the trail from a long way back. They might think she knows something about the Medusa that no one else does. Or maybe they know something themselves, and that's why they want to kill her. I hope she can explain it all to me."

"And I hope you'll tell me everything after she does."

"I can do better than that. Why don't you come and meet her?"

"I have to finish off a couple of things with the CHR folks, but I'll join you just as soon as I can."

"Don't be long," Jaime said, heading toward the elevator. "Paloma could change her mind and run off."

"Are you sure Paloma's the one who would do something like that?"

"Whatever do you mean, Presidenta?"

30

The feeling of a new presence in the room brought her back from the land of dreams. Paloma's eyelids flickered and then slowly opened, revealing her honey-colored eyes. The presence she'd felt was of two people. One was familiar. The other was a woman of about forty, with serious green eyes and a cascade of curly reddish hair. Though Paloma had never met this person before, she knew exactly who she was.

"Hello, Laura."

Arcadia's editor nodded, a dimple forming in each cheek as she gave a faint smile.

"I've heard a lot about you," Paloma said, still half-asleep. "It has always surprised me that such a young woman could become editor of such an important magazine."

"I'm flattered." Laura tried unsuccessfully to keep from blushing.

Jaime handed Paloma the glass of lime flower tea. "I'm afraid it's gone cold."

"It doesn't matter." Paloma sat up in the chair. "Obviously I didn't need it."

Laura suggested they go to her office so they could talk more comfortably. There, she gave Paloma her usual seat and settled herself into an armchair while Jaime leaned against the wall beside her. "Jaime told me what happened to you."

"It's been a nightmare. The thing is, I've been living in a nightmare for a long time."

Paloma sipped the cold infusion. Her hand was trembling. "I don't know what to do anymore . . . I'm desperate. I don't even recognize myself."

"Paloma, you can talk to us."

"We want to help you," Jaime said. Paloma appeared to him less cagey than she had been the other day. She was still on edge, but no longer seemed defensive. Now she acted more like a woman defeated by her own obstinacy than one tired of hiding a secret. "Will you tell us?"

Paloma glanced around, as if looking at something only she could see. Finally she fixed her eyes on Jaime. "What do you want to know?"

"We could start with the guy who tried to kill you."

"I'm not sure who that was, Jaime, I told you earlier. It could be the same person who broke into my apartment. At first I blamed that on Oscar Preston, but now I'm not so sure it was him."

"Who's Oscar Preston?"

"He's my rival at the museum. The director of my department is going to appoint a deputy in less than two months, and each applicant has to submit an original art history research project. I have reason to think Preston isn't playing fair, but I don't think he would take things this far on his own. Whoever broke in was searching for something, and when they didn't find it, they decided to get rid of me."

"That makes no sense. If they didn't find what they were looking for, the logical thing would be to keep you alive so you could tell them where it is. What were they after?"

Paloma rubbed her forehead, letting her fingers run through her dark bob. As Jaime and Laura waited, she picked up her glass and took another sip of tila. "It's better cold," she said and then sighed. "Do you remember you told me that the person who wanted to kill you had a copy of our essay?"

"You mean *your* essay."

"Same thing. It's because of the Medusa. All of this is because of the Medusa."

Paloma's answer came as no surprise to Jaime, but it didn't explain why someone would go to such lengths over a virtually unknown bust by one of the least fortunate sculptors of seventeenth-century Italy.

Jaime rested a hand on her shoulder. She avoided his gaze. She seemed about to burst into tears but managed to maintain her composure.

"It's true." Paloma rubbed her face with her hands as if to clear her mind. "I've been working on this for a long time, prompted by the study we did in college. That's what the people who searched my home wanted: my research."

"What research? Does it have to do with the Medusa?"

"Yes."

Jaime tried to focus on just Paloma's words and not be distracted by the sound of her voice or her gestures. Both of these reminded him of the past, and the past filled him with guilt.

"What's so special about the Medusa?" he asked.

"In the faculty library I found a reference to a book entitled *Mythological Sculpture in Italy*, written by Cosimo Rizzoli of Rome. The volume was a copy of a book published in 1789, and I couldn't resist ordering it from the warehouse. It was filled with fabulous illustrations of mythological pieces from the Renaissance to the rococo period. The section on Gian Lorenzo Bernini included some splendid prints of his most famous works: *Apollo and Daphne*, *Aeneas and Anchises*, *Neptune and Triton*. The biggest surprise was that, alongside the illustration of the goat *Amalthea*, which you know Bernini sculpted when he was just twelve, there was a print of the Medusa."

Jaime raised his eyebrows. "Of our Medusa? Wasn't it supposed to have been sculpted by Bolgi?"

"When I found the print, I was so surprised I went to talk to Professor Pérez-Ramírez about it. I'm sure you've heard of him."

"He was one of the best lecturers I ever had—and I barely went to his classes."

"You missed out, Jaime. When I told him about my discovery, his eyes lit up, the way they always do when something piques his interest. He invited me over to his house, where he showed me an old book with yellowing pages that turned out to be Andrea Bolgi's diary."

"Bolgi kept a diary?"

"Well, not a diary, exactly; rather, a sort of book of notes and sketches. One of Pérez-Ramírez's hobbies is collecting biographies of artists from every period, and he's particularly passionate about diaries and notes made by the artists themselves. He has notebooks by Leonardo and Michelangelo; Giorgio Vasari's *Lives of the Artists*, of course; Baglione's biography of Caravaggio; and tons of notebooks that belonged to various painters, sculptors, and architects. He told me he'd been collecting them for forty years and had invested a great deal of effort and money in them.

"Anyhow, in his diary, Bolgi explains how he sculpted the bust of Medusa, and says that when his patron, a rich collector named Domenico Corsini, told him he didn't like it, he asked for permission to start again. When Bolgi showed Corsini the new statue, his patron loved it and gave it pride of place in his garden of mythological sculptures. When we read that, Pérez-Ramírez and I looked at each other and immediately knew what had happened."

Jaime scratched his head. He was following what Paloma was saying, more or less, but his brain ached from so much thinking and he was struggling to grasp the full implications of her words.

"Are you saying that Bolgi's Medusa—?"

"Isn't really Bolgi's." With that one simple phrase, a massive weight lifted from Paloma's shoulders. "The damn Medusa belonged to Gian Lorenzo Bernini's workshop."

"That would explain a lot," Jaime said as he thought about it. "A Bernini sculpture would stir up far more interest than one by Bolgi. And it'd sell for a much higher price."

Paloma gripped the glass of lime flower tea that was beginning to warm in her hands. "That's all true," she said. "But the thing is, the sculpture isn't by Bernini."

"It isn't? But you just said—"

"I said it belonged to Bernini's workshop. The master kept it there along with other sculptures from classical times that he used as models. It actually was a Hellenistic piece, from the third century BC. Captivated by its chilling naturalism, Bolgi stole it from Bernini's workshop and took it to Naples. When Corsini commissioned him to sculpt a bust of Medusa for his garden, Bolgi was tempted to offer up the ancient piece as his own, but he didn't have the nerve. Instead he made a copy, but it wasn't to Corsini's liking. When his patron gave him permission to try again, Bolgi forgot whatever scruples he had left and presented the original bust."

"Incredible," Jaime said. "And how has it been masquerading as a seventeenth-century piece all this time?"

"Bolgi retouched it so that it would look like a piece contemporary to his time. The expressive qualities shared by Hellenism and the baroque played in his favor. Domenico Corsini took the bait, and, ever since, it has been catalogued as a sculpture by Andrea Bolgi. There was never any reason to doubt it."

Jaime looked at Laura out of the corner of his eye to see how she was taking the revelation. The *Arcadia* editor was listening attentively to Paloma and seemed to be doing some kind of mental calculation. "I don't get it. We have a sculpture from Hellenistic times passing itself off as a baroque piece, but it's not by Bolgi or Bernini or any other known artist. It's got a strange history, but that doesn't explain why someone would go to so much trouble to get their hands on it."

Paloma swallowed hard. "The answer has to do with something I discovered when the initial clues made me think the sculpture was, in fact, a piece by a young Bernini."

"But it isn't."

"No. It's ancient, as I said."

"So?"

"Remember the book I mentioned earlier? The text that accompanied the print of the Medusa linked it to a third-century-BC physician and a document known as the *Chronicle of Asclepius*. With Pérez-Ramírez's help, I followed that document's trail and eventually found it listed in the bibliography of an exhibition on mythological sculpture held a few years ago at the National Gallery in London. Thanks to Pérez-Ramírez's influence, I was able to gain access to it. It turned out to be a compendium of classical myths that related to medicine: a curiosity of minor historical interest. But one of the chapters mentioned a Medusa's head and the magic that Asclepius imbued it with."

Jaime gave a hint of a sardonic smile. "Asclepius? What does a Roman god of medicine have to do with Medusa?"

"Well, according to the legend," Paloma said with excitement, "when Perseus cut off Medusa's head, the blood that spilled out of her caused a number of extraordinary phenomena—natural wonders like Red Sea coral and Saharan cobras. It's also said that the winged horse Pegasus and the giant Chrysaor were born from this blood at the moment she was beheaded. But the most interesting thing is that the blood was supposed to have curative properties. Asclepius used it to cure the sick. According to the *Chronicle of Asclepius*, a quartz vial filled with it was hidden in a bust of Medusa that had been carved from marble in the third century before Christ."

"In a bust of Medusa? In *our* bust of Medusa?"

"That's what the documents seem to indicate."

Now it was Jaime who was excited. "So we're dealing with a myth."

"The blood of Medusa isn't just a myth!" Paloma said. "We're talking about one of the most important relics in Greek mythology, comparable to Christ's crown of thorns or the Holy Grail."

"And there are plenty of wackos who are looking to collect those things."

"Come on, Jaime! Surely you of all people aren't going to go all skeptical on me."

"The role reversal is as surprising to me as it is to you. Do you really believe what you're saying?"

"Of course I don't believe the bust contains the magical blood of Medusa! But I do believe that the sculpture is the same bust that the *Chronicle* references. That in itself makes it valuable, and not just to me. These people are after my research because it can prove to them it's the same statue."

"Or prove it to someone else," said Jaime.

"What do you mean?"

"Clearly the people who stole the sculpture already know its secret. I bet they plan to sell it, but they know they'll get a better price if they can establish that it's the piece referred to in the *Chronicle of Asclepius*."

"My notes cover the entire research process, including every step that led to the *Chronicle* and its link to the bust. My goal has been to shape the material into something solid within the next month and submit it to Ricardo. What I don't understand is why they attacked me if I still have what they want."

"Good point. If they don't have your work, then they need you alive. Unless . . ."

"Unless what?"

"Paloma, are you sure they don't have it?"

"Completely. I always carry my work on me and I have a copy hidden in a safe place. I don't even keep the document on my hard drive."

"When was the last time you saw that copy?"

"I was working on it last night."

"Did you go home for lunch today?"

"No, when I left the museum I went for a walk to clear my head. I was on my way back when—" Paloma's face grew pale.

Jaime jumped to his feet. "Right, you stay here. Laura, keep her company."

"Where are you going?" his boss asked, alarmed.

"To Paloma's apartment." He turned toward his former girlfriend. "Keys."

"What are you going to do?"

"Give them to me."

Paloma hesitated before taking her keys from her bag and throwing them to Jaime.

"Where do you keep it?"

"On a disk hidden among my music CDs. *Water Music*, by Handel."

"You still have good taste," Jaime said. "I'll call you later. Now you two behave yourselves. And don't open the door to strangers."

31

As Jaime rode in a taxi to Paloma's apartment, he felt a strange mixture of euphoria and fear. On the one hand, he was excited by the idea of the Medusa statue supposedly containing the magical blood of the mythological creature—though he lamented having been unaware of this angle when he wrote his article about the curse. At the same time, as a journalist and as Paloma's friend, he had a nagging feeling he was speeding toward a new danger: the person who was pulling the strings in this sinister plot.

Was it Alvino Nascimbene? The Carrera family? Either way, Jaime was getting closer to finding out, and he knew from experience that it was at just such moments that he needed to be most prepared. He couldn't let down his guard now.

He rode the elevator up to the fourth floor and found Paloma's door bolted. A good sign.

He let himself in with the keys. At first everything appeared to be in order. The computer was still in the same place, as was the furniture. However, the bookshelf at the back of the room, where the music CDs had been, was empty.

Bingo.

Jaime saw it all clearly. Someone had broken into Paloma's apartment and taken all the CDs, ensuring that they got the one containing the research document. The perpetrators had the research in their hands, and now they wanted Paloma dead. But why? What threat did she pose to them?

The past continued to nag at him, and Jaime thought again of how he hadn't behaved well toward Paloma all those years ago. It would be a lie to say that he hadn't known then how she felt about him, and he had completely disappeared from her life. He'd never introduced her to his mother. For heaven's sake, he'd never even referred to her as his girlfriend around his friends. Despite everything, she had loved him. But Jaime had begun to feel something else: a suffocating sensation, as if he had become someone's property. He had tried to distance himself from her gradually, so he could breathe more easily, and in the end he had untangled himself completely.

There must have been a better way to do things.

He was about to leave her apartment when the doorbell rang. Jaime froze for a moment, his heart racing. He hoped that whoever it was would give up and leave. After an extended silence he relaxed. And then there it was again: the bell, followed by the faint sound of keys clinking together on the other side of the door.

He slipped off his shoes and tiptoed to the entrance hall. Looking through the peephole, he could see a blurry figure fiddling with the lock. Instinctively, he reached out for a vase that stood on a nearby sideboard and lifted it above his head. Whoever was trying to sneak into Paloma's place was about to get a nasty surprise.

Jaime held his breath as the door opened. Slowly, someone edged through the threshold. "Paloma?" a quivering voice whispered.

Then the woman turned her head and saw Jaime standing with his arms raised. Her scream was followed by a sudden fall to the floor, and she hit the sideboard on her way down.

Jaime approached the figure sprawled on the ground and studied her for a moment. Then he put the vase back in its place, closed the door, and helped her to her feet.

"Y-you? Here?" Amanda Escámez could barely stand, her legs were trembling so badly. "What do you want?"

"I wanted to smash your head in. Isn't that obvious?"

"Me? Why? I—I came to see Paloma."

"Paloma's not here. How come you have keys to her apartment?"

"I've had them for a while. We used to be roommates."

"I don't think that gives you the right to let yourself in and take whatever you want."

"I haven't stolen anything!"

"I never said you did."

Amanda stared back at Jaime, looking as suspicious of him as he was of her.

"Well, what are *you* doing here? What do you want?"

"It looks like we're both a bit slow about this, don't you think? Let's relax and start again. I'm Jaime, and you're . . ."

"Amanda. I remember you, from the restaurant. Paloma started crying when she saw you."

"Not exactly; she wasn't crying because of that. Come on in and sit down. Since we're both here already, I doubt Paloma will mind."

When they sat down on the sofa, Amanda broke down and began to talk and cry. She told Jaime about her friendship with Paloma, describing how it had gone downhill in the last week and how strange her friend had been acting.

"None of that surprises me, but I'm wondering what it is you came here to do."

Amanda swallowed hard and bowed her head, like a teenager admitting to her dad that she'd skipped school for a week. "You were right. I came to steal something."

"Steal something?"

"I need to find some kind of document that Paloma's been obsessed with. I don't know what it is, and I don't care, but . . . I'm so sorry. Normally, I'd never do this to Paloma, but—"

"But?"

"That bastard's making me do it."

"Who?"

"Oscar Preston. He works at the museum, and he's blackmailing me to make me find out what Paloma's working on. I have to hand over the document to him by Wednesday or . . ."

Jaime could see that the woman was on the verge of falling apart. "Don't worry, Amanda. Paloma's told us everything."

"She has? So you know about my boy."

"What boy?"

"They've kidnapped my son! Oscar says that if I don't hand the document over by Wednesday, I won't see Hugo alive again."

Jaime couldn't believe how far this whole business had gone. Over nothing more than a legend, someone was willing to both kill and kidnap. Paloma had already mentioned Preston, and from the disparaging tone she'd used Jaime had gathered just what kind of person he was. It didn't take much imagination to figure out that the man was using blackmail to muscle in on the deputy director position. But how had he found out about Paloma's research in the first place? Jaime took a tissue from his pocket and handed it to Amanda.

"Thank you," she snuffled.

"Why didn't you tell Paloma about this?"

"I did. And she went nuts. She didn't tell me anything about her document; she's obsessed with this project, whatever it is."

"Hasn't she done anything to push back against this Preston?"

"It's not Preston's doing. The kidnapper forced him into blackmailing me."

"You must've at least told the police."

"Preston warned me not to. He says they're watching me. God, I'm so scared!"

Jaime tried to keep a clear mind. "You say you have to give the document to Preston by Wednesday."

"Yes. Or—"

"Don't worry. Paloma has decided to cooperate. I'm sure she'll help you now. Anyway, someone got here before you did."

"What do you mean?"

"Paloma's research isn't here anymore. They've taken it."

"How do you know?"

"Because I came to get it, too. It looks like someone else has a key to this apartment. Do you know who it could be?"

"Well . . . I didn't exactly tell you the whole truth before. I was Paloma's roommate—that part's true. But I took these keys from her at the museum. I had another set at home, but I couldn't find them."

"Things are becoming clearer," Jaime said. "This Preston, how are you meant to get the document to him?"

"We're supposed to meet on Wednesday, at the entrance to work. But what am I going to tell him now? I don't have anything to give him!"

"Don't worry about that. Just make sure you meet him. What are you doing right now?"

Amanda gave him a curious look. "Nothing. Why?"

Jaime finished shaping the idea he'd been working out in his head. As bad as the situation seemed, this new information helped him know which way to go next. "How about a guided tour of the official headquarters of *Arcadia* magazine? Wait there a second, and I'll take you."

"Where are you going?"

"To Paloma's room," Jaime said. "I have to find my shoes."

32

The clouds that had flown over the city all day long now made good on their threat to unload their contents onto the streets, enveloping the Prado Museum in a cloak of lead-colored rain. As he parked nose-to-curb on Calle de Felipe IV, Roberto Barrero reached over and switched on the windshield wipers in his Fiat Dobló. In the seat beside him, Jaime spoke to Paloma on his cell phone.

"You'll see us as you come up the road. A white van covered in bird crap."

"Hey!" Roberto protested. "Let the rain do its job, and then we'll see whether there's any bird crap."

A panoramic view of the main entrance to the museum stretched out before them. Jaime's mind hadn't stopped working since his conversation with Amanda, and he had carefully worked out a plan whose top priorities were keeping Paloma safe and Oscar Preston under observation. It was now the day when Amanda had to hand over Paloma's work to Preston, and Jaime and Roberto wanted to make sure there were no complications.

A moment later, a purple umbrella emerged from the grassy slope that separated the museum from the parking area, with Paloma under it. At the sight of her, Jaime's heart skipped a beat. She looked like a little mouse coming out of her burrow, well aware she was surrounded by hungry cats.

"Is that her?" asked Roberto. "She's not the kind of girl I pictured you with."

"That's because you have no imagination. Give her a beep."

Roberto honked his horn a couple of times and Paloma turned and ran toward them. Jaime climbed out and opened the rear door for her. "How did it go?" he asked as Paloma settled into the backseat.

"No one tried to kill me, if that's what you mean." Paloma turned to the driver's seat and was surprised by the sight of Roberto's shaved head, goatee, and black T-shirt. He looked like a member of the Hells Angels. "Hello. I'm Paloma."

"Pleased to meet you at last. Jaime's always going on about you."

Paloma was taken aback by the comment, but she smiled. "I'm surprised you put up with him."

"You know how it is: you grow fond of the little shit."

Jaime looked at Paloma. Her eyes betrayed a nervousness that was less about the threat to her life and more about the knowledge that someone wanted to take away everything she'd worked so hard for.

"What is it?" she asked. "Why aren't we leaving?"

"I'm waiting for your friend Preston." Roberto kept his eyes fixed straight ahead. "He leaves through the side door, right?"

"Yes. When I came out, he was just getting ready to leave. It can't be long now." Paloma looked at the two men, an eyebrow raised. "Why do you want to see him?"

"It was your boyfriend's idea," Roberto said. "I'm just providing logistical support."

"My boyfriend?"

"He means the muscle of this operation," Jaime said. He looked at Roberto. "Can't you turn the heat on? My toes are like ice."

"As the señorita wishes."

Roberto turned the control knob and warm air flowed from the vents.

Five minutes later, Jaime watched Amanda Escámez's unmistakable figure leave the museum accompanied by a man with curly hair and glasses. Amanda's expression was one of contempt, while the man displayed a tepid smile. It was obvious to Jaime that this was the odious Oscar Preston.

"Amanda and Preston seem to be getting along nicely," he remarked.

"He makes me sick," Paloma said. "Look at him, all happy to be getting his hands on my work."

Jaime kept his eyes fixed on Amanda and Preston. "After this he'll deliver it to whoever told him to get it. Then we'll know for sure who we're dealing with."

Paloma looked at Jaime. "Is that why you insisted we give him a printed copy?"

"Exactly. Something he couldn't send via email, so he has to go out on the street and actually hand it to someone."

"He could send it by regular mail," Paloma said.

"I doubt it. Whoever it is will want it as soon as possible."

"But they already have it. They took it from my apartment. Why haven't they told Preston to cancel the mission?"

"I don't know. But the fact that we know something he doesn't is our trump card."

"If you ask me," Roberto said, "I reckon they intend to cancel *him*."

Paloma looked appalled.

"Kill Preston?"

"It'd be great, wouldn't it?"

"How can you say that?"

"Roberto's an animal," Jaime said. "But he's right about one thing: these people don't mess around. They tried to kill me first, and then you. It's possible they want to get rid of Preston, too. Anyone linked to the Medusa is at risk."

"But Preston doesn't have anything to do with the Medusa."

"Not directly. But these murderers don't seem to care about tiny details like that."

They watched as Amanda and Preston stopped in the middle of the parking lot and she handed him a folder. "He has it," Paloma lamented. "I hope you enjoy it, you rat."

Jaime turned to her. "It won't do him any good. The people who blackmailed him already have it, and Ricardo Bosch will know that the work and the discovery are yours entirely."

"How will he know? He doesn't want us to submit anything until the deadline."

"But you'll do it anyway. Tonight you'll email him your work and in the subject write 'Do not open until such-and-such a day.' It'll be like a Christmas present."

"Wouldn't it be better to tell him the whole story?"

"Not until Amanda's son is safe. You've seen what they're like. The moment they sniff danger, they get trigger-happy. Or train-happy. Or walk-in-freezer-happy."

"In that case, I don't understand what we're doing here. I'm sure these people are watching Amanda to make sure she doesn't let the cat out of the bag. If they figure out that we're trying to mess up their plans—"

"There's nothing suspicious about this. You and I are friends, and I've come to meet you. Anyway, we're being careful. The other day, after Amanda left your apartment, I waited for almost twenty minutes before leaving. I doubt they know we're planning something together."

"I can't believe this jerk!" Roberto interrupted. "Is that sports car his?"

Paloma followed Barrero's gaze and saw that Preston and Amanda had stopped near a blue BMW Z4 with gleaming bodywork. "The pig sure does love to show off."

They watched from their seats as Preston pointed at the car and appeared to offer Amanda a ride home. After first spitting on his suit, Amanda turned and, with her customary sway of the hips, stalked off through the heavy rain. The American wiped off the gob of spit and then climbed into his car and started the engine.

Roberto found it easy enough to follow the conspicuous sports car down Paseo de la Castellana. Once the museum was behind them, he positioned himself at a cautious distance and kept his eyes on the target. Oblivious to being followed, Preston drove calmly to a pretty, landscaped area near Calle de Arturo Soria. As he parked in a private space outside a thirteen-story tower surrounded by yellowing trees, Roberto double-parked the van on the street.

"Now what?" Paloma asked. "Are we going to sit here all night?"

"You won't," Jaime replied. "And neither will I. We'll get a taxi and go somewhere safe. Now that we know where he lives, the main thing is to keep you out of danger. We have a tough day ahead of us tomorrow, and you should rest."

Though Paloma had no idea what Jaime had arranged for that night, she did know his plans for the next day. Missing work for an indeterminate period wasn't the best way to secure the job she wanted, but the conversation she'd had with Jaime and Laura at the CHR had convinced her that leaving the country was the only way to stay safe. As much as Jaime wanted to protect her, the fact was, she would always be an easy target in the city. Amanda had promised to cover for Paloma and tell their boss that she'd left in a hurry to take care of her sick mother.

Jaime and Paloma got out of the van, and she took refuge from the rain under a bus shelter while he spoke to Roberto through the open window.

"You sure you're okay with this?"

"I'm sure. I'd been thinking of heading to my grandma's village for vacation, but this is way more fun."

"Thanks, Roberto. I don't say this often, but you're a true frie—"

"Hey! Get away from my car. You're drooling all over it."

Jaime chuckled. "Keep me posted, okay?"

"If someone dies, you'll be the first to know."

Roberto closed the window, blew them a kiss, and disappeared behind a curtain of rain.

Jaime raised his hand to hail a taxi, and within minutes he and Paloma were comfortable in the backseat of one, on a course for the CHR building.

"What exactly is your friend going to do?" she asked.

"We're sharing the workload. I'll be protecting you; Roberto gets Preston." He smiled and pushed aside the wet hair on her forehead. "Looks like I'm the winner in this situation. And I guess you lucked out, too."

Paloma didn't answer.

Wearing pajamas and a dressing gown, Oscar Preston finished the last of his turkey sandwich and left the plate in the sink. It was almost midnight, but he couldn't sleep. He had read the document that Amanda had given him, and he couldn't believe what it said. If he was interpreting the information correctly, Paloma had discovered that the sculpture stolen from the museum in Verona last month was much older than previously thought and was also linked to the legend of the blood of Medusa and its alleged magical properties. Talk about a bombshell! If this research came to light, it would cause an uproar in the media and would be featured on TV and in newspapers all over the world. Not to mention that it would put Paloma automatically in the deputy director's chair.

Until now, Preston had felt sure of himself. His recently resuscitated work on *The Colossus*, the controversial painting traditionally attributed to Goya, cleared up many doubts surrounding the old debate. Preston had centered his attention on the brushstrokes found in the bottom left-hand corner of the painting, which some historians believed to be numbers, but others claimed were the initials of the painter Asensio Juliá. The analyses, reading, and interviews he had been carrying out for months went a long way toward answering the question of whether it had been a mistake to remove the painting from the catalogue as a result of its attribution being brought into doubt.

Now he knew that Paloma's research ran circles around his.

He felt pathetic. He felt a tightness in his chest that he couldn't alleviate with medicines or food. From the beginning, he had been certain that his work would bring him victory. Then this Clark had appeared with his veiled threats and murky deals, sowing seeds of doubt. Now Preston knew the truth: he was a failure who, on top of everything else, was up to his neck in thievery, kidnapping, and extortion. Just what his high blood pressure needed.

He was passing the plate under the faucet when the telephone rang. "Hello?"

"Hello, Oscar. Can you come down?"

It was Clark. His voice made Preston shiver. "Yes. I have it."

"Marvelous. Now shut up and come down."

He got dressed and went down to the street. The gray car was parked near the entrance, under the incessant rain. Without asking for permission, Preston opened the door and sat beside the man with the familiar mustache and nose plaster.

"Good evening, Oscar. Shall we go for a drive?"

"Now? It's late. I was about to go to bed."

"This won't take long. Do you have the document?"

Feeling a pain in his heart, Preston put the folder on the dashboard.

"Excellent."

"Now you'll do your part, right? You'll let me publish this work? It's—"

"It's fabulous, I'm sure. Honestly, I have no idea what it's about—I'm just a messenger—but I trust your opinion. Sadly, though, I'm afraid you won't be able to publish it."

"What do you mean? We had a deal."

"Yes, we did."

"And Amanda's son? Where's the boy?"

"The boy's fine. We'll keep him safe until we know that what you've given us is good. But don't worry, he'll be free tomorrow."

Preston looked Clark in the eyes and was surprised to find Clark's usual friendly glint wasn't there. Before he could say anything, Clark started the engine and drove to a street near Plaza de España full of bars with neon signs that advertised drinks and girls. He parked in front of a Chinese discount store and they got out of the car. They walked past a police station, dodged a group of drunks, and headed toward a tall, dark building just opposite the Torre de Madrid.

Bolts of lightning lit up the graffiti-covered exterior and an old *Telefónica* billboard, imbuing the scene with a desolate, science fiction–like atmosphere. The glass in the door had been smashed to pieces, as had the bulb that at some point in the past must have lit the building's interior. Strewn about was all manner of junk: paper, bottles, assorted packaging, and condoms. The strong smell of filth was nauseating.

There was nothing but a cavity where the elevator had once been. Clark gestured to Preston to climb up one of the rusty old staircases. On the first landing, Preston was shocked to find beggars sleeping under cardboard boxes. The place was like the scene of a nuclear disaster.

Clark told Preston to keep climbing. He had noticed the man's growing unease some time before, and he placed a hand on his shoulder to calm him.

"Easy, Oscar, everything's fine."

"What is this place? I hope you're not taking me for tapas again."

"No, no. There's no tapas here. Just drugs and hookers, but unfortunately we don't have time for that. The boss wants to talk to you."

"The boss?" Preston didn't understand. His clothes were soaked from the rain and his glasses had misted up.

"The man who's paying us," Clark said with a wink. "Come on, it's time to forget that wimpy art stuff and meet some *really* important people."

They climbed several more flights of stairs to the ninth floor, where Clark pushed open a metal door with a loud screech. Preston stepped through, panting from exertion and anxiety. During the climb he had seen it all: immigrant families huddled under blankets, ragged young people with dreadlocks, and haggard individuals smoking something pungent. What was he doing there? All he wanted was to go back to his apartment. If these men wouldn't let him publish Paloma's work, then he'd just have to investigate the history of the Medusa himself and write his own study.

He hurried through the door that Clark had pushed open, hoping to reach safety as quickly as possible, but his new surroundings didn't look any more promising.

The windows were devoid of glass, and nothing in the room resembled furniture. The remains of wallpaper hung from the walls. Rain was streaming in through every opening, soaking the floor and making the room uninhabitable. The only door was the one they'd come through, and nothing suggested this was somebody's office.

Preston looked at Clark. "What's happening now? Where's this boss?"

"I lied, Oscar. I'm the only boss here."

A clap of thunder sounded at that moment, making it seem as if they were in a scene from a horror movie.

Preston spun around, suddenly fearful someone was hiding behind him. Seeing no one, he turned back to face Clark again. "I don't understand what all this is about."

"Consider it a farewell. You've done your job, and it wouldn't be a good idea for us to be seen together anymore."

In the neon-tinted light, confusion reflected back from Preston's eyes. "But—you can't mean you're going to kill me. I called Amanda, I kept your identity a secret, and I handed over the document. I did everything you asked!"

"That's all true. Unfortunately for you, we don't need the document anymore."

"What do you mean?"

"I'm afraid I don't have time to chat, Oscar. I'm sorry. You seem like a stuck-up nitpicker, but over time I've grown quite fond of you."

Another thunderclap. Preston felt a shudder. Clark's icy tone and the sudden contempt in his voice could mean nothing good. He tried to speak, but the words stuck in his throat. He swallowed hard. "Look, Clark. I don't know what you want or who you are. You asked me to do something and I did it. I don't understand why you're saying now that—"

"Hands in the air, shithead!" Clark whipped an automatic pistol out from under his arm and aimed it at Preston.

"What are you doing? There's no need for that!"

"Then don't make me do it."

"I don't know what any of this is about, I swear to God. Please, don't kill me!"

"Like I said, we don't need you, Oscar. The boss already has what he was looking for."

"He has it? But you asked me to get it. And I did! It's there, in your car, in the fold—"

"I've got my orders. The boss was quicker than you were. I'm sorry, Oscar, but you're excess baggage now." Clark pointed the weapon at Preston's head. "Stand in front of that window facing the street. The views are awesome from here."

Preston was trembling. He put his hands on his head and walked toward the glassless window. Nine floors below, the storm-battered Plaza de España looked deserted. "Don't do it," he said. "I don't know who you are, I don't know anything, I won't say anything, please don't kill me, don't—"

"I'm not going to kill you. I just want you to jump."

Preston closed his eyes against the fate that awaited him. He began to sob uncontrollably.

"Come on, Oscar. It's just a little jump. Just one! Don't make me help you."

"No, listen. We can make a deal. Let me live and—"

"Aw, fuck it."

There came the thud of a silenced pistol and then a cracking sound. Preston felt his strength fail and sensed he was falling forward into the void. Then something clutched him by the back of his neck and stopped him from tumbling through the window. Preston dropped onto the dirty floor and lay there in shock alongside the unconscious body of the man who'd been about to kill him.

33

Clark hadn't expected his time to come so soon. He'd known that, extraordinary endurance notwithstanding, he bled like anyone else, and one day his luck would run out. It was simply a question of whether the weapon would be bullet, bomb, or blade. But the funny thing was, he couldn't recall any of those fates befalling him.

The cold rain dripped down his face. He opened first one eye, then the other, and he was left staring into the blackness before him, feeling stunned and confused. Pain seared the base of his skull and a terrible burning sensation raced across his face. The water was running in the direction of his forehead, and his body seemed to be swinging without touching the ground. Despite the darkness, he could just make out a face in front of him. A man with a mustache and a nose in plaster. He was looking at himself, reflected in a windowpane.

Something wasn't right. He tried to look up and saw the surface of the road some distance away. He looked toward his feet, and saw that they were tied to a rope that hung from a glassless windowpane. Beyond that was a stormy sky full of clouds.

He understood that he was hanging upside down from the ninth floor.

He wanted to scream, but no sound came from his mouth. He looked back toward his feet again; now the sky was partially blocked by a dark, oddly shaped head.

Clark blinked again, convinced his eyes were playing tricks on him. The head was black and it had two pointy ears at the top. Despite the darkness, the treacherous height, and the fear he felt, Clark recognized that he was looking at a mask with holes for the mouth and eyes.

"Good evening," the man in the mask said.

Clark blinked furiously.

"Who are you? Where am I?"

The stranger seemed offended. "What do you mean, who am I? I'm fucking Batman!"

"Batman?"

"Are you blind?"

"Please, get me down from here. I mean, pull me back up! This isn't funny."

"Tell that to your friend."

"My friend? What friend?"

"The one you tried to kill a moment ago. It's not nice to play with people's lives like that."

"I know, I know. Please, pull me up and we'll talk."

"We're already talking. Tell me why you were going to kill him."

"I was following orders. Please, pull me up. My mouth's filling with water."

"So's your nose. That plaster cast is pretty handy."

"I'm begging you . . ."

"You said you were following orders. Orders from whom?"

"I don't know!"

"You don't know or you don't want to know?"

Clark's body suddenly dropped two meters down the exterior wall and then stopped again. "Bastard! Son of a bitch!" he yelled. "Let me go!"

"As you wish."

Clark fell another meter. He screamed. "No! Get me up, get me *up*!"

"Are you going to play nice or not?"

"Pull me up." Clark began to make sniveling noises. "I'll tell you everything! Everything!"

He groaned and screamed a bit more before he noticed that the man was pulling the rope and his body was beginning to climb back up the wall.

"Now give me your hands," Batman instructed him when he was fairly close. "And don't try anything stupid, or I'll send you straight to Arkham Cemetery."

"Okay, okay . . . but don't let me go, please. Just don't let me go."

Clark stretched out his arms and bent at the waist in order to reach the man's hands. Once the man had him, he pulled Clark through the window into the building. Clark lay on the ground, trying to get his breath back as he looked at his captor in astonishment.

He was a broad-shouldered, heavily built man wearing a Batman suit that was too small for him. Below the bat printed on the chest, Clark could see a bulging stomach and lint-filled belly button sticking out.

"Who are you, clown?" Clark challenged him as soon as he'd recovered from his fright.

"I told you once. Don't make me repeat it."

"Batman, huh? More like some perverted old queen."

"Whatever. Just answer my questions. Where's Amanda's son?"

"Fuck you."

"Oh, so it's going to be like that. You want me to string you up by your feet again?"

"Do what you want. I won't tell you a thing."

"You don't need to. I know everything about you."

"You don't know shit about me."

"All right." Batman feigned indifference. "I know that shithead on the floor's named Oscar Preston. You kidnapped Amanda's son and you're blackmailing her to get your hands on Paloma Blasco's work. Suddenly it occurred to you to search Paloma's music CDs, and, once you found what you were looking for, you decided you didn't need either of them anymore and planned their murders. Have I left anything out?"

"I don't know anything about any CDs. How do you know any of this? Was it that son of a bitch?" Clark gestured toward Preston.

"No need. Paloma and Amanda filled me in. You were about to do away with Preston with your little pistol when I arrived and smacked you in the head with a metal bar."

Clark gingerly felt the bump while a distant memory struggled to the surface of his consciousness. "Azcárate . . . You're Jaime Azcárate, Paloma's boyfriend."

"Me, that scrawny poseur? Don't insult me or you'll find yourself back out the window."

"No, you can't be him." Clark looked pointedly at the human bat's bulging paunch. "The other guy looked like he was wasting away, and you're a fat bastard. I'm gonna kill you."

"And I'll take you to my cave so you can try Alfred's soup," the masked man said dryly. "Enough dicking around: Where's the boy?"

"Ha! At Disneyland."

"I see. And the sculpture?"

"What sculpture?"

"The Medusa everyone's looking for. Where is it?"

"What the fuck are you talking about? I don't know anything about a Medusa."

"Who's paying you?"

"Go fuck yourself!"

"It was a serious question."

Voices and the sounds of running could be heard through the door. Batman smiled. "It seems we've woken up the tenants."

"Then you're about to get your ass whooped, asshole."

"Or *you* are."

Clark was beginning to think he could make it out of this. *He* looked like a normal guy, while the other man looked like some kind of freak. A gang of angry beggars would see him as a clear target. "You're an idiot," he said to buy time. "While you're here making a fool of yourself, your friend Paloma's about to be killed."

For a moment, Clark thought his captor was going to lose his temper, but the guy's relaxed body language made him realize he was mistaken. "Right now, two of my men are heading to your friend's apartment to give her a nasty surprise," he tried again. "We have what we wanted, so she has to disappear. The attempt in the metro went wrong, but this time there won't be any mistakes. Do what you want with me, but you can kiss that whore good-bye." Clark looked closely for the man's reaction. First the guy looked up thoughtfully, as if he was reflecting on what he'd just heard. Then he stared Clark in the eyes, his expression inscrutable behind the black mask.

"She's a pain in the ass, that woman," he said finally. "She has it coming."

Clark was thrown. Suddenly the door opened and five young squatters in raincoats burst in, two of them brandishing lead pipes. "Fuck me!" one of them exclaimed. "It's Batman!"

With bemused looks on their faces, the other four surveyed the scene from the entrance, then burst into laughter. As did Clark.

"Oh my God, I'm glad you guys showed up. This crazy man cornered me up here and he's trying to kill me."

The first squatter took a step forward and raised an eyebrow. "Oh, yeah?"

The man dressed as Batman walked toward them. "Of course not. Our friend here's a thug who tried to murder that man sleeping there on the floor. He's also kidnapped a little boy. I'm trying to find out where he's hiding him."

"Don't listen to him!" Clark snapped. He'd begun to sweat. "Just look at him. It's obvious he's out of his mind."

The squatter and Batman looked intently at one another. "Man, I've seen some crazy people in this building, but you might just be the craziest."

"I'm telling you the truth: he's the criminal. By the way, that's one cool badge. Coprophagous Sphincters, am I right?"

The squatter looked down at his chest and smiled. "2012 Tour. You into them?"

"I was a bouncer at one or two of their gigs. Their cover of Karina's 'El baúl de los recuerdos' is off the charts."

The squatter grinned again and turned to his friends. "He might be nuts, but this Batman seems okay."

Clark's expression changed. "What? Are you as insane as he is?"

"Shut it, dick! Is it true about the boy?" the squatter asked Batman.

"I swear on the Sphincters' bass player."

The squatters formed a circle around Clark, who curled into a ball against the wall.

"Let's hear it, asshole. Where's the boy? Spill it or we'll send you down the elevator shaft."

While they kicked and Clark screamed, Roberto Barrero lifted Oscar Preston's limp body onto his shoulder. The first squatter came over to him.

"That piece of shit says the boy's in a warehouse between Calle Aníbal and Calle Sofora. Will that work?"

"That'll work. Thanks."

"Is Batman going to go rescue him?" one of the other squatters asked with a grin.

"I think Batman's done enough for one night." Roberto exhaled, feeling the weight of Oscar Preston's body across his shoulder. "It's time to hand things over to Commissioner Gordon."

34

The police found Hugo at ten past two in the morning, in a warehouse belonging to a bar that had closed down four months earlier. The commissioner on duty had been right to take the anonymous call seriously, and he was delighted he'd made that decision when he reunited the boy with his mother. Aside from a slightly upset stomach—his captor had fed him on a diet of Orangina and potato chips—Hugo was physically safe, and he narrated his adventure to the police as if it were the plot of a movie.

Amanda was shocked and overcome with emotion. She hugged and kissed her son, not wanting to let him go even for an instant, and told the commissioner about the kidnapping, the kidnappers' warning not to report it, and the attack on Señora Julia without mentioning Oscar Preston's role in the affair. Though her first instinct was to tell them everything, doing so would have put Paloma in a predicament. She and Jaime had specifically asked Amanda to be discreet and stick with the story of Paloma's mother being sick, in order to justify her absence from the museum for a few days. If Amanda had told the police about Preston, all the beans would have been spilled.

But so what? What loyalty did she owe to Paloma? Paloma hadn't behaved like a true friend. She'd put her interests before their friendship—and before Hugo. Still, Jaime Azcárate seemed to know what he was doing, and it was possible that Paloma remained in danger. It was clear to Amanda now that Preston wasn't the bad guy—or at least not the worst guy—in this matter, so the threat was still real. She also had reason to believe that Hugo had been saved by Jaime and that friend of his, Roberto Barrero. Who, incidentally, hadn't seemed at all bad. When he returned from his secret mission, maybe she would ask him out.

The policeman promised her he'd investigate the kidnapping and catch those responsible, and she assured him she'd contact him if she remembered anything. Once he was gone, Amanda cried for a while with Hugo in her arms, until the boy asked for permission to play video games. As usual, his mother gave it to him and lay on the sofa to enjoy a few moments' peace after all the tension.

The sound of the telephone made her jump.

"Jaime?" she said upon hearing the voice at the other end.

"Hello, Amanda. Sorry to call at this hour, but I'm guessing you have good news."

"Hugo's here," she said happily. "How did you do it?"

"It's best if you don't know too much. Did the police pester you for long?"

"No, it all went fine. Where are you?"

"With Paloma. Getting ready for tomorrow's trip. I just wanted to make sure everything had gone the way we hoped."

"Thanks, Jaime."

"We'll talk when we get back. Have a good night."

"You, too."

After she'd hung up, Amanda wondered how Paloma had never before mentioned this extraordinary guy who seemed just as likely to threaten to smash someone over the head with a vase as to phone her to make sure everything was all right. Though he hadn't admitted it, she was sure he'd had a hand in freeing Hugo. She closed her eyes and smiled at the sound of laser pistols and insults coming from her son, who was settled into a beanbag chair in front of the television.

She let him play for another hour and then decided it was time for him to go to bed. She was ready to do the same. All she wanted was to climb under the sheets and forget the nightmare they'd been through. She was putting Hugo to bed when she heard someone banging on the door.

"Señora Escámez?" came a voice from the hallway.

"Who is it?" she said, frightened. Through the peephole she could see a blurry human form.

"It's Inspector Serrano. I have a couple of questions for you about the kidnapper."

A few seconds later Amanda would regret her carelessness, but at that moment she saw no reason to be distrustful, even though the person she'd spoken to an hour before was named Commissioner Carneiro. As soon as she opened the door, someone shoved a foot inside. A man with a face full of bruises, his nose in plaster, burst into the apartment. He pushed her against the wall and locked the door.

"I lied," he said. "I'm not a policeman. But I do have a couple of questions for you."

35

Cagliari—Sardinia

Rosa Mazi woke when her cell phone began to vibrate under her pillow. Beside her, Dino woke up, too.

"What time is it, Rosa?" he murmured in the darkness of the bedroom.

"Almost three. Go back to sleep."

"Who's calling you at this time of night?"

"Business. Sorry, Dino."

Rosa pushed aside the comforter and climbed out of bed. She and Dino had worked late at the gallery before going back to his house for dinner and a drink. They'd fallen asleep in each other's arms after making love, and this interruption was like getting a bucket of cold water—or something much worse—thrown on their evening.

Rosa locked herself in the bathroom and took the call sitting on the toilet seat. "Clark, what is it?"

"Where are you? Why aren't you on the yacht?"

"What's it to you? Just tell me why you're calling at this time of night."

"Preston got away."

"Clark, if the best you can do is botch things up, like you did with Paloma in the metro, it's not going to come as a surprise when everything else goes wrong, too."

"The incident with Paloma was a mistake, I admit it. I planned to follow her to her apartment, but when I saw her wander down the platform it seemed like the perfect opportunity. I took a big risk, and I messed up. But can you imagine it, Rosa? That bitch's body, crushed between the train and track . . . It would've been a work of art, and I know how much you love art."

"Clark, I'm going to hang up and vomit now. Not necessarily in that order."

"Okay, okay. I was better prepared with Preston, but he had help. Some idiot dressed like Batman got me cornered. I think he was a friend of that Azcárate or his girlfriend. They've rescued the kid, I got the crap beat out of me by some homeless guys, and the police are out looking for me. And now those troublemakers are going after you, Rosa."

"Me? Where did you get that idea?"

"I just came from Amanda Escámez's apartment. She told me everything. She says they planned the handover of Paloma's document so they could watch me. They're planning to leave in the morning to go investigate the theft of the Medusa."

"What have you done to Amanda?"

"Relax. I didn't hurt her or her son. But she was so scared she spilled everything. I had to put the squeeze on the kid a little, but he's fine, I swear."

"And you're worried about me just because they're going to investigate the theft? Have you told them who or where we are?"

"Of course not."

"So why do you think I'm in danger?"

"Don't you get it? If they go to Verona and ask after you—"

"I don't have anything to do with that museum anymore."

"They're stubborn bastards, Rosa. But don't worry; I'll get them off your back. Tell your father I haven't failed. Not yet."

"All right, Clark," Rosa agreed, although she couldn't help feeling some apprehension. The last thing she needed now was a bunch of amateur detectives showing up at her door. "Do what you have to do, but don't call me again."

"Are you with your boyfriend?"

"Good-bye, Clark."

Rosa turned off her cell phone and went back to bed. Dino was still awake. "What is it that couldn't wait until morning?"

Rosa considered the good and simple man who'd shown up at the gallery one afternoon looking for work. A deep bond, built on their shared dreams for the future, had grown between them. The problem was, Rosa hadn't told him a thing about her family's illegal activities, much less the role she still played in them.

"A cousin of mine's visiting Sardinia," she said. "He was worried because he'd been trying to call me all day. It was nothing important."

"A cousin? Fantastic! We can meet him tomorrow for a coffee, if you want. I still haven't met anyone in your family. I'm beginning to think you're ashamed of me." Dino yawned. "Now let's get some more sleep. We don't have to get up just yet."

Dino made himself comfortable on his side of the bed and started snoring while Rosa turned off the light and was left staring up at the dark ceiling.

What did she have to do to free herself once and for all? She felt trapped between two worlds: one with Dino, the gallery, and the art school she planned to set up, and the other with the organization run by her father, who would only allow himself to be "seen" through his portrait. It was driving her crazy, and now on top of everything else, with Leonardo gone, Clark had begun looking to her as second in command.

She was tempted to run away from it all, but she knew she wouldn't get far. Her father's extensive contacts would quickly find her. And she couldn't ignore the possibility that Alvino Nascimbene, her family's mortal enemy, was still alive and looking for her.

That night she slept. But from the way she felt the next day, she could've sworn she'd spent the hours with one eye open.

36

En route to Verona

Once Jaime and Roberto left behind the morning rush-hour traffic and turned on to the Zaragoza road, the day brought them a brief rain shower that subsided and left the sky clear.

From his position at the wheel of Roberto's Fiat Doblò, Jaime Azcárate looked in the mirror every few seconds to make sure no car was following them. He shook his head and tried to free it of his fears. He was going to need his mind completely clear. He searched through Roberto's music, hoping to find something that would help him relax, but he didn't recognize any of the bands: *Vicious Brutality, Coprophagous Sphincters, Pepito the Fundamentalist* . . . He shook his head and looked out of the corner of his eye at Roberto, who was asleep beside him with his head back and mouth open.

"I'll admit, you're a brave man," he said, even though he knew Roberto wouldn't hear him. "But we're going to have to work on your taste in music."

To his surprise, Roberto stuck a hand in the pocket on the passenger door and then held a CD out to Jaime: the soundtrack to *Out of Africa*.

"What's this?" Jaime asked in amazement.

"You never know when some mama's boy is gonna be driving your car."

With that, he fell back asleep. It had been a long night.

As the soft chords began to play, Jaime stretched in his seat. Behind him, Paloma and Oscar were also sleeping, having first positioned themselves carefully to make sure they wouldn't accidentally touch each other. Jaime sighed. Four people in a car, and it was still going to be the loneliest and most boring of drives.

The plan that he'd been working on when he first learned that Paloma was in danger had centered on taking her somewhere remote, like a mountain lodge, in order to put distance between her and her pursuers. However, he and Roberto had ultimately decided to kill two birds with one stone and head to the Pontecorvo House Museum to see if they could find a connection between the former museum director, who was the daughter of Angelo Carrera, and the theft of the Medusa.

The previous night, while Roberto was saving Preston's life and locating Amanda's son, Jaime and Paloma had ruined their backs on a sofa at the Center for Historical Research, which they assumed was a safer location than either of their homes.

"You haven't changed," Paloma had said just before they tried to get some sleep. "Always trying to solve things by yourself."

"You must admit it makes things exciting. Anyway, I have Roberto to back me up."

"A fat geek who thinks he's Batman. How reassuring for you."

"That's not completely fair. Sometimes he thinks he's Chuck Norris." Jaime put his arm around her shoulders. "What have you told Amanda?"

"That we're going away until the danger's passed."

"Did you tell her where, exactly?"

"No," Paloma lied. Jaime had insisted that, for everyone's safety, no one could be told where they were going. But Paloma had already hidden too much from her friend, and in the telephone conversation they'd had that afternoon, she'd let slip that they were going to investigate the theft of the Medusa.

"Good. And the copy of your work for Ricardo Bosch?"

"I emailed it from Laura's office. I hope I'm not risking my job by doing all of this."

"Quite the opposite—you'll see."

At six in the morning, Roberto Barrero arrived to collect them in the van. In the trunk were the few pieces of luggage they'd loaded up the day before. And in the passenger's seat was Oscar Preston, unwilling to be separated a single centimeter from the man who had saved his life.

Roberto woke up when Jaime stopped at a toll point.

"Where are we?"

"Just past Alfajarín. We should reach Girona in about three hours."

"Do you think the police have nabbed our friend with the mustache yet?"

"If they have, he'll have already told them everything he knows." Jaime looked through the water-stained windshield. "Being interrogated by a police inspector isn't quite the same as talking to a bat with a beer belly."

"A few minutes more and he'd have told me everything he knew. And for your information, I don't have a beer belly. Those are my abs."

"Yeah, sure. You really had him scared; that's why it took five squatters to make him talk."

"So what? All superheroes have sidekicks. Besides, that criticism's pretty ironic, coming from you. You're practically a Perseus tribute act. At least we know Hugo's back home."

The truth was, that was all they knew. From the description Roberto had given him, Jaime had gathered that Preston's attacker was the same guy who'd tried to freeze him to death in El Burgo de Osma and who had tried to kill Paloma on the metro. Another member of Angelo Carrera's family or a hit man for his organization, no doubt.

Oscar Preston leaned forward and put his head between the two front seats. His bloodshot eyes had dark rings around them.

"The guy called himself Clark. He didn't tell me his real name."

"That's because not even *he* trusted you," Paloma said from the other side of the backseat. "I'll ask again: Why did we have to bring this slug with us?"

"He didn't want me to leave him at his apartment," Roberto explained. "He started crying like a little baby and left me with no option but to bring him with me. It's like that Chinese code of honor: if you save a life, you become responsible for it. This includes puppets and brownnosers."

"Please, I think we've already discussed this enough. I don't want to go home. I'm not safe there. I promise I'll do what you say." Preston looked at Paloma. "I think it's time to put an end to our rivalry; we're in the same boat now."

"As far as I'm concerned, you can drop dead."

"Stop bickering back there," Jaime said in a tired voice. "Preston's right. These people are after both of you. For the moment at least, it's best to put aside your differences and stick together."

"I'd rather be stuck with a dung beetle," Paloma replied.

Roberto grinned. "Is there a difference?"

"Mind your own business, jerk!"

Jaime looked at Preston in the mirror.

"Have some respect. Roberto saved your life, so shut your mouth. If you get bored, count yellow cars."

Preston grumbled, settled back in his seat with his arms crossed, and looked back out the window.

"I feel sorry for Amanda," Paloma said. "Poor girl! She's going to get bombarded with questions about this creep, and about me. I don't like disappearing at a time like this, but at least I know Preston won't be there, kissing Ricardo's ass while I'm gone."

The tension in the backseat was thick. Jaime and Roberto tried to ignore it and concentrate on the immediate future. Roberto took the wheel for the next leg of the drive and tortured the others with one of his underground rock CDs.

"By the way," he asked Jaime, "what exactly do you expect me to do on this trip? I hope I'm not just here as a bodyguard for your girl and the brownnoser. I'll remind you that even though the security guard gig pays the bills these days, I'm really a man of adventure."

"Don't worry. Not only have you proven yourself to be the most unsavory superhero this side of Gotham, you've demonstrated you have a real flair for investigation. I want you to help me make a timeline of everything we've established so far: details, dates, events, people—"

"I see. So you want me to write your report for you." Roberto turned to Paloma. "Old habits die hard for this guy."

"I'm sure you'd love it if I asked you to write the article for me," Jaime said. "But that's not what the timeline's for. I was going to do it in Madrid, but then everything got crazy. I figured that if we put together a good outline of all the information we have, it might help us find the Medusa."

Preston stopped gazing at the damp landscape they were passing and turned to Paloma.

"The Medusa? Is that what we're looking for? Paloma, is all that stuff true? The thing about the blood and—"

"That's none of your business," Paloma snapped back, practically tearing Jaime to pieces with her glare.

But Preston persisted. "I have to congratulate you. There's no doubt you deserve the deputy director's position more than I do. How did you do it? I mean, how did it all start? What made you suspect that the Medusa was older than the catalogues said?"

Roberto answered for Paloma. "You heard what she said: it doesn't concern you. You're here because someone wanted to turn you into a spot on the pavement, so you'd better shut your mouth or we'll throw you out of the window with a flare up your ass to make it easy for them to find you."

Though Paloma wasn't in a good mood, she laughed heartily at that. Red with rage, Preston sat back again and resumed watching the scenery with a sulky expression.

They spent the night in Arles, and the next day they set off again very early, skirting the Mediterranean coast in Roberto's car. Like they had the day before, Jaime and Roberto took turns at the wheel. At around one in the afternoon, they stopped to stretch their legs by Lake Garda, and an hour later they arrived in Verona.

Guided by Roberto's GPS, they crossed the River Adige at Vittoria Bridge and soon arrived on Piazzale Aristide Stefani, in front of an imposing hospital building. There, by a busy bus stop, was the bed-and-breakfast where Jaime had booked their reservations.

When Paloma saw the building, she shook her head in disbelief.

"Here? I don't believe it, Jaime."

"What's wrong with it?" He gave her a wink.

Not understanding the exchange, and because parking on the street proved impossible, Roberto left the others at the entrance and drove the van to a parking lot on the other side of the river. The hotel was on the third floor of the building, and Jaime, Paloma, and Preston carried their luggage up to the front desk. There they were met by a friendly, red-bearded young man who spoke perfect Spanish. The place was clean and modern, and everything smelled new. The doors were white, and no mark blemished the immaculate paint on the walls. After requesting their identity documents and explaining the rules of the establishment, the friendly owner accompanied them to the two adjacent rooms that Jaime had booked the day before.

"Paloma and I will sleep here," Jaime said to Preston. "You and Roberto can take that one."

"Why can't I have my own room?" Preston complained.

"Because Roberto is your life insurance. In fact, if I were you, I wouldn't breathe easy until he gets back."

Enjoying the look of fear on Oscar Preston's face, Jaime walked toward his and Paloma's room and gestured for her to go inside.

The room was spacious and minimalist, with a padded headboard secured to the wall; furniture with clean, straight lines; and shaded lamps. Paloma put her hands on her hips and looked at Jaime with irritation.

"You did this on purpose."

"What?"

"Are you going to tell me there are no other hotels in Verona?"

"There are plenty of others. But I have good memories of this one. Don't you?"

"You're unbelievable, Jaime Azcárate." She might have been flirting with him, but it sounded more like a scolding. "I suppose now you'll tell me you didn't know the twin beds would be pushed together."

"It seemed presumptuous to ask for a double. We still have a lot to work out."

"Don't hold your breath." She slammed the bathroom door behind her.

Jaime left the luggage on the floor and lay faceup on one of the beds, his arms crossed under his head. The bathroom door opened and Paloma reappeared.

"Are you being serious?"

Jaime tipped up his head so he could look at her.

"As a matter of fact, yes. I . . ." He didn't know where to begin, so he let the words guide his thoughts and not the other way round. "I suppose this is as good a time as any to say I'm sorry. I know it sounds absurd for me to say it now, but I've finally realized how much I hurt you."

The look on Jaime's face didn't go unnoticed by Paloma. It was that sparkling look he got sometimes that made people wonder whether he was being serious or joking. She'd experienced it before. She had also felt the breathlessness to which this man was able to drive her, and she wasn't about to take the bait.

"Don't you think it's a bit late to suddenly realize something like that? There's a time and a place for everything."

"Those times and places aren't fixed. They can change over the course of a person's life."

"Sure. That's why at thirty-four you still act like a fifteen-year-old. Sorry, Jaime, but it doesn't work like that."

"Do you remember a letter you wrote to me toward the end of our relationship? You told me that, one day, with the help of a psychologist, I'd realize how egotistical and insensitive I was, and how little I cared about other people. I just want you to know that I've saved a bundle on shrinks, because I haven't needed them to make me see all those things. I know now. I know how much I hurt you, and I'm sorry. I was a different person back then."

Paloma's eyes filled with tears. The last thing she'd expected to happen on this trip was for them to reconcile. Since they'd broken up years before, she had often wondered if she had pressured him too much.

She wanted to tell him that, but this didn't feel like the time or the place. She picked up her purse and went back into the bathroom.

Jaime grabbed a pillow and rested his head against it. The fresh smell of the sheets was tempting him to take a nap when Paloma came back out and planted herself on the bed in front of him.

It was hot in the room, and she'd taken off her woolen pullover, leaving her in a black nylon top that showed off her small, firm breasts. Jaime looked at her in surprise. Her eyes gave nothing away, but her parted lips suggested she had something to say, despite the silence. A question was trying to find its way to his lips, but he bit it back and sat up on the bed, leaning so that all his weight was supported by his left arm.

Paloma moved closer, her messy, ebony-colored hair falling against her cheeks. Jaime studied the stretch of smooth skin left exposed by the black top, from Paloma's neck to the top of her breasts, and he felt something he hadn't expected.

Paloma stretched out her bare arm toward the bed and Jaime did what was expected of him. He took her by the wrist and gently pulled until she was lying on top of him. "Hello," he whispered.

"Hello."

Paloma's lips brushed against his and Jaime felt his desire grow. He pulled her closer to him as she let go of any last misgivings. He had almost forgotten her nibbles, the way her lips and teeth devoured his mouth with tiny, exciting bites. Her soft, moist tongue slid over his in little circular motions. They kissed passionately as two pairs of hands searched desperately for a way past clothing, to naked flesh.

The first two buttons on Jaime's shirt flew off through the air seconds before Paloma pulled off her top. While she unbuttoned the rest of his shirt more carefully, Jaime concentrated on the fastener of the navy-blue bra that held Paloma's hidden charms.

The first time, he failed, but the second attempt was a success, and he uncovered the two delicate mounds, their nipples rising provocatively. While Paloma wrapped her arms around his neck, Jaime slowly savored those delicacies, seasoned with a sharp layer of nostalgia. Tears of yearning rolled down Paloma's cheeks as her fingers slid into Jaime's pants, searching for the fruit that had been so abruptly snatched from her years before.

"Does this mean you accept my apology?" he asked.

Paloma laughed and climbed onto Jaime as they kicked away the comforter, which fell to the floor like a parachute.

37

Verona

Verona, along with Venice, is one of the tourist destinations favored most by lovebirds travelling to Italy. If those lovebirds are also art lovers, then experiencing Verona is like walking among the clouds.

Twelve years earlier, two such lovebirds had walked among the clouds on the same streets that, according to tradition, were once walked by Romeo and Juliet. The bright young lovers ate gelato on the Piazza delle Erbe, enjoyed the panoramic view from the Lamberti Tower, and drank white wine at the Castel San Pietro as they watched the sun go down. They visited Roman monuments, medieval churches, the vast Castelvecchio Museum, and the breathtaking gothic tombs of the Scaliger family. And as tacky and as touristy as some traditions may be, there was one these two lovers couldn't skip. So before they left the city, on the railings on the same side of the square as Juliet's historic balcony, they locked a padlock inscribed with the names Paloma and Jaime along with a date that now seemed as distant as the time of Shakespeare's tale.

Their current trip to Verona bore little resemblance to the first, thought Paloma, as she walked with Jaime. Once again, he seemed both distant and alert, as if the episode in the hotel had never happened. Or perhaps precisely because it had. They walked in silence, as if they were simply enjoying the stroll through the medieval streets, though the same question was in both of their minds: What now?

It was October, so the streets were clear of the hordes of summer tourists, and the walk to the Pontecorvo House Museum was quick. After crossing the river by the Garibaldi Bridge, they walked down Via Rosa and turned left toward the Church of Sant'Anastasia, beside which stood the palatial old house. It was a two-story building with a façade that was white at the bottom and reddish at the top. Some of its windows were triangular, and others featured curved finishes. As they walked through the entrance, a curly-haired young woman behind a desk asked if they wanted to buy two tickets. Paloma was about to say yes, but Jaime talked first. "We're Jaime Azcárate and Paloma Blasco, from the Center for Historical Research in Spain. We wanted to see the director."

The young woman seemed surprised. "Do you have an appointment?" she asked in excellent Spanish.

"He's not expecting us."

"He couldn't be," she said. "Signor Ugolini isn't here right now. He's at a conference at the University of Milan."

"I see. When would it be possible for us to speak to him?"

"If you go to Milan and he has time, he might see you there. Or you could wait and see him here, but he won't be back for five days."

Jaime and Paloma exchanged a look that said *Where there's a will, there's a way.*

"If you tell me what it is you want to discuss and how to contact you," said the woman, "I'll pass the message on to Signor Ugolini. He checks in most days."

"It's about the Medusa that was stolen from here," Jaime said before Paloma could stop him. "We're helping the EHU with the investigation, and we'd like to talk about the night the theft took place."

The museum employee looked taken aback. "Seriously? The police came when it happened and they questioned all the staff."

"We know. But none of those investigators was an expert on the piece in question. Señorita Blasco, on the other hand, is a specialist."

"Oh, really?"

"Very much so." Jaime kept talking without letting Paloma so much as open her mouth. "It was a strange case. Someone went to a lot of trouble to break in and make off with the bust in the middle of the night. I understand a security guard was killed."

"Poor Massimo! He was a good man."

"Did you know him well?"

"I was with him the afternoon before the robbery. I went home at closing and left him here alone. I felt awful later, but I never imagined things would end like that."

"Can we come in?" Jaime asked.

The young woman looked at her watch.

"It's nearly closing time, but we can stay awhile longer if you want. By the way, I'm Sabina."

The museum was built around a central courtyard surrounded by Doric columns, and its exhibits offered a concise but complete overview of the history of the city, including archeological remains, artifacts from the Roman era, and other works of considerable artistic significance. Jaime had never seen the Medusa exhibited there, but Paloma experienced a profound feeling of emptiness when they entered the room where it had once stood.

"Do you remember anything in particular about the night of the robbery?" Jaime asked Sabina.

"Just what I told the police. Massimo had to stay to keep watch that night, and that always put him in a bad mood, but he was having financial difficulties and needed the extra hours. That night he was particularly grumpy, but that was nothing new. He was always a cantankerous old devil." Sabina gave a sad smile. "A big heart, but a bad temper."

"From what I hear, he liked a drink."

"I imagine whoever said that was exaggerating. He was sober whenever I saw him. Maybe a drink every once in a while, but I never saw him overdo it."

"I'm not judging him. But I understand that on the night of the theft, he took a flask of liquor to work."

"It was Spritz. Just mineral water with a little wine and liqueur."

"Spritz laced with hallucinogens."

"That wouldn't be Massimo's doing. Someone must have spiked his drink."

"Where did he keep his things?"

"In a room upstairs. I'll show you, if you want."

They stepped into the courtyard and climbed a timber stairway that led to the upper floor, where there were more exhibition rooms. In one corner was a door with a "Staff Only" sign on it. Sabina opened it and led them into a small room that looked like it was used partly as an office and partly for storage.

"This is where we leave our things when we come to work."

"Who has access?" Jaime asked.

"Just the staff. It's usually locked."

"And was it locked on the night of the theft?"

"Yes. Massimo was very cautious; he had a thing about privacy."

Jaime looked at Paloma. "Are you sure you're not related?"

"Very funny."

"Did you have many visitors that day?"

"The museum never has a lot of visitors. People prefer to go and grope Juliet's statue and stick a padlock on the railings. That day was as boring as any of them. I remember clearly that the only thing that broke the monotony, at least for Massimo, was a smudge on the glass cabinet containing the Lombard crowns. That, and the noise that strange visitor made with his feet."

"What visitor?"

"Just a guy wearing rubber soles that squeaked. It drove Massimo crazy. He even gave the man a nickname: the Pirate."

"The Pirate?"

"Massimo was always calling people things like that, based on how they looked or acted. He thought this guy looked like a pirate, because he wore an earring and a red handkerchief on his head."

Jaime swallowed hard. "What did this Pirate do at the museum?"

"I don't know, exactly. He arrived at about seven that night and spent about an hour here. It was a relief when he left. I thought Massimo was going to throttle him."

"You didn't know him from anywhere?"

"No. Should I have known him?"

"And Rosa Carrera? Do you know her?"

"Rosa Carrera . . . Do you mean Rosa Mazi?"

"I mean the woman who was director of the museum until a year ago."

"Yes, Rosa Mazi."

"Dark-haired, attractive, big eyes?"

"Yes, that's her. I didn't know her for long. I don't think she was happy here. She had dreams of setting up her own business, expanding a gallery her father had in Sardinia or something. Plus I think she had a fiancé, and it was hard for her to live so far away from him."

"Have you heard from her since?"

"Not much. She has my email address and sometimes sends me things, but they're invitations, petitions . . . the kinds of things people send out to everyone in their address books. In fact, a couple of days ago she sent an invitation to an exhibition opening this Saturday at her gallery. It's of a graphic artist, Giuliano Fiore; I don't know if you've heard of him."

"Sure, Giuliano Fiore. He's very well-known," Jaime lied. "Do you still have this invitation?"

"I think so. Just a second."

While Sabina sat at the computer and searched for Rosa's email, Paloma gave Jaime a questioning look. He threw back an expression that said *I'll explain later.*

"Here it is. Do you want me to print you a copy?"

"I'd be very grateful if you could," said Jaime. Before long he held the printed sheet of paper in his hands. "Thank you very much for your help, Sabina. I'm sorry to have bothered you. You must be starving by now."

"Not at all. I'm sorry I couldn't be more useful."

"On the contrary," Jaime said in a cheerful voice. "You've made our visit well worth the trip."

Outside the museum, the temperature had dropped a few degrees and the sky was overcast. Without asking permission, Jaime put his arm around Paloma and pressed her close to him. As they walked back to the hotel over the Garibaldi Bridge, she asked, "Are you going to tell me what all that was about? I can't see how that girl was any use to us."

"She was nice, wasn't she?"

"Hey, if my presence is getting in the way of your plans, you can pretend I'm not here."

"Not at all. My plans are coming together quite nicely. Now we know what door to knock on next."

"Rosa Mazi's? How do you know she's dark, attractive, and the rest of it?"

"Because I've seen her up close. You're not jealous, are you? I'm absolutely certain now that she and her handkerchief-wearing brother were behind the theft of the sculpture. I'd bet the pension I'll never get that he was the one who drugged poor Massimo's drink and stole the statue. He had access to the museum because his sister was the director. He must have stolen or copied the keys. All the cool kids are stealing keys these days, you know."

"Very funny. But why would they steal the sculpture from their own museum?"

"It wasn't Rosa's anymore. And to tell you the truth, I'm not completely sure that she was involved. The statue had been a gift from her father: Angelo Carrera."

"Angelo Carrera?" Paloma said. "The historian?"

"He's not a historian. He was a shady businessman."

"But a history enthusiast. He wrote an article about the Medusa kept at the Capitoline Museums. I went to visit him when I was in Rome, and he was very interested in my theory that Bolgi's sculpture could have been Bernini's."

Jaime stopped and grabbed hold of the bridge's handrail.

"You know Angelo Carrera?"

"Was I not speaking clearly just now?"

"I understood everything. But why didn't you say this before?"

"I did. The other day, at *Arcadia*, when I told you and Laura everything."

"Sorry but no. I'd remember something like that."

"You'd remember if you actually listened to me."

"I was listening to you. I'm sure you never said the man's name."

"I did!"

"Shit, Paloma. It's a shame I didn't have my tape recorder on me at the time. At least now we know how he found you and why he was so interested in Bolgi's Medusa." Jaime looked up at the sky like an illuminist who'd just received the favor of the gods. "He also verified that, as you suspected, it wasn't Bolgi's, but was from Bernini's workshop. That was why he bought the Medusa and donated it to his daughter's museum, to keep it safe. And later he stole it back, probably because he found a buyer. For some reason, Rosa must have refused to return it to him and—"

"What are you talking about? There isn't enough evidence to claim all that. And anyway, I think Angelo Carrera died a few years ago."

"Yeah, another victim of the famous curse of Medusa."

"The curse!" Paloma held her hands to her head. "For God's sake! How can anyone be expected to do serious scientific work with theories like that getting thrown around?"

"You say that, but you're the one who's in this mess because you're convinced the Medusa possesses magical blood."

"But I'm talking about a legend. You actually believe that stuff."

"You know what your problem is, Paloma? You don't consider every angle. A lot of people died because of the supposed evil influence of this creature, including poor Massimo, who was poisoned, and Angelo Carrera, murdered on board his yacht."

"How do you know he was murdered?"

"Well, it sure wasn't an accident. He was a nasty piece of work, and a lot of people wanted him dead. But there was one man in particular who wouldn't stop until he saw Carrera's boat sink to the bottom of the sea."

"I see bad luck, but I don't see curses anywhere."

"There's also the janitor who died of a heart attack while watching soccer, and the EHU investigators who were burned to death on board the *Artemis*. Not to mention Domenico Corsini, the supposed original owner of the piece. And now if we're not careful, Preston, Roberto, you, and I will be next on the list. The next issue of *Arcadia* is going to be packed with dead bodies."

"*Arcadia*? Is that all you can think about? Publishing another of your sensationalist stories?"

"No." Jaime dropped his playful tone. "I'm thinking about your safety. And your work. When we find the Medusa, it will be you and you alone who breaks the news to the world, but don't forget I have to earn a living, too."

"And what will happen to Preston?"

"He'll get what he deserves. He'll get to sit in the front row, watching and biting his nails with rage, while you get named Doctor *honoris causa* or awarded the Nobel Prize."

"I'll be more than happy if I get the deputy director's job."

"It's yours," Jaime said with complete confidence.

"But how? Those bastards have my work."

"You have it, too. And so does Ricardo Bosch, if you sent it to him by email like I asked you to."

"Of course I did."

"Well, there you go. Whatever anyone else does, there's more than enough evidence to show that the work is yours and yours only. But first, my almond-eyed girl, let's go find this Medusa and take a couple of nice pictures of you and her together."

38

After Jaime and Paloma had eaten with Roberto and Preston at a trattoria near the hotel, the four of them returned to their rooms. While Paloma and Preston each went to take showers, Jaime sat at the desk and drew up a timeline of events related to the Medusa, including his latest findings.

"So you've found your old flame from El Burgo de Osma?" Roberto stretched on the bed where just a few hours earlier Jaime and Paloma's bodies had been reunited. "What are you going to do? Turn up at her gallery with a bouquet of flowers?"

"No. I told you, she was a bit frosty on our first date."

"You think she has the Medusa?"

"Unless she's sold it, it's a good bet she still has it. But first she'll want to polish up Paloma's work. In the short time I knew her, she struck me as someone who pays attention to detail."

"You're made for each other. You should take her out dancing."

"Oh, she'll be begging me to take her out. Out of *jail*, that is. How's your guest behaving?"

"Well enough, I suppose. All he does is watch TV. But I call dibs on the room with the girl next time. The hotel manager has come by twice to offer us a gay tour of the city."

Jaime laughed. "Patience. You'll be free of him soon enough."

"He's such a sissy! When this is over I'll bet he tries to hire me as a bodyguard. What about you and Paloma? The bed wasn't looking too professionally made when I got in here. Did you—"

Roberto punched away the cushion Jaime threw at him.

"What? Can't I even ask?"

"Some things, no."

"Fine. Then try this question: Do you really think that statue contains the blood of Medusa?"

"I don't know, Roberto. We've seen stranger things."

"That's for sure. For example: the similarities between the myth and your life right now."

Jaime narrowed his eyes. He wasn't sure whether he liked what Roberto was insinuating. "What do you mean?"

"Oh, come on. The myth of Medusa is about the fear men have of being possessed by strong women. From the way you act in front of Paloma, it's obvious you still feel bad about what you did to her."

Jaime didn't take the bait. He just looked toward the bathroom door, behind which Paloma was showering, and imagined her naked body. Deep inside him, nostalgia and desire swirled in a bubbling cocktail. He shook his head to return to the present.

"That's a very interesting theory. Now, why don't you go find a computer with Internet access and book us a lovely hotel in Cagliari?"

Roberto smiled. "Sardinia, huh? Let me guess: you want to visit that other strong woman—the one who almost turned you into an ice sculpture. And you still have the nerve to deny that the Medusa story bears any resemblance to your life."

"I'm not denying anything. And yes, I think it would be good to pay her a visit. How could it not be, given how hospitable she was last time we met?"

"You're a hopeless romantic." Roberto got up from the bed. "All right, a hotel in Cagliari. With three rooms, a pool, and a gym. Batman's getting pudgy."

When he was alone, Jaime reviewed the notes he had made based on Paloma's research and his own.

> *Third century BC. An unknown artist sculpts the bust of Medusa, possibly on commission from a physician who wants to use it to store the creature's blood. Origin of the blood? No idea.*
>
> *Circa 1630–50. Bernini acquires the bust of Medusa and uses it as a model for his piece, now exhibited at the Capitoline Museums.*
>
> *1656. Bolgi, who had stolen the ancient Medusa from Bernini's workshop, presents it to Domenico Corsini as his own work. Soon after, a plague ravages Naples. Corsini, seized by the delirium of the illness, dies in his garden (first victim of the "curse"). Bolgi dies the same year.*
>
> *1799. Pietro Parodi buys the Medusa for his private collection. It's passed down through his heirs until 1940.*
>
> *1940. Luca Parodi takes it from Naples to Rome.*
>
> *1970. Before his death, Parodi sells it to the Leoni Antique Center.*

1998. The Leoni Antique Center burns down. The Medusa survives.

2009. The Petrarca Gallery buys part of the Leoni collection, including the Medusa. Angelo Carrera buys it from the Petrarca and takes it to the museum run by his daughter in Verona.

2010. Angelo Carrera dies when his yacht sinks.

2012. Rosa Mazi leaves the Verona museum, probably to focus on an art gallery in Cagliari (Sardinia) which she runs with her fiancé (?).

2013. Rosa Mazi's brother steals the Medusa from the museum in Verona. A security guard dies during the robbery after being drugged.

These were the facts only, without any hypotheses or conclusions, though for some time Jaime's mind had been exploring much deeper avenues than his notebook suggested, and a picture made up of ghostlike snippets had begun to take shape. Now he just needed to find out what Rosa Mazi intended to do with the sculpture and Paloma's work. Sell them to someone, no doubt. But who?

He was about to reread his notes again when the door opened and Roberto appeared, looking like a man who'd just swallowed a live toad.

"What's the matter?" asked Jaime, looking back down at his notes. "No hotels with a pool?"

"Worse," his friend replied. "You'd better come see this."

. . .

Oscar Preston was lying naked on the ceramic shower floor. A stream of blood flowed into a large red pool that was gradually pouring down the drain. A bar of soap lay a few centimeters from his right foot.

"I came in for my wallet and found him like this." Roberto sounded apologetic. "An accident?"

"Yeah, like the accident I had in El Burgo de Osma."

Jaime did a quick check of the room and saw that the window was ajar. The temperature outside was cold, and he doubted Preston would have opened the window to let air in. A terrible hunch suddenly pierced his soul.

"Paloma." He ran back out and toward the other room, cursing himself for not checking the bathroom window before she went to take her shower.

The door was locked and he could hear the sound of running water inside.

"Paloma!" he yelled. Receiving no reply, he stepped back and kicked the doorknob, breaking the door open with one blow, and rushed inside.

In the shower stall, two pairs of eyes looked back at Jaime: those belonging to Paloma, who was naked and terrified, and those of the mustachioed man who had one hand around her throat. As Jaime ran in, the man aimed a pistol between his eyes.

"Stop right there, Jaime Azcárate. Move and I'll blow your brains all over the walls."

Jaime raised his hands and froze.

"A gunshot isn't a bar of soap," he said, trying to control his voice. "It won't look like an accident."

"It doesn't have to. You just hold still and do what I say."

"Jaime, what's going on?" Roberto called from the bedroom.

Jaime opened his mouth to sound the alarm, but Clark's menacing expression stopped him. Jaime realized that this guy had a broken nose thanks to him, and he'd taken a beating courtesy of Roberto. The look in his eyes didn't suggest that any of them could hope to receive mercy.

Clark gestured for Jaime to call Barrero to the room. "Come on in, Roberto," Jaime said. "Everything's fine."

"That's great," Roberto answered.

But instead of simply walking into the bathroom, he jumped in and aimed a pistol at Clark.

Jaime gave a defiant smile. Paloma screamed and Clark burst into laughter.

"Well, look at that. Now the fat Batman thinks he's Dirty Harry. By the way, that gun's mine."

"The fuck it is. It's the spoils of war." Roberto kept the weapon trained on him. "And for your information, I'm not fat. My last BMI test was—"

"Drop the gun," Clark ordered. "If you shoot, first the girl will die, and then your friend."

The smile slid from Jaime's face. Roberto had made a mistake in entering the bathroom rather than saving himself and going for help. The thug was right. If Roberto pressed the trigger, Paloma could get shot just as easily as Clark.

"Do what he says," he told Roberto.

"Yeah, right."

"Roberto, put the gun down."

When he didn't obey, Clark stopped aiming at Jaime and raised the gun to Paloma's temple.

"Roberto, please!" Jaime cried out.

Barrero spoke in a tone of exaggerated calm. "Don't worry, Jaime. This bastard's screwed. I've called the police. They'll be here any minute."

Clark's expression changed, but only momentarily.

"Do you think that scares me? When the police come they'll find an open-and-shut case. Paloma and Preston hate each other; everyone knows it. They argued, things went too far, and they killed each another."

"And what about us?" Jaime asked. "I suppose we were trying to stop the fight and just walked into a couple of doors?"

"Make your friend drop his weapon or I swear I'll kill her right now." Clark pressed the barrel against Paloma's terror-stricken face.

Jaime couldn't take it. He knew this man would try to make the scene look like an accident if he could. But this was the same guy who'd tried to push Paloma onto the subway track from a platform packed with people. Discretion wasn't his strong point. If he had to kill them the hard way, he would. Preston had been easy prey. They were next, and there was no room for negotiation.

"How did you find us so fast?" he asked in a desperate attempt to buy time.

"It was easy. Paloma's friend couldn't resist my charms."

Paloma went pale. "Amanda? What have you done to her?"

"We just talked. Don't worry; I didn't hurt her or her little brat. It's you three I'm interested in. Now drop the weapon or I swear I'll kill you all. You've got until three. One . . . two . . ."

Jaime grabbed Barrero's gun by the barrel and threw it in the garbage can beside the sink.

"What the fuck are you doing?" Roberto protested.

"The right thing," said Clark, leading Paloma out of the shower. "Now, in there, the two of you. On your knees."

As they crawled into the shower beside one another, Roberto looked at Jaime like he was the one he wanted to kill. Keeping his gun on Paloma the whole time, Clark stepped out of the way and took the second pistol out of the garbage.

"Now you get in there with them," he said to Paloma, who followed the others into the shower. The three were then cramped together in the tight space. Clark laughed. "What a bunch of pervs. The three of you in the shower! I should make you strip and put on a show."

"Why don't you join us?" Roberto dared him. "You seem to like what you see."

"I can see plenty from here, Batman. Now, everybody say 'Cheese.'"

Jaime saw Clark shift position to try to get a better line of sight.

"Hang on," Jaime asked. "I thought you were going to stage this like it was a fight between Paloma and Preston."

"You pointed out yourself that your presence would make that story a hard sell. So I'd better just finish the job as quickly as possible."

Clark's mocking smile was chilling. His blue eyes bulged madly over the plaster cast and the extravagant mustache. He aimed at Paloma and prepared to fire.

"Just one more question," Jaime said. "How much is Rosa Mazi paying you for this?"

Clark's eyes betrayed surprise.

"Rosa? How do you know—"

Roberto Barrero took advantage of the momentary confusion and launched his sizable body toward Clark, who staggered back toward the window. The pistol, now pointing upward, went off, shattering the glass shower door.

Several shards fell on them. One stuck in Clark's scalp, but he didn't seem to notice as he clutched the butt of the gun, holding it high enough that Barrero couldn't snatch it from him.

Taking advantage of the gunman's precarious position, Jaime climbed to his feet and rammed his elbow into the man's stomach. Clark grunted in pain and bent forward just in time to receive Roberto's fist in his mouth.

"Get out of there, come on!" Jaime shouted to Paloma while he and Roberto held the thug down. Despite everything, he managed to cling to the weapon.

Paloma climbed out of the shower and threw on a bathrobe as she ran into the hallway to call for help. She was distraught to find no one at reception. The hotel, which took up the entire third floor and had been nearly empty when they'd arrived, now seemed completely abandoned. The low season that had made it possible for them to get a last-minute reservation now threatened to contribute to their deaths.

"Hey! Is there anyone there?" she cried in desperation. Then she heard footsteps coming from the hallway and Jaime and Roberto appeared at a run.

"No time!" said the journalist, taking her by the arm and pulling her toward the exit.

"Hey!" Paloma protested. "I'm half-naked!"

Jaime held out her boots. "I came prepared."

The three of them ran out the door and down the stairs. On their way out, they bumped into the owner of the hotel, who at that moment was coming up with a package.

"Eh, che sta succedendo qui?"

"There's man with a gun in there!" Paloma screamed in Spanish as she tried to pull her boots on. "Hide, and call the police!"

"Are you serious?" the bewildered hotel owner asked.

Before they could reach the front door, they heard footsteps at the top of the stairs and Clark appeared with a gun in each hand. At the sight of him, the hotel owner dropped the package and threw himself to the floor.

"Run!" Jaime cried, throwing open the front door.

Roberto and Paloma did not need him to say it twice. They ran out onto the street with Jaime close on their heels.

It was nighttime, and the few pedestrians who were walking through the little park in front of the hotel were bewildered to see two men and a woman running at full speed toward the hospital.

"We'll be safe there!" Jaime shouted to the others before looking back to see Clark sprinting out of the building.

They ran to the other side of the square, leaving the park behind them. Then Jaime spied a bus at the stop beside them, about to close its doors.

"The bus!" he shouted, suddenly changing his mind.

Roberto heard him, took Paloma by the arm, and banged on the door, which had just closed. The driver gave them a bad-tempered look, but seeing Paloma's fraught expression he took pity on them and reopened it. Roberto helped Paloma onto the bus and blocked the door with his large frame, keeping it from closing until Jaime could catch up and board. As the bus pulled out, they watched out of the window as Clark followed in their steps and was left panting at the stop. Jaime let out a euphoric burst of laughter.

"It looks like our friend missed the bus," he exclaimed. "The perfect getaway!"

"Right out of a movie," Roberto agreed, trying to get his breath back.

The driver glowered at them. Jaime noticed and inserted coins in the ticket machine while Roberto and Paloma made their way to the back of the vehicle.

The few other passengers looked at them in bewilderment, particularly at Paloma in her white bathrobe and brown boots. While Jaime finished paying for the tickets, Roberto and Paloma sat down to avoid attracting more attention, but all eyes remained fixed on them even after Jaime joined them.

"Is it true about Oscar?" Paloma trembled with fear and cold. "The rat told me he'd killed him before he came in through my bathroom window."

"I'm afraid it's true."

"The bastard," she said, tears in her eyes. "Oscar was a creep and an asshole, but he didn't deserve to die."

In his aisle seat, Roberto gave her a serious look.

"Yeah, it's a shame, but I suggest we focus on ourselves. What do we do now?"

Jaime looked at the electronic sign that announced the stops.

"This bus is heading toward the Castelvecchio Museum. There are tons of restaurants and cafés in that area. We'll get off and go in one of them."

"That's your idea?" Paloma sounded upset. "Dinner?"

"My idea," Jaime said, "is to hide somewhere safe while the police sort things out and arrest the murderer." He looked at Roberto. "Hey, you: Chuck Norris. Did you really have time to call for help before you came to our rescue?"

"Are you kidding? That was a bluff. I could hear someone in there with you and I figured you needed me. There was no time for a call." Roberto pulled his cell phone from his pocket. "But there is now." He looked around at the other passengers. "Hey, does anyone know what the emergency number is? *Emergenchi?*"

Paloma translated the question and a woman sitting behind them answered: *"Uno, uno, due."*

"Grazie mille." Roberto dialed the number and passed the phone to Paloma.

When she'd finished speaking to the police, Jaime gave her a questioning look.

"They told me that the owner of the hotel already called them. I explained where we are and they said to stay on the bus and get off at the Castelvecchio stop, where a car will be waiting for us."

"Is this Castelvecchio place very far?" Roberto asked, looking out of the rear window. His tone was urgent.

"Five or ten minutes, why?"

"Because the guy behind us might get to us first."

Jaime and Paloma turned at the same time and they froze in horror.

A few meters behind the bus, Clark was following on a red Ducati.

39

"You have to give it to him: he has good taste in bikes," Jaime remarked, his voice tense. "Who'd he steal that bike from?"

"What does that matter?" said Paloma. "He's coming after us!"

"Don't worry; he can't get on the bus while it's moving. And when we reach our destination, he'll have to deal with the police."

"Sure, but *that's* not our destination."

Paloma pointed ahead at the next stop. The driver had already begun to slow down the bus.

"Oh, shit . . ." Jaime leapt up from his seat and ran to the front of the bus. "No! Don't stop! *Non si fermi!*" But the driver gave him a look of disdain and halted the bus.

Roberto and Paloma watched through the window as Clark jumped off the motorcycle and ran to the bus door. "Don't let that man on!" Jaime cried. "He's a murderer! *Assassino!*"

Though his shouting unnerved the passengers, no one did anything but look back at him in surprise. As the driver opened the doors, Clark shoved the other people at the stop aside, climbed onto the bus, and advanced down the aisle like a shark swimming toward a school of fish. Jaime retreated to the back.

"*Eh! Il biglietto!*" shouted the driver, even as the gunman ignored him and continued toward his victims. "*Eh!*"

Clark stopped in front of his prey. "Nice try," he said in a threatening tone. "Now get off the bus, unless you want a bloodbath right here."

Jaime's lips were trembling with rage.

"You wouldn't start shooting here."

"Try me."

Jaime looked at his companions. Paloma looked spent and Roberto, though still defiant, might as well have had the word *defeat* tattooed on his forehead. Slowly, they began to stand. Then Roberto suddenly started screaming. "A gun! A gun!"

The passengers gave him looks of incomprehension, but his message became clear when they saw a fat guy with a goatee lift his right arm and brandish a weapon—the one he had just extracted from Clark's belt. Everyone froze, not knowing how to react, until Roberto pressed the trigger. At the sound of the loud bang, a bullet passed through the roof of the bus. This was enough to make all of the passengers leap out of their seats and scream as they rushed for the bus's rear door. A torrent of people flooded down the aisle, knocking Clark to the ground. Jaime, Roberto, and Paloma were among those who trampled him as they made a sprint for the door.

"The Ducati!" Jaime yelled, seeing the motorcycle lying on its side by the bus stop.

Roberto, who was already on the street, understood what Jaime meant and took Paloma by the hand, though she didn't need any guiding. The bike's engine was still running. Between the two of them, they pulled it upright and Roberto sat his large frame on the front part of the seat. "Get on!" he shouted to Paloma, who jumped on behind him. Roberto sped over to the bus door, where Jaime was waiting.

When they'd pulled up to a stop, Jaime straddled as best he could the tiny section of bike that wasn't already occupied and clutched

Paloma by the shoulders. "Go, Roberto!" he yelled, seeing Clark stumble from the bus. "Step on it!"

Roberto did as he was told and the motorcycle, carrying three passengers, shot down the street.

"Forget what I said earlier!" Jaime cried, sounding euphoric. "*This is the perfect getaway!*"

As they bounced along the cobblestones, Jaime's fingers dug into Paloma's shoulders.

"I'm pretty sure it's illegal to have three people on a bike!" said Roberto.

"I don't know about illegal," Jaime replied, trying hard to stay in his seat. "But it sure is uncomfortable!"

Roberto rode with skill, occasionally swerving to dodge a pedestrian attempting to cross the lamp-lit street. Once he thought there was enough distance between them and Clark, he looked over his shoulder toward Paloma. "Which way to Castelvecchio?"

"Just a bit farther. Follow the bus stops and—Look out!"

Roberto turned back and had to steer sharply to the right to avoid an oncoming taxi. He swerved two more times before managing to get back into his own lane.

For some reason, the bike felt lighter to him now, and he took the opportunity to accelerate hard.

"Roberto, stop!" Paloma cried out desperately.

"Stop? Why?"

"We've lost Jaime!"

Roberto hit the brakes and skidded toward the sidewalk in a small arc. He looked back and saw Jaime sitting on the road a short distance behind them. "You can't be serious!" he exclaimed. "Can't you even keep your butt on a seat? Good thing you're a skinny runt; if you were my size . . ."

Paloma jumped off the bike and ran to help Jaime up. He had hit his lower thigh hard, and he grimaced as he stood.

"Are you all right?"

"Honestly, I was more comfortable on the bus." He answered through clenched teeth as he hobbled along, holding Paloma's arm.

Roberto tried to scoot up closer to the handlebars to leave more space in the back, but before Paloma and Jaime could get on, a gunshot rang out and a bullet struck the pavement a few centimeters from the bike's rear wheel.

Turning around, Roberto saw Clark approaching on an electric bicycle, his pistol aimed in their direction.

"Motherfucker! Is this guy gonna steal every kind of vehicle in Verona?"

Paloma leapt onto the motorcycle, but before Jaime could do the same, Roberto had already started to ride off.

"What are you doing? Turn around! We don't have Jaime!"

Roberto made a U-turn, but Jaime was already running toward the sidewalk to escape the bullets.

"Jaime!" Paloma called after him. "Come on, get on!"

"There's no time," Roberto said as Clark pedaled toward them and fired again. He switched direction and rode away from the threat, ignoring Paloma's cries of protest.

"No! We have to go back for him!"

"That bastard will blow our heads off if we do."

As if to support his hypothesis, a bullet whistled past them and shattered the bike's rearview mirror. Cursing his bad luck, Roberto accelerated and steered away from the danger, in the direction of their designated meeting place with the police.

From his hidden location behind a trash container, Jaime watched the red bike speed down the street, relieved to know that Paloma and Roberto were safe. But then he turned his attention to his own problems.

Clark's electric bicycle was drawing close and approaching at full speed. Jaime crouched down beside the container, but Clark jumped the curb and rammed him. The bike's front wheel struck Jaime on the ankle, making him howl with pain as Clark circled back around to run him down again. Trapped between the container and the wall of a building, Jaime had no choice but to flip himself backward and sideways into the road, where a car driving close to the curb almost ran him over.

The driver laid on his horn and spat a stream of insults out of the window. As Jaime shrugged and climbed to his feet, he saw something long and thin protruding from the garbage container. Just then, Clark rounded the container with the bicycle and took aim, but Jaime snatched the object out of the garbage and swung it at the killer's head.

The broom handle struck Clark full on the temple, knocking him clean off his bicycle. He hit the ground face-first.

Jaime threw away the handle and, trying to ignore the pain in his leg, ran off down the sidewalk in the direction the motorcycle had taken. He was exhausted and injured, but adrenaline made him run faster than he had ever thought possible. No pain or fatigue would keep him from doing what he needed to do: lead Clark to the police who were waiting at Castelvecchio.

Without slowing down, he turned his head to see whether the hit man was still in pursuit. Seeing that he was right on his heels, Jaime pushed his legs to go faster.

What Jaime was seeing didn't seem possible. He was about to keel over, and yet Clark looked like he could run all night without even breaking a sweat. Jaime was beginning to think the man wasn't human. *A bit farther,* he told himself. *Just a bit farther and you'll be able to lie down and sleep in a hospital or a police interview room.*

The mantra spurred him on, but his lungs hurt and it was hard to catch his breath. His heart was beating like a Keith Moon drum solo, and he was breathing through his mouth now, but he kept on running, determined to stop only if he dropped dead—something that could very well happen if the psychopath behind him fired again.

The psychopath fired again.

The bullet whistled past Jaime and embedded itself in the glass of a shop window. He ran from one sidewalk to the other, dodging honking cars and seeking out the shelter provided by shadows, parked cars, and trash containers.

His body was just about to give up when one of the towers of the Castelvecchio appeared in the distance. Unfortunately, he saw no signs of police lights and no trace of a red Ducati. He was still too far away. He ran a few meters more, but his legs failed him, and he was close to collapsing. This was enough to allow Clark to catch up and block off his route to the castle.

"Stop right there!" the gunman yelled. "This is as far as you go."

"How about . . . we sort this out . . . like civilized . . . people?" Jaime gasped for breath.

"Sure, that's what we'll do," Clark gestured toward a narrow side street off to the right, beyond a classical-style building constructed of gray stone. "Down there."

"In that palazzo?"

"No, you idiot. The street."

"I didn't think you cared about witnesses."

"Witnesses, no. The police that your friends went to find, yes. Now move!"

Clark gave Jaime a shove, and he had no choice but to obey. The narrow one-way street led to a little elevated park that ran alongside the river. Clark made him climb the marble steps and walk toward the low stone wall, beyond which flowed the dark waters of the Adige.

Suddenly Jaime understood. "One bullet and into the river, huh?"

"And good luck finding your body. A stroke of genius, don't you think?" Clark nodded toward the wall. "Up there."

Jaime had run out of options. He was exhausted, sore, and saw no possibility for escape. He climbed the parapet and balanced there. He could sense, more than see, the river some distance below his feet. He considered jumping before Clark had a chance to fire. If he survived both the fall and the freezing water, perhaps he could then swim back to the riverbank. Then he lifted his gaze, and what he saw filled him with hope. He broke into a smile that developed into an actual laugh.

"What's so funny?" asked Clark.

"Nothing. Have you noticed where we are?"

"Oh, sure, another trick. Very funny. Listen, asshole: earlier it was three against one, and you caught me off guard, but now it's over. Say good-bye."

"If you say so." Jaime raised his arms in the air and waved them around as if he was doing stretching exercises. Then he started jumping up and down on the wall.

"What the fuck are you doing?"

"Can't you tell? I'm waving at the camera."

Clark was fed up with being taken for a fool and aimed his gun to fire. Suddenly the area was lit up by a powerful beam, bathing victim and executioner in a blanket of yellow light that streamed from the back of the palazzo they'd passed on the way to the park.

"What the fuck?"

Two figures appeared silhouetted against the bright light, shouting in Italian. Clark shaded his eyes with his hand, trying to make out what was happening. As it turned out, they were standing in the lot behind the Banca d'Italia, and the security cameras had alerted the night guards to their presence. Looking shaken, Clark couldn't decide what to do. He aimed the gun at the two approaching police officers and then at Jaime, who'd climbed down from the wall and taken cover behind a concrete pillar.

"What are you going to do now, Clark?" Jaime asked. "Kill us all? Face down an entire city's police force? Whatever the Carreras pay you, it's not worth your life."

A carabinieri car emerged from a side street, and two more armed officers climbed out. Behind them, the roar of the red Ducati announced the arrival of Roberto and Paloma.

Clark let out a curse, stuffed the pistol into his belt, and climbed onto the low wall.

"Non si muova!" shouted one of the police officers.

But Clark had already made his decision, and after a quick Iberian slap, he cast a defiant look at the crowd and threw himself from the wall. A moment later, a splash was heard and the policemen ran over and pointed their flashlights down at the water.

Paloma and Roberto ran to embrace Jaime. One of the police offers approached them with an ill-tempered expression.

"Qualcuno mi può spiegare cosa è successo qui?" he said.

Even a person who didn't speak Italian could tell what the man was asking. Jaime looked at his two friends.

"You explain it," he said, still trying to catch his breath. "If you don't mind, I'm going to sit on this bench and rest."

PART IV
CASSIOPEIA

40

Cagliari—Sardinia

Though she took care of herself, Rosa Mazi was not a woman obsessed with her appearance. However, when she came out of the shower that morning and studied her reflection in the mirror, what she saw was a strong exterior that masked the weakness that had been growing inside. At that moment, as she watched the water drip from her hair onto her shoulders, she realized there might be three new corpses in the world. Rosa forced herself to smile, but she managed only a pathetic grimace. That morning would be the first day of the rest of her life, she had told herself. A life without stealing, threats, or killing. Those three dead bodies would be the last. She promised herself.

    Her father's business and power had given her a life without limitations, one that had been hard to resist until now. She had a yacht, a luxurious apartment she never used, and the premises that had housed the former family art gallery and would now be used for a new initiative: Cassiopeia. All of this, she was aware, she owed to her father, but she had made a decision. As soon as she received her cut for the Medusa, she and Dino would buy another place and live solely from their trade. If her father objected, she would be forced to send him to a home or divulge the truth that he still lived. The one thing she was sure of was that she would never return to her old life. The criminal empire of Angelo Carrera would die with him.

She dried her hair with a towel and pulled on a sweat suit before heading to the yacht's main deck, where a servant had served her usual breakfast: freshly squeezed fruit juice, a bowl of high-fiber cereal, and a cup of coffee with skimmed milk. She had a view of the seafront promenade and the maze of narrow streets packed with restaurants and souvenir shops directly under the old citadel and the Rampart of Saint Remy. She was enjoying that moment of solitude when her cell phone vibrated on the table.

"Hullo, Dino."

"How are you, my princess? Do you feel like having breakfast with me?"

Rosa looked at her half-eaten bowl of cereal.

"Sure, where will you be?"

"I'm at La Loggia. I hardly slept last night, I was so nervous."

"Same here. See you in half an hour?"

"Perfect. See you soon, gorgeous."

Rosa drank her coffee in two gulps, excited by the idea of meeting Dino. La Loggia was very close to the gallery, on Corso Vittorio Emanuele, just a ten-minute walk from the harbor. She was about to set off when her cell phone rang again. She thought it would be Dino again and was disappointed when she saw the screen.

"Clark, I thought I told you not to call me again."

For the next two minutes, she stood as still as a photograph: mute, expressionless, with an inscrutableness broken only by a slight elevation of the eyebrows.

"And what do I care about your beginner's mistakes?" she finally said. "Whatever you have to say to your uncle, say it to him. Don't use me as the messenger for your screwups."

She listened for a while longer, until her pulse sped up and she began to feel dizzy. She held her hand to her forehead to keep her balance.

"All right, I'll tell him. But he's not going to like it."

As she walked into the lounge on the bottom deck, she cursed under her breath. Clark had let the family down again, and now she would have to take the flak for it.

"*Failed?*" asked the most irritated voice Rosa had ever heard.

"Clark will live. He called from the airport, and he'll be here in a couple of hours. Listen, Papà, there's something I have to tell you—"

"*No, you listen to me, Rosa. These people have screwed everything up for us too many times. We can't allow them to mess with us. I want you to wipe any evidence that might incriminate us from the yacht's computers. Then come to the apartment and pack up the bust. As soon as Clark arrives, he can help you. We have to get it out of here and take it on board.*"

"I don't understand. Why such a rush?"

"*We might have to leave, go somewhere else. I was going to tell you, but you got to me first.*"

"What's going on?"

"*They've arrested Dr. Galliano.*"

"What?"

"*The police kept the operation secret, but one of my informers got news to me this morning.*"

"But how did it happen?"

"*Someone tipped them off. One of the men who hijacked the* Artemis *with your brother wanted to sell some sculptures to the doctor, and unfortunately the mansion was under surveillance. Now, with the doctor behind bars, our chance to sell the Medusa is significantly smaller.*"

"That's not true. We can find another buyer. It's an ancient sculpture, with a legend attached to it and—"

"There's no time! We have to get the bust out of here as soon as possible and go into hiding. We'll figure out then what we need to do next, but for now the most important thing is to escape. How long before we can be ready?"

Rosa had been about to tell her father that she did not intend to do any more jobs for him, that the next day her gallery was opening its first exhibition, and that as soon as the doctor made his payment she would be out of the game. But now she felt her legs tremble and her lungs fight for air. She couldn't leave her father in the lurch. If this mission failed, there would be no profits from the Medusa, and she would be unable to meet her costs. Her future and her dreams would be lost.

"How long, Rosa?"

"I don't know! A while. We have to pack it, load it up, get rid of—"

"Make sure you're quick. Galliano will have told them everything, and they'll be preparing to come after us. He doesn't know where we are, but the police are bound to find a connection. Be as quick as possible. When Clark arrives, tell him not to waste any time. You continue with your gallery as normal, as if nothing was happening. If they detect unusual movements, they'll suspect. Don't let me down, Rosa. This time, there's not just a lot at stake. Everything is at stake."

41

Madrid

Laura Rodríguez was in for a surprise as she rode her bicycle in the area surrounding the auditorium of the University City. The day was cold, but the editor was determined to embrace a healthy lifestyle after twenty years of smoking and nearly forty of inactivity. Though the streets were flat, she struggled to keep up a respectable pace. Still, she worked hard, knowing—or at least hoping—that someday her suffering would be rewarded.

Exhausted after her fifth lap around the sports grounds, she stopped at the south end of the park and sat on a bench to drink some water from her bottle. She was wiping her lips on her sleeve when the branches of some nearby bushes moved. Laura gave a start as two men in suits suddenly emerged. They looked at her cautiously, like two huntsmen afraid to startle a deer.

"Laura Rodríguez?" asked one. He had coppery hair and wore an alert expression.

"That's me. Do I know you?"

"I'm Inspector Víctor Giner. This is Officer Ramón Ezquerra. We're from Heritage Squad."

Laura took a good look at Ezquerra, a well-built man with a broad forehead.

"Don't we know each other?"

"We sure do. That business with the antipaganists."

Laura thought back several years to when Ezquerra had helped Jaime with an investigation into Egyptian reproduction stores that had been sabotaged by religious fanatics.

"It's been a while. Please, sit down." She politely waved at the bench.

The men exchanged amused expressions and, eschewing formalities, sat on the back of the bench with their feet resting on the seat.

"We apologize for bothering you here, but we had to speak to you urgently," Giner said. "Is it a Silvertrip?"

"Sorry?"

"The bike. A Silvertrip?"

"I don't know, it was a gift. Listen, it's cold out, and I have to get to work. How can I help you?"

"Okay, I'll cut to the chase. Three nights ago, the police received an anonymous call from a man who was adamant that someone had kidnapped a nine-year-old boy and was holding him captive in a warehouse up for sale in the Tetuán district. The tip-off, initially, seemed implausible, but it turned out to be true. A patrolman went there and found the child."

"Yes, I heard it in the news. But what does that have to do with me?"

"The boy is the son of Amanda Escámez, a Prado Museum employee and colleague of Paloma Blasco, Jaime Azcárate's ex-girlfriend."

Laura swallowed hard. Jaime. It was always Jaime.

"Please, go on."

"That same night, a few hours earlier, the police went to a derelict building on Plaza de España because local residents had complained about a racket coming from it. Squatters live in that building, along with families of Romanian immigrants and other homeless people. When the police arrived, some of the squatters claimed they'd helped a guy dressed as Batman get the address of the warehouse from the alleged kidnapper." Giner broke off when Ezquerra began to laugh.

"What's so funny?"

"I'm sorry, Inspector. But if you could hear how what you said sounds!"

"I know how it sounds; I was the one who said it."

Laura felt a bit bemused. She was beginning to think these two men had been out all night drinking and were just taking her for a ride. "A kid rescued by Batman," she said. "At least that's good news. Is there anything else you want to tell me? Did Spiderman intercept a drug delivery or—?"

"The thing is, Laura, we believe this Batman could really be a security guard named Roberto Barrero who works at the Center for Historical Research."

Laura closed her eyes, her heart sinking. The image of the Batman mannequin she'd seen in Roberto's living room popped into her head. "And how did you come to that conclusion?"

"Based on statements by the owner of a nearby Chinese store. He said he heard screams and went outside to check things out. A van parked at the door to his store caught his attention; its rear was blocking off half of the entrance. He memorized the license plate. It turned out to belong to a Fiat Doblò owned by Roberto Barrero."

"I can see why you'd suspect him."

"There's one other matter," Inspector Giner said. "Two weeks ago, the Italian police reached out to warn us that one of the Alessandro Algardi fountains, stolen in the 1950s from the Granja gardens, may have shown up at a mansion in Bergamo. Officer Ezquerra and two other squad members went there to join the surveillance team the Italians had already set up."

"Hang on, this is a lot at once."

"I'll give you the short version. The mansion's garden was filled with a great many copies of mythological sculptures, but we had doubts about the possible authenticity of the fountain. We were right to be suspicious."

"Did you find something?"

Ezquerra took over the explanation from Giner. "The mansion belonged to a rich neurosurgeon named Umberto Galliano," he said.

"A neurosurgeon mixed up in art theft?"

"No, a collector. We've done a thorough background check on him, and his interest goes back a long way. His great-grandfather started bringing artifacts back from the Acropolis of Athens. The tradition of collecting continued for generations, until the authorities started cracking down on heritage theft. Federico Galliano, Umberto's father, focused on obtaining works from auctions and galleries, and he passed his interest down to his son. But Umberto was lazy and didn't share his father's patience. He couldn't be bothered to travel around hunting for antiques, so he decided to pay others to bring the pieces to him. He somehow wound up making contact with the most powerful and dangerous art-trafficking organization Europe has ever seen."

"The Pole's gang."

"Exactly."

"But they were dismantled a few years ago."

"Yes, but they managed to cause some significant havoc first. We now know that Dr. Galliano was their best customer. Incidentally, he's not quite right in the head. Like any fanatical collector."

An elderly lady with a little dog passed the bench and said hello to them. Ezquerra replied with a wave and stopped talking until she'd walked past.

"After we found all this out, we obtained a warrant and searched the mansion. That place would make most of the world's museums look about as exciting as my living room. You wouldn't believe all the stuff that was in there: medieval panel paintings, classical sculptures, altarpieces, gold artifacts, furniture, armor. Pretty much anything you can imagine."

"All stolen?"

"About forty percent of it."

"Did you arrest the doctor?"

"He and his wife were both arrested and questioned. At first they denied everything, but the rich aren't used to tough interrogations, and in the end the doctor broke down and talked." Inspector Giner looked proud. "Now we know who supplied them with the objects."

For some reason, two disparate thoughts came together in Laura's mind, and she imagined a stone woman with serpents for hair slowly descending the stairs in Dr. Galliano's mansion. "Did the Algardi fountain prove to be genuine?" she asked.

"Our experts confirmed as much."

"Did they find any other important pieces?"

"All stolen artwork is important."

"I mean pieces by well-known artists. Were there others besides the Algardi?"

"There was a Renaissance panel painting by Fra Bartolommeo, but we believe Galliano's father acquired that piece legally. The rest weren't by particularly well-known artists."

Laura hesitated to ask the crucial question. Out of loyalty, she was reluctant to reveal Jaime and Paloma's secret. However, she thought better of the situation and took a deep breath before asking. "Tell me something: among the sculptures you found at the mansion, was there by any chance a bust of Medusa?"

The men's mouths dropped open and they looked at each other in astonishment. Giner spoke first. "A bust of Medusa? What do you know about that?"

"What do *you* know?"

"The commissioner leading the investigation in Bergamo was absolutely sure we'd find a bust of Medusa at the mansion. He must've meant the one that was stolen in Verona last month."

"Exactly. It wasn't at the mansion?"

"There was no Medusa," Ezquerra assured her. "I helped with the inventory myself, and I can tell you that we didn't find anything vaguely like a Medusa, other than the one that was part of the copy of Cellini's Perseus. There was just about every mythological piece you could want: Hercules and Antaeus, Jason and Medea, a nude Aphrodite . . . but no woman with snakes on her head."

Laura thought for a moment. It seemed that nobody yet suspected the significance of the sculpture. She considered explaining it to the officers, but Jaime had explicitly asked her not to speak to anyone about it, no doubt to protect Paloma's research. Exercising her renowned caution, she looked for another way to arrive at the heart of the matter. "You said that the doctor admitted who had supplied the stolen art."

"That's right," answered Giner. "Apparently, it's an organization headed by a family that manages the details of every operation and hires assorted mercenaries to do their dirty work. We have reason to believe that one of these mercenaries led the hijacking of the freighter *Artemis*. It's likely that another was responsible for kidnapping Amanda Escámez's son, and was later tormented by this . . . Batman and his army of squatters."

Ezquerra gave another laugh, and Giner silenced him with a glare.

"Do you know what family it is?" Laura asked.

"We have some information."

"So you have them in custody."

"Not yet. There's a small hitch." The two policemen looked at each other in discomfort.

"I see. I guess that's why you're here."

"Right again. We know that your contributor Jaime Azcárate has been conducting his own investigations."

Laura shrugged. "What can I say? What Jaime does outside of office hours is his business."

"Nobody's blaming you. Or him. However, it has been brought to our attention that Azcárate and three others—whose descriptions fit those of Paloma Blasco, Roberto Barrero, and a Prado Museum researcher named Oscar Preston—left on Wednesday for Verona, the city from which, 'coincidentally,' the Medusa you mentioned was stolen. Last night one of them was found dead. Murdered, probably."

Laura's heart skipped a beat. "Who?"

"Preston. He died from a blow to the head while showering in his hotel. We've spoken to Amanda Escámez, who initially was very guarded. In the end, she broke down and told us everything. The details are still unclear, but apparently Preston had something to do with her son's abduction."

"The others—what happened to them?"

"They managed to get away after a dramatic escape through the streets of Verona."

"Are they all right?"

"All three are unscathed. And that, partly, is what worries us."

Laura felt as if her nose was beginning to freeze. She took a tissue from her pocket and blew it loudly. "What are you implying?" she asked.

"Dr. Rodríguez, it's possible the three of them are in trouble with the law."

"Trouble? What kind of trouble? If it's true what you say, it was thanks to Roberto that you discovered the whereabouts of the boy. And

I'm certain that, were it not for Jaime, Paloma would be dead. Where are they now?"

"The Italian police questioned them for a few hours before releasing them. But it's possible they'll be charged with illegal possession of firearms."

"What?"

"In the hotel room and on the bus, there were cartridges from two different pistols."

"They must be the killer's."

"That's the most logical hypothesis. However, one of the shells matched another found in the building on Plaza de España, where our Batman went into action. We believe Roberto Barrero stole the weapon from the murderer and took it with him. And clearly he used it."

Laura could feel her heart beating.

"What worries us, Dr. Rodríguez, is that soon after making their statements and being released, Azcárate and the others disappeared."

"What's the problem with that? You said yourself: they were released."

"Do you know where they've gone?"

"No. Jaime hasn't contacted me since Monday."

"We suspect they're in Cagliari, the capital of Sardinia. At least, that's what the search history on the computer at their hotel in Verona would suggest."

"Why Sardinia?"

"You tell me, Laura. You know Azcárate. What's he intending to do?"

"Write an article," Laura said, knowing that she was telling only half the truth.

The fact was, she knew Jaime Azcárate well and was aware that for him, his work for the magazine was just an excuse to embark on romantic adventures like this one. Jaime was out to solve the mystery of the blood of Medusa, find the sculpture, and—perhaps—win back Paloma's affection.

She decided to end on a good note with Giner and Ezquerra. "Gentlemen, I can assure you that Jaime won't jeopardize your investigation, if that's what you're worried about. As soon as I get back to my office, I'll reach out to him to see if he's gone off script. If he has, I promise I'll call him back immediately. You have my word."

"Let's hope he listens to you," said Inspector Giner. He scratched his earlobe and gave Laura a piercing look. "Because if he keeps sticking his nose into these people's business, there's a very good chance that they're going to make him disappear."

42

Cagliari—Sardinia

Blue neon letters spelled out the word *Cassiopeia* outside the street-level business in a three-story building on Corso Vittorio Emanuele, near Piazza Yenne, at the south end of the city. The old art gallery, which had been owned by Angelo Carrera, had since been converted by his daughter into two bright sections: a café whose classic decor made tasteful concessions to modernity, and an exhibition room where work by artists of all kinds could be showcased. Their debut exhibition, featuring works by the young painter Giuliano Fiore, was scheduled to open that night. This would be Cassiopeia's first public event, and its owners saw this as their opportunity to build the gallery's reputation within the city's cultural circles.

Though establishments of its kind were not common in Cagliari, Cassiopeia's sophisticated yet friendly atmosphere had drawn an enthusiastic crowd made up largely of young people looking to enjoy a pleasant evening out listening to music, drinking coffee or cocktails, and admiring the art show.

None of the revelers knew that the business was a front for the murky activities of Angelo Carrera and his tormented daughter. Not even Dino, who at that moment was working behind the bar alongside a young waitress, was aware of the true nature of the business or of his lover's double life.

Rosa Mazi was tense, but her beauty that night still eclipsed any work of art they could have exhibited. She wore a sleeveless, navy-blue dress that emphasized her figure, and she was attentive to every detail, working hard to make sure the guests felt relaxed in a way she herself could not afford to feel.

She had spent the day removing all evidence of the family's criminal activities from the yacht and packing up the artwork stored in her father's apartment just a few meters above the gallery in which she now stood. The gallery owner side of her was trying to edge out the thief. The businesswoman ached to erase the criminal. Not even a gleaming smile could hide the princess's desire to kill the monster.

Standing beside her, holding a glass of wine, a short young man with dark skin and an unkempt black beard wavered between his hostess's words and the visitors' reactions to the paintings. His fashion style—red shoes, yellow capri pants, and a green shirt with a waistcoat covered in some sort of badges—went way beyond eccentric.

"I don't think I've had the chance to thank you, Rosa." He took her hand and kissed it delicately. "You don't know what this means to me."

"I should be thanking you, Giuliano. Look how many people have come to the opening!"

"No, no, you've misunderstood me," the painter insisted. With a husky sigh he added, "What I mean is, I hope I can find a way to thank you." A wine-stained tongue emerged from between his lips and moved suggestively. Rosa took a step back.

"You can discuss that with Dino. I'm sure he can think of a way."

"Forget Dino. I thought you were the boss."

"I am. But I'd rather talk about art."

The painter stood up on his toes—Rosa was a full head taller than him—and put an arm around her neck. "And what are we talking about, if not art?" he asked with a broad smile.

"The guy's all over her." Roberto Barrero spoke with the bottle of Ichnusa beer he'd just ordered from the bar raised in front of his lips.

"What do you expect?" Jaime said. "He's Italian and an artist."

"Yeah," Paloma agreed. "It's in the genes."

The three stood partially hidden behind some Ionic pillars that set the bar apart from the main gallery, observing the happenings around them and trying not to attract attention. They'd ordered and paid for their drinks separately, and crossed paths only briefly before disappearing back into the crowd of exhibition goers, of whom there fortunately were many.

Dressed in jeans, a dark jacket, and black shirt, with a slightly loosened red tie hanging around his neck, Jaime had no trouble recognizing the woman who'd almost killed him in El Burgo de Osma. That "Sandra" seemed like a clumsy teenager compared to this elegant gallery owner. But he would have to keep his guard up. Beneath her refined exterior was hidden a monster he should fear—and would confront, if necessary.

Miles Davis's "Seven Steps to Heaven" drifted from a set of speakers, making Jaime wish he could enjoy the event in a more relaxed way. But there wasn't time to hang around. He had a criminal to unmask, an art treasure to recover, and a legend to unveil. All of that was more exciting to him than the music. The buzz it gave him was physically tangible. This startled him until he realized that he was actually feeling his cell phone vibrating in his jacket pocket. He took a sip of his margarita and made for a group of young people who were drinking and chatting in a corner, using them for cover as he took the call.

"Tell me something I want to hear," he said.

"It's your lucky day. A door marked 'Private' and a storeroom."

"And Paloma?"

"It doesn't say 'Paloma.' Just 'Private.'"

Jaime took a deep breath and gathered his patience. "I mean, is Paloma with you?"

"I know, you idiot. But, no. I thought she was with you."

"I'll find her and we'll catch up with you."

Jaime began looking around the gallery. He was worried she might be wandering about in plain sight, despite being Carrera's main target. He'd tried to persuade her to stay behind and fly back to Madrid, but she'd flatly refused. She hadn't wanted to meet the same fate as Preston, but, more than that, she wanted to be with them in the event that they found the Medusa.

He'd tried to convince her that putting her head in the lion's mouth might not be the best way to secure a permanent future for herself at the Prado Museum, but Paloma had made her decision, and Jaime knew from experience how stubborn she could be.

Confident that no one was paying attention to him, he left his half-finished margarita on a table and headed to the exhibition area, where he found Paloma standing in front of one of the paintings, completely absorbed by it.

"This guy must be sick in the head," she said, barely looking at Jaime.

"Why do you say that?"

"Why? Have you *seen* these paintings?"

"Artists have their own perspectives on the world."

"Were you and I really in the same program at school? This guy's a grade-A wacko. What about Roberto?"

"Don't use our names," Jaime said, barely moving his lips.

"Sorry. What about . . . Batman?"

"He's found something. Let's go."

Jaime took Paloma by the arm and they headed across the room, but just before they reached the other side someone put a hand on his shoulder. *"Eh, amico!"*

Jaime clenched his fists and turned. In front of him stood the esteemed artist Giuliano Fiore. He was holding a half-empty glass, and judging from his glassy eyes and lack of balance, he was well on his way to getting smashed—no doubt to help him forget the brush-off he'd just received from Rosa Mazi.

"Excuse me," Jaime said, trying to push past him.

"Ah, *spagnolo*! I love Spain! Wine, women, Real Madrid!" He looked at Paloma. "Eh, hello. *Bella ragazza. Spagnola? Io sono l'artista.*"

Jaime gave a nervous smile and tried to pull Paloma away. This man was the star of the night, and they shouldn't stand near him if they didn't want their pictures to show up in the newspapers' art sections. Besides, if word got around that there was a Spanish couple at the gallery, Rosa might suspect it was them.

"*Eh, anche io ce l'ho, una bella moglie. Ma lei non mi ama.*"

This guy's loud behavior was becoming more conspicuous than his dreadful paintings, and several guests had already turned to look at him. Jaime considered dropping him to the floor with his fist, but that would just make things worse. Suddenly the painter grabbed Jaime by the arm and began to pull him toward a corner of the room. Jaime's stomach clenched when he saw that the artist was leading him straight to where Rosa Mazi stood, speaking to a journalist.

"*Vieni con me. Si chiama Rosa. É bella, come la tua ragazza.*"

His horror mounting, Jaime tried to pull away from the inebriated pain in the ass who was dragging him into the very jaws of his enemy. He dipped his head down just as Rosa lifted hers, and for a second he was afraid their eyes had met.

In that one eternal, apocalyptic instant, he gave everything up for lost.

Then a man and woman stepped into their line of sight. Jaime took the opportunity to kick Giuliano in the shin and slip off into the crowd, confident that Rosa was so focused on the journalist, she hadn't recognized him.

He took Paloma by the hand and, not caring whether anyone was watching, slipped with her behind a set of red curtains draped over the wall across from the entrance.

"Narrow escape," he whispered, his heart thumping in his chest.

"What happened?" said Paloma.

"Later."

In front of them stood the metal door Roberto had discovered on his first sweep of the premises. Careful not to make any noise, Jaime opened it, and they followed the hallway down a set of stairs that led to a dark storeroom. Roberto was inside inspecting the basement room with a small LED flashlight.

"Welcome to the Batcave," he said in greeting.

"Seriously?"

"Just be glad I didn't bring the suit."

"You're such a dork," Jaime said. "Wouldn't it be more appropriate to say it was the Minotaur's labyrinth, or—"

"There you go again with your bullshit. Batman's no less of a myth than Perseus."

"Perseus? It was Theseus who killed the Minotaur."

"I know that, smart ass. Perseus killed *Medusa*."

"Can you two stop?" Paloma said. "You're making me nervous."

"The lady's right," Roberto exhaled. "What the fuck took you so long?"

"We were chatting with the artist."

"That guy? He should be locked up. His paintings are a pile of shit."

Paloma looked at Jaime. "See?"

"If they find us here, we're the ones who are going to get locked up." Jaime glanced around him at the near-empty storeroom. "What is this? You said you'd found something."

"I did find something. A storeroom!"

"And the Medusa?"

"Fuck me, you don't ask much, do you? Behind that door, there's a garage with a truck in it, but I already looked inside and it's empty. Look what I found in the corner, though: an elevator."

"Do I look like a guy who's hunting for elevators?"

"Maybe you should be, shithead. Your building doesn't have one, and it's the stairs or nothing. Where's your girlfriend?"

"Busy with the press, but I don't know for how long. We have to be quick."

Paloma looked around. "Quick with what? There's nothing here."

"I think I get it," said Roberto. "Go up in the elevator and see where it takes us. If this storeroom's empty, there must be a floor that isn't. If Jaime's right, the Medusa's waiting for us somewhere in the building."

"Let's go then. Got the camera?" Jaime said.

"In my jacket pocket."

"And the jacket?"

"Shit!" Roberto turned back to an old table and grabbed the cinnamon-colored jacket they'd bought, like Jaime's clothes, at a discount store in the city's shopping district. "Sorry. It got hot in here."

The plan to crash the opening and search the Cassiopeia Gallery had occurred to Jaime while at the Pontecorvo House Museum the very moment Sabina handed him the invitation. The information he'd gleaned from their conversation had convinced him there was a good chance that the Carreras hid their stolen goods at the gallery before selling them to their clients. An art gallery was the perfect front. The stolen works could come and go in full view without anyone noticing a thing.

After being released by the Verona police, the three companions had returned to the hotel to collect their luggage and pay the bewildered owner whose unlucky establishment had lost a shower door and gained a dead body. Next, they climbed into Roberto's van and travelled west to Livorno, where they caught the ferry to Olbia, on the northeast coast of the island of Sardinia, and then drove over two hundred kilometers south.

Jaime had come to the conclusion that they should avoid hotels along the way, not wanting to leave too obvious a trail after Laura Rodríguez's call telling him about her meeting with the inspectors and warning that the police were looking for them.

"Don't worry, Presidenta," he had said. "I'm a journalist and I'll do my job: nothing more, nothing less."

"You'll be careful?"

"As careful as always."

"God help us, then."

After he'd talked to Laura that afternoon, they'd located the gallery on a city map and gone to a department store on Via Regina Elena to buy clothes appropriate for an art gala: elegant, but not too eye-catching. They had cleaned themselves up as best they could in a restaurant bathroom, but wound up having to make a quick exit after the owner caught Roberto standing on a soaking wet floor, smothering himself in deodorant and free cologne samples.

The storeroom elevator Roberto had discovered turned out to be a freight elevator, which added weight to the theory that works of art were stored in the building.

"Can't you imagine the Medusa riding up in this thing?" Jaime said in excitement.

Roberto wasn't so optimistic. "What about riding down? Can't you picture it leaving this place forever? The bust and the magical blood are probably in the hands of a collector already. That, or they were never here."

"Batman sure is a downer," Paloma observed.

"At least he's more realistic than Perseus," Roberto said.

Jaime ignored the exchange. A shiver ran down his spine as he walked into the service elevator. A second shiver followed when he saw his own face in a mirrored elevator wall. Though he'd dressed up and shaved, his reflection showed the strain and exhaustion of the last few days. He felt sore and depleted, but at the same time was as excited as a teenager on his first date. The Medusa was close. He could feel it.

There were three buttons on the panel. When Roberto pressed the middle one, Paloma shuddered. Jaime took her by the hand. "Don't worry. We'll be fine."

"How do you do it?" she asked.

"What?"

"Stay so calm. I've watched you get chased, beaten, and shot at, Jaime. And instead of running home you go back for more."

"Seriously? I was under the impression that you thought I lived in a fantasy world."

"Well, maybe I was wrong about that."

"That's a relief." Jaime gave her a little half smile. "Anyway, you're hardly the queen of the chickens. You had the chance to call it a day, and here you are."

"Yeah, but I'm peeing my pants."

"You think I'm not?"

Paloma turned to Roberto. "What about you?"

"Me? Let's just say this isn't the first time I've done this sort of thing. In situations like this, the important thing is to focus on stealth and caution."

"And what if they discover us anyway?" Paloma asked as the freight elevator stopped with a shudder.

"Then fuck stealth and caution, and run like hell," Roberto said.

43

The elevator doors opened onto a gloomy hallway. Across from them, a pair of abstract paintings by an unknown artist hung over a wooden credenza. Roberto shined his flashlight on the paintings and screwed up his face.

"So, art historians, what do you think?"

"They're not exactly straight out of MoMA," Jaime said. "They look like they were painted by someone's nephew. Hey, Dark Knight, have you got a spare flashlight? I can't see a thing."

"I bought this one for myself while you were wasting time looking at clothes. But you can borrow my lighter." Roberto pulled a plastic cigarette lighter from his pocket and passed it to Jaime. "It's no Zippo, but you might be able to get it to work."

"What a cheapskate."

On the floor, resting against the wall, were two suitcases with combination locks.

"It looks like your girlfriend's ready for a trip," said Roberto.

Beyond the entrance hall was a spacious living room without a single decorative element, just a bare table and some chairs. One side of the room opened up into an unfurnished kitchen. It was clear nobody lived there.

With Roberto in the lead, shining his flashlight, they crept down a long hallway with doors on either side. The first door led into a small study containing a walnut desk with several thick folders piled on top. Jaime picked one up and asked Roberto for some light. There was nothing inside but invoices and documents related to the gallery and bar. Also on top of the desk was a framed photograph of a luxurious yacht, the name *Phoenix* painted in black letters on its side.

Jaime was about to try his luck with the next door when Paloma called to them from the other side of the hallway. "Look at this!"

Jaime walked into the room and froze when he found himself facing the almond-shaped eyes of Rosa Mazi. Once he'd recovered from his fright, he stepped closer to the bedside table to study the photograph more closely. The young woman in the picture must have been about seventeen years old, and she'd struck a smiling pose beside a racehorse. Though it was clearly the same person, this woman had little in common with the one now entertaining her guests below them or the one who'd tried to turn Jaime into a human Popsicle in El Burgo de Osma.

"Your girlfriend's a looker, but she's a bit weird." Roberto studied the shelves along one wall of the room. "What kind of woman would put the complete works of Nora Roberts next to *The Aeneid*?"

"The same kind of woman who's capable of holding a gun to a guy's head after seducing him: a real romantic." Jaime took in the room with a quick glance, saw that there were no sheets on the bed, and concluded that no one had slept there for some time.

There was just one door they hadn't yet tried. Before opening it, the three of them looked at each other anxiously. What if they were wrong? What if what they'd thought they would find wasn't there?

Their fears proved true when they found themselves in a completely empty room: no furniture, no wallpaper, not even a light bulb.

"I don't know how I could've gone along with such an idiotic plan," Paloma said, disheartened. "Jaime and his fantasies."

"You said you were wrong about them."

"I've changed my mind. There's nothing in this apartment."

Certain what they sought was not there, they retraced their steps back to the elevator, got in, and pressed the top button. There was still one more floor to search, a chance that Jaime's hunch had been right. When the doors opened after a few seconds, they were faced with what looked like a wooden board blocking the exit. Jaime knocked lightly with his knuckles, and a hollow sound echoed back.

"Is the whole floor walled off?" Paloma asked.

"I don't think so."

Jaime took a deep breath, put a hand on the board, and slowly pushed until there was a crack big enough to look through.

With the help of Roberto's flashlight, they determined that the room was small and, like the apartment below, had been abandoned long ago. It smelled damp, there were large water stains on the gray walls, and water dripped from the ceiling. They pressed their ears against the wooden panel and, hearing nothing, pushed it aside and stepped out of the elevator. The panel turned out to be a false door that, from the other side, disguised the elevator as a closet. They found themselves in a hallway identical to the one in the apartment below, but with one subtle difference: all the doors in this hallway were locked.

Paloma looked at Jaime. "Now what?"

"A locked door's always a good sign. Roberto, do you have your Swiss Army knife?"

"Right here. But why do you need it?"

Before Jaime could stop him, Roberto kicked the doorknob, breaking the lock, and the door swung open. "Good work," Jaime grumbled. "Nice and quiet."

"I don't mess around."

Upon entering, they found countless packages sealed in bubble wrap piled up against one wall. Carefully Jaime tore the wrapping off of one. It appeared that his suspicions had been right. Paloma copied his actions and was stunned to find a Van Gogh painting identical to one stolen in Amsterdam and subsequently destroyed by the thief. "Is it a copy?" she asked.

"Either that, or the one that got destroyed was the copy." Jaime shook his head. "These people are ingenious."

Roberto didn't seem as impressed as they were. "Well, that's all fine and good. But where's the Medusa?"

"This must be the picture gallery," Jaime said. "I bet you anything the sculpture room's not far away."

"I'll take that bet. Show us the way. I'll get my door-smashing boot ready."

Back out in the hallway, Roberto noticed that one of the doorknobs had no lock. Without a word he approached and opened it. It was a bathroom. "Excellent. I need to take a piss."

"Now?" Paloma sounded shocked.

"A joke. But . . ."

"What is it?"

Roberto shined his flashlight on the washbasin's countertop, upon which lay a number of items: toothbrush, soap, razor, a can of deodorant. There was a smell of pine in the air and they could hear water running in the toilet tank, as if someone had recently used it. And everything was clean. Too clean for an apartment used only for storage.

The hairs on the back of Jaime's neck stood up.

"I think someone lives here," whispered Paloma. The knot forming in the pit of her stomach tightened when she heard the sound of a door opening at the end of the hallway.

Jaime gestured for his friends to retreat silently to the room where the paintings were stored, but before he could catch up, he heard a gravelly voice from somewhere behind him.

"Rosa? Rosa, is that you?" The words were spoken in Italian.

He had heard no footsteps, but Jaime knew someone was in the hallway, right behind him. Somebody switched on a light. Slowly, Jaime turned around. What he saw seemed like something out of a pulp fiction novel.

In the middle of the hallway stood an elderly woman with dark, wrinkled skin, dressed in a maid's uniform. Her hands rested on an electric wheelchair that held the shell of what must have once been a complete man.

He was at least eighty, with a long face, prominent chin, and large ears that supported the arms of the tinted glasses he wore. These were the only parts of his anatomy that Jaime recognized as being human. The rest looked more like the body of a grub. The burgundy pajamas the man wore did not hide the absence of both legs or the grotesque curve of his right arm, which had been amputated below the elbow.

Jaime felt a combination of caution, apprehension, and pity. It did not escape his notice that, in addition to being paralyzed and mutilated, the man was virtually blind. Behind him, through an open doorway, Jaime could see a small television monitor and microphone set.

"Rosa, is that you?" repeated the old man with growing unease. "Signora Rizzo, what's happening?"

The maid looked at Jaime, wide-eyed. "There's a young man in the hallway, Signor Carrera."

"A young man? Do you recognize him?"

"No. I don't think so. Signor Carrera, it's time for your juice."

"Forget the juice for now. I have to take care of this."

"But your vitamins—"

"The vitamins can wait. Who's there? Answer me!"

Jaime thought it would be absurd not to say anything now when he had come so far. He mustered his courage and took a step forward. "I'm a friend of Rosa's," he said in Italian.

The elderly man's eyebrows rose behind his dark glasses, perhaps the most expressive gesture he was able to perform. "A friend? Rosa never brings friends here. No one comes up to this floor. What do you want?"

Figuring he had nothing to lose in this situation and much to gain, Jaime decided against trying to hide his identity. Switching to Spanish, he said, "My name's Jaime Azcárate. I'm working on a story for *Arcadia* magazine."

The man's eyebrows rose again, and stopped there, his surprise and alarm clear. "Signora Rizzo," he said, "go in the other room and wait for my instructions."

The aide frowned, her eyes fixed on Jaime. "Don't keep him. It's time for his juice and medication."

"Don't worry," said Jaime. "We won't be long."

Once the maid had disappeared through the door at the end of the hallway, Carrera approached in his wheelchair, which he controlled with his right arm. He stopped in front of Jaime. "Azcárate? How did you get here?"

"I see you speak excellent Spanish. I've come to photograph the Medusa."

"I don't know what you're talking about."

"Sure you do." Suddenly there was a clicking sound. Jaime turned and saw that Roberto had just snapped a photo from the doorway.

Sorry, he mouthed silently.

"This is private property," the elderly man said. "Get out right now or I'll call the police."

"Call them," Jaime said. "They'll be thrilled to know that the Van Gogh from Amsterdam's still intact. Along with all the other pieces you have stashed here."

. . .

As Jaime continued to speak, Roberto and Paloma retreated stealthily to the room through which they'd entered the apartment. Roberto carefully closed the door behind them and took out his cell phone.

"What are we doing in here?" asked Paloma.

"Let Jaime do the talking, he's got a knack for it. Meanwhile, an apartment with a hidden elevator, a collection of stolen paintings, and an old wreck in a wheelchair means it's time for us to call in the cavalry."

"But, the Medusa—"

"If it's here, we'll find it before the police arrive. But we should cover our asses; we don't need a repeat of Verona."

Roberto had just started to unlock his phone when suddenly he froze. The elevator behind him had begun to whirr. "What the fuck?"

"Someone's coming up!" Paloma said. "We have to hide."

But before they could return to the hallway, the freight elevator stopped at their level and the false closet door opened. A man in a suit with blue eyes and a scar-covered face walked through and regarded Roberto and Paloma with a look of disbelief.

"Who are you?" he asked.

Roberto positioned his large frame between Paloma and the stranger. "Who are *you*?"

"I'm Vicente Amatriaín. I work for the EHU."

Roberto relaxed. "I was about to call you." He showed Amatriaín the hand that still held his cell phone. "I'm Roberto Barrero and this is Paloma Blasco."

"What's going on? Is Jaime Azcárate with you?"

Roberto threw Paloma a look of annoyance. "Why does your boyfriend always take all the credit?"

Amatriaín grew impatient. "Where is he?"

Roberto pointed at the door.

"Stay here," the policeman ordered. "And don't do anything stupid. I'll speak to you later."

"Don't worry," Roberto called after Amatriaín as he set off down the corridor. "At this point, we're almost completely out of stupid things to do."

44

Jaime didn't waste any time. Certain that his friends were in the process of alerting the authorities, he figured he'd try to get as much information out of the old man as possible. "I suppose the Medusa's here, behind one of these doors."

"The Medusa?" the man asked. "I don't know what Medusa you mean."

"Sure you do. Bolgi's Medusa, which you ordered stolen from the Pontecorvo House Museum. Of course, you already know that it's not by Bolgi, and that it's much older than people think. You still have it stored here because your buyer, Dr. Galliano, was arrested before you'd gotten your hands on the document that proves that the sculpture is also a reliquary containing the blood of Medusa."

Jaime was disappointed not to see any surprise register in the old man's face. The lips remained firm, the eyes under the dark glasses did not blink, and not a drop of sweat appeared on the wrinkled brow. "Suit yourself. I'm calling the police."

"That won't be necessary," said a voice from the end of the corridor. Jaime turned and was stunned to see the figure approaching them. "Azcárate, step aside please."

Jaime moved out of the way. He could just make out Paloma and Roberto at the end of the hallway, watching from a safe distance. Then he looked at Amatriaín. The sight of him pointing a handgun at an old, profoundly disabled man was almost absurd.

"What's happening?" the man asked. "Who are you?"

"I'd keep quiet if I were you," Amatriaín said. "Don't make the situation worse for yourself."

"There's been a mistake. I don't know what you've been told about me, but I'm not who you think I am."

"Oh but you are." Amatriaín advanced until the barrel of his gun was less than an arm's length from the old man's head. "You're what was left of Angelo Carrera after his boat sunk. Are you going to deny it?"

"What is it you want?" the man asked.

"You know exactly what. Where's the Medusa?"

"You as well? You're all obsessed."

The appearance of Amatriaín had taken Jaime by surprise, but it also put him in an awkward situation. It was clear that he had little choice. He could either stay and watch as the conversation deteriorated or leave with his friends before the shooting started. The first choice could be one he would regret; the second might mean losing the Medusa forever. He decided to take a risk.

"If I may, I suspect that—"

"Shut up, Azcárate, and don't underestimate this old man. He's tricked us all since he faked his death in that shipwreck. Unfortunately for him, he almost died for real before his son and daughter gave him oxygen and got him to dry land. After they managed to get him out of the water, a stroke turned him into a vegetable."

"How do you know any of this?" the old man asked.

"I can answer that." Jaime threw a few glances at Roberto and Paloma, trying to warn them of what was coming. He took a deep breath. "He knows because he's the one who tried to kill you."

Angelo Carrera looked confused. "What do you mean?"

"So this is the historic moment," Jaime said, "when Angelo Carrera and Alvino Nascimbene finally come face-to-face." To judge from Amatriaín's face, one would think that time had stopped. The expression on his tanned, scar-covered face was ice-cold. Unblinking and apparently unmoved by Jaime's words, he continued to point the gun at the old man. Though he remained silent, his lips began to tremble.

That was when Jaime knew he had struck a bull's-eye. Paloma and Roberto had gotten the message and retreated, which bolstered his confidence. Now he just had to stay brave. He wished now that he'd finished his whole margarita.

"Nascimbene?" Angelo Carrera stammered. "You're Alvino Nascimbene?"

"That's ridiculous," Amatriaín said, his lips still trembling.

Jaime slapped him on the shoulder. "Come on now, Vicente. We know each other! Oh, sorry!" he apologized, realizing he'd struck the injured shoulder. "I didn't mean to call you Vicente—or to hurt you. Are you all right?"

"I'll say it for the last time, Azcárate: step away and let me do my job."

"And what is your job? To kill this old man like you killed his son on board the *Artemis*? To steal the Medusa and then take credit for finding it? Or perhaps to destroy it, along with the dreams of this man you hate so much? Don't be fooled, Signor Carrera," Jaime said to the man in the wheelchair. "This person's name is Alvino Nascimbene, and he's no policeman, or secret agent, or anything close to it. He was a security guard. He's married and has a daughter and a little house in Trujillo. His last known employment was at the Leoni Antique Center, until it burned down in a fire. A fire that *he* started."

"You're out of your mind, Azcárate."

"Oh, really? And what do you call murdering your classmate just to get your hands on a statue he knew absolutely nothing about?"

"Classmate? What are you talking about?"

"An old friend you studied art curation with: an agent who specialized in the recovery of stolen artifacts. His name was Vicente Amatriaín."

"I'm Vicente Amatriaín!"

"Well, that's what your face says, and no doubt your identity card and Europol badge, too. Documents can be forged, and plastic surgery can work wonders. And fingerprints, as you well know, disappear if you have a convenient sulfuric acid accident, for which no records, anywhere, exist. However, there's one thing you were unable to completely erase: your talent for drawing. As an art historian, I could tell that the sketch of the Medusa that you showed me in El Burgo de Osma was by the same hand as the portrait you did of your wife."

The man who had been passing himself off as Vicente Amatriaín turned and trained his weapon on Jaime. His eyes were bloodshot, and spotless dentures showed through what appeared to be a demented grin. "I thought you were intelligent, Azcárate, but you've proven yourself a total idiot. What are you hoping to achieve? You could've just left and I wouldn't have had to kill you."

"You're right about that," Jaime admitted with a defiant smile. "But you're forgetting about my friends."

45

While Jaime was doing his Hercule Poirot act, Clark entered the Cassiopeia Gallery and looked around in horror at the crowd of artsy intellectuals. Dino, who was serving customers behind the bar, noticed the newcomer and went to meet him. "Hey, can I help?"

"Yeah, I'm looking for your bimbo."

"Excuse me?"

"My cousin Rosa. Where is she?"

Dino wrinkled up his nose. The man wore a dirty baseball cap and a grimy brown raincoat and smelled foul. With his bruised face, broken nose, and scabby hands, he looked like he'd been in some kind of accident.

"You're Rosa's cousin? The one that called in the middle of the night? It's good to meet you. Rosa has never introduced me to anyone in the family."

"No shit, dickhead. So, run along and get her, will you? And bring me a beer or I'll help myself."

Dino was unaccustomed to being spoken to this way, but he put up with it since it was a relative of Rosa's. He went grumbling to the bar, served Clark a bottle of Peroni from which he drank deeply, and then Dino pointed toward the exhibition area. Clark found Rosa doing her best to dodge the advances of a short young man who seemed rather drunk.

"Hello, Rosetta. Your boyfriend has very bad manners."

"Clark! You're here already?"

"No, I'm a hologram. Who's this dwarf?"

Giuliano Fiore puffed his chest out and clenched his fists. "Who are you calling dwarf, asshole?"

Clark smiled like a barracuda and opened his raincoat to reveal the butt of the pistol he wore under his armpit. All hostility drained from the painter's expression.

"Excuse me, Rosa. I'm going to . . . speak to the press." Fiore scuttled off with a few backward glances.

"Who was that idiot?" Clark asked.

"Giuliano Fiore. The artist."

Clark looked around him. "These paintings are his?"

"Yes. Why?"

"I like them. They have style."

Rosa gave a restless sigh. "How are you, Clark?"

"Wiped out, as always." He winked at his cousin and lifted his bottle. "Although I feel much better now."

Rosa screwed up her nose and noticed that some nearby guests were throwing side glances at Clark and matching her expression. With his appalling appearance, dirty clothes, and bad odor, he stuck out like a skunk in a parade of pedigree dogs. She took her cousin by the arm and led him to a corner. "This is my last night of family business, Clark. If we get through this, I'm done."

"Come on, Rosa. This work is hard for me, too. I've been loyal to your father for twenty years, and to tell you the truth, I've fucking had it with getting the crap kicked out of me for the sake of some old cripple. But I'm still here."

"That's because you're an idiot. And don't push it; that's my father you're talking about."

"I don't give a shit. How'd it go on the boat?"

"There's nothing left. I copied everything onto an external drive and infected the computers with a virus so the data will be impossible to recover."

"Good work, cousin."

"I hope so. Now go up there and get everything ready to bring down to the truck. And while you're at it, take a shower."

"A shower?" He sniffed his underarm. "What for?"

As Clark elbowed his way past the guests who looked at him with irritation and disgust, Rosa stepped outside for some air. In less than an hour, they would usher the people out and close the doors to the gallery. She and Clark would then bring down the works of art that her father kept in the apartment upstairs and load them onto the truck to take them to the family's warehouse at the port.

She sighed, hating herself for having been unable to cut free from her bonds sooner. Now her special night stood to be ruined by her father's absurd ambition—his damned obsession with accumulating more money and power than he could ever use, especially since he was supposed to be dead. She turned to go back into the gallery and found herself looking at Clark's flushed face.

"What is it now? Weren't you going upstairs?"

"I was, but come and see what I've found."

Rosa followed Clark to the basement storeroom. There, tied to each other with rope, were a stout man with a shaved head and goatee and a dark-haired woman.

"What's this?" Rosa asked, perplexed.

"*This* is Paloma Blasco and Roberto Barrero," said Clark. "And if you let me kill them right now, you'll make me the happiest man on earth."

46

"All right, Jaime. How long have you known?"

Jaime was surprised that Alvino Nascimbene was admitting so openly that he'd been unmasked, but he was even more amazed that he was being given the opportunity to keep talking. "Didn't you hear what I said? My friends heard our conversation. The police will be on their way."

"Do you think the police will believe your ridiculous story? I'm Vicente Amatriaín, the EHU officer with an impeccable reputation in the field of stolen art recovery."

"Sure, that's Amatriaín. But you screwed up in Amsterdam. Admit it."

"And you've screwed up by coming here. But what do you mean? I'm curious."

"It wasn't difficult to figure out." Jaime tried to control the trembling in his voice. The man's cool demeanor, the way he seemed to think he'd beaten everyone else to the punch, made Jaime think he was prepared for any eventuality. "We tracked the history of the Medusa up to the fire at the Leoni Center."

"It's true," Carrera cut in. "This worm set fire to the center and blew up my yacht. He's a lunatic and a murderer."

"You're one to talk, Angelo," Jaime said. The only thing he could think of that might keep the bullets in the clip was for him to keep talking. "I know about the war that's been going on between you two since Alvino was a boy. He has it in for you, Angelo. Your abandonment, his mother's beatings, and his time in care left him seriously disturbed, to the point that revenge became his purpose in life. That's why he burned down the Leoni Center: because he knew there was something there that you'd been obsessed with ever since Paloma Blasco went to visit you in Rome.

"After your conversation with Paloma you began making your own inquiries, and you too concluded that the sculpture was much more valuable than the catalogues reported. Nascimbene realized the same thing. He knew that the most important thing in the world to you was the Medusa, so he decided to strike where it would hurt you most and burn down the gallery, hoping that the bust of Medusa would be destroyed. Fortunately the sculpture survived, and the Petrarca Gallery acquired it soon afterward. Now that I think of it, a guy would have to be a bit shortsighted to attempt to destroy a marble statue with fire."

"Not bad, Azcárate. Have you thought about opening a private detective agency?"

"What for? I'm a journalist. You know what they say: the media is the fourth branch of government, or something like that."

"Go on with your story. I was finding it quite fascinating."

That's what worries me, Jaime thought. But he had no option but to keep talking. "Carrera remained interested in the statue until he decided to buy it for the museum where his daughter worked as director. His interest was such that he was willing to pay a huge sum of money for it, and not long after he transferred it to Verona, his yacht sank under mysterious circumstances. Or maybe not so mysterious.

"You, Alvino, caused the explosion on the boat, and like everyone else, you assumed Carrera had died. Mission accomplished. But one thing kept nagging at you: the Medusa. Why had Carrera paid so much for that lump of marble? The whole thing smelled fishy to you, and you took your suspicions to an old university friend: Vicente Amatriaín. And don't tell me you're the real Vicente Amatriaín, because no one's buying it anymore."

"I wasn't going to."

"So much the better. A year later, Angelo determined that the Medusa could become the biggest deal of his life if he could find the right buyer. And he found Dr. Galliano, an eccentric collector from Bergamo who was obsessed with Greco-Roman mythology. As it happened, he also had been the best customer of the Pole's gang. Galliano knew that a sculpture and reliquary linked to the legend of the blood of Medusa would be the jewel of his collection, but he needed to be sure it was the genuine article. Angelo decided he'd deal with that later and first asked his daughter Rosa to return the bust. But she refused and left the museum to come back here and run this gallery with her fiancé. Then Angelo planned the robbery and sent his son to carry it out."

"Leonardo." Carrera made a groaning sound. "This bastard killed him, too."

"That was self-defense," Nascimbene argued.

"We'll get to that," said Jaime. "We know that you, Angelo, needed to persuade the doctor that the sculpture was what you'd been told it was. So you watched Paloma, discovered my relationship with her and our university essay, and sent your daughter and that mercenary with the mustache after us. Meanwhile, the EHU launched an investigation led by one of their most distinguished officers: Vicente Amatriaín. But you, Alvino, had other plans for him. Here I admit I don't fully understand the details. What made you kill Amatriaín and steal his identity?"

"Are you expecting a full confession, Azcárate?"

"I'm curious. But it's not important. I imagine you met up with Amatriaín at some point, and he told you that he was on deck to join the new EHU. You hoped that would put you on the trail of the most notorious art thieves. Maybe you even suspected that Angelo Carrera was still alive, and that he and his son and daughter were behind some of the more spectacular robberies, so you didn't think twice. Or maybe you thought long and hard about it. You figured you'd kill Amatriaín and assume his identity in order to get to the Carrera family and finish them off. You wanted to see them rotting in jail or massacred in a firefight. Whichever it was, you wanted to be responsible for it. That was the extent of your bitterness toward the man who abandoned you to a psychopathic mother. So you told your family you were going to take a training course in Paris, but, before you left, you went to ask your adoptive mother for money. Money that would help you pay for an operation to transform you into a carbon copy of your friend Amatriaín. Dr. André Fournier obviously did a first-class job."

Alvino Nascimbene had listened to Jaime's suppositions, guesses, and stabs in the dark with quiet interest, but this last sentence seemed to take him aback. "André? How—?"

"Your wife mentioned him."

"You spoke to Isabel?"

"I sure did. She told me André Fournier was a regular customer at the Leoni Center. I looked him up on the Internet and learned that in the early nineties, he opened a plastic surgery clinic in Paris. I also made inquiries with the private security firm where you worked: there was no required course held in France or anywhere else that year." The rage that flashed in Nascimbene's eyes told Jaime he had guessed right again.

"The physical similarities between you and Amatriaín were striking," Jaime continued, "and that suited your plan in two ways. First, it ensured the cosmetic surgery was a success, and second, it meant that when you killed Amatriaín, you could put his body in your car and set fire to it, faking an accident in which you supposedly died. As far as anyone was concerned, the charred body belonged to Alvino Nascimbene, the security guard. As Amatriaín, you were in charge of the investigation, so you were able to switch DNA samples and close the case. You involved yourself in various operations, including the one in which you managed to conveniently lose your fingerprints so that you couldn't be identified. A person would have to be pretty sick in the head to go to such lengths to get revenge—which you clearly are."

"Incredible," Angelo Carrera exclaimed. "Did he really do all that?"

"Believe it or not, Angelo, he did. When it comes to revenge, this guy makes the Count of Montecristo look like an amateur. After all this, the fake Amatriaín reappeared: ready to lead the mission despite his gloved hands and a face covered in scars as a result of an accident with acid. But the truth is, he wasn't interested in finding the sculpture. He wanted the man he suspected of stealing it: the despised Angelo Carrera. The only thing I don't understand is why you came to me. Why did you need me to help you?"

"I believe you've answered your own question." Nascimbene's voice betrayed hints of both fury and admiration. "Your sharpness, audacity, and recklessness suited my purposes perfectly—though it was my superiors who wanted you to write the report. I came here today to recover the Medusa and arrest these thugs so you'd make me out to be a hero. Instead, your big mouth has just ensured that you'll have to share the same fate as this son of a bitch in the wheelchair."

"That's why you saved my life on the *Artemis*. You're the one who hired those second-rate mercenaries to steal the artifacts and blow the ship."

"My son Leonardo." Carrera groaned again. "He betrayed me to help a miserable rat like you."

"The idiot took the bait." Nascimbene couldn't resist bragging. "Not only did he do my dirty work for me, he also served up the perfect chance to eliminate another Carrera. You should've seen his body," he said to the man in the chair. "He looked like a stuck pig."

"You set up the whole thing," Jaime to Alvino. "There wasn't a single stolen work of art on the ship and you knew it. It was all a trap that you laid to eliminate almost the entire team—emphasis on the 'almost.' After our full day of work, you kindly took the team to dinner so that Leonardo's men could hijack the ship and lay the explosives. When we returned, the show began, and that's just what it was: a show fueled by smoke bombs that, for one thing, created an eerie atmosphere and tied the events to the Medusa and, for another, ensured there was virtually zero visibility on the ship."

Nascimbene smiled. "That wasn't too hard to guess. No one in their right mind would believe the story of the curse."

"I never did. I assumed the attack had been organized by someone on the outside until I understood the meaning of the words spoken by the man in the handkerchief: when he arrived at death's door, he said the name of his murderer. He understood he'd been tricked, and knew the person who'd done it could only be Alvino Nascimbene. You killed him, just like you killed the ship's crew, and the EHU team, and Kraniotis. And for what? So they wouldn't get in the way while you conducted your own search for the Medusa. The only reason you saved me was so you could use me as a friendly witness, and so I'd write a report that would make you look good. You were just another dumbass who figured the key to everything was in my university essay and *Arcadia* article. That's why you tried to stop me going down to help the poor people who were burning to death down below: you hoped I might lead you to the Medusa. I bet you've been keeping an eye on me ever since. That's why you're here today."

"You're right about almost everything." Nascimbene aimed his weapon between Angelo Carrera's eyes. "All right, old man. Let's get to it. I couldn't give a damn about the junk you've been gathering over the years. I just want to know one thing. Where's the Medusa?"

"The Medusa's not here." Carrera managed to sound calm.

"Bullshit! You're not going to trick me again. Tell me where the sculpture is or I'll blow your head off." Nascimbene's eyes were burning and the hand in which he held the gun trembled. He was so determined to frighten an answer out of the man in the wheelchair, he didn't even realize that he was about to lose control of the situation. His index finger applied slight pressure to the trigger, but he stopped halfway, before the gun fired.

"There." Carrera gestured with the only hand he had left. "In that room."

"Good. I'll still kill you, but first I want you to see what I do with your precious statue."

The words confirmed Jaime's suspicions. Nascimbene's search for the Medusa had nothing to do with its material, artistic, or historical value. This was a quest for vengeance, an elaborate exercise whose purpose was to cause his adversary as much pain as possible. These two men had lost control of themselves a long time ago, and all either of them desired was to see the other destroyed, to inflict the maximum amount of suffering.

Rage had blinded Nascimbene, so much that he didn't notice a figure appear at the end of the hallway. "Open that door, old man," he ordered Carrera. "Open it right now or I'll put a bullet in your head."

Angelo Carrera was beginning to show signs of fear. A drop of sweat slid down his forehead and face and onto his pajamas.

That was when the first gunshot rang out, and the situation took an interesting turn.

47

Jaime didn't know where the sound had come from, but he didn't hang around to find out. He leapt into the nearest room, hit his head on something hard, and rolled onto a mat. As he sat up, he realized that the object was a washbasin, and he was in the bathroom.

Meanwhile, on the other side of the door, Alvino Nascimbene had turned and fired two rounds at the new arrival. But the gunman was quick and threw himself to the floor even before the trigger was pulled. Two bullets found Nascimbene's chest. A third passed through his throat and he dropped to the ground, a pool of blood expanding around his body.

Someone stepped out of the shadows, strode toward the body, and gave it a kick to make sure its owner was dead. Persuaded that this was the case, he approached the wheelchair, took a handkerchief from his pocket, and dried the elderly man's face.

"Clark, what took you so long?" Carrera was panting.

"I was downstairs, with Rosa. We found some intruders going down in the elevator."

"Intruders?"

"Roberto Barrero and Paloma Blasco. Don't worry, Uncle Angelo. Rosa's watching them."

"Thank God you showed up. We have to be quick. Load the truck and let's get out of here."

Clark turned to the bathroom door and looked inside. "If you don't mind, I have some unfinished business with this guy."

"There's no time, Clark! Get the sculpture on the freight elevator and—"

"Right away, Uncle Angelo." Clark reloaded his pistol. "This won't take long."

Down in the basement storeroom, Roberto and Paloma felt their hearts thump when they heard the shots. Rosa, who was standing guard, felt the same thing. The two captives were bound together around the waist with some packing twine Clark had found in the storeroom. There was also a bruise on Roberto's forehead, the result of a blow he'd received when he tried to defend himself.

"What's that shooting?" Rosa asked in alarm. "Was anyone else with you?"

"There sure was." Roberto glared at her. "Captain America, Iron Man, Hercules, Perseus, and the X-Men. Your daddy and cousin should be pushing up daisies by now."

Anxiety got the better of Rosa. She couldn't believe that the night she had waited so long for was going to be stained with blood. The possibility she feared most was that the shots had come from the trigger-happy Clark. She had asked him to go upstairs only because if she'd left, he would have blown the two captives' brains out. Now she regretted not going herself.

"It's Jaime Azcárate, right? He's the only one up there."

"Don't underestimate Jaime. I hear he wiped the floor with you up in that village near Soria."

"I'm not underestimating him." Rosa sounded concerned. "Now keep quiet, and you might just make it out of this alive. Unless you want me to tell Clark he can do whatever he wants to you."

"Who's going to hear us?" Roberto said. "Anyway, between the music playing out there and the gunshots happening upstairs, all we have to do is wait for the carabinieri."

Rosa looked around in desperation. From the half-open cupboard where Clark had found the twine, she took a handful of thick paper that she wadded into a ball and shoved in Roberto's mouth, in the process receiving a bite to her hand that she repaid with a loud slap. About to repeat the process with Paloma, she noticed the woman's frightened expression and hesitated. "Do I need to do this?" she asked.

Paloma shook her head.

"Good. Now stand up. I can't leave you here."

Rosa took Paloma by the arm and helped her to her feet, forcing Roberto, who was bound to her like a conjoined twin, to also stand. She led them to one side of the storeroom and opened an old trunk. "In there! Come on, do it!"

Paloma rushed to obey first, and as a result, had to suffer Roberto's weight on top of her.

Rosa closed the chest and headed to the elevator. Having given up as lost her plans to start a new life, the best she could hope for now was that it wasn't too late to prevent a massacre.

As soon as Clark started toward the bathroom, Jaime Azcárate slammed the door shut and bolted it.

"What are you doing to do now, journalist?" Clark called from the other side. "Throw yourself into the toilet and flush?"

Jaime didn't answer. Clark was out there with a loaded gun and a venomous desire to take revenge on the person who'd repeatedly thwarted him. A simple door lock wouldn't stop him for long. He glanced around, then made a dash for the shower. On one wall, a small rectangle of frosted glass allowed the light from the streetlamps to filter in. Jaime opened the tiny window and looked out. The opening was too tight for him to pass through, and, at any rate, the fall to the street was three floors. If he jumped, he'd break more than a few bones.

A gunshot rang out and a bullet passed through the door. Jaime ran out of the shower, knowing he was a sitting duck there, though the bathroom offered no better options. A second bullet made a hole just above the lock and Jaime threw himself to the floor. He stretched his arm out to grab the edge of the washbasin and his fingers found a cylindrical object. He took hold of it and dragged himself back to the shower.

He had just closed the opaque shower screen when the bathroom door opened with a violent crash. Clark appeared in the doorway with a sadistic expression on his ruined face. The plaster cast on his nose was filthy, a monstrous snout that went with the blood and grime on his face and hands.

Clark stood at the shower for a moment, assessing the situation. There was no one in view. Without a second thought, he fired twice at the screen, making two holes that spidered out into tiny cracks. No sound came from inside.

He fired again at two different points. Same result. Slowly he approached and laid his hand on the aluminum knob. Holding the pistol firmly in one hand, he reached out with the other and jerked the screen open.

A jet of pressurized deodorant doused his face a second before becoming consumed by a sudden burst of flames. Clark only had time to fire once before his hands flew to his blazing head. Screaming horribly, he ran to the sink and doused himself under the faucet.

From where he was crouched in the shower, Jaime put Roberto's lighter back in his pocket, dropped the can of deodorant, and struggled to his feet. He ran out of the shower and stood over Clark, who was now writhing in pain on the floor in a puddle of water.

"I'm sorry," Jaime said, genuinely regretful for what he was about to do.

Then he put the sole of his foot on the back of the attacker's head and crushed his face against the floor. Clark stopped moving.

There was nobody in the hallway. Angelo Carrera had disappeared, and there was no sign of the maid, either. All that was there was the bleeding corpse of Alvino Nascimbene. Jaime was about to return to the elevator, but then he changed his mind. There was one thing he had to do first. He owed it to Paloma.

He retraced his steps and kicked the lock on the door to the room beside the one where the paintings were stored. But he had nothing like the brute force of Roberto Barrero, and the door didn't budge. The only reward for his efforts was the pain in his foot so intense he was afraid he'd broken every bone in it. "The key! The fucking key!" he muttered through clenched teeth.

He knew Carrera must keep the key somewhere in the apartment, but there was no time to search for it. He went to Nascimbene's body, took his pistol, and fired twice at the lock before—using the other foot this time—he kicked the door again. This time it burst open.

The room was small and virtually empty. Through the darkness Jaime could make out a prismatic object leaning against the back wall. He flicked the light switch, and as the object became illuminated, his eyes lit up, too. The object was a meter and a half tall and was draped in a sheet.

Jaime approached and pulled off the covering, and he suddenly felt as if the ground had vanished from under his feet.

From on top of a square base, the white head of a woman stared back at him with fierce eyes and wild hair, looking furious to find herself there. To Jaime, she appeared to be screaming to be set free.

"Medusa . . ." He was overcome with emotion and added more quietly. "Why aren't you here, Paloma?"

For a moment it felt as though the danger had dissolved in that mystical space. The fear and tension had disappeared. Jaime felt just one thing: pride at reaching the end.

Since the beginning of this adventure, Jaime had encountered several pairs of eyes that had been full of hatred, brimming with rage and pain. But none of them had been equal to the expression of wrathful violence that some long-ago Greco-Roman master—with Andrea Bolgi's later, unsolicited assistance—had managed to confer upon on the marble.

Jaime dialed Roberto's cell phone, but his friend appeared to have turned his phone off. He took a few photos of the bust from various angles. So absorbed was he in savoring the feeling of triumph that he didn't notice the sound of footsteps hurrying down the corridor.

Rosa Mazi burst in. "Where's my father?"

"Hiding in his bedroom, I presume." Jaime continued to take photographs.

"And Clark?"

"In the bathroom. Cooling off."

Jaime turned and faced her, standing up as tall as he could. He didn't remember her being so tall and sinewy, but he was long past being impressed. He felt his strength and confidence returning, as if the Medusa were passing him some of her power.

"Long time no see, 'Sandra.'"

Rosa hesitated. She felt uneasy. This tense situation was not exactly of her design, but she certainly had contributed. "Who killed Amatriaín?"

"It's not Amatriaín. That was Alvino Nascimbene."

"What?"

"Your father will explain it to you from his prison cell."

"The hell he will! Help me get it out of here."

It took Jaime a moment to understand what she was asking. Once he did, he gave Rosa a mocking smile. "Don't you get it? It's all over. Your father, your brother, Clark—your whole stinking organization has gone to shit. All you are now is a headline in tomorrow's papers."

"That's not true! Tonight's the night everything is supposed to change. We have to clear out this apartment and get rid of anything that might implicate us. I just want a normal life—A *normal* life!"

"Rosa, what's going on here?"

They turned toward the voice. In the doorway was a slim man in a close-fitting suit with very short hair. He stood there looking at them.

"Dino!"

"I couldn't find you, so I went down to the basement to look for you. The police are here."

Rosa went pale.

"The police?"

"Someone complained about the noise. Who are those two people in the trunk? And the body in the corridor? Good God, Rosa—is there something you want to tell me?"

"What people?" Jaime asked. "What trunk?"

"What have you done with them?" Rosa asked.

"I left them there; I didn't know whether they were dangerous. I don't understand any of this, honey. What's going on?"

"She can explain later," Roberto Barrero said, shoving Dino into the room. Behind him, Paloma was wearing an expression of indignation that disappeared as soon as she followed Roberto into the room and spied the Medusa.

"Jesus . . ."

Jaime opened his arms to indicate the breadth the room. "I don't think Jesus is in here, but it *is* beginning to get a bit cramped. Did you two get yourselves into trouble?"

"Clark found us and tied us up," Roberto said. "Then your girlfriend stuck us in a fucking trunk. Her fiancé found us, but he left us there. Good thing the rope was so ancient."

"Jaime, you're bleeding!" Paloma cried. Jaime touched his side, and his hand was bloody when he pulled it away. One of Clark's bullets had found him, but, to his surprise, he hadn't felt any pain. As he bent over to examine his wound, Rosa swung around and snatched Nascimbene's pistol from him. She walked over to the doorway and blocked the exit.

"Right, everyone at the back of the room!" She aimed the weapon at them.

Dino appeared stunned. "Honey!"

Jaime gave him a sympathetic look. "New to the family, huh?"

"Shut up!" Rosa screamed, aiming at Jaime's chest.

Everyone in the room stood as still as the Medusa herself. Then Rosa raised the gun to her own temple.

"What are doing, Rosa?" Dino looked and sounded horrified. "Honey, don't do anything stupid. Let's talk about it."

"It's too late." She began to sob. Her hands were trembling, and she beat the pistol against her head. "Everything's lost, Dino."

"No, that's not true."

"Listen to Dino. Every situation has a solution." Jaime tried to ignore his wound, but he was beginning to feel dizzy.

"Rosa, my darling!"

Rosa stood in the same position for what seemed like an eternity. She looked at Jaime, then Dino, and then the Medusa, an expression of hatred gradually forming on her face. Then she turned the gun away from her head and pointed it at the creature. "This is all your fault."

"No!" screamed Paloma as Rosa opened fire on the sculpture.

Turned to Stone

• • •

Angelo Carrera quickly understood that he was running out of time. As soon as he heard Clark shooting at the bathroom door, he steered his electric wheelchair to the apartment at the end of the hallway. In one of his private rooms was the control panel he used to communicate with the *Phoenix*. Unfortunately, there was no one on the boat who could help him now. If the police weren't already on their way after questioning Dr. Galliano, they would be as soon as a neighbor reported the gunshots. The need for escape was urgent.

Signora Rizzo, resigned to postponing her boss's juice and vitamins for the time being, had taken their luggage down to the garage and would be back to collect him shortly. But first, it was essential that Clark and Rosa help him with the Medusa.

"For the love of God!" he called out. "Where is everyone?"

The door opened and someone entered the room. From the smell of mothballs, he gathered it was the maid.

"Signora Rizzo. And my daughter?"

"I don't know, Signor Angelo," the woman said in a plaintive tone. "But we have to go now."

"Not without the Medusa!"

"I am responsible for looking after you. Not your toys."

Signora Rizzo took the wheelchair by the handles and briskly pushed him from the room, ignoring his loud protests. They went around Alvino Nascimbene's body and bolted for the hidden elevator, descended to the basement, and continued on to the garage. With a great deal of effort, Signora Rizzo managed to cram the wheelchair into the cab of the truck. It was the first time in years that Carrera had left his gloomy apartment, and even the fluorescent lights were too bright for his ruined eyes. After securing the wheelchair in place, the signora closed the door and went off in search of Rosa.

Angelo was afraid Clark and Rosa wouldn't manage to carry out his plan. The packages were in the entrance hall, and the paintings were packed up and ready to be transported. There was just one other thing he needed: something more important and valuable to him than all the paintings cached in that apartment. But he couldn't get it down without help.

That damned Clark. And where was Rosa? Why were they taking so long?

So much work, sacrifice, and money would be wasted if they didn't hurry. They had to get rid of all the merchandise, and the only way to do it was to hide it in the warehouse until they could transport it by road or sea. The paintings and gold artifacts were the least of the treasure. One item above all others had to be saved.

Then all of a sudden, his hopes were shattered.

He heard the sound of the garage door opening, and half a dozen men with automatic weapons surrounded the vehicle and yelled at him to freeze. Angelo Carrera protested, but he knew it was useless. With a heavy heart, he lowered his head and sat motionless.

His dream of power and wealth was over.

48

"The Medusa!" Paloma couldn't believe what she was seeing. "What have you done?"

The bullet had penetrated the marble and was lodged there, right between the creature's eyes. Rosa dropped the pistol and fell to her knees, sobbing like a child. Dino crouched beside her and took her in his arms.

Jaime moved to do the same with a stricken Paloma. "They'll be able to repair it," he assured her. "The important thing is that we've found it. Consider this my way of saying I'm sorry."

Paloma gave him a sad look. "Most people give flowers, or chocolates, or a spa day. Or diamond rings."

"I've always been more original than that."

"I'm touched by the gesture." Paloma shrugged off Jaime's arm and began to pace around the bust. "But I doubt they'll let me keep it."

As Jaime watched, Paloma stopped in front of the spot where the bullet had lodged. She appeared to be trying to look past it to some greater truth about the lump of marble that had been so neatly carved some twenty-four centuries before.

So absorbed were they by the moment's magnificence, they didn't even notice that Rosa was crying on the floor, in a panic. Dino still crouched beside her, unable to grasp even a fraction of what was going on.

"Can you explain to me what's happened here?" he begged them.

"There's not much to explain." Roberto took his camera from his jacket pocket. "The monster has been freed. Paloma, get in the shot. Not you, Jaime, you'll ruin it."

Seeming to have shrugged off her agitation, Paloma straightened her dress, smoothed down her hair, and went to pose with the Medusa. That piece of marble was entwined with the story of her life, and it was only right that she appear in the photographs that would document this historic discovery.

"That's it, stand beside her. Like a huntress with her prey." Roberto pressed the shutter release. "That's it."

Paloma endured having several photos taken with the bust, but her anxiety began to grow. "Stop, Roberto, I have to check." She took the bust in her hands and tried to shift it on its pedestal. "We have to find out whether the legend's true."

Jaime looked at her in surprise. "You think the blood's in there?"

"We have to consider all the possibilities," Paloma said.

Jaime and Roberto exchanged glances and smiled. "Does it have an opening mechanism?" Roberto picked up Rosa's pistol. "Maybe our friend wants to shoot it a couple more times. Or I could just do it."

"What on earth are you talking about?" Dino exclaimed.

"Nothing important. You mind your own business."

"It's your decision, Paloma." Jaime took her by the arms and looked her straight in the face. "Do you want to see if the Medusa bleeds?"

"No . . . I don't know. I suppose I can wait until the lab tests. Scans, X-rays . . ."

Roberto cocked the weapon and aimed at the marble. "Are you sure? Make up your mind quickly."

"No! Don't do it, Roberto."

"Really? Last chance."

"Really."

"It's your call."

Just as Roberto lowered the gun, there came a bang that made the room shake.

Jaime and Paloma watched, stunned, as Roberto dropped the pistol and collapsed. A grotesque apparition with a blackened face walked into the room, carrying a smoking gun.

"No, Clark!" Rosa screamed.

"Shut up, cousin."

Shaken by Roberto's fall, Jaime was all but paralyzed, but he managed to push Paloma down behind the statue's pedestal. He remained standing, with no possibility of escape in any direction.

Clark planted himself in front of Jaime and smiled like a condemned man who'd survived being charred by the fires of hell. "You and I have some unfinished business. I'm gonna love seeing your face when this whore dies." He looked down at Paloma and aimed the gun at her head.

"No, please. Not her—"

"Arrivederci, brown-eyed girl!"

Clark curved his finger over the trigger, but before he could press it, he sensed movement above his head. Looking up, he came face-to-face with the fierce Medusa. He opened his mouth to scream, but before any sound could come out, the block of heavy marble struck his forehead.

Clark reeled and fell to the floor, his skull ruined. Jaime didn't care whether he was dead or alive. He dropped the bust of Medusa, which fell to the floor with a loud thud, and grabbed Paloma's trembling hand to help her up.

"Are you all right?" Jaime asked.

"I think so. What did you do to the Medusa?"

"I'm sorry. There was nothing else within reach."

Only then did they remember that on the other side of the pedestal, next to a traumatized Rosa and Dino, lay Roberto's body.

He was lying facedown above an expanding pool of blood. Jaime pressed his jacket against the wound and applied direct pressure, trying to stop the profuse bleeding.

"Roberto . . . Roberto, can you hear me?"

A weak nod of the head told Jaime that Roberto could.

"How do you feel?"

"Like shit."

"Try to save your strength. We'll get you out of here."

"No. Jaime. Listen—"

"You can talk and move. That means the bullet didn't hit your spine or lungs. So if you try to stay still—"

"Forget it. It's game over for me."

"What are you talking about?" But Jaime knew what his friend was saying. He just couldn't accept that Roberto might really be dying.

Roberto smiled and blood spilled from his mouth.

Jaime's eyes filled with tears. It seemed impossible that after so many dangers, his friend would end his days like this. But the wound was serious, and time was running out. "An ambulance!" he cried out in distress. "For God's sake, someone call an ambulance!"

Dino and Rosa watched the scene unfold from where they sat on the floor, rendered immobile by shock. Jaime looked at Paloma, who was equally distressed. Her eyes were welling up, and all signs of the hope she'd shown earlier had been erased. Jaime knew that they needed to pick Roberto up, carry him to the building's garage, get a vehicle, and drive him to the nearest hospital.

His friend was dying, and he wasn't about to just sit there with his arms crossed while that happened.

Then, as if guided by a spell, his teary gaze fell upon Medusa's head, lying forgotten on the floor a few meters away. The blow had split the marble around the bullet hole, leaving a cavity surrounded by cracked stone.

Jaime leapt to his feet and, without thinking twice, threw the head against the wall with all his might. Some chunks of marble broke away and fell to the floor. Looking distraught, he picked the bust up once more and threw it again. A terrified Paloma, crouched next to Roberto, just watched.

"Come on!" Jaime picked up the head again and threw it to the ground with even more force. "Come on! Where are you?"

Five more times, he struck the head against the walls and floor, until Paloma took him, crying and panting, in her arms. "Leave it," she whispered, stroking his hair. "Leave it, my love, please."

Defeat showed in Jaime's eyes. His best friend was going to die, the sculpture that had been Paloma's passion was now a pile of broken marble—and all of it was his fault.

In one final attack of fury, he kicked the head, which rolled to the opposite corner of the room and broke apart beside Roberto's dying body.

"Oh God." Jaime collapsed on the ground, consumed by grief. "Oh God, what have I done?"

"Jaime." Paloma's voice took on a strange edge.

Her eyes focused intently on the lump of marble, as if she was somehow communicating with it. Following her gaze, Jaime at first saw nothing more than the mess that had once been a coveted work of art. But when he looked more closely, he realized something about the coloring of the biggest piece of marble had changed. He dragged himself closer to the remnants of the bust, and then he saw it: a small area inside the piece contrasted subtly with the white of the outer surface.

With Paloma's help, he picked up the head again and struck the side sharply against the floor. On his third attempt, a small, pink crystal sphere broke away from the main lump of stone.

Paloma looked at it in amazement. "Oh my God."

"Yeah." Jaime returned to Roberto's side, carrying the small translucent object.

"Listen, fatso. Open your mouth."

But Roberto's strength had faded and he showed no sign of understanding. Jaime struggled with the strange vessel, looking for a way to open it. He was certain that the key to it lay in some sort of internal rod that protruded a few millimeters from the rock crystal, but his nerves prevented him from figuring out how it worked. "Shit," he muttered.

Desperate, he did the only thing he could think to do. The tiny ball was no bigger than a pill and looked to him like it was something that should be swallowed. Jaime took it between his fingers and inserted it in Roberto's mouth, letting it fall to the back of his throat. But Roberto coughed and expelled the vial, now covered in his blood.

"No! Roberto, you have to swallow it. It's the only thing that can—"

Roberto's hand grabbed Jaime's own. "Stop being . . . a prick," he said. "It's not the Holy Grail. And you're not . . . Indiana . . . Jones."

"I know! But—"

"Listen . . . Paloma's worth more . . . than any . . . legend." Roberto coughed again and his hand let go of Jaime's, all its strength gone. "Write that report . . . And fix . . . your . . . relationship."

Jaime wanted to reply with something fitting, but the words eluded him. And then Roberto closed his eyes and stopped moving, and the chance to speak was past.

"No!" Jaime groaned. "It can't be . . . He can't . . . He can't . . ."

Paloma took him in her arms as silence and sorrow filled the room. Jaime continued to clutch the pink-tinted vial in his hand, as if by merely holding it he could save his friend's life. Roberto's breathing was now barely perceptible.

Suddenly the sound of several pairs of booted feet could be heard running down the hallway.

PART V
TYING UP LOOSE ENDS

49

December 2013—Madrid

By eleven in the morning, the increase from the previous night's near-freezing temperatures made cycling around Complutense University's main auditorium bearable. At least, that was what Laura Rodríguez kept telling herself. She wanted to keep her vow to lead a healthy life, but this weather was enough to make her want to put the whole idea on hold until spring.

    Laura would have preferred to stay warm and cozy in her office, but she was determined to continue with her fitness regime, and so—dressed in a windbreaker, thermal cycling pants, and earmuffs—she pedaled along the red track that encircled the sports field. When she'd completed a lap and a half, she noticed another cyclist riding beside her. Despite his helmet and polarized sunglasses, she recognized the attractive face of Inspector Víctor Giner.

    "Do you mind if I join you?" he asked in a polite voice.

    "Not at all. But I'm nearly two laps ahead."

    "Don't worry, I'll catch up."

They pedaled together in silence, and, at the end of her tenth lap, Laura suggested they get a coffee at the *Arcadia* office. He gladly accepted and, without making the slightest effort to make up the extra two laps, followed Laura to the nearby CHR building. After they'd locked up their bicycles and Laura had made the coffee, she sat down at her desk and Giner took a seat opposite her.

"I didn't have a chance to speak to you after the business in Sardinia," he said.

"Are you going to give me a lecture? Or arrest me?"

"No, no. Nothing like that. I wanted to congratulate you on having such an extraordinary contributor. If Azcárate and his friends hadn't kept Angelo Carrera's daughter and nephew busy, Carrera would have escaped."

"You should meet Jaime."

"I'd like that. Officer Ezquerra told me about him. He says he's nuts."

"That's one way of putting it. I like to say he follows his own rules."

"That isn't always a good thing, Laura. This time he was lucky, but next time things could turn out much worse."

"I think he's aware of that."

"I still admire him for it." Giner's expression darkened. "I'm sorry about what happened to Roberto Barrero. He took some big risks, too."

"They both knew what they were doing."

"Too much risk to take for a legend."

"Again: you don't know Jaime." Laura sipped her coffee and contemplated the winter scene outside her window. "And your crew? I imagine there's a lot of work left for you to do."

"What do you mean?"

"I mean that, even though I've heard the damn story from just about every angle, there are still a lot of loose ends. Like, why did those people want to kill Jaime in El Burgo de Osma? He hadn't even been hired by the EHU yet."

"He hadn't, but Vicente Amatriaín had. In their confessions to the Italian police, Angelo Carrera and his daughter explained that the family had been on Amatriaín's tail for some time." He paused. "The *real* Amatriaín, I mean. Especially since he'd started following the trail of the Medusa. Rosa Mazi, who was following Amatriaín—the *phony* Amatriaín, at that point—saw him talking to Jaime Azcárate and figured he was one of Amatriaín's contacts. That's why she tried to eliminate him."

"But I heard Jaime found a copy of his essay in the criminals' van."

"It was there because the Carreras had a double mission. First, they were going to get rid of Amatriaín, and from there they planned to immediately travel to Madrid in search of Paloma Blasco's research. Angelo Carrera knew that the essay was hers, so he gave his daughter and nephew a copy of the journal."

"He was very shrewd, this Angelo."

"He had to be. He and his family had been smuggling stolen goods right under our noses for years." Giner cleared his throat. "They're the direct heirs to the Pole's ring. Even though they never worked together closely, the Carreras' criminal operations were on a par with those of the legendary organization. But there was one seemingly unimportant, but in fact absolutely brilliant, difference."

"What?" Laura asked.

"The mastermind of one group's operations was dead."

"Angelo Carrera."

"It was all meticulously planned over a period of years. The Carreras had always dealt in stolen artifacts, but at first it was on a very small scale. They rarely got their hands dirty. When Carrera discovered that Paloma Blasco was paying so much attention to the Medusa at the Leoni Antique Center, he decided to look more closely at both Paloma and the Medusa. Then he found out about the legend of the blood and realized that he could be looking at the art deal of the century. He didn't want to run the risk of stealing the sculpture from the gallery, so he bought it for his daughter's museum and then later snatched it back.

"Not long after that, Nascimbene tried to murder him, an attempt that left him paralyzed but also gave him the opportunity to run his operations from the darkest shadow that exists: the grave. It was a brilliant move. No one could suspect a dead man. He locked himself in his luxurious apartment, where his only company was a maid who looked after him, and he began to control the operation from there."

"How could he do that?"

"He was in constant contact with his two children and nephew. Angelo had ordered them not to contact him directly under any circumstances. They spoke to him through a communication link to the family yacht. Here's an example of the old man's personality for you: he spoke to his son and daughter through an oil portrait that portrayed him as young and brimming with health."

"Was the yacht searched?"

"Yes, and just like at the gallery and Rosa's apartment, there was nothing much there to find. I must admit, it was another brilliant strategy. If the police had suspected any of the Carreras and searched the yacht, they would have nothing but a few decorative pieces that the family acquired legitimately. No one could have imagined that the stolen artwork was stashed in the deceased Signor Carrera's abandoned apartment, which had been registered under a false business name."

"Well, it occurred to Jaime," Laura said. "The gallery was the perfect front."

"True. A neighbor even said that he'd once helped Rosa unload a shipment of paintings and carry them up to the apartment. Who would have suspected it was anything but a legitimate gallery business?"

"Have the police questioned Rosa?"

"They certainly have. The poor woman was a mess and quickly confessed everything. She had wanted to leave the organization and devote herself to the gallery and to starting an art school with her fiancé, but her father's emotional blackmail was too powerful. She also admitted that Dr. Galliano was their organization's best customer."

"I guess he was willing to pay a tidy sum for the Medusa."

"You can't even imagine. Galliano is fanatical about Greek mythology, particularly all things medical. His collection includes sculptures of Apollo, Asclepius and his sons Machaon and Podaleirio, the centaur Chiron . . . all the mythological gods. When he heard about the existence of a bust of Medusa referred to in the *Chronicle of Asclepius*, he went crazy with desire. Of course, Carrera just saw opportunity—and money."

"And now he'll be seeing prison bars." Laura turned to the window and looked outside just as it began to snow.

50

El Burgo de Osma

The giant polychrome wooden Christ by Juan de Juni looked down on the visitors as they advanced along the side nave, stopped to gaze at the series of medieval panels adorning the broad aisle, and then continued in the direction of the Baroque chapel that contained paintings and sculptures from three centuries later. The *Ars Homini* exhibition was running like clockwork. Hordes of visitors took the same route day after day, always stopping in front of the same pieces. All of the tourists, regardless of their nationality, seemed cut from the same cloth.

If the wooden Christ were able to think and see, it would have noticed that two visitors stood out from the rest. The man was tall and walked with a slight stoop, and his arm was draped around a woman slightly shorter than him. Their faces looked like ones from a Greek tragedy.

The couple progressed at a snail's pace through the cathedral, examining each painting with equal interest and diligence. Though they looked like people who had suffered a lot, they seemed happy despite whatever ordeal had befallen them. At one point he whispered something into her ear, and she laughed. Then she held him gently by the neck and kissed his lips.

Jaime Azcárate thought about how much his life had changed since the last time he was in El Burgo de Osma. That time, he'd been alone, he'd been unable to get into the cathedral, and he had almost been frozen alive. Now he was enjoying the exhibition in the arms of a woman he never expected to see again, much less under such affectionate circumstances. Their recent experiences had been so intense that, though two months had passed, neither of them had yet fully recovered.

Medusa hadn't fared so well. Jaime was present when the bust was provisionally taken into storage at Cagliari's National Archeological Museum, and he'd witnessed the experts' expressions of disgust as they examined the shattered marble and their surprise when they discovered a hidden mechanism that activated a small, round cavity whose purpose remained a mystery. After it had been carefully restored—the bullet hole and the damage Jaime wrought had left it virtually unrecognizable—the bust was returned to the museum in Verona, but there was much ongoing debate about its future.

But Jaime and Paloma gave all this little thought. After all they'd been through, what mattered most to them was the fact they were together again.

Newspapers and tabloids had immediately spread the news about the Medusa, and the weeklies published lengthy stories about every phase of the adventure from Paloma's initial discovery to the events at the Cassiopeia Gallery. Due to the dubious ethics involved in the operation, some details had to be concealed or altered—a feat accomplished through the long arm of Herbert Monfort, the EHU man who'd planned the operation and was indebted to the CHR for his organization's part in how the tragic events had unfolded.

Arcadia published a full exposé, written by Jaime Azcárate, entitled "Turned to Stone," which was a huge success in both its print and digital versions. Paloma, meanwhile, drew up an exhaustive study recounting the more scientific and scholarly aspects of the case: the true origin of the sculpture and the subsequent fraud committed by Bernini's disciple, Andrea Bolgi. The publication of her essay in several national and international journals was a defining moment for her as a historian. The legend of Medusa's blood and the statue's curse also attracted more fanciful minds, extending her essay's success beyond academic circles and earning it a featured place in everyday conversations and TV chat shows for almost a month.

All Jaime and Paloma wanted now, however, was to enjoy a few days of peace—together, if at all possible. That was why they'd escaped to El Burgo de Osma to see the exhibition. In a week, Jaime had to be back at *Arcadia* headquarters to prepare the next issue, and Paloma would take up her new post as deputy director of research and conservation at the Prado Museum. Everything had changed. Medusa had changed them.

After seeing the exhibition, they stopped for a coffee near the cathedral and then, feeling no rush, slowly strolled back to the hotel. When they got to their room, Paloma's cell phone rang, and she excused herself to take the call.

Five minutes later, when she'd hung up, Jaime asked, "Is he walking?"

"Not yet. Amanda says he can almost eat without help, but he keeps trying to do more than he should, and it's slowing down his recovery. That friend of yours is pigheaded."

"He sure is. Though I'm sure he's thrilled to have Amanda looking after him. How's she taking it?"

"She's delighted. She liked him immediately when you introduced them, and she's happy to be able to repay him for saving her son. Roberto was extremely lucky. When I saw him lying there, I honestly didn't think he'd live to tell the tale."

"It was a pretty small bullet to be taking on all that flesh. He'll never go on a diet now."

"He's a superhero. He can do whatever he wants."

The comment amused Jaime; he could afford to laugh now. He hadn't thought Roberto would make it, either. If Roberto had died, Jaime's life and work would never have been the same. In fact, they still wouldn't be the same; Roberto's doctors weren't sure Roberto would ever lead a normal life again. At the very least, he would have to stop playing at being Batman.

Mercifully, the Cassiopeia Gallery's neighbors had reported hearing gunshots, and the police and ambulance had shown up just in time. They'd quickly extracted Roberto from the scene and taken him to the nearest hospital, where doctors removed the bullet and stabilized him. He'd lost a lot of blood and suffered severe tissue damage, but no vital organs had been affected, and he responded well to the hemostatic gauzes, antibiotics, and blood transfusion with which he was treated.

All this had taught Jaime a valuable lesson: superheroes, as tough as they might seem, were vulnerable, too. It was a lesson that, given his tendency to frequently risk his own neck, he would do well to etch into his mind.

Jaime sat on the bed and gazed up at the ceiling. He felt exhausted but content. "This is where it all began."

Paloma sat beside him and stroked his chest under his shirt. "Yeah, but this time the story will have a very different ending. Hopefully, one with no curses."

"Definitely no curses." Jaime pushed aside the throw pillows on the bed and looked into Paloma's honey-colored eyes. "I was thinking this might be a good time to do something I should have done years ago."

"What's that?"

Jaime gave her a timid smile. He couldn't believe what he was about to say. "Introduce you to my mother. I know she'd love to meet you."

Paloma burst into laughter, tipping her head back. Around her neck was a silver chain, and at the end of the chain was a rock-crystal vial, no larger than a pearl, filled with pink liquid.

AUTHOR'S NOTE

I often explain that Jaime Azcárate appeared to me in a daydream one morning when I was in class and said, "Don't tell your story, tell mine." And that's what I did.

This is absolutely true. What I haven't said before now is that, though the character has been through many adventures and will go through many more, the first story that came to me was the one you've just read, hopefully with satisfaction and with a smile on your face.

In mythology, Medusa was defeated after seeing her face mirrored in Perseus's shield. Today, I aspire to make Jaime Azcárate a more or less fictitious—and most importantly an entertaining—reflection of those of us who look at life with curiosity and passion instead of worrying too much that we might be turned to stone or have our heads cut off.

The classical heroes accepted their fate without questioning it. We question ours (as we should!), but that doesn't mean we ignore the singing sirens that call us to adventure, or the muses who whisper in our ears, suggesting mad quests, voyages, mysteries, and treasures. The boldest of us run headlong into the labyrinths of our lives, braving the monsters our minds generate until, at the end, we find ourselves. The important thing is that we learn and have fun along the way.

Turned to Stone is one of those stories that, because it was an idea born in my youth, might never have seen the light of day. But now it's here, and it serves as an example of the truth that every step taken is an important one. As it was for Jaime and as it was for me. If reading it has been such a step for you, too, my satisfaction will be threefold.

Jorge Magano

ABOUT THE AUTHOR

Guided by his fascination with museums and love of Indiana Jones, award-winning writer Jorge Magano graduated with a degree in art history. Since then, he has worked at the University of Madrid and participated in archeological excavations that have taken him all over the world. Magano is the author of *La Isis dorada* (*The Golden Isis*), *Donde nacen los milagros* (*Where Miracles Are Born*), and *La mirada de piedra* (*Turned to Stone*).

Photo © 2014 Gonzalo Jerez "El Selenita"

ABOUT THE TRANSLATOR

Simon Bruni is a literary, academic, and general translator from Spanish. In a career that has seen him translate everything from video games to sixteenth-century Spanish Inquisition manuscripts, he has found the pull toward literary translation irresistible. In 2011 he won a John Dryden Prize for his slang-driven translation of Francisco Pérez Gandul's cult prison thriller, *Celda 211*. He has translated several novels for AmazonCrossing.

TURNED TO STONE